For Roger, Our

Call Me Titan—Old gods don't die, they just fade away . . . or do they? From bestselling author Robert Silverberg, the tale of an immortal Titan's search for revenge against Zeus . . . in the late twentieth century.

Slow Symphonies of Mass and Time—Multiple award winner Gregory Benford puts his talents of scientific extrapolation and deft characterization to use in an enthralling game of cat-and-mouse at the center of the galaxy.

Only the End of the World Again—Acclaimed writer Neil Gaiman takes a fresh look at the timeless battle of good and evil—a battle in which the last, best hope of mankind just happens to be a werewolf.

Lethe—In a riveting meditation on love, memory and identity, Walter Jon Williams asks what it means to be human in a future where cloning is widespread and what people feel and remember has become a matter of choice.

The Outing—From SF legend Andre Norton, a story of old debts and older secrets . . . and the price a young girl must pay to satisfy both.

Calling Pittsburgh—Some wars are fought on battlefields; others across a table. Steven Brust takes us to a high stakes poker game in which the fate of the Earth rides on the skill of one man . . . and the luck of the draw.

LORD OF THE FANTASTIC

STORIES IN HONOR OF
ROGER ZELAZNY

EDITED BY MARTIN H. GREENBERG

AVON · EOS

Permissions for each individual story appear on pages 371–373, which constitute an extension of this copyright page.

AVON BOOKS, INC.
1350 Avenue of the Americas
New York, New York 10019

Copyright © 1998 by Avon Books, Inc., for the Estate of Roger Zelazny
Interior design by Kellan Peck
Published by arrangement with the editor
Visit our website at **http://www.AvonBooks.com/Eos**
ISBN: 0-380-78737-7

Library of Congress Cataloging in Publication Data:

Lord of the fantastic : stories in honor of Roger Zelazny / edited by Martin H. Greenberg.
p. cm.
1. Fantastic fiction, American. 2. Zelazny, Roger. I. Greenberg, Martin Harry.
PS648.F3L67 1998   98-18521
813'.08766—dc21   CIP

First Avon Eos Trade Printing: September 1998

AVON EOS TRADEMARK REG. U.S. PAT. OFF. AND IN OTHER COUNTRIES, MARCA REGISTRADA, HECHO EN U.S.A.

Printed in the U.S.A.

QPM 10 9 8 7 6 5 4 3 2 1

CONTENTS

INTRODUCTION
Fred Saberhagen

IT MAY BE TAKEN AS GIVEN THAT ANY WRITER WHO SUCCEEDS IN selling fiction has a large ego—it takes one to negotiate that process. Roger Zelazny managed to combine that essential inner toughness with an excellent wit, and almost self-effacing courtesy, that made him a near-perfect friend, host, guest, companion on a panel or at a party. The same qualities, combined with his awesome talent, made him a near-perfect collaborator, too, in works of fiction. (Exactly what the *perfect* friend, collaborator, guest, etc., would be like is a philosophical question; that man or woman has not yet been observed in the flesh.)

For perhaps two decades, give or take a few years, Roger's nonfictional life and my own ran on roughly parallel tracks. We both started selling stories around the beginning of the sixties. In a few years he moved from the Middle West to Santa Fe, New Mexico, with his wife and small family. Six months later, with no idea that the Zelaznys were anywhere around, Joan and I left a different city in the Middle West and arrived in Albuquerque with *our* offspring.

We happily renewed acquaintance with Roger at a local convention, and thereafter saw each other with some frequency, living as we did only about sixty miles apart. My kids (one daughter, two small sons) being a few years the older, got in some practice as baby-sitters for his (two small sons, one daughter). Now and then,

1

when our families were at the zoo or on some similar joint excursion, mine did yeoman service carrying small Zelaznys on their backs. And for years to come the Saberhagen goldfish remembered the experience of being fed by three-year-old Trent Zelazny, who served the tank an entire container of fish food at one sitting (one swimming?), enough to turn the water to a gel.

As I recall, it was during one of these family visits to our house that Roger began to tell me about a story idea that had been growing in his mind. Somehow it was decided that the idea was to be a subject of collaboration between us—but *how* that decision was reached I do not remember now, nor, I suspect, did I remember a day after it happened.

"Let me borrow your typewriter," said Roger, and closeted himself in my office for perhaps half an hour, emerging with about ten pages that contained the heart of the book that was going to be *Coils*. Certainly his ten pages would have served as a salable proposal, but by that time we were after more. After a little more discussion on chapter breaks, motivation, and so on, he left those pages with me, and after putting in some labor I sent back to him in Santa Fe about fifty pages, forming a kind of narrative skeleton.

Meanwhile, publishing arrangements had been concluded with Tor Books. So Roger sat down with my fifty pages, his typewriter[1] in his lap I have no doubt, and let flow the series of nicely polished chapters that made up the finished book. I marveled at a distance; he could always make that stage of things look easy, like a highwire artist strolling across close up under the big top.

I had never tried book-length collaboration before, and I probably never will again—I've been spoiled. It was for each of us the easiest book that we had ever finished . . . maybe too easy, now that I look back at the experience. It is quite possible that both *Coils* and our second joint production, *The Black Throne,* would have been better books, and would have sold more copies, had we struggled more with the stories, and with each other, during their production.

But struggle? With Roger?

He was one of the least contentious of men, and in many ways one of the most generous. His martial art of preference was *aikido,* so purely a defensive system that any direct contest between practitioners is impossible.

[1]This was around 1980. Not that the date would have made much difference. As far as I know, no one ever persuaded Roger that writing on a computer is easier and more efficient than making marks directly on the paper. Joan and I once talked him into *buying* a Macintosh, but then it just sat there. We had some fun with dueling chess programs, his computer's against mine.

Dwelling as we did in different cities, leading what were in many ways quite different lives, there were often long gaps between meetings. He traveled the world a great deal more than I did, but both of us were busy, and our schedules all too frequently failed to mesh. Avoiding quarrels as he did, he also disliked confrontations; and a further extension of this principle led him to steer clear of saying or doing anything that might produce an unpleasant reaction in whoever was around him, particularly friends or loved ones. This behavior made him an unfailingly pleasant companion.

But it also had a downside, when it denied people information they would have deemed of great importance, however unpalatable—such as the fact that Roger Zelazny was dying of cancer.

When he died I was angry at him, and now, almost two years later, I think I still am, not only for leaving us all here Rogerless but for keeping the imminence of his departure such a secret. But I'll get over it. After all, he didn't do it on purpose.

Someone someday will do a thorough biography. This is not the place to attempt even an outline of that. Rather it is the place to see what kind of reflections a spirit like Roger's can evoke in the minds of other talented writers, what sparks his talent can strike from theirs. And to hear from those others about his impact on their lives. And on the world.

True love can never be forgotten—or can it?

■

LETHE
Walter Jon Williams

DAVOUT HAD HIMSELF DISASSEMBLED FOR THE RETURN JOURNEY. HE had already been torn in half, he felt: the remainder, the dumb beast still alive, did not matter. The Captain had ruled, and Katrin would not be brought back. Davout did not want to spend the years between the stars in pain, confronting the gaping absence in his quarters and surrounded by the quiet sympathy of the crew.

Besides, he was no longer needed. The terraforming team had done its work, and then, but for Davout, had died.

Davout lay down on a bed of nano and let the little machines take him apart piece by piece, turn his body, his mind, and his unquenchable longing into long strings of numbers. The nanos crawled into his brain first, mapping, recording, and then shut down his mind piece by piece, so that he would feel no discomfort during what followed, or suffer a memory of his own body being taken apart.

Davout hoped that the nanos would shut down the pain before his consciousness failed, so that he could remember what it was like to live without the anguish that was now a part of his life, but it didn't work out that way. When his consciousness ebbed, he was aware, even to the last fading of the light, of the knife-blade of loss still buried in his heart.

* * *

4

The pain was there when Davout awoke, a wailing voice that cried, a pure contralto keen of agony, in his first dawning awareness. He found himself in an early-Victorian bedroom, blue-striped wallpaper, silhouettes in oval frames, silk flowers in vases. Crisp sheets, light streaming in the window. A stranger—shoulder-length hair, black frock coat, cravat carelessly tied—looked at him from a gothic-revival armchair. The man held a pipe in the right hand and tamped down tobacco with the prehensile big toe of his left foot.

"I'm not on the *Beagle*," Davout said.

The man gave a grave nod. His left hand formed the mudra for <correct>. "Yes."

"And this isn't a virtual?"

<Correct> again. "No."

"Then something has gone wrong."

<Correct> "Yes. A moment, sir, if you please." The man finished tamping, slipped his foot into a waiting boot, then lit the pipe with the anachronistic lighter in his left hand. He puffed, drew in smoke, exhaled, put the lighter in his pocket, and settled back in the walnut embrace of his chair.

"I am Dr. Li," he said. <Stand by> said the left hand, the old finger position for a now-obsolete palmtop computer, a finger position that had once meant *pause,* as <correct> had once meant *enter,* enter because it was correct. "Please remain in bed for a few more minutes while the nanos doublecheck their work. Redundancy is frustrating," puffing smoke, "but good for peace of mind."

"What happens if they find they've made a mistake?"

<Don't be concerned.> "It can't be a very large mistake," said Li, "or we wouldn't be communicating so rationally. At worst, you will sleep for a bit while things are corrected."

"May I take my hands out from under the covers?" he asked. "Yes."

Davout did so. His hands, he observed, were brown and leathery, hands suitable for the hot, dry world of Sarpedon. They had not, then, changed his body for one more suited to Earth, but given him something familiar.

If, he realized, they were on Earth.

His right fingers made the mudra <thank you>.

<Don't mention it> signed Li.

Davout passed a hand over his forehead, discovered that the forehead, hand, and the gesture itself were perfectly familiar.

Strange, but the gesture convinced him that he was, in a vital way, still himself. Still Davout.

Still alive, he thought. Alas.

"Tell me what happened," he said. "Tell me why I'm here."

Li signed <stand by>, made a visible effort to collect himself. "We believe," he said, "that the *Beagle* was destroyed. If so, you are the only survivor."

Davout found his shock curiously veiled. The loss of the other lives—friends, most of them—stood muted by the intensity of his own previous, overriding grief. It was as if the two losses were weighed in a balance, and the *Beagle* found wanting.

Li, Davout observed, was waiting for Davout to absorb this information before continuing.

<Go on> Davout signed.

"The accident happened seven light-years out," Li said. "*Beagle* began to yaw wildly, and both automatic systems and the crew failed to correct the maneuver. *Beagle*'s automatic systems concluded that the ship was unlikely to survive the increasing oscillations, and began to use its communications lasers to download personality data to collectors in Earth orbit. As the only crew member to elect disassembly during the return journey, you were first in the queue. The others, we presume, ran to nano disassembly stations, but communication was lost with the *Beagle* before we retrieved any of their data."

"Did Katrin's come through?"

Li stirred uneasily in his chair. <Regrettably> "I'm afraid not."

Davout closed his eyes. He had lost her again. Over the bubble of hopelessness in his throat he asked, "How long has it been since my data arrived?"

"A little over eight days."

They had waited eight days, then, for *Beagle*—for the *Beagle* of seven years ago—to correct its problem and reestablish communication. If *Beagle* had resumed contact, the mass of data that was Davout might have been erased as redundant.

"The government has announced the loss," Li said. "Though there is a remote chance that the *Beagle* may come flying in or through the system in eleven years as scheduled, we have detected no more transmissions, and we've been unable to observe any blue-shifted deceleration torch aimed at our system. The government decided that it would be unfair to keep sibs and survivors in the dark any longer."

<Concur> Davout signed.

He envisioned the last moments of the *Beagle*, the crew being flung back and forth as the ship slammed through increasing pendulum swings, the desperate attempts, fighting wildly fluctuating gravity and inertia, to reach the emergency nanobeds . . . no panic, Davout thought, Captain Moshweshwe had trained his people too well for that. Just desperation, and determination, and, as the oscillations grew worse, an increasing sense of futility, and impending death.

No one expected to die anymore. It was always a shock when it happened near you. Or *to* you.

"The cause of the *Beagle*'s problem remains unknown," Li said, the voice far away. "The Bureau is working with simulators to try to discover what happened."

Davout leaned back against his pillow. Pain throbbed in his veins, pain and loss, knowledge that his past, his joy, was irrecoverable. "The whole voyage," he said, "was a catastrophe."

<I respectfully contradict> Li signed. "You terraformed and explored two worlds," he said. "Downloads are already living on these worlds, hundreds of thousands now, millions later. There would have been a third world added to our commonwealth if your mission had not been cut short due to the, ah, first accident . . ."

<Concur> Davout signed, but only because his words would have come out with too much bitterness.

<Sorry>, a curt jerk of Li's fingers. "There are messages from your sibs," Lib said, "and downloads from them also. The sibs and friends of *Beagle*'s crew will try to contact you, no doubt. You need not answer any of these messages until you're ready."

<Understood>

Davout hesitated, but the words were insistent; he gave them tongue. "Have Katrin's sibs sent messages?" he asked.

Li's grave expression scarcely changed. "I believe so." He tilted his head. "Is there anything I can do for you? Anything I can arrange?"

"Not now, no," said Davout. <Thank you> he signed. "Can I move from the bed now?"

Li's look turned abstract as he scanned indicators projected somewhere in his mind. <Yes> "You may," he said. He rose from his chair, took the pipe from his mouth. "You are in a hospital, I should add," he said, "but you do not have the formal status of patient, and may leave at any time. Likewise, you may stay here for the foreseeable future, as long as you feel it necessary."

<Thank you> "Where is this hospital, by the way?"

"West Java. The city of Bandung."

Earth, then. Which Davout had not seen in seventy-seven years. Memory's gentle fingers touched his mind with the scent of durian, of ocean, of mace, cloves, and turmeric.

He knew he had never been in Java before, though, and wondered whence the memory came. From one of his sibs, perhaps?

<Thank you> Davout signed again, putting a touch of finality, a kind of dismissal, into the twist of his fingers.

Dr. Li left Davout alone, in his new/old body, in the room that whispered of memory and pain.

In a dark wood armoire Davout found identification and clothing, and a record confirming that his account had received seventy-eight years' back pay. His electronic inbox contained downloads from his sibs and more personal messages than he could cope with—he would have to construct an electronic personality to answer most of them.

He dressed and left the hospital. Whoever supervised his reassembly—Dr. Li perhaps—had thoughtfully included a complete Earth atlas in his internal ROM, and he accessed it as he walked, making random turnings but never getting lost. The furious sun burned down with tropical intensity, but his current body was constructed to bear heat, and a breeze off the mountains made pleasant even the blazing noontide.

The joyful metal music of the gamelans cluttered from almost every doorway. People in bright clothing, agile as the siamang of near Sumatra, sped overhead along treeways and ropeways, arms and hands modified for brachiation. Robots, immune to the heat, shimmered past on silent tires. Davout found it all strangely familiar, as if he had been here in a dream.

And then he found himself by the sea, and a pang of familiarity knifed through his heart. *Home!* cried his thoughts. Other worlds he had built, other beauties he had seen, but he had never beheld *this* blue, *this* perfection, anywhere else but on his native sphere. Subtle differences in atmospherics had rendered this color unnatural on any other world.

And with the cry of familiarity came a memory: it had been Davout the Silent who had come here, a century or more ago, and Katrin had been by his side.

But Davout's Katrin was dead. And as he looked on Earth's beauty, he felt his world of joy turn to bitter ashes.

<Alas!> His fingers formed the word unbidden. <Alas!>

He lived in a world where no one died, and nothing was ever lost. One understood that such things occasionally occurred, but never—hardly ever—to anyone that one knew. Physical immortality was cheap and easy, and was supported by so many alternate systems: backing up the mind by downloading, or downloading into a virtual reality system or into a durable machine. Nanosystems duplicated the body or improved it, adapted it for different environments. Data slumbered in secure storage, awaiting the electron kiss that returned it to life. Bringing a child to term in the womb was now the rarest form of reproduction, and bringing a child to life in a machine womb the next rarest.

It was so much easier to have the nanos duplicate you as an adult. Then, at least, you had someone to talk to.

No one died, and nothing is ever lost. But Katrin died, Davout thought, and now I am lost, and it was not supposed to be this way.

<Alas!> Fingers wailed the grief that was stopped up in Davout's throat. <Alas!>

Davout and Katrin had met in school, members of the last generation in which womb-breeding outnumbered the alternatives. Immortality whispered its covenant into their receptive ears. On their first meeting, attending a lecture (Dolphus on "Reinventing the Humboldt Sea") at the College of Mystery, they looked at each other and *knew,* as if angels had whispered into their ears, that there was now one less mystery in the world, that each served as an answer to another, that each fitted neatly into a hollow that the other had perceived in his or her soul, dropping into place as neatly as a butter-smooth piece in a finely made teak puzzle—or, considering their interests, as easily as a carbolic functional group nested into place on an indole ring.

Their rapport was, they freely admitted, miraculous. Still young, they exploded into the world, into a universe that welcomed them.

He could not bear to be away from her. Twenty-four hours was the absolute limit before Davout's nerves began to beat a frustrated little tattoo, and he found himself conjuring a phantom Katrin in his imagination, just to have someone to share the world with— he *needed* her there, needed this human lens through which he viewed the universe.

Without her, Davout found the cosmos veiled in a kind of uncertainty. While it was possible to apprehend certain things (the usefulness of a coenocytic arrangement of cells in the transmission of information-bearing proteins and nuclei, the historical significance of the Yucatán astrobleme, the limitations of the Benard cell model in predicting thermic instabilities in the atmosphere), these things lacked noesis, existed only as a series of singular, purposeless accidents. Reflected through Katrin, however, the world took on brilliance, purpose, and genius. With Katrin he could feast upon the universe; without her the world lacked savor.

Their interests were similar enough for each to generate enthusiasm in the other, diverse enough that each was able to add perspective to the other's work. They worked in cozy harmony, back to back, two desks set in the same room. Sometimes Davout would return from a meeting, or a coffee break, and find that Katrin had added new paragraphs, sometimes an entire new direction, to his latest effort. On occasion he would return the favor. Their early work—eccentric, proliferating in too many directions, toward too many specialities—showed life and promise and more than a hint of brilliance.

Too much, they decided, for just the two of them. They wanted to do too much, and all at once, and an immortal lifetime was not time enough.

And so, as soon as they could afford it, Red Katrin, the original, was duplicated—with a few cosmetic alternations—in Dark Katrin and later Katrin the Fair; and nanomachines read Old Davout, blood and bone and the long strands of numbers that were his soul, and created perfect copies in Dangerous Davout, later called the Conqueror, and Davout the Silent.

Two had become six, and half a dozen, they now agreed, was about all the universe could handle for the present. The wild tangle of overlapping interests was parceled out between the three couples, each taking one of the three most noble paths to understanding. The eldest couple took History as their domain, a part of which involved chronicling the adventures of their sibs; the second couple took Science; the third Psyche, the exploration of the human mind. Any developments, any insights, on the part of one of the sibs could be shared with the others through downloads. In the beginning they downloaded themselves almost continually, sharing their thoughts and experiences and plans in a shared frenzy of memory. Later, as separate lives and more specialized careers developed, the downloads grew less frequent, though there were no interruptions until Dangerous Davout and Dark Katrin took their first voyage to another star. They spent over fifty years away, though to them it was less than thirty; and the downloads from Earth, pulsed over immense distances by communications lasers, were less frequent, and less frequently resorted to. The lives of the other couples, lived at what seemed speeded-up rates, were of decreasing relevance to their own existence, as if they were lives that dwelled in a half-remembered dream.

<Alas!> the fingers signed. <Alas!> for the dream turned to savage nightmare.

The sea, a perfect terrestrial blue, gazed back into Davout's eyes, indifferent to the sadness frozen into his fingers.

"Your doctors knew that to wake her, after such an absence, would result in a feeling of anachronism," said Davout's sib, "so they put you in this Victorian room, where you would at least feel at ease with the kind of anachronism by which you are surrounded." He smiled at Davout from the neo-gothic armchair. "If you were in a modern room, you might experience a sensation of obsolescence. But everyone can feel superior to the Victorians, and besides one is always more comfortable in one's past."

"Is one?" Davout asked, fingers signing <irony>. The past and the present, he found, were alike a place of torment.

"I discover," he continued, "that my thoughts stray for comfort not to the past, but to the future."

"Ah." A smile. "That is why we call you Davout the Conqueror."

"I do not seem to inhabit that name," Davout said, "if I ever did."

Concern shadowed the face of Davout's sib. <Sorry> he signed, and then made another sign for <profoundly>, the old *multiply* sign, multiples of sorrow in his gesture.

"I understand," he said. "I experienced your last download. It was . . . intensely disturbing. I have never felt such terror, such loss."

"Nor had I," said Davout.

It was Old Davout whose image was projected into the gothic-revival armchair, the original, womb-born Davout of whom the two sibs were copies. When Davout looked at him it was like looking into a mirror in which his reflection had been retarded for several centuries, then unexpectedly released—Davout remembered, several bodies back, once possessing that tall forehead, the fair hair, the small ears flattened close to the skull. The gray eyes he had still, but he could never picture himself wearing the professorial little goatee.

"How is our other sib?" Davout asked.

The concern on Old Davout's face deepened. "You will find Silent Davout much changed. You haven't uploaded him, then?"

<No> "Due to the delays, I'm thirty years behind on my uploading."

"Ah." <Regret> "Perhaps you should speak to him, then, before you upload all those years."

"I will." He looked at his sib and hoped the longing did not burn in his eyes. "Please give my best to Katrin, will you?"

"I will give her your *love*," said Old Davout, wisest of the sibs.

The pain was there when Davout awoke the next day, fresh as the moment it first knifed through him, on the day their fifth child, the planet Sarpedon, was christened. Sarpedon had been discovered by astronomers a couple centuries before, and named, with due regard for tradition, after yet another minor character in Homer; it had been mapped and analyzed by robot probes; but it had been the *Beagle*'s terraforming team that had made the windswept place, with its barren mountain ranges and endless deserts, its angry radiation and furious dust storms, into a place suitable for life.

Katrin was the head of the terraforming team. Davout led its research division. Between them, raining nano from Sarpedon's black skies, they nursed the planet to life, enriched its atmosphere, filled its seas, crafted tough, versatile vegetation capable of withstanding the angry environment. Seeded life by the tens of millions, insects, reptiles, birds, mammals, fish, and amphibians. Re-created themselves, with dark, leathery skin and slit pupils, as human forms suitable for Sarpedon's environment, so that they could examine the place they had built.

And—unknown to the others—Davout and Katrin had slipped their own genetics into almost every Sarpedan life-form. Bits of redundant coding, mostly, but enough so that they could claim Sarpedon's entire world of creatures as their children. Even when they were junior terraformers on the *Cheng Ho*'s mission to Rhea, they had, partly as a joke, partly as something more calculated, populated their creations with their genes.

Katrin and Davout spent the last two years of their project on Sarpedon among their children, examining the different ecosystems, different interactions, thinking of new adaptations. In the end Sarpedon was certified as suitable for human habitation. Preprogrammed nanos constructed small towns, laid out fields, parks, and roads. The first human Sarpedans would be constructed in nanobeds, and their minds filled with the downloaded personalities of volunteers from Earth. There was no need to go to the expense and trouble of shipping out millions of warm bodies from Earth, running the risks of traveling for decades in remote space. Not when nanos could construct them all new on site.

The first Sarpendans—bald, leather-skinned, slit-eyed—emerged blinking into their new red dawn. Any further terraforming, any attempts to fine-tune the planet and make it more Earthlike, would be a long-term project and up to them. In a splendid ceremony, Captain Moshweshwe formally turned the future of Sarpedon over to them. Davout had a few last formalities to perform, handing certain computer codes and protocols over to the Sarpedans, but the rest of the terraforming team, most fairly drunk on champagne, filed into the shuttle for the return journey to the *Beagle*. As Davout bent over a terminal with his Sarpedan colleagues and the *Beagle*'s first officer, he could hear the roar of the shuttle on its pad, the sustained thunder as it climbed for orbit, the thud as it crashed through the sound barrier, and then he saw out of the corner of his eye the sudden red-gold flare . . .

When he raced outside it was to see the blazing poppy unfolding in the sky, a blossom of fire and metal falling slowly to the surface of the newly-christened planet.

There she was—her image anyway—in the neo-gothic armchair:

Red Katrin, the green-eyed lady with whom he in memory, and Old Davout in reality, had first exchanged glances two centuries ago while Dolphus expanded on what he called his "lunaforming."

Davout had hesitated about returning her call of condolence. He did not know whether his heart could sustain *two* knife-thrusts, both Katrin's death and the sight of her sib, alive, sympathetic, and forever beyond his reach.

But he couldn't *not* call her. Even when he was trying not to think about her, he still found Katrin on the edge of his perceptions, drifting though his thoughts like the persistent trace of some familiar perfume.

Time to get it over with, he thought. If it was more than he could stand, he could apologize and end the call. But he had to *know* . . .

"And there are no backups?" she said. A pensive frown touched her lips.

"No *recent* backups," Davout said. "We always thought that, if we were to die, we would die together. Space travel is hazardous, after all, and when catastrophe strikes it is not a *small* catastrophe. We didn't anticipate one of us surviving a catastrophe on Earth, and the other dying light-years away." He scowled.

"Damn Mosheshwe anyway! There were recent backups on the *Beagle,* but with so many dead from an undetermined cause he decided not to resurrect anyone, to cancel our trip to Astoreth, return to Earth, and sort out all the complications once he got home."

"He made the right decision," Katrin said. "If my sib had been resurrected, you both would have died together."

<Better so> Davout's fingers began to form the mudra, but he thought better of it, made a gesture of negation.

The green eyes narrowed. "There are older backups on Earth, yes?"

"Katrin's latest surviving backup dates from the return of the *Cheng Ho.*"

"Almost ninety years ago." Thoughtfully. "But she could upload the memories she has been sending me . . . The problem does not seem insurmountable."

Red Katrin clasped her hands around one knee. At the familiar gesture, memories rang though Davout's mind like change-bells. Vertigo overwhelmed him, and he closed his eyes.

"The problem is the instructions Katrin—we both—left," he said. "Again, we anticipated that if we died, we'd die together. And so we left instructions that our backups on Earth were not to be employed. We reasoned that we had two sibs apiece on Earth, and if they—you—missed us, you could simply duplicate yourselves."

"I see." A pause, then concern. "Are you all right?"

<No> "Of course not," he said. He opened his eyes. The world eddied for a moment, then stilled, the growing calmness centered on Red Katrin's green eyes.

"I've got seventy-odd years' back pay," he said. "I suppose that I could hire some lawyers, try to get Katrin's backup released to my custody."

Red Katrin bit her nether lip. "Recent court decisions are not in your favor."

"I'm very persistent. And I'm cash-rich."

She cocked her head, looked at hm. "Are you all right talking to me? Should I blank my image?"

<No> He shook his head. "It helps, actually, to see you."

He had feared agony in seeing her, but instead he found a growing joy, a happiness that mounted in his heart. As always, his Katrin was helping him to understand, helping him to make sense of the bitter confusion of the world.

An idea began to creep into his mind on stealthy feet.

"I worry that you're alone there," Red Katrin said. "Would you like to come stay with us? Would you like us to come to Java?"

<No, thanks> "I'll come see you soon," Davout said. "But while I'm in the hospital, I think I'll have a few cosmetic procedures." He looked down at himself, spread his leathery hands. "Perhaps I should look a little more Earthlike."

After his talk with Katrin ended, Davout called Dr. Li and told him that he wanted a new body constructed.

Something familiar, he said, already in the files. His own, original form.

Age twenty or so.

"It is a surprise to see you . . . as you are," said Silent Davout.

Deep-voiced, black-skinned and somber, Davout's sib stood by his bed.

"It was a useful body when I wore it," Davout answered. "I take comfort in . . . familiar things . . . now that my life is so uncertain." He looked up. "It was good of you to come in person."

"A holographic body," taking Davout's hand, "however welcome, however familiar, is not the same as a real person."

Davout squeezed the hand. "Welcome, then," he said. Dr. Li, who had supervised in person through the new/old body's assembly, had left after saying the nanos were done, so it seemed appropriate for Davout to stand and embrace his sib.

The youngest of the sibs was not tall, but he was built solidly, as if for permanence, and his head seemed slightly oversized for his body. With his older sibs he had always maintained a kind of formal reserve that had resulted in his being nicknamed "the Silent." Accepting the name, he remarked that the reason he spoke little when the others were around was that his older sibs had already said everything that needed saying before he got to it.

Davout stepped back and smiled. "Your patients must think you a tower of strength."

"I have no patients these days. Mostly I work in the realm of theory."

"I will have to look up your work. I'm so far behind on uploads—I don't have any idea what you and Katrin had been doing these last decades."

Silent Davout stepped to the armoire and opened its ponderous mahogany doors. "Perhaps you should put on some clothing," he said. "I am feeling chill in this conditioned air, and so must you."

Amused, Davout clothed himself, then sat across the little rosewood side table from his sib. Davout the Silent looked at him for a long moment—eyes placid and thoughtful—and then spoke.

"You are experiencing something that is very rare in our time," he said. "Loss, anger, frustration, terror. All the emotions that in their totality equal *grief*."

"You forgot sadness and regret," Davout said. "You forget memory, and how the memories keep replaying. You forgot *imagination*, and how imagination only makes those memories worse, because imagination allows you to write a different ending, but the world will not."

Silent Davout nodded. "People in my profession," fingers forming <irony>, "anyway those born too late to remember how common these things once were, must view you with a certain clinical interest. I must commend Dr. Li on his restraint."

"Dr. Li is a shrink?" Davout asked.

<Yes> A casual press of fingers. "Among other things. I'm sure he's watching you very carefully and making little notes every time he leaves the room."

"I'm happy to be useful." <Irony> in his hand, bitterness on his tongue. "I would give those people my memories, if they want them so much."

<Of course> "You can do that." Davout looked up in something like surprise.

"You know it is possible," his sib said. "You can download your memories, preserve them like amber or simply hand them to someone else to experience. And you can erase them from your mind completely, walk on into a new life, *tabula rasa* and free of pain."

His deep voice was soft. It was a voice without affect, one he no doubt used on his patients, quietly insistent without being officious. A voice that made suggestions, or presented alternatives, but which never, ever, gave orders.

"I don't want that," Davout said.

Silent Davout's fingers were still set in <of course>. "You are not of the generation that accepts such things as a matter of course," he said. "But this, this *modular* approach to memory, to being, constitutes much of my work these days."

Davout looked at him. "It must be like losing a piece of yourself, to give up a memory. Memories are what make you."

Silent Davout's face remained impassive as his deep voice sounded through the void between them. "What forms a human psyche is not a memory, we have come to believe, but a pattern of thought. When our sib duplicated himself, he duplicated his pattern in us; and when we assembled new bodies to live in, the pattern did not change. Have you felt yourself a different person when you took a new body?"

Davout passed a hand over his head, felt the fine blond hair covering his scalp. This time yesterday, his head had been bald and leathery. Now he felt subtle differences in his perceptions—his vision was more acute, his hearing less so—and his muscle memory was somewhat askew. He remembered having a shorter reach, a slightly different center of gravity.

But as for *himself,* his essence—no, he felt himself unchanged. He was still Davout.

<No> he signed.

"People have more choices than ever before," said Silent Davout. "They choose their bodies, they chose their memories. They can upload new knowledge, new skills. If they feel a lack of confidence, or feel that their behavior is too impulsive, they can tweak their body chemistry to produce a different effect. If they find themselves the victim of an unfortunate or destructive compulsion, the compulsion can be edited from their being. If they lack the power to change their circumstances, they can at least elect to feel happier about them. If a memory cannot be overcome, it can be eliminated."

"And you now spend your time dealing with these problems?" Davout asked.

"They are not *problems,*" his sib said gently. "They are not *syndromes* or *neuroses.* They are *circumstances.* They are part of the condition of life as it exists today. They are environmental." The large, impassive eyes gazed steadily at Davout. "People choose happiness over sorrow, fulfillment over frustration. Can you blame them?"

<Yes> Davout signed. "If they deny the evidence of their own lives," he said. "We define our existence by the challenges we overcome, or those we don't. Even our tragedies define us."

His sib nodded. "That is an admirable philosophy—for Davout the Conqueror. But all people are not conquerors."

Davout strove to keep the impatience from his voice. "Lessons are learned from failures as well as successes. Experience is gained, life's knowledge is applied to subsequent occurrence. If we deny the uses of experience, what is there to make us human?"

His sib was patient. "Sometimes the experiences are negative, and so are the lessons. Would you have a person live forever under the shadow of great guilt, say for a foolish mistake that resulted in injury or death to someone else; or would you have them live with the consequences of damage inflicted by a sociopath, or an abusive family member? Traumas like these can cripple the whole being. Why should the damage not be repaired?"

Davout smiled thinly. "You can't tell me that these techniques are used only in cases of deep trauma," he said. "You can't tell me that people aren't using these techniques for reasons that might be deemed trivial. Editing out a foolish remark made at a party, or eliminating a bad vacation or an argument with the spouse."

Silent Davout returned his smile. "I would not insult your intelligence by suggesting these things do not happen."

"So how do such people mature? Change? Grow in wisdom?"

"They cannot edit out *everything*. There is sufficient friction and conflict in the course of ordinary life to provide everyone with their allotted portion of wisdom. Nowadays our lives are very, very long, and we have a long time to learn, however slowly. And after all," smiling, "the average person's capacity for wisdom has never been so large as all that. I think you will find that as a species we are far less prone to folly than we once were."

Davout looked at his sib grimly. "You are suggesting that I undergo this technique?"

"It is called Lethe."

"That I undergo Lethe? Forget Katrin? Or forget what I feel for her?"

Silent Davout slowly shook his grave head. "I make no such suggestion."

"Good."

The youngest Davout gazed steadily into the eyes of his older twin. "Only you know what you can bear. I merely point out that this remedy exists, should you find your anguish beyond what you can endure."

"Katrin deserves mourning," Davout said.

Another grave nod. "Yes."

"She deserves to be remembered. Who will remember her if I do not?"

"I understand," said Silent Davout. "I understand your desire to feel, and the necessity. I only mention Lethe because I comprehend all too well what you endure now. Because,'' he licked his lips, ''I, too, have lost Katrin.''

Davout gaped at him. ''You—'' he stammered. ''She is—she was killed?''

<No> His sib's face retained its remarkable placidity. ''She left me, sixteen years ago.''

Davout could only stare. The fact, stated so plainly, was incomprehensible.

''I—'' he began, and then his fingers found another thought. <What happened?>

''We were together for a century and a half. We grew apart. It happens.''

Not to us it doesn't! Davout's mind protested. *Not to Davout and Katrin!*

Not to the two people who make up a whole greater than its parts. Not to us. Not ever.

But looking into his sib's accepting, melancholy face, Davout knew that it had to be true.

And then, in a way he knew to be utterly disloyal, he began to hope.

''Shocking?'' said Old Davout. ''Not to us, I suppose.''

''It was their downloads,'' said Red Katrin. ''Fair Katrin in particular was careful to edit out some of her feelings and judgments before she let me upload them, but still I could see her attitudes changing. And knowing her, I could make guesses by what she left out . . . I remember telling Davout three years before the split that the relationship was in jeopardy.''

''The Silent One was still surprised, though, when it happened,'' Old Davout said. ''Sophisticated though he may be about human nature, he had a blind spot where Katrin was concerned.'' He put an arm around Red Katrin and kissed her cheek. ''As I suppose we all do,'' he added.

Katrin accepted the kiss with a gracious inclination of her head, then asked Davout, ''Would you like the blue room here, or the green room upstairs? The green room has a window seat and a fine view of the bay, but it's small.''

''I'll take the green room,'' Davout said. I do not need so much room, he thought, now that I am alone.

Katrin took him up the creaking wooden stair and showed him the room, the narrow bed of the old house. Through the window he could look south to a storm on Chesapeake Bay, blue-gray cloud, bright eruptions of lightning, slanting beams of sunlight that dropped through rents in the storm to tease bright winking light from the foam. He watched it for a long moment, then was startled out of reverie by Katrin's hand on his shoulder, and a soft voice in his ear.

"Are there sights like this on other worlds?"

"The storms on Rhea were vast," Davout said, "like nothing on this world. The ocean area is greater than that on Earth, and lies mostly in the tropics—the planet was almost called Oceanus on that account. The hurricanes built up around the equatorial belts with nothing to stop them, sometimes more than a thousand kilometers across, and they came roaring into the temperate zones like many-armed demons, sometimes one after another for months. They spawned waterspouts and cyclones in their vanguard, inundated whole areas with a storm surge the size of a small ocean, dumped enough rain to flood an entire province away . . . We thought seriously that the storms might make life on land untenable."

He went on to explain the solution he and Katrin had devised for the enormous problem: huge strings of tall, rocky barrier islands built at a furious rate by nanomachines, a wall for wind and storm surge to break against; a species of silvery, tropical floating weed, a flowery girdle about Rhea's thick waist, that radically increased surface albedo, reflecting more heat back into space. Many species of deep-rooted, vinelike plants to anchor slopes and prevent erosion, other species of thirsty trees, adaptations of cottonwoods and willows, to line streambeds and break the power of flash floods.

Planetary engineering on such an enormous scale, in such a short time, had never been attempted, not even on Mars, and it had been difficult for Katrin and Davout to sell the project to the project managers on the *Cheng Ho*. Their superiors had initially preferred a different approach, huge equatorial solar curtains deployed in orbit to reflect heat, squadrons of orbital beam weapons to blast and disperse storms as they formed, secure underground dwellings for the inhabitants, complex lock and canal systems to control flooding . . . Katrin and Davout had argued for a more elegant approach to Rhea's problems, a reliance on organic systems to modify the planet's extreme weather instead of assaulting Rhea with macro-tech and engineering. Theirs was the approach that finally won the support of the majority of the terraforming team, and resulted in their subsequent appointment as heads of *Beagle*'s terraforming department.

"Dark Katrin's memories were very exciting to upload during that time," said Katrin the Red. "That delirious explosion of creativity! Watching a whole globe take shape beneath her feet!" Her green eyes looked up into Davout's. "We were jealous of you then. All that abundance being created, all that talent going to shaping an entire world. And we were confined to scholarship, which seemed so lifeless by comparison."

He looked at her. "Are you sorry for the choice you made? You two were senior: you could have chosen our path if you'd wished. You still could, come to that."

A smile drifted across her face. "You tempt me, truly. But Old Davout and I are happy in our work—and besides, you and Katrin need someone to provide a proper record of your adventures." She tilted her head, and mischief glittered in her eyes. "Perhaps you should ask Blonde Katrin. Maybe she could use a change."

Davout gave a guilty start: she was, he thought, seeing too near, too soon. "Do you think so?" he asked. "I didn't even know if I should see her."

"Her grudge is with the Silent One, not with you."

"Well." He managed a smile. "Perhaps I will at least call."

Davout called Katrin the Fair, received an offer of dinner on the following day, accepted. From his room he followed the smell of coffee into the office, and felt a bubble of grief lodge in his heart: two desks, back-to-back, two computer terminals, layers of papers and books and printout and dust . . . He could imagine himself and Katrin here, sipping coffee, working in pleasant compatibility.

"How goes it?" he asked.

His sib looked up. "I just sent a chapter to Sheol," he said. "I was making Maxwell far too wise." He fingered his little goatee. "The temptation is always to view the past solely as a vehicle that leads to our present grandeur. These people's sole function was to produce *us,* who are of course perfectly wise and noble and far superior to our ancestors. So I have to keep reminding myself that these people lived amid unimaginable tragedy, disease and ignorance and superstition, vile little wars, terrible poverty, and *death* . . ."

He stopped, suddenly aware that he'd said something awkward—Davout felt the word vibrate in his bones, as if he were stranded inside a bell that was still singing after it had been struck—but he said, "Go on."

"I remind myself," his sib continued, "that the fact that we live in a modern culture doesn't make us better, it doesn't make us superior to these people—in fact it enlarges *them,* because they had to overcome so much more than we in order to realize themselves, in order to accomplish as much as they did." A shy smile drifted across his face. "And so a rather smug chapter is wiped out of digital existence."

"*Lavoisier* is looming," commented Red Katrin from her machine.

"Yes, that too," Old Davout agreed. His *Lavoisier and His Age* had won the McEldowney Prize and been shortlisted for other awards. Davout could well imagine that bringing *Maxwell* up to *Lavoisier*'s magisterial standards would be intimidating.

Red Katrin leaned back in her chair, combed her hair back with her fingers. "I made a few notes about the *Beagle* project," she said. "I have other commitments to deal with first, of course."

She and Old Davout had avoided any conflicts of interest and interpretation by conveniently dividing history between them: she would write of the "modern" world and her near-contemporaries, while he wrote of those securely in the past. Davout thought his sib had the advantage in this arrangement, because her subjects, as time progressed, gradually entered his domain, and became liable to his reinterpretation.

Davout cleared away some printout, sat on the edge of Red Katrin's desk. "A thought keeps bothering me," he said. "In our civilization we record everything. But the last moments of the crew of the *Beagle* went unrecorded. Does that mean they do not exist? Never existed at all? That death was *always* their state, and they returned to it, like virtual matter dying into the vacuum from which it came?"

Concern darkened Red Katrin's eyes. "They will be remembered," she said. "I will see to it."

"Katrin didn't download the last months, did she?"

<No> "The last eight months were never sent. She was very busy, and—"

"Virtual months, then. Gone back to the phantom zone."

"There are records. Other crew sent downloads home, and I will see if I can gain access either to the downloads, or to their friends and relations who have experienced them. There is *your* memory, your downloads."

He looked at her. "Will you upload my memory, then? My sib has everything in his files, I'm sure." Glancing at Old Davout.

She pressed her lips together. "That would be difficult for me. *Me* viewing *you* viewing *her* . . ." She shook her head. "I don't dare. Not now. Not when we're all still in shock."

Disappointment gnawed at his insides with sharp rodent teeth. He did not want to be so alone in his grief; he didn't want to nourish all the sadness by himself.

He wanted to share it with *Katrin,* he knew, the person with whom he shared everything. Katrin could help him make sense of it, the way she clarified all the world for him. Katrin would comprehend the way he felt.

<I understand> he signed. His frustration must have been plain

to Red Katrin, because she took his hand, lifted her green eyes to his.

"I *will*," she said. "But not now. I'm not ready."

"I don't want *two* wrecks in the house," called Old Davout over his shoulder.

Interfering old bastard, Davout thought. But with his free hand he signed, again, <I understand>.

Katrin the Fair kissed Davout's cheek, then stood back, holding his hands, and narrowed her gray eyes. "I'm not sure I approve of this youthful body of yours," she said. "You haven't looked like this in—what, over a century?"

"Perhaps I seek to evoke happier times," Davout said.

A little frown touched the corners of her mouth. "*That* is always dangerous," she judged. "But I wish you every success." She stepped back from the door, flung out an arm. "Please come in."

She lived in a small apartment in Toulouse, with a view of the Allée Saint-Michel and the rose-red brick of the Vieux Quartier. On the whitewashed walls hung terra-cotta icons of Usil and Tiv, the Etruscan gods of the sun and moon, and a well cover with a figure of the demon Charun emerging from the underworld. The Etruscan deities were confronted, on another wall, by a bronze figure of the Gaulish Rosmerta, consort of the absent Mercurius.

Her little balcony was bedecked with wrought iron and a gay striped awning. In front of the balcony a table shimmered under a red and white checked tablecloth: crystal, porcelain, a wicker basket of bread, a bottle of wine. Cooking scents floated in from the kitchen.

"It smells wonderful," Davout said.

<Drink?> Lifting the bottle.

<Why not?>

Wine was poured. They settled onto the sofa, chatted of weather, crowds, Java. Davout's memories of the trip that Silent Davout and his Katrin had taken to the island were more recent than hers.

Fair Katrin took his hand. "I have uploaded Dark Katrin's memories, so far as I have them," she said. "She loved you, you know—absolutely, deeply." <Truth> She bit her nether lip. "It was a remarkable thing."

<Truth> Davout answered. He touched cool crystal to his lips, took a careful sip of his cabernet. Pain throbbed in the hollows of his heart.

"Yes," he said. "I know."

"I felt I should tell you about her feelings. Particularly in view of what happened with me and the Silent One."

He looked at her. "I confess I do not understand that business."

She made a little frown of distaste. "We and our work and our situation grew irksome. Oppressive. You may upload his memories if you like—I daresay you will be able to observe the signs that he was determined to ignore."

<I am sorry>

Clouds gathered in her gray eyes. "I, too, have regrets."

"There is no chance of reconciliation?"

<Absolutely not>, accompanied by a brief shake of the head. "It was over." <Finished> "And, in any case, Davout the Silent is not the man he was."

<Yes?>

"He took Lethe. It was the only way he had of getting over my leaving him."

Pure amazement throbbed in Davout's soul. Fair Katrin looked at him in surprise.

"You didn't know?"

He blinked at her. "I *should* have. But I thought he was talking about *me,* about a way of getting over . . ." Aching sadness brimmed in his throat. "Over the way my Dark Katrin left me."

Scorn whitened the flesh about Fair Katrin's nostrils. "That's the Silent One for you. He didn't have the nerve to tell you outright."

"I'm not sure that's true. He may have thought he was speaking plainly enough—"

Her fingers formed a mudra that gave vent to a brand of disdain that did not translate into words. "He knows his effects perfectly well," she said. "He was trying to suggest the idea without making it clear that this was his *choice* for you, that he wanted you to fall in line with his theories."

Anger was clear in her voice. She rose, stalked angrily to the bronze of Rosmerta, adjusted its place on the wall by a millimeter or so. Turned, waved an arm.

<Apologies>, flung to the air. "Let's eat. Silent Davout is the last person I want to talk about right now."

"I'm sorry I upset you." Davout was not sorry at all: he found this display fascinating. The gestures, the tone of voice, were utterly familiar, ringing like chimes in his heart; but the *style,* the way Fair Katrin avoided the issue, was different. Dark Katrin never would never have fled a subject this way: she would have knit her brows and confronted the problem direct, engaged with it until she'd either reached understanding or catastrophe. Either way, she'd have laughed, and tossed her dark hair, and announced that now she understood.

"It's peasant cooking," Katrin the Fair said as she bustled to the kitchen, "which of course is the best kind."

The main course was a ragout of veal in a velouté sauce, beans cooked simply in butter and garlic, tossed salad, bread. Davout waited until it was half consumed, and the bottle of wine mostly gone, before he dared to speak again of his sib.

"You mentioned the Silent One and his theories," he said. "I'm thirty years behind on his downloads, and I haven't read his latest work—what is he up to? What's all this theorizing about?"

She sighed, fingers ringing a frustrated rhythm on her glass. Looked out the window for a moment, then conceded. "Has he mentioned the modular theory of the psyche?"

Davout tried to remember. "He said something about modular *memory,* I seem to recall."

"That's a part of it. It's a fairly radical theory that states that people should edit their personality and abilities at will, as circumstances dictate. That one morning, say, if you're going to work, you upload appropriate memories, and work skills, along with a dose of ambition, of resolution, and some appropriate emotions like satisfaction and eagerness to solve problems, or endure drudgery, as the case may be."

Davout looked at his plate. "Like cookery, then," he said. "Like this dish—veal, carrots, onions, celery, mushrooms, parsley."

Fair Katrin made a mudra that Davout didn't recognize. <Sorry?> he signed.

"Oh. Apologies. That one means, roughly, 'har-de-har-har.' " Fingers formed <laughter>, then <sarcasm>, then slurred them together. "See?"

<Understood> He poured more wine into her glass.

She leaned forward across her plate. "Recipes are fine if one wants to be *consumed,*" she said. "Survival is another matter. The human mind is more than just ingredients to be tossed together. The atomistic view of the psyche is simplistic, dangerous, and *wrong.* You cannot *will* a psyche to be whole, no matter how many *wholeness* modules are uploaded. A psyche is more than the sum of its parts."

Wine and agitation burnished her cheeks. Conviction blazed from her eyes. "It takes *time* to integrate new experience, new abilities. The modular theorists claim this will be done by a 'conductor,' an artificial intelligence that will be able to judge between alternate personalities and abilities and upload whatever's needed. But that's such *rubbish,* I—" She looked at the knife she was waving, then permitted it to return to the table.

"How far are the Silent One and his cohorts toward realizing this ambition?" Davout said.

She looked at him. "I didn't make that clear?" she said. "The technology is already here. It's happening. People are fragmenting their psyches deliberately and trusting to their conductors to make sense of it all. And they're *happy* with their choices, because that's the only emotion they permit themselves to upload from their supply." She clenched her teeth, glanced angrily out the window at the Vieux Quartier's sunset-burnished walls. "All traditional psychology is aimed at integration, at wholeness. And now it's all to be *thrown away* . . ." She flung her hand out the window. Davout's eyes automatically followed an invisible object on its arc from her fingers toward the street.

"And how does this theory work in practice?" Davout asked. "Are the streets filled with psychological wrecks?"

Bitterness twisted her lips. "Psychological imbeciles, more like. Executing their conductors' orders, docile as well-fed children, happy as clams. They upload passions—anger, grief, loss—as artificial experiences, secondhand from someone else, usually so they can tell their conductor to avoid such emotions in the future. They are not *people* any more, they're . . ." Her eyes turned to Davout.

"You saw the Silent One," she said. "Would you call him a *person?*"

"I was with him for only a day," Davout said. "I noticed something of a . . ." <Stand by> he signed, searching for the word.

"Lack of affect?" she interposed. "A demeanor marked by an extreme placidity?"

<Truth> he signed.

"When it was clear I wouldn't come back to him, he wrote me out of his memory," Fair Katrin said. "He replaced the memories with *facts*—he knows he was married to me, he knows we went to such-and-such a place or wrote such-and-such a paper—but there's nothing else there. No feelings, no real memories good or bad, no understanding, nothing left from almost two centuries together." Tears glittered in her eyes. "I'd rather he felt anything at all—I'd rather he hated me than feel this apathy!"

Davout reached across the little table and took her hand. "It is his decision," he said, "and his loss."

"It is *all* our loss," she said. Reflected sunset flavored her tears with the color of roses. "The man we loved is gone. And millions are gone with him—millions of little half-alive souls, programmed for happiness and unconcern." She tipped the bottle into her glass, received only a sluicing of dregs.

"Let's have another," she said.

When he left, some hours later, he embraced her, kissed her, let his lips linger on hers for perhaps an extra half-second. She blinked up at him in wine-muddled surprise, and then he took his leave.

"How did you find my sib?" Red Katrin asked.

"Unhappy," Davout said. "Confused. Lonely, I think. Living in a little apartment like a cell, with icons and memories."

<I know> she signed, and turned on him a knowing green-eyed look.

"Are you planning on taking her away from all that? To the stars, perhaps?"

Davout's surprise was brief. He looked away and murmured, "I didn't know I was so transparent."

A smile touched her lips. <Apologies> she signed. "I've lived with Old Davout for nearly two hundred years. You and he haven't grown so very far apart in that time. My fair sib deserves happiness, and so do you . . . if you can provide it, so much the better. But I wonder if you are not moving too fast, if you have thought it all out."

Moving fast, Davout wondered. His life seemed so very slow now, a creeping dance with agony, each move a lifetime.

He glanced out at Chesapeake Bay, saw his second perfect sunset in only a few hours—the same sunset he'd watched from Fair Katrin's apartment, now radiating its red glories on the other side of the Atlantic. A few water-skaters sped toward home on their silver blades. He sat with Red Katrin on a porch swing, looking down the long green sward to the bayfront, the old wooden pier, and the sparkling water, that profound, deep blue that sang of home to Davout's soul. Red Katrin wrapped herself against the breeze in a fringed, autumn-colored shawl. Davout sipped coffee from gold-rimmed porcelain, set the cup into its saucer.

"I wondered if I was being untrue to *my* Katrin," he said. "But they are really the same person, aren't they? If I were to pursue some other woman now, I would know I was committing a betrayal. But how can I betray Katrin with herself?"

An uncertain look crossed Red Katrin's face. "I've downloaded them both," hesitantly, "and I'm not certain that the Dark and Fair Katrins are quite the same person. Or ever were."

Not the same—of course he knew that. Fair Katrin was not a perfect copy of her older sib—she had flaws, clear enough. She had been damaged, somehow. But the flaws could be worked on, the damage repaired. Conquered. There was infinite time. He would see it done.

"And how do your sibs differ, then?" he asked. "Other than obvious differences in condition and profession?"

She drew her legs up and rested her chin on her knees. Her green eyes were pensive. "Matters of love," she said, "and happiness."

And further she would not say.

Davout took Fair Katrin to Tangier for the afternoon and walked with her up on the old palace walls. Below them, white in the sun, the curved mole built by Charles II cleaved the Middle Sea, a thin crescent moon laid upon the perfect shimmering azure. (Home! home!, the waters cried.) The sea breeze lashed her blond hair across her face, snapped little sonic booms from the sleeves of his shirt.

"I have sampled some of the Silent One's downloads," Davout said. "I wished to discover the nature of this artificial tranquillity with which he has endowed himself."

Fair Katrin's lips twisted in distaste, and her fingers formed a scatologue.

"It was . . . interesting," Davout said. "There was a strange, uncomplicated quality of bliss to it. I remember experiencing the download of a master sitting zazen once, and it was an experience of a similar cast."

"It may have been the exact same sensation." Sourly. "He may have just copied the zen master's experience and slotted it into his brain. That's how *most* of the vampires do it—award themselves the joy they haven't earned."

"That's a Calvinistic point of view," Davout offered. "That happiness can't just happen, that it has to be earned."

She frowned out at the sea. "There is a difference between real experience and artificial or recapitulative experience. If that's Calvinist, so be it."

<Yes> Davout signed. "Call me a Calvinist sympathizer, then. I have been enough places, done enough things, so that it matters to me that I was actually there and not living out some programmed dream of life on other worlds. I've experienced my sibs' downloads—lived significant parts of their lives, moment by moment—but it is not the same as *my life,* as *being me.* I am," he said, leaning elbows on the palace wall, "I am myself, I am the sum of everything that happened to me, I stand on this wall, I am watching this sea, I am watching it with you, and no one else has had this experience, nor ever shall, it is *ours,* it belongs to us . . ."

She looked up at him, straw-hair flying over an unreadable expression. "Davout the Conqueror," she said.

<No> he signed. "I did not conquer alone."

She nodded, holding his eyes for a long moment. "Yes," she said. "I know."

He took Katrin the Fair in his arms and kissed her. There was a moment's stiff surprise, and then she began to laugh, helpless peals bursting against his lips. He held her for a moment, too surprised to react, and then she broke free. She reeled along the wall, leaning for support against the old stone. Davout followed, babbling, "I'm sorry, I didn't mean to—"

She leaned back against the wall. Words burst half-hysterical from her lips, in between bursts of desperate, unamused laughter.

"So that's what you were after! My God! As if I hadn't had enough of you all after all these years!"

"I apologize," Davout said. "Let's forget this happened. I'll take you home."

She looked up at him, the laughter gone, blazing anger in its place. "The Silent One and I would have been all right if it hadn't been for you—*for our sibs!*" She flung her words like daggers, her voice breaking with passion. "You lot were the eldest, you'd already parceled out the world between you. You were only interested in psychology because my damned Red sib and your Old one wanted insight into the characters in their histories, and because you and your dark bitch wanted a theory of the psyche to aid you in building communities on other worlds. We only got created because *you were too damned lazy to do your own research!*"

Davout stood, stunned. <No> he signed, "That's not—"

"We were *third,*" she cried. "We were *born in third place.* We got the jobs you wanted least, and while you older sibs were winning fame and glory, we were stuck in work that didn't suit, that you'd *cast off,* awarded to us as if we were charity cases—" She stepped closer, and Davout was amazed to find a white-knuckled fist being shaken in his face. "My husband was called The Silent because his sibs had already used up all the words! He was third-rate and knew it. It *destroyed* him! Now he's plugging artificial satisfaction into his head because it's the only way he'll ever feel it."

"If you didn't like your life," Davout said, "you could have changed it. People start over all the time—we'd have helped." He reached toward her. "I can help you to the stars, if that's what you want."

She backed away. "The only help we ever needed was to *get rid of you!*" A mudra, <har-de-har-har>, echoed the sarcastic laughter on Fair Katrin's lips. "And now there's another gap in your life, and you want me to fill it—*not this time.*"

<Never> her fingers echoed. <Never> The laughter bubbled from her throat again.

She fled, leaving him alone and dazed on the palace wall, the booming wind mocking his feeble protests.

"I am truly sorry," Red Katrin said. She leaned close to him on the porch swing, touched soft lips to his cheek. "Even though she edited her downloads, I could tell she resented us—but I truly did not know how she would react."

Davout was frantic. He could feel Katrin slipping farther and farther away, as if she were on the edge of a precipice and her handholds were crumbling away beneath her clawed fingers.

"Is what she said true?" he asked. "Have we been slighting them all these years? Using them, as she claims?"

"Perhaps she had some justification once," Red Katrin said. "I do not remember anything of the sort when we were young, when I was uploading Fair Katrin almost every day. But now," her expression growing severe, "these are mature people, not without resources or intelligence—I can't help but think that surely after a person is a century old, any problems that remain are *her* fault."

As he rocked on the porch swing he could feel a wildness rising in him. *My God,* he thought, *I am going to be* alone.

His brief days of hope were gone. He stared out at the bay—the choppy water was too rough for any but the most dedicated waterskaters—and felt the pain pressing on his brain, like the two thumbs of a practiced sadist digging into the back of his skull.

"I wonder," he said. "Have you given any further thought to uploading my memories?"

She looked at him curiously. "It's scarcely time yet."

"I feel a need to share . . . some things."

"Old Davout has uploaded them. You could speak to him."

This perfectly sensible suggestion only made him clench his teeth. He needed *sense* made of things, he needed things put in *order,* and that was not the job of his sib. Old Davout would only confirm what he already knew.

"I'll talk to him, then," he said.

And then never did.

The pain was worst at night. It wasn't the sleeping alone, or merely Katrin's absence: it was the knowledge that she would *always* be absent, that the empty space next to him would lie there forever. It was then that the horror fully struck him, and he would lie awake for hours, eyes staring into the terrible void that wrapped him in its dark cloak. Fits of trembling sped through his limbs.

I will go mad, he sometimes thought. It seemed something he could choose, as if he were a character in an Elizabethan drama who turns to the audience to announce that he will be mad now, and then in the next scene is found gnawing bones dug out of the family sepulcher. Davout could see himself being found outside, running on all fours and barking at the stars.

And then, as dawn crept across the windowsill, he would look out the window and realize, to his sorrow, that he was not yet mad, that he was condemned to another day of sanity, of pain, and of grief.

Then, one night, he *did* go mad. He found himself squatting on the floor in his nightshirt, the room a ruin around him: mirrors smashed, furniture broken. Blood was running down his forearms.

The door leapt off its hinges with a heave of Old Davout's shoulder. Davout realized that his sib had been trying to get in for some time. He saw Red Katrin's silhouette in the door, an aureate halo around her auburn hair in the instant before Old Davout snapped on the light.

Afterwards Katrin pulled the bits of broken mirror out of Davout's hands, washed and disinfected them, while his sib tried to reconstruct the green room and its antique furniture.

Davout watched his spatters of blood stain the water, threads of scarlet whirling in Coriolis spirals. "I'm sorry," he said. "I think I may be losing my mind."

"I doubt that." Frowning at a bit of glass in her tweezers.

"I want to *know*."

Something in his voice made her look up. "Yes?"

He could see his staring reflection in her green eyes. "Read my downloads. Please. I want to know if . . . I'm reacting normally in all this. If I'm lucid or just . . ." He fell silent. *Do it,* he thought. *Just do this one thing.*

"I don't upload other people. Davout can do that. *Old* Davout, I mean."

No, Davout thought. His sib would understand all too well what he was up to.

"But he's me!" he said. "He'd think I'm normal!"

"Silent Davout, then. Crazy people are his specialty."

Davout gave a laugh. "He'd want me to take Lethe. Any advice he gave would be . . . in that direction." He made a fist of his hand, saw drops of blood well up through the cuts. "I need to know if I can stand this," he said. "If—something drastic is required."

She nodded, looked again at the sharp little spear of glass, put it deliberately on the edge of the porcelain. Her eyes narrowed in thought—Davout felt his heart vault at that look, at the familiar lines forming at the corner of Red Katrin's right eye, each one known and adored.

Please do it, he thought desperately.

"If it's that important to you," she said, "I will."

"Thank you," he said.

He bent his head over the basin, raised her hand, and pressed his lips to the flesh beaded with water and streaked with blood.

It was almost like conducting an affair, all clandestine meetings and whispered arrangements. Red Katrin did not want Old Davout to know she was uploading his sib's memories—"I would just as soon not deal with his disapproval"—and so she and Davout had to wait until he was gone for a few hours, a trip to record a lecture for Cavor's series on *Ideas and Manners*.

She settled onto the settee in the front room and covered herself with her fringed shawl. Closed her eyes. Let Davout's memories roll through her.

He sat in a chair nearby, his mouth dry. Though nearly thirty years had passed since Dark Katrin's death, he had experienced only a few weeks of that time; and Red Katrin was floating through these memories at speed, tasting here and there, skipping redundancies or moments that seemed inconsequential . . .

He tried to guess from her face where in his life she dwelt. The expression of shock and horror near the start was clear enough, the shuttle bursting into flames. After the shock faded, he recognized the discomfort that came with experiencing a strange mind, and flickering across her face came expressions of grief, anger, and here and there amusement; but gradually there was only a growing sadness, and lashes wet with tears. He crossed the room to kneel by her chair and take her hand. Her fingers pressed his in response . . . She took a breath, rolled her head away . . . He wanted to weep not for his grief, but her hers.

The eyes fluttered open. She shook her head. "I had to stop," she said. "I couldn't take it—" She looked at him, a kind of awe in her wide green eyes. "My God, the sadness! And the *need*. I had no idea. I've never felt such need. I wonder what it is to be needed that way."

He kissed her hand, her damp cheek. Her arms went around him. He felt a leap of joy, of clarity. The need was hers, now.

Davout carried her to the bed she shared with his sib, and together they worshiped memories of his Katrin.

"I will take you there," Davout said. His finger reached into the night sky, counted stars, *one, two, three* . . . "The planet's called Atugan. It's boiling hot, nothing but rock and desert, sulfur and slag. But we can make it home for ourselves and our children— all the species of children we desire, fish and fowl." A bubble of happiness filled his heart. "Dinosaurs, if you like," he said. "Would you like to be parent to a dinosaur?"

He felt Katrin leave the shelter of his arm, step toward the moonlit bay. Waves rumbled under the old wooden pier. "I'm not trained for terraforming," she said. "I'd be useless on such a trip."

"I'm decades behind in my own field," Davout said. "You could learn while I caught up. You'll have Dark Katrin's downloads to help. It's all possible."

She turned toward him. The lights of the house glowed yellow off her pale face, off her swift fingers as she signed.

<Regret> "I have lived with Old Davout for near two centuries," she said.

His life, for a moment, seemed to skip off its internal track; he felt himself suspended, poised at the top of an arc just before the fall.

Her eyes brooded up at the house, where Old Davout paced and sipped coffee and pondered his life of Maxwell.

"I will do as I did before," she said. "I cannot go with you, but my other self will."

Davout felt his life resume. "Yes," he said, because he was in shadow and could not sign. "By all means." He stepped nearer to her. "I would rather it be you," he whispered.

He saw wry amusement touch the corners of her mouth. "It *will* be me," she said. She stood on tiptoe, kissed his cheek. "But now I am your sister again, yes?" Her eyes looked level into his. "Be patient. I will arrange it."

"I will in all things obey you, madam," he said, and felt wild hope singing in his heart.

Davout was present at her awakening, and her hand was in his as she opened her violet eyes, the eyes of his Dark Katrin. She looked at him in perfect comprehension, lifted a hand to her black hair; and then the eyes turned to the pair standing behind him, to Old Davout and Red Katrin.

"Young man," Old Davout said, putting his hand on Davout's shoulder, "allow me to present you to my wife." And then (wisest of the sibs) he bent over and whispered, a bit pointedly, into Davout's ear, "I trust you will do the same for me, one day."

Davout concluded, through his surprise, that the secret of a marriage that lasts two hundred years is knowing when to turn a blind eye.

"I confess I am somewhat envious," Red Katrin said as she and Old Davout took their leave. "I envy my twin her new life."

"It's your life as well," he said. "She is you." But she looked at him soberly, and her fingers formed a mudra he could not read.

He took her on honeymoon to the Rockies, used some of his seventy-eight years' back pay to rent a sprawling cabin in a high valley above the headwaters of the Rio Grande, where the wind rolled grandly through the pines, hawks spun lazy high circles on the afternoon thermals, and the brilliant clear light blazed on white starflowers and Indian paintbrush. They went on long walks in the high hills, cooked simply in the cramped kitchen, slept beneath scratchy trade blankets, made love on crisp cotton sheets.

He arranged an office there, two desks and two chairs, back-to-back. Katrin applied herself to learning biology, ecology, nanotech, and quantum physics—she already had a good grounding, but a specialist's knowledge was lacking. Davout tutored her, and worked hard at catching up with the latest developments in the field. She—they did not have a name for her yet, though Davout thought of her as "New Katrin"—would review Dark Katrin's old downloads, concentrating on her work, the way she visualized a problem.

Once, opening her eyes after an upload, she looked at Davout and shook her head. "It's strange," she said. "It's *me,* I know it's me, but the way she thinks—" <I don't understand> she signed. "It's not memories that make us, we're told, but patterns of thought. We are who we are because we think using certain patterns . . . but I do not seem to think like her at all."

"It's habit," Davout said. "Your habit is to think a different way."

<Possibly> she conceded, brows knit.

"You—Red Katrin—uploaded Dark Katrin before. You had no difficulty in understanding her then."

"I did not concentrate on the technical aspects of her work, on the way she visualized and solved problems. They were beyond my skill to interpret—I paid more attention to other moments in her life." She lifted her eyes to Davout. "Her moments with you, for instance. Which were very rich, and very intense, and which sometimes made me jealous."

"No need for jealousy now."

<Perhaps> she signed, but her dark eyes were thoughtful, and she turned away.

He felt Katrin's silence after that, an absence that seemed to fill the cabin with the invisible, weighty cloud of her somber thought. Katrin spent her time studying by herself or restlessly paging through Dark Katrin's downloads. At meals and in bed she was quiet, meditative—perfectly friendly, and, he thought, not un-happy—but keeping her thoughts to herself.

She is adjusting, he thought. *It is not an easy thing for someone two centuries old to change.*

"I have realized," she said ten days later at breakfast, "that my sib—that Red Katrin—is a coward. That I am created—and the other sibs, too—to do what she would not, or dared not." Her violet eyes gazed levelly at Davout. "She wanted to go with you to Atugan—she wanted to feel the power of your desire—but something held her back. So I am created to do the job for her. It is my purpose . . . to fulfill *her* purpose."

"It's her loss, then," Davout said.

<Alas!> her fingers signed, and Davout felt a shiver caress his spine. "But I am a coward, too!" Katrin cried. "I am not your brave Dark Katrin, and I cannot become her!"

"Katrin," he said. "You are the same person—you *all* are!"

She shook her head. "I do not think like your Katrin. I do not have her courage. I do not know what liberated her from her fear, but it is something I do not have. And—" She reached across the table to clasp his hand. "I do not have the feelings for you that she possessed. I simply do not—I have tried, I have had that world-eating passion read into my mind, and I compare it with what I feel, and—what I have is as nothing. I *wish* I felt as she did, I truly do. But if I love anyone, it is Old Davout. And . . ." She let go his hand, and rose from the table. "I am a coward, and I will take the coward's way out. I must leave."

<No> his fingers formed, then <please>. "You can change that," he said. He followed her into the bedroom. "It's just a switch in your mind, Silent Davout can throw it for you, we can love each other forever . . ." She made no answer. As she began to pack grief seized him by the throat and the words dried up. He retreated to the little kitchen, sat at the table, held his head in his hands. He looked up when she paused in the door, and froze like a deer in the violet light of her eyes.

"Fair Katrin was right," she said. "Our elder sibs are bastards—they use us, and not kindly."

A few moments later he heard a car drive up, then leave. <Alas!> his fingers signed. <Alas!>

He spent the day unable to leave the cabin, unable to work, terror shivering through him. After dark he was driven outside by the realization that he would have to sleep on sheets that were touched with Katrin's scent. He wandered by starlight across the high mountain meadow, dry soil crunching beneath his boots, and when his legs began to ache he sat down heavily in the dust.

It was summer, but the high mountains were chill at night, and the deep cold soaked his thoughts. The word *Lethe* floated through his mind. Who would not choose to be happy? he asked himself. It is a switch in your mind, and someone can throw it for you.

He felt the slow, aching droplets of mourning being squeezed from his heart, one after the other, and wondered how long he could endure them, the relentless moments, each striking with the impact of a hammer, each a stunning, percussive blow . . .

Throw a switch, he thought, and the hammerblows would end. *"I am weary of my groaning . . ."*

"Katrin deserves mourning," he had told Davout the Silent, and now he had so many more Katrins to mourn, Dark Katrin and Katrin the Fair, Katrin the New and Katrin the Old. All the Katrins webbed by fate, alive or dead or merely enduring. And so he would, from necessity, endure . . . *So long lives this, and this gives life to thee.*

He lay on his back, on the cold ground, gazed up at the world of stars, and tried to find the worlds, among the glittering teardrops of the sky, where he and Katrin had rained from the sky their millions of children.

AFTERWORD

I've realized, on reflection, that I've met three Roger Zelaznys in my life.

The first I met in a convenience store in 1969, when I found a copy of *Lord of Light* in a wire rack behind the comic books. This first Roger displayed a completely original blend of mind-staggering concepts, wide-ranging knowledge, and a singular grace of expression.

It is hard to overstate how important a figure Roger Zelazny was in the science fiction field at that time. No one who encountered *Lord of Light* or *The Dream Master* during that period will ever forget the experience. Roger was, literally, a revolutionary: he entered the field, remolded it, and left it in his image. If Roger's later works did not achieve the impact of his earlier work, possibly it was because the center of the field had shifted in Roger's direction: his work stood out less because everyone else's work had become more like Roger's.

My second Roger was the man I met at a science fiction convention in the early seventies. He was gracious, soft-spoken, witty, and (when he wanted to be) screamingly funny. He gave the two funniest guest-of-honor speeches I've ever heard, and it is my eternal regret that no one ever thought to record them. He spoke with eloquence—in long, spontaneous, unrehearsed, grammatically correct complex sentences—on subjects ranging from poetry to philosophy to particle physics. His public persona demonstrated the same originality and wide-ranging knowledge shown by his work.

When I became a writer, I found Roger an amiable senior colleague: we cheerfully plotted the evil that befell one another's characters in the *Wild Cards* series, and when Martin Harry Greenberg had the notion of asking me to write a sequel to one of Roger's stories for the Tor Doubles series, Roger graciously allowed me to follow his own "The Graveyard Heart" with my "Elegy for Angels and Dogs." We talked about collaborating on a novel, and once spent an airline flight plotting it, but it never came about. We thought we'd have plenty of time to get around to it.

But outside of our professional engagements we rarely saw each other, even though we lived only 65 miles apart. He was at heart a very shy man, and did not seek out company.

I met my third Roger about a year before his death. This third

Roger was my friend, and a treasured one. Though already weakened by the illness that later killed him, Roger seemed to achieve a kind of flowering in the last year of his life—he reached out to touch us, and none of us could ever doubt that we had been *touched*. I saw more of him in that last year than I had in all the previous years of our acquaintance. I remember his kind and faultless presence at barbecues, at parties, at games, at my wedding reception and housewarming.

It was clear that in his last year Roger was a happy man, and it was a joy to watch him. In intimate surroundings as well as anywhere else, he demonstrated his remarkable originality of thought, his wide-ranging knowledge, and his singular grace of expression.

It was a privilege to know him. It is a continuing tragedy that he is gone.

He was an utterly singular being, and those who were privileged to know him miss him every day.

*Roger never said that it happened this way. Then again, who's
saying that it didn't?*

■

THE STORY ROGER NEVER TOLD
Jack Williamson

HE WAS LATE, RUSHING TO WORK ON THAT GRAY NOVEMBER
morning in 1962, when a car coasted to the curb beside him. A
man slid out of it, lifting an imperative hand to stop him. The
driver got out and darted around the car. A woman, she held his
eye. Slenderly perfect in figure and style, she was made up like a
matinee queen, every blond curl precisely in place. The man caught
her arm and spoke to him in a language that sounded like Russian
or perhaps Greek.

"Are you lost?" he asked. "Can I help?"

The woman spoke, her inflections just as puzzling. He stepped
back, staring. The man was too film-star handsome. They both
looked far too hep and chic for the traffic noise and diesel reek of
this busy Cleveland street. He dodged back when the woman
pounced at him, reaching with both hands to clap him on the sides
of his head.

"Hey—"

In a moment she had glided away. Catching a startled breath,
he found that she had left a cloud of some rich perfume and two
hard little objects clinging to his temples. They vibrated briefly
and felt slightly warm. She spoke to him again, her voice now
musically clear.

"You are Security Agent 850–28–3294?"

He retreated again, blinking in startled bewilderment at them and their car, a 1958 Ford sedan. It looked too new, the sky-blue paint too bright, the whole shape not quite right, though it had a 1962 license plate.

They stood intently waiting.

"I do have a job with Social Security," he told them. "And that is my Social Security number. But I'm no agent—"

"A clever attempt at cover." The woman glanced down the street and made a face of shocked disgust. "And a very strange place to hide. You almost escaped us."

He backed farther away. Though he saw no weapons, they both looked alert and superbly fit, poised and ready for anything. Her green eyes narrowed, she watched him like a crouching cat. Hostile or not, they made no sense here in downtown Cleveland.

"What's this all about?" He blinked at them and the sky-blue Ford. "Who are you?"

She made a sound he didn't understand.

"Security," the man said. "We are here from Security Command."

"What's that?"

"If you've forgotten—" Impatiently, she sniffed something, perhaps a name or a title, that he didn't get. "We're here to get you back to your duty."

"You've got me wondering." He turned to the man, who seemed less demanding. "Do you have some identification?"

The woman tilted her ivory wrist to display a little object that flickered for a moment with rainbow color.

"Do you want our individual designations?"

Blankly, he nodded.

"They don't translate." The man shrugged as if in apology. "Not into any local dialect. You may call me Paul." He smiled ambivalently at the woman. "Lilith, perhaps, from the local folklore? Call her Lil."

"What, exactly, are you after?"

"If you have forgotten who you are," the woman was severely ironic and no longer charming, "your record here has been abysmal since the day you were placed. You've failed to file reports and ignored your recall. We are here from the command to pick you up."

"You must have made some mistake—"

"We don't make mistakes." Her voice had the cold snap of breaking ice. "We're here to stop your own."

"If you want to see my record—" He appealed to the man. "Just come down to the office with me. I'm still the new man there, but you won't find anything—"

"You'll come with us." Sharply, she cut him off. "At once."

"Wait a minute." He edged back, prepared to run. "Let's call a cop to straighten this out."

"Get him in the car," she told the man. "I'm sick of this hideous hellhole."

"I've got to get on to the office." He backed farther. "Let me call a lawyer—"

"Your native ways are no concern of ours, and you won't be returning to any office here." The woman grew stern. "Not after your miserable fiasco."

"However," the man was more patient, "we are required to record any statement you may wish to make."

Looking up and down the street, he found no police car, no taxi, no visible escape.

"Let's get on with it," the man urged him. "We have your earlier duty record, apparently satisfactory and complete up until your assignment here. What we need is an account of what you have been doing since."

"In particular—" The woman paused, holding out her wrist as if that flickering dial might conceal a microphone. "Have you compromised the service? Have you revealed yourself?"

"What could I reveal?" He dug for his wallet. "I'm an American citizen. Here's my driver's license. Roger J. Zelazny, born right here in Cleveland, May 13, 1937."

"Born?" Her perfect eyebrows lifted. "What does that mean?"

"Remember we're out on a frontier rim world," the man told her. "Among primitive exotics. Natural procreation is evidently still allowed."

She made a face and shrank away.

"Thank you." With a noncommittal nod, the man glanced at the license and gave it back. "Will you continue?"

"Just what do you want to know?"

"Your own account of what you have been doing."

"Briefly," the woman said. "I've got to get out."

"Mostly, I've just been in school." He spoke slowly, watching the street for a chance to break away. "At Noble School and high school out in Euclid. Then Western Reserve for the B.A. in English. I finished my M.A. at Columbia earlier this year. I write a little poetry—"

"A bard?" The man turned to the woman. "A native bard!"

The woman shrugged with impatient disdain.

"A native informant!" The man's voice quickened. "Or native enough, if he's been here since we set up the station."

She said something he didn't catch and gestured at the Ford.

"Please forgive us, Mr. Zelazny." The man was suddenly affable. "Lil is my superior. The service is her career. My own main interest is cultural anthropology. The service affords me a splendid opportunity for field work while I'm fulfilling a civil duty. Whatever your excuses, your extended experience here can make you a very useful informant." His voice turned harder. "You will find yourself far more comfortable if you don't resist."

The woman reached for him with red-nailed talons.

"Help!" Yelling, he gestured wildly at a passing taxi. "Help me! They're—"

Her steely fingers gripped his arm. He felt a sharp vibration in the objects she had stuck to his temple. His yell was cut off. Suddenly limp, he let them drag into the Ford. The man got in the backseat beside him. The doors closed with oddly solid thumps. He heard a puzzling hiss of air. The woman drove them, silently and fast.

Feeling numbed and groggy, he tried to see where they were going. The familiar buildings gave way to suburbs, farms, finally woods. Then the woods were gone. He craned to the window and saw the earth falling away below.

"Where—"

His voice only a croak, but the man answered helpfully:

"The first stop is your proper post at the signal station out on the satellite. The second is Galactic Security High Command."

He gulped and tried to wet his mouth.

"Really—" His throat ached, but he found a papery voice. "Can't you just pretend I'm really who I say I am?"

"Why not?" The man shrugged. "If you want to work as my informant, I'll play whatever game you choose."

"Anything!" he gasped. "Please."

"The unmanned signal station was set up here when we began observing artificial fires. The first nuclear explosions triggered a more urgent alert. Agent 850–28–3294 was assigned to watch duty here. Though the blasts had been increasing in frequency and power, he never filed a report. He ignored official inquiries and even his final notice of recall."

The man's grin turned sardonic.

"That's what you have to explain, if you persist in your denial."

Stunned by that, too sick to think what it might mean, he sank weakly back in the seat. The man said nothing more to him. When the woman spoke, their exchange was not translated. The sky outside darkened to purple and black. Stars blazed out. He watched in dull wonderment and finally went to sleep.

When he woke, feeling almost himself again, they were falling

out of that black sky, down to the gray blaze of the sunlit Moon.
The craters swelled and multiplied till the man pointed to one with
a bright metal rim.

"The signal station," he said. "Underground."

The woman was pecking at a keyboard where the steering wheel
had been. They hovered near it till a tower of darkness stood suddenly above it, a beam of blackness that shone toward the stars.

"The transit tube," the man said.

The woman steered them into it, and out again above another
landscape, so barren and crater-pitted that he thought for a moment
that they were still on the Moon. The sun that lit it, however, was
huge and dimly red, turning the craters into scarlet pools.

"Security Command." The man pointed. "And your own destination. The oxygen-breathers' complex at the security academy."

Turning, he saw an enormous mirror dome rising out of barren
desolation. Inside it, he found himself in a line of oxygen-breathing
bipeds shuffling down endless gray-walled corridors, following
arrows of flashing light, Some looked almost humanoid, but none
resembled him or his captors. Most were grotesquely different,
many of them apparently new recruits, a few veterans back for
retraining.

They all wore translators, but the slouching thing ahead had a
scent that sickened him and the shell-cased thing behind merely
stared though multiple eyes when he turned and tried to talk. He
did make out scraps of talk from others, but their native worlds
had been so diverse that they seemed to find little in common and
less to say.

The corridors branched and branched again until he sat alone in
a narrow booth. A rapid metal voice rattled out of the wall, in
structing him to press his open hands to the plate in front of him
and look into the lens. It asked questions he seldom understood.

"Number 850–28–3294," it droned at last, "you are found
grossly unqualified for any security service. Your earlier field assignment was a gross and inexplicable error. You will proceed to
the exit and await final disposition."

"Final? What does that mean?"

The wall did not explain. The maze of corridors led him on to
a little room where the man he might call Paul sat waiting behind
a bare glass desk.

"You're out of the service?" With a sympathetic smile, he rose
to offer his hand. "That tends to support the story you told us,
though it does leave you in devil of a spot. A bonanza, however,
for me. At least I can get you off your feet."

He gestured at a chair. Zelazny collapsed into it gratefully.

"Want a drink? A rum cola? My favorite drink on your planet."

With only a stale doughnut and instant coffee for the breakfast he hardly remembered, Zelazny felt readier for nearly anything else, but he accepted the glass and waited silently.

"My informant!" Paul waved his glass expansively. "I did the research I could during the weeks it took to run you down, but I never really got to know a native. For my graduate project, I'm planning an animated exhibit of the culture of Earth, displayed through the story of your own life."

He sipped cautiously at the rum and cola, wishing it had been steak and eggs, while he tried to answer interminable questions about his life, his family, his friends, his experience in the Ohio National Guard, his travels, his studies in school, his political interests, his poetry awards, his plans for the future.

"Back when I had a future," he interrupted bitterly. "I'm starving. Can I have something to eat?"

"Certainly. We've only begun."

Paul left him alone in the room for an anxious hour and came back with a sandwich of imitation bread with slices of imitation ham and imitation cheese, dressed with imitation margarine and imitation mustard. The imitations were less than perfect, but he ate it while Paul resumed the interrogation. When he demanded a rest, Paul showed him into an Earth-type bathroom that adjoined the room, and took him later to a high galley where he could look far across the red-lit waste landscape to another dome rising into the dead-black sky like a huge silver moon.

"The marine complex," Paul said. "For water-breathers."

Walking with him there, Paul continued the interrogation till he begged for a break. Back in the little room, a cot had replaced the desk, and dishes on a table beside it were filled with imitation salad and imitation mutton stew.

The room became a prison. He was sometimes left alone there, battered with never-ending questions from a machine behind the wall. His watch still ran, but Earth time meant nothing here. Paul came unpredictably to wake him for a walk or another meal, always demanding more about his planet and its peoples. He was dreaming that he was back on Earth, shuffling papers for Social Security, when Paul shook him awake.

"Come see yourself!"

Paul ushered him into a vast hall at the top of the dome.

"Your replicate!" He gestured proudly. "A splendid likeness, don't you think, created to play the central role in my animated diorama of your culture. The grand climax of my studies! The entire faculty seems enormously impressed, and I expect it to make my career."

Any likeness was hard to see. The replicate looked too dark and too tall. Strangely garbed, with beads strung around its neck and huge rings in its ears, a long spear lifted, it stood guard at the entrance to an enclosure woven of thorny brush. Beyond it a half-naked woman, clad and jeweled just as strangely, grinned from the doorway of a mud-plastered hut.

He stared at Paul.

"What is that meant to be?"

"Don't you like it?" Paul looked hurt. "I have designed it to portray you as the symbolic prototype of your culture."

He shook his head.

"Your own life story! I present you as a Masai warrior. The Masai, as you know, are magnificent runners. As the narrative unfolds, your extraordinary abilities are recognized by an American professor who has been searching Kenya for fossil relics of your evolutionary origins. He takes you back to America and obtains an athletic scholarship for you at his university. You win great races. You excel in scholarship. You lecture to share the history and folkways of your people. You win influential friends. You become rich and famous, and finally return to a happy reunion with the woman you had loved when you were children.

"Please say you like it."

"It's interesting." He nodded reluctantly. "But that's not me. It has nothing to do with me."

"Just open your eyes! You must recognize the star role I have given you in the basic myth shared by nearly all your tribes? The mythic hero leaves his home, faces great dangers and crippling handicaps, endures severe ordeals, learns profound truths and discovers new strengths, defeats powerful enemies, creates the genius of his people, and returns at last to enjoy his due rewards. The diorama reveals you as the spirit of your world! Dramatized, of course, but you must recognize that fiction can convey more truth than bare fact can. Don't you see?"

Paul waited impatiently for him to nod again.

"I knew you would! You would share my elation if you could stay to see the whole diorama in motion. Unfortunately, however, you are leaving. My superior, whom you remember as Lil, has admitted her terrible blunder. She mistook you for an actual agent, a man she thought had been assigned to the warning station on your satellite. He was given another duty post instead, from which he has just come home."

"You mean—"

"A matter of transposed digits in the designation of Agent 850–28–3294. His number should have been 3249. As a result, your satellite station has never been manned at all. Lil's career is in grave jeopardy unless she is able to correct the error at once."

"Correct?"

"It can be done."

"How?"

"Simply enough." Paul grinned at his anxiety. "Technology exists for very severely limited navigation into the past. So long as we create no paradoxical interruptions in established sequences of cause and effect, we can return you to the space-time coordinates where we found you. Lil has arranged for us to leave immediately."

Waiting for them in the sky-blue Ford, she nodded at him with no apology, and took them up at once, diving back into the transit tube and emerging over the Moon. He napped again during the flight back to Earth, but he was wide awake before she pulled them to the curb on his Cleveland street.

Nearly an hour late to work that morning, he never tried to explain the delay, but as time went on he found that his philosophy of life and art had changed. Poetry had been his first great love. He returned with a new language: his far-ranging and often mythic fiction.

AFTERWORD

I met Roger at SunCon in 1977. He later moved to New Mexico and become a loyal friend, but New Mexican roads are long and I knew him best from teaching his work. That changed in a remarkable way. "A Rose for Ecclesiastes" and other early stories are finely crafted works of art, brilliantly imagined, full of poetry and literary allusion. The later novels, such as the Amber series, have the same daring originality, the same poetic imagination, but they flow almost in the easy-seeming manner of a chanting epic bard.

"The Story Roger Never Told" story was suggested by that shift, which revealed a second side of Roger's genius. In these latter days, nobody makes a living writing great short stories. Novels are generally more profitable. The shift may have been commercially impelled, but this story presents an alternative explanation.

Isle of the Dead *presented a universe in which godlike terra-formers reshape worlds to their clients' bidding. In Nina Kiriki Hoffman's tale of ghosts and science, a new player takes a hand in the process.*

■

THE SOMEHOW NOT YET DEAD
Nina Kiriki Hoffman

"I KNOW IT'S HARD TO BELIEVE," SAID CRANSTON. HE PEERED INTO the bottom of his glass, then glanced up at me from under bushy dark brows. He looked like a man who should be smoking a pipe—weathered, squint-eyed from sun-staring, contemplative.

"And ironic," I said. "A consummation devoutly to be wished by most of the people I know, I bet." I picked up my glass for the first time since he had set it in front of me. He stared. I smiled at him and said, "Explain that!"

"Uh," he said. He opened and closed his mouth a couple times. Ghosts weren't supposed to be able to pick things up, I was pretty sure. "Jake, I'm not saying I'm an expert on death. I really don't know much about it. All I know is I watched them bury you three days ago, so I don't know what you're doing here now."

I looked out the view window in the back of Cranston's apartment at green-edged sunlight touching green-brown sand and an ice-green stream swollen with spring rain. The forest beyond looked like black ink trees on wet green paper. On Emery, the soil was greenish tan or greenish brown or greenish red, the sky was greenish blue, and the water various shades of green; the plants here were reddish purple, magenta, lavender, or purple-black, though the flowers came in a lot of colors.

I was the first human to die on Emery since we had started the colony three years earlier.

You would think death would be pretty much the same everywhere, but apparently it wasn't.

I sipped my drink. It tasted different. Brighter, wider, with strange edges to it. It sparkled against the back of my throat.

"Uh," Cranston said again, "Jake? Were you . . . well, were you experimenting on yourself before you died?"

I glared at him with narrowed eyes. I had been gradually retrofitting the colonists to match the planet—that was my job. First you picked a planet that was a pretty close match for the colonists, then you tinkered. Incorporate local molecules into our food, tailor messenger RNA to accomplish specific intracellular tiny tasks, that sort of thing, all baby steps so people wouldn't be too startled when they woke up in the morning and looked in their mirrors.

I tried everything on myself first. Animal testing and computer modeling could only take you so far.

Besides, since Diane had moved out of my apartment and in with Roy, who was there to care what became of me?

This was not adequate colonial thinking. Cranston had already pointed out to me that everyone cared, because, although others had bits and pieces of the same training I had, I was the ablest organism engineer the colony had. I was needed, whether anyone liked me or not.

I guess I took a pretty big hit with that last modification. I had thought it would give me the power to eat the local fruit without risk. I mean, those peach things had been ripening every year on the spoonleaf trees, sitting there in all their red, orange, and yellow glory, smelling more inviting than anything the synthesizers could come up with, ripening and dropping to the ground, where rabbit-squirrels feasted on them and got drunk. Dragon-birds ate them and flew erratically, if at all.

Getting drunk had seemed like a good idea.

I had analyzed the peaches the first year after we landed, mapped everything that made them dangerous and incompatible with human digestive systems. Plotted the adjustments we would need in our physiologies so the native peaches and other local fruits and vegetables would be nutrition instead of poison, planned carefully so no one step would be too giant a leap. Initiated the series of modifications in the general population, slow shifts across weeks and months, with downtime in between for acclimation and acceptance.

The last step was too big; I should have broken it down into three; but I wasn't feeling patient. The peaches were ripe now. I could smell them. What was I waiting for?

So I'd leapt.

Some leaps fail.

The fruit did get me drunk fast, though. And it had sure tasted good.

"Who decided to bury me? It's not like we have an unlimited amount of Terran material around," I said. Nagging everyone to recycle our resources was another crusade of mine. True, I was shifting everyone around so that we would be as close to indigenous as possible, but it was early yet in our Emeryforming, and I still had enough Terran in me to be rare, maybe even precious here.

"I don't know," said Cranston.

"And for that matter, how did I die? My memory goes dark for a while, and then I wake up underground."

"You do? You did?" Cranston leaned closer and studied my clothes. Standard colony issue shirt and trousers in my color, silver, the cloth designed to repel all kinds of dirt and stains. My clothes were clean. I scratched my head and shed a sprinkle of dry green dirt on his table.

"Under some dirt, anyway, though fortunately not in a coffin," I said. "Who pronounced me dead?"

"Roy," he said.

"Where were *you* when all this was going on?" Cranston and I played chess every Fourday evening. He was one of the colony scouts; he went out every week to map new areas, locate resources, and search for and record new species. It gave him an expanded perspective. He was one of the few people in the colony I could spend time with who didn't get annoyed with me right away.

"Roy's the G.P. It never occurred to me to question his judgment."

"What about the burial? You know I would rather donate my parts wherever they might be needed, in whatever form. At least I could have been fertilizer. For that matter, what about preserving my work? Did anybody check to see what I was working on when I died, and whether an autopsy was indicated? What if I had just discovered some key thing?"

"There *was* an autopsy," Cranston said. "Eva said—" He stared at me and shook his head. "I don't understand this at all. I thought you had been autopsied and harvested in accordance with your wishes. So naturally I still think you're a ghost."

"What did Eva say?"

"She said you didn't leave notes on the last phase of your work, and that she couldn't figure out what you had done to yourself even after she examined you."

Not enough notes? I took detailed notes with every modification! Maybe she hadn't looked in the right file. Possibly I had called them eccentric filenames. Possibly I had locked or hidden them. "Cause of death?" I asked Cranston. "Did she mention one?"

"Your gut was full of half-digested fermented peaches. She ruled it a suicide. Jeez, Jake. You're the one who told everyone not to eat those things. And it was pretty inconsiderate of you leaving the rest of us half fish, half fowl."

Eva knew I had eaten peaches. Therefore she had actually done the autopsy. Feeling strange, I opened the stiktites on my shirt and studied my belly. I couldn't detect the marks of laser surgery at all. I patted my gut. No gaping wounds or even any soreness.

"You saw them bury me three days ago?" I said.

"Yeah."

"How long have I been dead?"

"You died on Oneday, they buried you on Twoday, and today is Fiveday," he said. He sighed and shook his head. "Theory number two: this is a very vivid dream."

"I'm not that anxious to be a figment of your imagination."

"I'm not that anxious for you to be my figment either," said Cranston, frowning. "I'd like to stick with the ghost hypothesis, but I don't believe in them. So what are you, why are you here, and what do you want?"

"You know me," I said. "You know who I am."

"I don't think so," he said. "And even if I did know who you were, I lost track of what you want a long time ago. Enlighten me."

What if he were right? What if I wasn't even myself? I drank the rest of my drink. It didn't taste like any drink I'd ever had, though as far as I knew, Cranston had poured me my usual bourbon.

"I've got a theory," I said. "You're a figment in *my* dream."

He pinched himself, shook his head. "I'm awake." He reached over and pinched the back of my hand.

"I'm awake," I said.

Cranston stared at his hand, at my hand. His mouth opened and closed again.

"Yeah," I said. "We're both awake, and you touched me. Who's a figment now?"

He stood up and paced away, then came back. "Jake, you look kind of green, and you smell funny—not bad, but not normal either. Would you check your pulse for me?"

Guess he didn't want to touch me again.

I glanced at his wall chrono, put my fingers on the pulse at my wrist, counted heartbeats for half a minute. "Normal," I said.

He shook his head, paced away, came back.

"Why'd you come here, anyway? To my apartment, I mean? Is this the first place you came after you woke up?"

"Of course," I said.

"Why?"

"You're—you're my friend. You used to be my friend. Has that changed?"

"I don't know."

"Since you don't think I'm myself. Okay, guess I can sit with that for now. Do you want me to leave?"

"No. No. I just want you to tell me the truth. What were you working on when you died?"

So I told him about the peaches and the three-in-one jump I had made.

He licked his lips. "The first year, I thought they stank," he said, "I hated when they were ripe. Such a stench, and it was everywhere! But yeah, this year I really wanted to try one." He glanced out the window. No spoonleaf trees in view, but there were some along the stream a little way. "So you can eat them now?"

"Well," I said. I realized I was a little hungry. I guessed I hadn't eaten in four days, but maybe being dead didn't take much energy. "I don't know. What if Eva was right, and that's what killed me?"

"Half digested, she said. So the first part of digestion went all right."

"I could eat now," I said.

"Let's go."

When we first arrived on Emery, everyone had to wear breathing masks. Too many allergens in the atmosphere. People could exhaust themselves with sneezing and scratching, and a few people couldn't even breathe without the masks. My first modifications had taken care of those problems, and I had done a nice job; lots of individual tailoring involved.

While I was working on people, Dreena Alexander, the botany engineer, was working on the Terran plants we had brought with us, and studying the local plants. We had coordinated efforts, though we didn't get along very well.

It would have been fun to leave Dreena with some kind of little allergy just to irritate her, but she was smart, if irritable and prickly. She would have figured it out and complained to the colonial council. They had a number of effective policing powers.

Dreena was in the spoonleaf grove when Cranston and I arrived. She squatted in sunlight with a peach in one hand and a portable analyzer in the other. She had thick dark hair that she bound into a lump at the back of her neck, pale skin, high Slovak cheekbones, and a single bar of eyebrow that crossed above both eyes and the bridge of her nose, which made her frowns look emphatic. She always reminded me of a frog, not because she was shaped like one, but because every pose she took seemed like one a frog might take. Now, for instance, squatting on her heels, her knees up, her torso leaning forward as she stared down at the peach in her right hand. The tip of her tongue touched her upper lip and lingered.

"Hi, Dreen," I said. I stooped, picked up a fallen peach, brushed green-tan dirt off it and bit. My mouth filled with an array of flavors and textures—mango, persimmon, peach ice cream, cinnamon applesauce; firm juicy flesh inside an envelope of fuzzy skin. The faint fizzy afterbite of an intoxicant. "Oh, god. You can't believe how good this tastes, Cranston."

Dreena licked her lips. The peach she was holding moved closer to her mouth.

"Stop that!" Cranston said, knocking her hand away.

"What?" She shook her head, stared at the peach in her hand, dropped it.

I took another bite of mine. I could already feel the ease working its way through me, telling me to smile and relax. I wondered how many of these I had eaten on Oneday. Maybe I had relaxed to death?

"He's eating one," Dreena said to Cranston.

"He's modified."

She stood and studied me. "Wait a minute. I thought he was dead."

"That too," said Cranston.

"Wait a minute! You *were* dead! Eva even cut you open!"

I finished the peach and licked my fingers. These peaches didn't have pits. I wasn't sure how the spoonleaf trees propagated—that was Dreena's department. I looked at the other fruits on the ground. They all looked delectable. I craved another, but figured I better quit.

"Well, I don't feel sick, not even a little bit. Just happy. Maybe we should go back to the lab and check this out," I said.

"Maybe we should tell the council that something strange is going on with you, Jake!" said Dreena. "I think the fact that you're not dead is fairly significant."

"She has a point," Cranston said. "I wonder why I didn't think of that."

She stepped closer to me, stared at my face, then my hands. I glanced at my hands. My skin did look greener than it had before.

"I want that mod," Dreena said. She licked her lips again.

"So do I," said Cranston.

"I have to restructure it."

"Why?"

"You guys said I died. I don't think killing everybody else is a good idea."

"Let's go to the lab first," Dreena said.

I grabbed a peach as we left the grove. "What do these things do, anyway, besides ripen, drop, and ferment?" I asked Dreena. "Do they have anything to do with reproduction?"

"No," said Dreena. "The spoonleaf trees reproduce in nodules underground; they're cross-fertilized by bee-shrews. I haven't been able to figure out a function for the peaches, aside from making animals drunk out of their gourds, which I also haven't figured out. Where's the payoff for the trees?"

"The first year we got here, the peaches did stink, didn't they?" I sniffed the peach I held. Nectar. Ambrosia. I remembered analyzing one the first year. It was one analysis among many, but Cranston was right; initially, I had found the peaches repellent. In fact, we had called them urine fruit. How odd.

"I assumed you modified our tastes," Cranston said.

"Not on purpose," I said. "Can I borrow your analyzer, Dreena?"

She handed it to me and I scanned the peach. Its profile was similar to the one I had gotten when I first analyzed a peach right after we arrived. Similar, but some of the spikes looked different. I thought. I couldn't be sure until I checked my records.

I began to have strange thoughts. I was a skillful organism engineer, true, but how skillful could I be? Emery was unlike any other world ever documented, and I had been inventing everything as I went along.

Well, that was my job. But the modifications had been going extremely well. None of the usual missteps you read about in case studies of other colonies. We could chalk this up to Dreena's and my expertise, or we could figure there was something else in the mix.

I saved the peach profile on Dreena's analyzer and handed it back to her as we walked. The forest ended and the colony began; the dividing line seemed unnecessarily sharp to me for the first time, though all our buildings, made from a combination of local soil and insta-hard foam, were different colors of local green.

Doors opened along the etched glass streets. People brought tables and chairs onto the front patios of apartment houses and office buildings. Others carried baskets of bread and pastries or trays with pots of tea, cups, napkins, sugar bowls, and cream pitchers on them. Tea time, a mandatory break in routine that had always irritated me. What if you were in the middle of a flare of inspiration and you had to stop for tea? Then again, lunch irritated me too.

Heck. Sleep irritated me most of all. What a waste of time.

"Jake?" said someone. We were headed toward the entrance to the medical building. Eva stood on the patio.

Eva and I had been involved for a while that first year, until little niggles every day added up to huge irritations we couldn't resolve or ignore. She still looked good to me, dark-skinned and soft-edged, and she smelled good too, though not the way she used to smell. Right now she smelled like spicy red peppers frying in hot olive oil. Odd.

She had a powder-blue teapot in her hand, for a couple seconds, anyway. She dropped it. It bounced, the lid flew off, and tea splashed everywhere.

I licked my fingers, realized I had finished the peach I had been carrying. Mild intoxication warmed me. I smiled, feeling like an idiot, though a relaxed and happy one. "Hi there," I said.

"You were dead," she said.

"So I've heard."

"I had my hands inside your body. I took sections. . . ."

"Strange way to restart a relationship," I said. "I thought you didn't like me anymore."

"I don't."

"So how much testing did you do? Did you stop looking for cause of death after you decided I had committed suicide?"

She nodded slowly. "Is this real?"

I glanced at Cranston. We had already been all through this.

"That's the hypothesis we're working with," Cranston said.

"Jake is going to show me his notes on his last modification," said Dreena, poking me in the back to get me moving toward the entrance.

"I want to see too," Eva said.

I grabbed the basket of scones from the table as we went into the building. I bit into one. Like everything else, the scone tasted different, more like dusty clay and less like bread. Hard to swallow. I hoped it wouldn't make me sick.

In my lab I went to my terminal. I pressed my thumb on the recognition plate, then accessed my work files.

"It knows you," said Cranston.

I waggled my eyebrows at him. "Better than you do." I selected and opened a file named "Uric." Schematics of mRNA, catalytic sites in various cell organelles, chemical formulae, computer-modeled 3-D molecule maps; I flicked through the frames, checked to see if they were in a format people without my background could follow. As far as I could tell, they were accessible enough.

"What's wrong with this file, Eva? Why couldn't you find it? Or did you just not understand it?"

"Why'd you call it 'Uric'?" she asked.

"Why not? You should have been able to pick it by the date stamp if nothing else."

"Stand away and I'll show you."

I stood up. She took my seat and pressed her thumb to the recognition pad, and the computer shut down and restarted. My filenames came up. More than half were missing; "Uric" wasn't there, for instance. "Why'd you hide it?" asked Eva.

No good explanation came to mind. I couldn't even remember doing it. Though I've never been fond of people snooping through my work. I'm not much of a team player.

Or maybe I'd hidden it because it was too revolutionary. If we still had the activities checks and balances we had had when we first got to Emery, every step of my work would have been evaluated by two other scientists before implementation. Those were bad old days, all right. People always looking over my shoulder. I had hated that.

They'd stopped after the first year. They trusted me. Everything I did worked, after all.

I opened the computer again myself and selected "Uric," then stood up to let Eva take a look at it. I watched as she paged through. Pretty elegant, really, but too much at once, for sure.

"Some of the best work you've done, Jake," she said after studying it. "I still don't see what killed you."

"Whose idea was it to bury me?"

"Mine," said Dreena.

"Why? Wasting me that way? Why?"

She shook her head. "It makes no sense to me now. At the time, it seemed vital. I argued in front of the whole council that we should establish a cemetery in the shade of the spoonleaf groove, as we'd be needing one sooner or later, and that you should be the first to be buried—just easy-to-break-down body, not closed up in a coffin—as some kind of offering to the planet."

"It made sense to me at the time too," Eva said. "Right now I can't imagine why. Obviously you belonged in reclamation. Dreena's thinking was muddled!"

"Muddled by what, though?"

"You think everyone's thinking is muddled," Dreena said to me.

"Well, sure," I said, "but in this case I believe something else was operating. Operating on everyone. Astonishing. Elegant."

"Something else?" asked Cranston.

I still couldn't figure out what I had died of. It seemed like maybe the most important thing had been to get me in the dirt somehow. "What exactly are bee-shrews, anyway?"

"Underground hive animals," said Dreena. "Pollinators. Gifton's going to study them when he finishes with the tree-grazers."

"Roy pronounced me dead. . . ." Roy had a better reason than most to want me dead.

"You *were* dead, Jake," said Eva. "You were absolutely dead. Your body had cooled to ambient temperature. There was no breathing, no brain or heart activity. And if you weren't dead before I started the autopsy, you were during and after." She stood up. "Come to my lab. I want to check this. It's too much."

I shut down my terminal and we all followed Eva to the lab in the basement where she cut up and examined and tested a lot of dead things. It was cold in her lab. She got a diagnosdoc out and pressed it against my neck. It monitored heart, lungs, temperature, and brain activity, and it could do blood panels if she asked it to. Which she did.

She looked at the readout. She swallowed. "Well, you're not dead anymore," she said.

"And the good news is?"

"I don't think you're human anymore either. Temperature is low, blood gases are different, and some of these other readings . . ."

I edged the diagnosdoc away from my neck and nodded.

"This isn't consistent with that last mod, Jake," Eva said. "It couldn't have changed you this much."

"It didn't," I said.

We came. We saw. We were seen. We were helped.

Dreena volunteered to try my final modification next. I didn't always like her, but I had to admire her, even though it turned out that the hardest part of the modification was shoveling her under the dirt and waiting three days, wondering if she would come back or not. She had really been dead, all right; her sojourn underground bothered us a lot more than it bothered her.

We don't know what it is the planet is doing to us, exactly. Roy wants to examine me more than I feel like being examined, especially by him. And people are taking their time about accepting this modification, so he doesn't have that many people to study.

If what I suspect is true, I'll have plenty of time to do everything *I* want, including things I wish I didn't have to do, like sleep. I don't seem to need as much sleep as I used to, though.

What I like doing the most right now is sitting around and thinking about how long I'll have to get on everybody else's nerves. It might just be forever.

AFTERWORD

I first met Roger Zelazny at Norwescon, where he was guest of honor in the early eighties. He was one of my favorite writers, and I stopped him on a staircase and asked him to sign my copy of *Doorways in the Sand,* one of my favorite books.

Roger was very gracious to a fan who had probably interrupted a conversation. (I was so star-struck I don't remember who he was with.) He gave me his autograph, and said *Doorways in the Sand* was a book he quite liked, too.

One of the last times I saw Roger was at Moscon, a small regional convention in Moscow, Idaho, where he was guest of honor shortly before his death.

Roger and Jane Lindskold and M. J. Engh and some others and I had dinner in the hotel coffee shop. I had just discovered temporary tattoos and I was passing them out. I remember Jane put a blue lightning bolt on her cheek, and I think Roger put a small blue star on his hand.

He was still gracious and shy and kind, a delight to be with.

Have you read *A Night in the Lonesome October?*

Roger is still one of my favorite writers, too.

In his introduction to the anthology Wheel of Fortune *Roger
comments that when taking a gamble "the statistical character
of reality seems usually to have the upper hand." Of course, if
you're like the narrator in Steven Brust's story, trusting to luck
just isn't enough.*

■

CALLING PITTSBURGH
Steven Brust

THE CYGNIAN CAREFULLY PLACED TWENTY IMUS IN FRONT OF HIM
and sat back all over his chair. The 'Geausian, on the small blind,
mucked his cards with a flash of tentacle. I had the big blind with
ten imus; the Cygian had the button, an aggressive bet, and probably nothing else.

Sorry. I'm not used to explaining this stuff to people who don't
play; stop me when you have to. I mean I had to make a forced,
"blind" bet, before seeing my cards—it goes around the table, see?
You take turns making a small blind bet, a big blind bet and like
that, and the guy with the "button" gets to act last. Does that
make sense? No? Well, never mind. In this hand the Cygnian, who
had the button, would be the last to act in every round of betting,
so that gave him the advantage of knowing what everyone else
was doing, and I was speculating that he might have nothing except
that advantage. Well, he also had a lot more chips—that is,
money—on the table than I did. I peeked at my cards: Q9 offsuit.
A good hand if and only if I was heads up against a pure steal,
which I probably was. Tempting, but . . . I mucked it. Wait for

the next hand. Except for a couple of hands at the end of the round, I had position on him (that's why I'd sat there; it always pays to have position on a Cygnian), so for that reason if no other it was best to wait.

What? Oh. No no, not your fault. By "position," I mean that most of the time I got to decide what to do after I knew what the Cygnian was doing; that's what "having position" on someone means.

You see, poker is all about decisions. A good player is someone who makes good decisions, that's all. And the more you know, the better decisions you can make. So if there's someone like your typical Cygnian who likes to steal a lot of pots and likes to make big, aggressive bets, you can make a better decision if you know what he's up to before you make your move. So I was being careful, and trying to play my best game.

The dealer washed the deck, I watched the Cygnian. I'd—what? "Washed"? Don't worry about it. He shuffled, okay? I'd spent the last hour throwing way some decent hands, winning a small pot now and then to stay even, and studying the other players, and it was true what I'd been told: you just can't get a read on a Cygian. His motions at the pot were small, precise, and absolutely the same whether he had the stones or nothing; except every time he'd been called he'd had the stones. The—

For G–d's Sake. All right.

"The stones." "The nuts." "The rocks." "The admirals." The best possible hand under the circumstances. When I was holding that Q9 in my hand, if, at the river—I mean, after the last card— the board had been, say, 4 5 8 10 J, without any three of them being of the same suit, I'd have had the stones. Okay?

I was saying, then, that every time the Cygnian had been called, he'd shown down the best possible hand. The Martian colonial had found that out and it had cost him everything he had on the table. But Martian colonials are gamblers.

Martian colonials are gamblers, Cygnians are emotionless odds machines that are impossible to read, 'Geusians are rocks, T'Cetians are calling stations, and on and on—I know I sound like a textbook on prejudice, but if prejudice is all you have to go on, that's the way to bet until you get more information, and I always bet with the odds. But then, I'm Jewish.

I put out five imus for the small blind (you're on the big blind, then the small blind, then the button, in that order, and then your position gradually gets worse again as the button moves around the table), the other 'Geusian, who I think was female, put out the big blind, and the dealer whipped the cards around. The dealer was certainly female, and human, and attractive. Captain Billy only hired dealers who fit this description, which was one reason the Captain's Quarter was *the* place to play on Titan. Another was that everyone trusted Billy to keep the game safe and, within limits, friendly.

I protected my hand with my lucky 1921 silver dollar. I'm not actually superstitious, but it pays to make the other players think I am. Across the table, in seat 1, the spacer made it forty to go; spacers are typically even bigger gamblers than Martian colonials, and this guy played too many hands in early position, and raised on hands that didn't merit it. He was going to get broken sooner or later and I hoped I was the one who broke him.

But it was the Cygnian I was worried about. It was the Cygnian I was there to break. It was the Cygnian who had what I wanted.

Hands hit the muck until it came around to seat 5, where a local, a small Oriental-looking woman, raised two hundred imus. Orientals, too, are often wild, hairy-eyed gamblers, but don't count on it; they can also be monsters, and I still hadn't quite gotten a read on this one. Two more hands hit the muck, and then it was up to the Cygnian, who peeked at his cards and quickly covered them again. Was that a tell? That extra quick hiding of his cards could mean he had a good hand, and if so, it would be the first tell I'd gotten off him . . . he mucked his hand. Crap. A "tell" is just some mannerism that gives you a clue about what the guy's holding. Anyway, the 'Geusian mucked his cards, and I looked at mine. 9–3 offsuit. Some hands are easier to play than others—I tossed it into the muck.

The spacer called, and the flop came J–7–6 rainbow. The spacer checked, the local tapped, about fifteen thousand imus. The spacer said, "Over-betting the pot just a bit there, honey?" She shrugged, and he threw his hand away. The dealer dropped 5 imus, the max rake, and pushed the pot.

Oh. The "rake" is the percentage Captain Billy takes out of each pot—it's where he makes his money. He gets ten percent up to maximum of 5 imus, which means that every ten hands he might make enough money to buy a piece of Mediterranean coastline. If you really wanted the Earth back, you'd open up a casino instead of trusting me to win it for you an acre at a time.

"How did you find me?"

"It wasn't easy. You move around a lot."

"Goes with the job."

"What do we call you? I can't pronounce—"

"Call me Phil. What do you want?"

"We want our planet back."

"Nice idea. How do you—"

"Poker."

"Poker?"

"It seems to be one of four aspects of Earth culture the bastards have decided they like. The others are—"

"I know. Chinese poetry, Spanish dancing, and South Indian music. Northern Italian cooking should have been on the list. And Japanese pottery. I'm starting to guess where this is going, guys, and I don't think you realize—"

"We realize. We're hoping you're as good as we've been told you are, that's all."

"Even if I am, what if I get unlucky?"

"Don't."

Now I had the button, so I could afford to take a chance, especially if the Cygnian was in. I had about twenty thousand—enough money to buy a small midwestern town, and say about the same as he had in cash—but he had a lot more on the table than his cash, so I had my work cut out for me if I was to break him. But that was what I was there for; that was why two people had died getting me this stake.

No, now was not the time to think about that.

This time the Martian colonial in seat 3 was up to his tricks again, making it a hundred to go. The Cygnian, with his small, mechanical motion, left arm relaxed in front of him, fingers still, head up and alert, eyes almost closed, pushed in a small, square, purple plaque and my heart skipped a bit. At the same time his voider said smoothly, "Raise. All of it." The dealer took the plaque, dropped it into the 'val machine and swung the screen so we could all read it. The screen flashed once then spelled out, "Padua, Italy: 19,385."

I had enough chips to call, but I'd have to hit the flop hard. To my surprise, the 'Geusian called. Well, that took out any notion of bluffing; for the 'Geusian to call that size of bet, he had to be sitting on a monster. I looked at my hand: 6–3 of spades. Ouch. I wanted to call so bad I could taste it, but even on the button . . . I sighed and threw it away, as did the colonial, who had apparently learned his lesson.

The flop came A–4–4, two spades, and I almost cried. The Cygnian checked with no more or less enthusiasm than he had when betting, and the 'Geusian slapped a tentacle down right behind him.

"Would you care for drink, sir?"

I turned around. Cocktail waitress. There was a world outside of this table after all. Odd. I glanced around the room. There were six other tables busy, and about that number empty. The other games, mostly small stakes limit hold 'em or seven stud, were being played just as earnestly as our own game; I was playing for a planet, some of them were playing to kill a few hours; but the game was the same either way; and the cards never cared. "Water, please."

I returned my attention to the universe in front of me. The turn was the nine of hearts, and there was no betting.

The river was the queen of diamonds, and I felt vindicated: no flush.

"Hands, please," said the dealer.

The Cygnian turned over the jack of diamonds and the ten of hearts; the 'Geusian showed two queens and took a lot of money along with Padua, Italy, and I felt a twinge. There was something there—something in the Cygnian's body language. If I could figure out what it was, it was worth half a continent.

For the next hour I folded vigorously, even when the Cygnian put London, Ontario, Canada, into the pot before the flop and I was sitting on KQ of clubs; I watched, hoping that whatever I'd half-noticed would jump up and bite me. As long as he didn't know what I was after . . .

"You have to try. He's one of the richest men in the Galaxy, and by now he owns almost twenty percent of the Earth, and wants more. And, as far as we know, this is his only weakness."

"Weakness?" I'd said. "It's not a weakness. He's good."

"We know. That's why we want your help. You're good, too. We don't know anyone else who can do it. Here, take this, and here's a ticket to Titan City, where he'll be showing up to play in a place called the Captain's Quarter, where they accept real estate—"

"But what if I lose?"

They'd shaken their heads. They hadn't wanted to think about that.

And it was the wrong thing for me to think about now. But how could I not think about it?

The hand where he bet London was shown down; he broke a local man in seat 6 who had AK when the flop came A–J–4, because the Cygnian had the jacks wired. It—sorry. I mean he had been dealt a pair of jacks, so when the jack hit he had three of a kind, whereas the local man had a pair of aces. Okay? It was a real bet this time, no bluff. If I could see him bluff, and see any difference in body language that indicated a bluff, I'd be set. If I could do it, that is, before my stake dribbled away, or I got clobbered with a good second-best hand, or some idiot made a bad draw that happened to hit.

No-limit poker is like that. No matter how good you are, you can get burned, and hard, and suddenly. It is terrifying. That's why I like it.

The next time the Cygnian was in the pot, I raised behind him with an offsuit 8–4, then bet the flop, was check-raised, and exposed my cards with a grin as I threw them away. Yessir, Mr. Cygnian; I bluff all the time. No, really.

A new dealer came on about then; a redhead with a no-nonsense attitude and a tattoo of some sort peeking out from her left sleeve. The Martian colonial went broke and left; the Oriental woman went broke and pulled out more money; the rest of us stayed about the same for most of an hour, then I got my break.

To make it short, I called an unraised pot in middle position with 7–8 of hearts, made the straight at the river against the spacer who was slow playing pocket rockets—I mean he had wired aces and decided to pretend he was weak, hoping to win a big pot— the 'Geusian who wouldn't bet me out with top set but was willing to call all the way to the river, and three others who were hoping to hit something as long as it was cheap, which it was until I hit my straight. When the smoke cleared, I'd been paid off big, and I had enough chips in front of me to take on the Cygnian.

As I stacked my winnings I glanced at my watch, looked like I was thinking about leaving, then shook my head and settled back. I don't know if anyone went for the act, but it didn't matter. I was ready, now. I had the chips I needed—now I needed either good information, or a lot of luck. I'd prefer the luck. I'd been lucky once against Doc Holliday and almost gotten shot at, and I'd been lucky once against Doyale Brunson and gotten a cheap lesson. But you can't count on luck; over the long run, it always evens out. And I know a lot about the long run.

For the next hour, I ran a few small bluffs and showed them off, win or lose, and I also played a couple of small pairs that I threw away when I didn't flop the set—I mean, when the card didn't show up in the first three that the dealer flopped—but nothing much happened. Then, with the button in front of the Oriental woman, the Cygnian made it twenty to go, and, with the rock folding, I checked my cards and saw two red nines. I have a fondness for pocket nines, because they're strong enough so I can feel confident if I make the set, but small enough so that I can throw them away with a clear conscience if I miss and someone bets an over-card; and if there are no over-cards, I can be pretty sure someone has a draw for a straight. Pocket jacks, for example, are just the kind of hand that gets me into trouble. Also, the nines work fairly well against a large field, but have the advantage of being a slight favorite heads-up against over-cards, and a big favorite against a smaller pair. In this case, I wanted to be heads up against the Cygnian so I kicked it two hundred. It folded back around to him, and he called; I tentatively put him on two over-cards, or maybe a suited ace. That means, like, the ace-three of spades.

The nine of clubs was the first card off, followed by the ace of

hearts and the six of clubs. The Cygnian, still leaning back, still
with his small, neat, precise movement, bet five thousand imus.

I had to think about it. I had no doubt that I had the best hand
right now; I'd be willing to bet my whole stack that he didn't have
the set of aces. But . . .

Okay, if he had Ax of clubs, which seemed most likely, he was
getting good odds to hit his flush, and would happily call a tap,
and might even tap off against me if I raised. Whereas I would
have two chances to pair the board to beat the flush even if he
made it. I liked my odds, and normally I'd make him put all his
money in and take my chances, only that wasn't what I was after
this time. I wanted what he had on the table. I needed what he
had on the table. The Association had puts its collective and individual necks in a noose to get me the chance to get what he had
on the table.

I was sweating. I was by G–d not showing it.

I raised him five thousand. He called. I wished I could read
his expression.

He *called*. What in blazes did that mean? What did he have?
How do you get a tell from a creature with different psychology,
different physiology? Why wasn't Madman Caro around to write
about how to play against a rust-browned, scaled creature from
thousands of light-years away? What would he have said? He'd
probably have said that there must be similar enough psychology
or the Cygnians wouldn't enjoy the game. Darn useful.

The burn and the turn, and we both leaned forward; his arms
resting, almost human-like, on the table before him. As the card
fell, I watched him, out of habit even though I couldn't read him,
and found him watching me. For the first time, I wondered what
tells of mine he was catching. I felt naked. What if he could read
me, and knew I couldn't read him?

Three of clubs. If he had the hand I put him on, that gave him
the flush, and I was chasing; I needed the board to pair. What
would he charge me to look for the pair?

Forty thousand.

I could afford that; it was a good bet with about half that much
already in the pot and the hopes that I could make a big score if
I hit. Except that he had probably put me on a hand, too, and, if
the board paired, he'd call me for the boat and wouldn't pay off,
which meant that it was a bad bet. I mentally sighed and started
to muck my hand—

—And noticed that his left arm hadn't moved. It was still out
there, on the table, covering his remaining chips as if he were
protecting them. It was his left arm—the beautiful hairless left arm,
with its two elbows and skinny little wrist. I was in love with his

left arm, and I watched it from beneath my baseball cap, keeping my eyes out of sight of his eyes. Baseball never made it off planet, but it was still played in empty lots and yards in places like Ontario, Canada.

Then there was a moment when my mind raced backward and forward, and put it together. He'd think I was putting him on this, so that he'd put me on that, so that . . .

"Call," I said.

And there it was: burn and turn: ace of spades. That's-a nice, as Chico Marx said. Marx Brothers movies should have made it off planet, too.

"I bet," said the Cygnian, moving another plaque forward. The dealer slipped it in: "Pittsburgh, Pennsylvania, USA, 1105,643."

Pittsburg. I'd been there. One of the most underrated cities in North America. People who'd never been there thought of it as a graveyard of abandoned steel mills, but it was a beautiful city, and it would be good to have it back. I could just cover the bet.

His left arm was in his lap; he was no longer bluffing.

But, a moment ago, he had been.

So he really thought he had the winning hand.

So . . .

Then there was the question of whether I trusted my judgment, or whether this tell was an elaborate ploy to get me to call down the nuts. What if he had, say, A6? Or even AA for that matter?

As I said, it was a question of whether I trusted my judgment.

"Call," I said, and turned over my cards.

What was it? It doesn't matter. It was a tell. No, I didn't see his hand; I didn't have to. I'd seen his left arm, out there resting on the table when he was bluffing, back in his lap when he really had it.

Yes, it was possible he'd had aces-up, and was bluffing the flush, and when the ace hit, that gave him aces full. But I just didn't think so. You see, when he bet the flush, he thought I had the flush, and he was representing a bigger flush. He was nervous about it, which meant he was afraid I had the best possible flush—which means I had the ace of clubs. And that meant he *didn't* have the ace of clubs. So what else could he have that he'd bet that way?

No, I never did see his hand, but it doesn't matter. He had pocket sixes, which meant when the ace paired he had a sixes full of aces, and he wasn't worried about my flush anymore. I called with nines full of aces and won. We'd both flopped sets—trips— three of a kind, only mine were bigger. Bad luck for him, good luck for you.

You still don't get it? Good. Want to play cards? Never mind.

I've given you Pittsburgh, and London, Ontario, and half a dozen smaller towns. The rest? Well, the Cygnian is going to be on Mars in a few months, and there are places to play there. Give me a stake and I'll bring you Paris.

AFTERWORD

No one can be familiar with my work and with Roger's and not realize how much influence he's had on me. Since I first encountered his writing it has been my desire to make others feel the way his work makes me feel. I hope I'm more than an imitator, but if not, well, I'm imitating one of the very best.

It was my great joy to know him in person as well as through his work, and I treasure every minute that we were able to spend together.

Ironically, perhaps, there is little in the above story that directly reflects his influence on me, except that I used the impoverished and sold-off Earth riff from "And Call Me Conrad"/*This Immortal,* and that one day at a World Fantasy convention I asked him how to write short fiction, which I've never been good at, and he said, "Write the last chapter of a novel," which is what I've tried to do.

I hope he'd have liked it.

I hope to someday write something half as good as his worst effort.

I hope new readers never stop discovering and falling in love with his work.

I hope.

Originally, Roger considered making Billy Blackhorse Singer in Eye of Cat *a Hopi. On later consideration, he made Billy a Navajo because of that nomadic people's legendary adaptability. In her tale, Kathi Kimbriel shows the compelling power of the more traditional, sedentary Hopi—a people whose myths contain the secrets of the future.*

■

IF I TAKE THE WINGS OF MORNING
Katharine Eliska Kimbriel

THEY WERE EARLY; THE SHUTTLE HAD BEATEN EVEN THE SUN TO Third Mesa. Silver sky was giving way to growing eastern light as the transport hatch swung open with a harsh metallic crack. Within the frame of rock and dry scrub before her, Brenna saw a jackrabbit shocked out of hiding; it plunged off into the brush, its white tail a flag of warning.

"Any regrets, woman?"

Duncan's choice of words caused her to tense; then she realized he had spoken in the tongue of her childhood, and her spine relaxed.

"Nay, Duncan," she answered in the same pidgin, conscious of the fresh-faced soldier behind them. "I told you I'd take this job for you, and neither drought nor death will sway me." Laying a delicate hand upon his bronzed, gnarled arm, she added. "Just because the military is here doesn't mean it wasn't an accident."

The old man grunted, stepping heavily from the open hatchway

65

into the dirt. "The problem with you, niece, is that you have no fear." Turning, he accepted the flight packs the silent private held out to him.

Smiling thinly, Brenna shook back her dark hair, trying to capture its fullness in a thong. Even lifted from her neck, it drew a line of warmth where it lay curling down her spine. "Ah, no, Duncan," she protested, this time in Englaz. "I'm a Celt, and we Celts fear only one thing—that someday the sky will fall upon us. Are we expecting thunderstorms?"

"The Hopi are," their pilot said suddenly. A tattooed arm gestured toward the foot of the mesa. "The caves are there, and Colonel Asbin's headquarters over by the road."

Brenna's gaze traveled up the sheer stone side of Third Mesa, up into the cloudless sky. Expecting rain? No one bothered to predict the weather out here, much less control it. She saw movement on the cliff; a farmer or shepherd descending a rocky footpath, ready for a day's work in the valley.

"Hopi sinom," Duncan said softly, setting the bags at her feet.

"Are they really the little people of peace?" Brenna asked, directing her words to no one in particular.

The pilot shrugged. "Other than making staff nervous with portents of doom, they've been harmless enough. At least they haven't firebombed this dig like the Navajos did the other." A vague gesture indicated that the aging geodesic tent closest to the cliff would be theirs.

Seizing the stiff strap, Brenna tossed her pack over one shoulder. Duncan's bad back meant they traveled light—very light, this trip. *I need no references, I know it blindfolded,* he had told her back in Flagstaff. Studying her uncle's bent, wiry frame, Brenna hoped so. The elderly man had been desperate for one last visit to the Hopi, and Brenna had wanted a light load after a year away from anthropology. This desolate slice of North America was as good a place as any.

From shadow to sun and then shadow again. The star was edging past the horizon, glittering like molten gold. It would be a standard August day, hot and dry. The green of the tiny farm plots was startling against the dust. *How long have they turned that soil?* she wondered. A village had existed on this site since 1150 A.D.: Oraivi, the oldest continuously occupied settlement on the continent. How much had the weather changed in that time?

"I recognize that lass," Duncan murmured suddenly, nodding toward the smiling, sloe-eyed girl who had just left another of the urethane tents. "Ling A-Ttavitt, a decent site artist. You glance inside, eh?" Straightening, the man moved agilely to greet the student, giving Brenna some of the solitude she needed for her observations. Grateful for his perception, Brenna moved quickly toward the slit in the rock.

It was up a wash of shale; sentries stood at the bottom.

Brenna climbed the rubble handily, dropping her bag before the opening. Slipping into the narrow crevice, she was momentarily startled by low-intensity floods blazing at her entrance. The light bounced among mirrors leading under the mesa. *So, Dr. Strand discovered the joys of electronic eyes. . . .*

A short, winding corridor lead to a wide chamber. . . . The silence was profound. Sifted dirt lay deep at her feet, mute evidence that neither animal nor water had invaded this sanctuary in centuries. Then a Hopi had discovered the new cave entrance. . . . This site might be too old for the memory of the tribe who lived above it, but it would be worth a try. She had no doubt Strand had not bothered to question the elders—only immutable history had interested him. A living tradition would have threatened old Strand.

Both pictographs and petroglyphs covered the walls of the chamber, the former in several colors, the latter deeply incised. Nodding absently, Brenna focused her eyes momentarily on the beckoning darkness beyond. She lowered herself onto a rock near the center of the grotto, studying the paintings in the indirect light. The color was still strong, indicating that the cave had been sealed a long time.

The pictures were interconnected, a story. . . . Curiosity quivered within her; it had been a long time since she had felt any interest in her work. The riots had killed more than bodies. . . . Brenna waited, listening for an inner voice. Nothing. It had been over a year since she had courted the ghosts of the past. Had her gift faded beyond recall? Was she finally—

A tendril of emotion touched her, like a finger of cold air. She shivered, oblivious to the rising temperature outside. There was something . . . Brenna stood, moving instinctively toward the inner corridor.

"It dead-ends." A-Ttavitt's voice was loud in the stillness, her presence startling Brenna.

Masking sudden annoyance, Brenna said coolly: "There's been shift, I can see some kind of small opening."

"Where Dr. Strand was injured." Brenna's head snapped around at her words. "It triggered the heart attack."

The feeling grew, drawing her. Not new ghosts; old ones. There was reverence, gentleness . . . the same uneasy sensation that touched her in cathedrals. Whirling abruptly, rejecting the thought, she rushed back down the corridor. A-Ttavitt hesitantly followed.

Duncan was waiting for them at the foot of the wash. "Ready

for the mesa?'' he asked, pausing to wipe sweat from his forehead with a bright red bandanna.

"Yes, old man, lead on and speak," she replied in the home tongue, slipping an arm around him as they walked. A-Ttavitt's face was a study in neutrality, hiding curiosity or confusion within.

"We came to this quickly," Duncan observed in the same speech. In their years of working together, a language of privacy had evolved—a mixture of Gaelic, Cymric, and smatterings of anything else convenient. They normally did not use it in the presence of others.

"This one may be hard to shake," she murmured, and then turned to the woman, who had moved up on their left. "Forgive me, Ms. A-Ttavitt, but I wanted to tell him of the pictographs, and my Englaz is sometimes a poor language for vivid description."

"Of course," A-Ttavitt said politely. Only her eyes held expression; they were wary.

Duncan stopped walking. "Ms. A-Ttavitt, there is no need to escort us. I haven't forgotten the way into Oraivi. Why don't you gather up all the disks on the dig, so we can examine them this afternoon. I know how they wander from the boxes."

Clearly relieved to be dismissed, the frail woman hurried back toward one of the tents.

"Why her distress?" Brenna asked in home-speech.

"She is afraid of the Hopi. Asbin has been spreading all kinds of rumors, including that Strand was murdered by the very people who called him in." Duncan placed his feet carefully as they continued up the dusty road.

"Any truth to the rumors?"

That slight shrug again, Duncan's way of indicating that they should mind their own business. "Was Strand a healthy man? Of his old students, you probably knew him best."

"A heart condition, completely controlled by medication. He was a tough old goat." She smiled to keep up the premise of their discussion. There might be no monitoring devices on the path, but recent years had taught Brenna caution.

"We are supposed to be discussing pictographs. What do you think of them?"

"From what immediately rose out of the memory tapes, I would say Hopi or Anasazi," she responded.

"Humph. Memory tapes. They can't be relied on. Feel anything?" This was intent; he knew her strange talent for "waking dreams," and what triggered it. Knew that the sense had been balky of late.

"Possibly. A feeling of . . . awe . . . touched me, as if I was in Jerusalem again." She considered the finger of presence that had beckoned. "There is more to the cave system than the front room. I'll start tonight. Anything from A-Ttavitt on how they were found?"

"Found or made?"

Brenna smiled at the sharp words. "I think found, if you mean made recently."

Duncan wheezed in reply. "Ms. A-Ttavitt says a shepherd found them—she doesn't know why Strand was called in. She respected the old man's solid technique, but she was no more blind to his limitations than you were."

They were nearly at the top of the mesa. "A people of peace," Brenna murmured in true Gaelic. "How certain can we be that it is still their way?"

"They managed to peacefully defeat the mineral exploiters and the Navajo," was Duncan's only answer.

By now Brenna was feeling the effort in her legs. "With the help of the government and the Navajos," was her wry response. "How far would they have gotten if the coal mining had not been destroying the water table? And only the Navajo know why the threat of destroying their ceremonial fetishes caused that land ownership appeal to be dropped." She stopped walking, leaning against the first rocky outcropping of the wall to catch her breath.

"It is a story they keep close to their hearts, how the Hopi came to be the keepers of the Navajo *tiponis*." Duncan had no false pride; he sank against the rock, his breathing slow and deep.

After a sharp glance told her the old man was fine, Brenna looked out over the expanse of earth below, watching it flood with color as the sun rose higher. Sculptured rocks, fleecy sheep, rows of cotton, maize, squash. . . . Heat baked them, light burning into their faces and reminding Brenna she had left her UV block in the camp. Feeling the slow pace steal into her bones, Brenna suddenly thought of her grandmother, and the woman's fierce love of her land. Land that Winifred Carey had died for, as she would have died defending her God. Brenna had not been in Wales during the riots; had not been present during either of the incidents that had destroyed both sides of her family. She'd found that absence had not eased the pain.

"Grana would have liked this place," she said aloud, lapsing into true Cymric even as she pushed her thoughts away.

"It's a beautiful region, and the lack of machinery would have pleased her," Duncan said tranquilly.

"No, I mean the living spirit of the lan—"

"What did you say?"

At the soft Englaz question, Brenna nearly jumped off the side of the mesa. She whirled, seeking a source. Only a few rolling pebbles. . . . Two sleek, dark heads slowly appeared at a hole in the wall, the children studying her thoughtfully.

"Whose words are those?" the older child asked, her Englaz precise.

Brenna smiled faintly. "It is the tongue of my mother's people," Brenna told her in Englaz. "Don't you have a language you use only with your people?"

As the girl nodded solemnly, Brenna continued: "We are the anthropologists who have come to study the cave pictures. I would like to talk to some of your elders, to see if any of them remember stories about the paintings." Bending her knees, Brenna peered through the opening in the wall. "Will you take us to them?"

Another moment, as if of decision, and then: "I'll take you to my *So'o.* Come!" A gesture as swift as her words, and the girl was up and running, vanishing into the pueblos beyond.

"Wait!" What color was her shirt, how tall— Then Brenna realized the younger child remained, shyly watching out of the corner of an eye. Studying the chubby toddler in turn, Brenna decided that it was male. "Will you take Duncan and me into Oraivi?"

The youngster nodded, waiting for Duncan to stand. Uncertain, Brenna slowly offered the boy her hand. The child considered the pale, slender fingers, the delicate silver bracelet, and then extended a small, round hand in reply. Looking up at her, he softly said something in Hopi, and then began to lead her into the village.

Brenna could hear chuckling from behind her. "All right, expert—what did he say?"

"The word means 'beautiful,' " Duncan answered in their home-speech, moving up to take her other arm. "I'll leave you to guess if he meant you or the bracelet. The older one is taking us to her grandmother. She used the word for clan mother, so we may get some history after all."

They were surrounded by sun-bleached adobe walls, jutting out of the mesa. If there was a pattern to the town, Brenna could not make sense of it; they were lost amid the narrow streets, following a cloud of dust.

The adults walking the streets and working before doorways politely averted their gazes, but Brenna heard the soft flow of Hopi voices behind them, and knew their presence had caused excitement. There had been trouble years ago, with outsiders entering the settlement at will—enough trouble that Oraivi had closed its doors even to scholars. Duncan had not visited the area in almost forty years.

It was a place of contrasts; a land dominated by smell and touch. A warm, capricious wind brought odors to her nose, of bread baking, ground cornmeal, newly washed wool; the sharp, familiar fra-

grance of sheep was strangely comforting. In a way, part of her
heart had come home. Around Oraivi all things orbited, the spiritual center of the Hopi universe.

Another corner, and they were among a group of children. Solemn, colorfully dressed in blue cloth pants and traditional long-
sleeved shirts, they actually stared at the newcomers in amazement,
and were no less awed by the urchin leading them in. Brenna had
a sudden fear of an irate Hopi mother rushing up to snatch away
her son, but no adults materialized. Duncan sat down on a bench
beside the small doorway, and gestured for her to do the same.
Before she could join him, the little girl suddenly appeared from
inside the pueblo, seizing her other hand.

"My So'o is asleep, but my brother is coming when his funny
computer finishes spitting up," the girl announced. "What's your
name?"

"Ah . . . Dr. Meghan Stewart," Brenna chose to say "What's
yours?"

This unleashed a flood of answers from the throng, rendering it
impossible for her to hear any one name. In the midst of the shouting children and Duncan's amusement, Brenna felt a tug on her
sleeve. She had to bend forward to hear the small boy's hesitant
Englaz.

"What your *real* name?"

The question so astonished Brenna she merely stared in response.
She did know that the Hopi were like many Amerindians, having
both Englaz and tribal names. But the protocol involved . . .

Duncan was fighting to control a laugh; he knew how nervous
children made her, with their wise eyes and cutting tongues.

Something in the small face, the dark eyes answered her.
"Brenna," she murmured to him.

"Renna?" the child attempted.

"B-erenna," the woman emphasized, making the soft "pop" of
the consonant.

"There is no 'B' in Hopi," Duncan explained.

"What means?" the tiny boy persisted, as if trying to understand
something obscure about her.

Means? Oh, yes— "It means 'raven-haired woman,' " she told
the pair holding her hands, hoping her voice did not carry to the
noisy group beyond. They were now about five bodies deep in
pushing, squirming youngsters.

"Appropriate," said a voice close to her ear. Both children lifted
their heads at the word, and the gathering began to quiet down.
Looking over her shoulder, Brenna saw a slender man. Dark eyes
studied her intently. Lifting her head to meet his gaze, Brenna
wondered how long he had been standing there. "Go on," he said

finally to the group of children. "They will be here for some time." Duncan helped a tiny girl vacate his lap, and the crowd began to melt away. The Hopi looked pointedly at the children holding Brenna's hands. Sighing, the young girl let go and grabbed for the little one. A few swift words in Hopi, and the child released Brenna.

The woman hesitantly waved goodbye, and the two children wiggled fingers back at her before running after their playmates.

"I hope you'll forgive their curiosity," the man said simply. "We have few visitors, and never . . . a fair, raven-haired woman. They are used to the military ignoring them."

"Of course," Brenna said, not wishing to turn aside any courtesy. Then her humor took hold. "Is your computer finished . . . spitting up?"

The man stared blankly at her a moment, and then a smile flashed across his face, revealing startling white teeth against polished copper skin. He pulled a small, square disk from his shirt pocket. "Schematics. When the laptop prints the final result—"

"I see," she answered, smiling shyly. "I'm Dr. Meghan Stewart, and this is—"

"One of the few people left who studies individual regions instead of just Amerindians," the man finished for her. "My grandmother cherishes the eight-part 3D series you did on Hopi culture. She will be pleased that she lived long enough for you to return. I am David Lansa. Will you come in for cool water or coffee?" With a faint smile, he backed into the adobe home. A moment of hesitation, and Brenna followed him.

The main room was larger than she had expected, its whitewashed ceilings higher. Brenna's eyes rested on the huge stone fireplace, the focal point of the area. Despite the growing heat a fire was burning brightly, water boiling in a pot. Ladders led up to a higher level; muted sunshine above hinted at solar panels. Other rooms stretched beyond the main living space, the narrow corridors bearing a vague resemblance to the passages below the mesa.

"Please, be seated," David suggested, ushering them to low seats by the cooler, inner wall. He paused by the fireplace mantel, retrieving several mugs, and took out a sealed tin. As he prepared the concoction, Brenna recognized the odor of real coffee. A strange blend of old and new, this man who carried schematics in his worn shirt pocket. A shagged, feathered haircut in the latest style, and faded indigo pants of a material she had not seen in years. Cotton clothing was something the average person could not afford. Rubbing her hand down the smooth, semipermeable fabric of her skin-tight, flaming red pants, she kept her thoughts to herself.

Finally David Lansa handed them mugs of steaming coffee and then folded cross-legged to the woven floor mats. "What address do you prefer, doctors?" He eyed Brenna steadily. "You have many names."

"Duncan will suffice for me, as always, but my niece will have to speak for herself." He glanced briefly at Brenna as he spoke.

She understood his meaning. She never introduced herself as Brenna; it was a nickname Grana had given her as a child, and had been kept within the family. Something in the little boy had called it from her.

"My parents named me Meghan," she started slowly. "Somehow I have never felt tough enough to be 'the strong one.' What name do you prefer?"

"I?" The Hopi studied her for a long moment. "Kúivato. David Lansa is simpler. Lansa means the spear or lance, and since the millennium my family has been the thrown weapon of the Hopi. We are almost a splinter clan unto ourselves, though we have no rites in the yearly cycle. We go out and abroad, paving the way to modern society, choosing the best of the new world to bring back to our people." After a moment, he added: "I do not know what 'David' means."

"Are you of your grandmother's clan, David?" Duncan asked, sipping at his coffee.

"Parrot," the man confirmed. Duncan nodded thoughtfully.

"The reason we have come, Mr. Lansa, is to ask if your elders can tell us anything about the pictures in the caves." Brenna leaned forward, balancing the mug of strong brew on the edge of her seat.

"Caves? I thought . . . there was just the one."

"There is something beyond the front grotto; we haven't examined it, yet."

David did not change expression. "Silena mentioned only the one room. He was the man who found it—he had lost a sheep, and thought a coyote might have dragged off the remains." The man paused to drink some coffee. "May I ask if you've spoken to Asbin yet?"

"Briefly," Brenna said, her mind's eye returning momentarily to the shadowed televid image of a man as neutral as his cinder-block building—silver hair, gray NorAmerican Forces uniform, eyes the color of old snow.

David Lansa's eyes seemed to smile grimly. "He told you little of the incidents here?"

"We know that two accidents have taken place," Brenna told him, her gaze never leaving his face. "And that Strand's work has been removed by estate authorities.'' This last grated; the legal intricacies were so involved Strand's results would be duplicated before the originals were released. After consideration, she added: "Asbin suspects the paintings and carvings are fakes, to hold up construction of the control site." It was a struggle to control a cynical smile; "control site" was such an innocent name for what was essentially a cluster of anti-terrorist launching silos.

Duncan leaned back against the wall, settling in. David's face was expressionless. One slender finger traced the rim of his mug; the pause was a long one.

"I sent for Dr. Strand," the Hopi said finally. "Not because of his reputation, but because I knew he had just finished a semester and could arrive immediately. I feared the military hearing of the site too soon and tampering with the paintings. I know what *I* think they are—at least the first chamber, I have not been deeper into the cave— but what matters is what you tell the military they are. The NorAmerican Forces intend to gut that cave for their control room."

When the silence had gone on too long, Brenna asked: "Has Asbin confronted your elders with his theory that Navajos or Hopis killed Dr. Strand?"

David's eyes hardened like basalt. "They questioned villagers for days. Desperation can drive people to horrible deeds, but no Navajo or Hopi killed Dr. Strand. Why would we? He was on the verge of proving the caves of Hopi origin, guaranteeing their safety." His voice softened. "But this would be the best site, and the political stability of both hemispheres deteriorates. I often wonder what Asbin's orders truly are."

Despite the growing heat, his words chilled Brenna. She had been naive enough to think that she'd left nuclear threats behind when she left Europe. War escalating among a myriad of ancient enemies scattered throughout Asia, Africa, Europe— *When will we learn we are Human first, and that all other names are merely changes of clothing?* She knew she had not kept up with international news, the past year or so, but information had only made her feel worse—

A woman stepped into the room, breaking off Brenna's thoughts. Nodding politely to their guests, she spoke swiftly to David in Hopi. The young man acknowledged her words by setting down his mug. "My great-grandmother is awake," he said softly. "I do not think she can help you, but she will see you now." With that, he rose to his feet, leading the way into the inner sanctuary of the house to a tiny, wizened woman whose memories spanned a thousand years.

Ten thousand years, Brenna thought. That, David had said, was how long people had lived on the mesas. The image held her silent as she followed Duncan carefully down the footpath, their halogen flashlights provided by the Hopi. An hour had stretched into meals and a day. David had been correct—the pictographs, even the caves, had been beyond the collective memory of the Hopi elders who came to speak. Brenna had sat enthralled by their stories, as they related their tales of the last hundred years and of legends older than themselves.

One clan history in particular intrigued her. All the clans had special ceremonies that demonstrated their powers, gifts from the Creator Taiowa to aid rainfall, fertility, planting, and healing. These ceremonies determined each clan's place in the pecking order of Hopi life, an order that began with the ruling Bear Clan and continued on down.

All except the Coyote Clan. They were as they had been from the very beginning: the guardian clan. The ones to scout ahead the paths of their people's journeys to be sure they were safe; the ones who brought up the rear of every ceremonial procession, guarding against evil. Coyote Clan was named in the ancient prophecies— the last to leave any legendary village along the path of the Hopi migration to Oraivi; the ones who would "close the door" upon this world, the Hopi's mythological fourth world. The ones to herald the end of all things.

"Where will they be if the legends die?" she murmured, and then caught herself up. Another saying of her grandmother's. Severed from her past, Brenna felt an elusive kinship with the Hopi, as they struggled to retain their beliefs in a world leeched of faith. To face every ghost, to learn from past lives, understand what those people were and meant to be . . . even as her own presence stirred latent images quiescent in the very air around her. Images engraved in the memories of the stones themselves.

Shivering in the cooling desert air, Brenna shoved the thoughts back into the depths of her mind. It was gone, all of it—no sense in raking through her own pain. It was but a grain of sand in the weathering of the world.

"Let's go to the caves," Duncan said suddenly. "The waxing moon beckons. Perhaps we should have taken David up on his offer of Coyote guards on the site."

"Were you planning on explaining it to Asbin, or were you going to leave it to me?" she murmured, considering her possible level of authority. Asbin had sent a soldier up earlier, to ask when she was returning to the camp. To ask, not to demand—it was not the usual military tone of voice. David's farewell threaded the river of her thoughts.

Kúivato, she had called him, and he had shown no surprise at her memory. *It means "Greeting the Sun"; David is simpler,* had been his response. *But you did not give me a name. Brenna,* she had told him, because it felt right. . . .

"I think they're grooming David to be chief. The elders obviously think quite a bit of him," Duncan went on as they neared the bottom.

"I thought chiefs must be of the Bear Clan," Brenna said, forcing herself to concentrate on his words.

"Bear Clan is dying out. The rulers of the next world will be Parrot Clan. David seems intelligent and farsighted; I think he'd make a good chief." Duncan paused before the entrance to the cave, flicking his small flashlight to wide beam. The young soldiers shifted nervously before it. "Go on in, Brenna. I want to talk to them."

Brenna did not argue. Military guards, no matter how distressed, held no interest for her. Lights blazed as she entered the passageway. She paused, watching the play of light and shadow flash across the rock walls. Vivid drawings leapt out at her, mellowed by the indirect radiance.

Old, extremely old . . . Brenna could feel the weight of eons in their lines. A-Ttavitt's readings were on filatape, carefully tacked beneath each image; Asbin was selective about what he would force them to repeat. Tomorrow Brenna would bring her black box in and start on the corridor paintings—thank the powers that be for the paintings; petroglyphs were harder to date—

"Blessings, child, here's an interesting sight," Duncan murmured as he came up behind her. "What's all the fuss about? These are plainly Hopi symbols. See, here is the *nakwách* of brotherhood," he began, pointing to the curious carving that was reminiscent of the Chinese yin-yang symbol. "Brenna, this is—this is the Creation Myth! I've never heard of it being on a cave wall. No wonder Strand was so excited. Damn it, what a time for this to turn up."

"What do you mean?" she asked softly in home-speech.

He did not look at her, his gaze on a carving. "There's a warhead in orbit."

The silence in the cave was absolute. Brenna directed her flashlight toward the ceiling, looking for more carvings or paintings. Ancient campfires had burned within this place . . . the carbon build-up needed measuring. . . . She considered asking who had launched the device, but thought better of it. Did it really matter what terrorist or nationalist group was flexing its muscles this week? Eventually one of them would launch a makeshift device, a faulty control box activating the head or damaging the targeting mechanism, and then . . .

"They can't declare an emergency overriding historical Class One statutes without a seven-day grace period," Duncan murmured, stepping farther into the cave. "There should be time to image them, date them . . . leave something for the future."

"Future?" The bitterness churning just beneath the surface welled up in her. Fragments of the past, obliterated in the name of age-old hatreds, divisions—"If we destroy the past, can we have a future without repeating every mistake we've ever made? What happens when we've killed all the legends? Grana always threw that in my face, when I told her religion was dead. What is left, now that reason, too, has failed us?"

"Not our question, lass. Clear your mind and reach out. I'm going to try and see into that second chamber." Without pause Duncan started patting his clothes, looking for the flashlight he'd snapped off and tucked into a pocket.

Wordlessly Brenna extended her own to him, touching his cheek in thanks for the anchor he had provided to her life. Piecemeal wars, ravaging the roots of humanity— Sighing, she tried to push it aside, settling on the big flat rock and opening her mind to whatever power lingered in the cave. All she could do was relax; the energy chose whether or not to acknowledge her presence.

Once again a feeling of unease. That gentle feeling of incredible strength, unfathomable depth—she drew back, pulling into her own consciousness. Usually it was visual images, 3D color imprints of the past, of the individuals who had painted and carved their records. This sensation had been present before, but never dominant, never overwhelming everything else. It reminded her too much of the state of meditation . . . prayer . . . of all she had lost when the Highlands burned, the land and all her father's family save Duncan. The sensation had vanished, then . . . *or did you cease to open yourself to it?*

Brenna had no desire to meet up with her own dead.

She heard Duncan rattling around in the back, sliding pebbles, his grumbling—a sharply caught breath.

"Brenna! Good Lord, Brenna, come and *look!*"

Leaping to her feet, Brenna moved into the passage. Duncan's legs were visible ahead, still protruding from the opening into the other chamber. Abruptly the light dimmed—a large beam had burnt out, only the flood by the outer door remaining. Brenna was plunged into murk, her reference point a needle slice of Duncan's reflected light.

"Ah, Duncan," she began quietly, uncertain where to put her feet. In response the man activated the back button of his flashlight, red light erupting briefly at her knees, and—

The ceiling broke loose, chunks of rock hailing down before her, dust rising in choking clouds, obliterating light and sound and—

*   *   *

Brenna spent the following day in the ancient dome. She accepted Duncan's death stoically, a selfish corner of her heart thinking it was inevitable—she had lost everyone else, why not Duncan? How ironic to finally meet Asbin over her uncle's body. Ignoring her cuts and bruises, she remained on the cot, clutching a piece of the rock that had fallen on them. It was a stalemate; she could scarcely think, but she would not leave.

She'd had nightmares; tons of rock, falling on her, annihilating the heritage of her people, destroying the remnants of Celtic history. A man with Asbin's face chipping away at hierogyphics, petroglyphs, erasing the past. Her grandmother's voice, arguing, scolding, warning her of people with agendas, how could she have been so foolish, scientists were always expendable— *Pe cymmerwn adenydd y wawr, a phe trigwn yn eithafoedd y môr: Yno hefyd y'm tywysai dy law, ac y'm daliai dy ddeheulaw.*

She woke with the words of the psalm on her lips, sitting bolt upright on the cot.

"Brenna, can you hear me?" David knelt beside her, shaking her gently.

"How long?" she whispered.

"This is the second morning. You were . . . chanting . . . in your sleep, in another tongue," he said quietly.

"Home-speech," was her terse reply as the dream flooded back to her. "From psalms. It's about—it's about running from God. 'If I take the wings of morning, and dwell in the uttermost parts of the sea, even there shall thy hand lead me, and thy right hand hold me.' David, I dreamt that the legends died."

"Have they?" After a moment he set his hand lightly over hers. "I am sorry. He was a fine man."

There was a long moment of silence, and then Brenna asked conversationally: "Perhaps the legends have not yet died. Where is Asbin?"

"Squatting in the blockhouse like a spider. There are six guards left; two on Asbin's quarters, four guarding the troop carrier and A-Ttavitt cataloging fragments, as you instructed." At her blank look, he said gently: "The last order you gave your assistant. All nations with missile capability have been put on alert, the Americas included. Only a half-dozen soldiers can be spared for rocks."

"Then I might as well continue working," Brenna whispered, exhaustion creeping through her bones.

"Asbin wants you to continue."

"Why?"

It was more rhetorical than anything else, but David said: "I think he hopes this is another false alarm, and that he will have time to entrench."

She heard the judgment in his voice. "But—"

David shrugged. "I think his superiors have abandoned him. And I am grateful we are in the middle of nowhere . . . the center of my universe."

Standing, Brenna moved past him, pausing in the open arch to greet the sunrise. No joy in it—"Please follow me." She walked briskly toward the cave opening.

One of the soldiers appeared as she neared the entrance. His young face was devoid of emotion. *Had he caused Duncan's death?* Paranoia was being passed like a virus. . . .

"Doctor, no outsiders are allowed to enter the cave unless—"

"David Lansa is an engineer. He is going to check the structural support, to try and anticipate landslides," Brenna announced, climbing the entry rubble. She stopped moving at the sight of three newcomers walking up the shattered rock behind her. Two of the Hopi were young men, perhaps David's age. The third man was much older, graying yet still hale, with the ageless eyes of all Hopi elders.

"This is Pamösi, Paul Fog, the leader of the Coyote Clan, and two *Qaletaqa*—Guardians. They have offered to watch outside the caves," David explained.

"For what?" the soldier asked, his reserve ruffled.

"Evil spirits?" Brenna suggested, and then propelled herself past him into the cave.

The passage was broader than she remembered; higher. The aging floods blazed on—the soldiers had patched the defective one back together, Brenna noted. The passage to the second chamber had been cleared of rock and reinforced, Duncan's body undoubtedly sealed in a bag and awaiting transport. The soldiers had created a ramp to reach the second chamber.

What was Asbin thinking of? What was he doing, supervising this crumbling site? *What am I doing here?*

"I am an ecological engineer, Brenna. But I will help you as I can," David said, coming up behind her. He had brought a pocket halogen, and was carefully examining the wall and ceiling portastruts in the brilliance of its white light.

Brenna reached for the only disconnected floodlight, wrestling it onto the ramp. She would see the second chamber—all of it—without any more delay. "Why did our pilot tell us your people are expecting rain?" she asked between shoves.

"Let me help. Because it is time for the Snake-Antelope Ceremony, to bring rain for the final maturity of the crops. It is almost complete; I will arrange for you to see the Snake Dance on the last day." David pushed the floodlight to the top of the ramp, switched it on, and shoved it ahead of himself into the grotto.

Brenna half-expected to see the carvings defaced, but the dream
had not been literal. There were no fresh scars—all was what Duncan must have seen. She climbed over the flood, wondering if she
had totally misunderstood Asbin; if he neither helped nor hindered
because it did not matter, it had never mattered, it was all
illusion . . . all mere appearances. In the end they would be
destroyed.

Before her were petroglyphs—an entire wall of them. Brenna sat
upon a ledge, carefully leaning back, her eyes taking in the details.
From the passage came a sound of exclamation. Flicking a glance
to one side, she realized that surprise, not injury, had prompted
the gasp—David was also staring at the wall. After watching him
sink down upon the ramp of rubble, Brenna turned back to the
carvings.

It was an unusual grouping; divided into four areas, each area
divided again, making a total of eight sections. One set of carvings
had a line jutting across a corner, as if to symbolize a break. Brenna
considered the designs . . . human figures, bear tracks, snakes,
cornstalks, *nakwách* brotherhood symbols. Stone dust lay in piles
beneath the mural, undisturbed for centuries.

One chip of stone was different—darker. Standing, Brenna
moved to the wall. After the rockslide, this would never be considered an undisturbed site. . . . She picked up the fragment. Portions
of carvings were on either side. "I wonder what this is from," she
said aloud. "David, you must be my Hopi source." Somehow she
couldn't trust A-Ttavitt now. "I know these carvings only in relation to world petroglyphs. I can determine their age, but without
something concrete leading to a known people, I can't begin to
prove their source is the Anasazi or any other prehistorical group."

"How do you normally determine source?" David asked, taking
the fragment from her. His face stilled as he looked at it.

Brenna considered the question, and then grinned without mirth.
Why not? Who would believe him, if she chose to deny it? "The
energy left in the carvings . . . reanimates . . . and shows me the
circumstances under which the image was created," she said
swiftly, embarrassed to hear the words spoken aloud. Only Duncan
had known for certain of her talent, although Brenna believed
Grana had suspected.

David did not smile. "You mean the spirits reveal themselves to
you?" he asked.

"Who said anything about spirits?" she retorted, moving to the
petroglyphs. "Are any of the carvings familiar?"

"I think I know precisely what they are. The Hopi have four
sacred tablets, stones of prophecy we have held in our hearts for
centuries. These carvings match the ones on the tablets."

Brenna swiftly turned. "Exactly? Your tablets are copies of this wall?"

"Or the walls are copies. Our legends say we entered this world at the spiritual center of the universe, but we had to make our migrations to the four corners of the continent to weed out all the latent evil of the previous world." This was half to himself. Brenna felt a chill as she watched David examine the dark rock fragment. "Oraivi is the site we finally returned to, all clans, dependent on our mighty Creator for rainfall and life. To think that our Emergence and Ending might be the same place."

He looked up, smiling, as if to reassure her he had not lost his mind. "Never laugh at a legend. It may come back to haunt you. May I borrow this? I'd like to take it to the leader of the Fire clan. We may be able to help you after all. And you, us."

Brenna nodded, mystified, as David stood to leave. "Interpret your dream, Brenna. I think it will answer almost everything." And he left.

The dream? First engineer, then mystic, and now psychologist—

"Dr. Stewart?" The light from the first chamber was blocked by several shadowy figures. It was the elusive Asbin, looking pinched, a living skull with haunted eyes. Ling A-Ttavitt was among the group amassed at his back.

"Colonel," she said neutrally.

"We must prepare to evacuate; our orders are to leave at 0600 hours. The defense effort has reached Crisis One proportions, and—"

"Where could be safer than a million miles from anywhere?" Brenna asked conversationally.

Asbin blinked, and then seemed to regroup his thoughts. "Surely you wish to be with your family at—"

"My family," she interrupted him, "died in this cave. If the world is changing irrevocably, let me try to save a piece of the past. I can be packed in five minutes." Her gaze flicked beyond him to the shade that was A-Ttavitt. "Bring me the black box. Put it in the first chamber, and start imaging the pictographs." To Asbin she said: "I am making progress, and prefer to remain here tonight." The look she gave the officer was direct as she gestured at the petroglyphs. "I'm a Celt, colonel, and Celts aren't afraid to die."

Asbin considered her a moment, and then pivoted toward his following. "Get the imager," he told the motionless A-Ttavitt.

Only then did the site artist start out the stone corridor.

Brenna left Ling A-Ttavitt working in the first chamber and strolled into the second, the black box swinging from one hand.

David Lansa was taking a long time. . . . She became conscious of hunger, of how long it had been since she had eaten. Dust sifted down into her hair. *Interpret your dream.* No, thank you. Her dreams were often frightening. Better to work on the walls. Carefully she positioned the instrument, sampling one of the incised lines, seeking trace elements from carving tools, exposure rates, organic materials. The light sequence flashed as the box began compiling information. Why had she taken this job? To please Duncan. And she would finish it, to honor his memory.

Where was David? Who could interpret these, now that Duncan—

She felt a pang at his name, the first real mote of grief she had allowed herself. The delicate chill slid around her, encouraging the emotion—*encouraging?* Shaking, Brenna set the black box down on the dirt floor. It hummed along, oblivious to her discomfort.

Something was aware of her thoughts, her feelings. Or someone. A question rose from her subconscious. Vainly she tried to suppress it. What if . . . what if what she had felt all these years was not pure energy, but cognizant spirit? What if . . . Brenna sat down in the deep dust, ignoring the waves of silt rising into the stale air. Soundlessly she felt the pieces of her dream fit themselves into a giant picture. The Celtic heritage destroyed, ripped apart by the Eurasian Forces. Her guilt at not being with her family . . . of living when they had died. Her fierce crusade to protect the relics of other pasts, other peoples. And her strange link to Grana, to the old woman's belief.

The scientist bowed her head to her knees, uncertain whether she was unbalanced by grief or one of the privileged few able to tap into the universal consciousness. What it was, why it spoke to her— Whispering aloud, she addressed it in a language she understood: "I have done nothing of myself. I am but a vessel to be filled with what must be remembered."

Amazingly, there was no bitterness in the thought; only wonder. Later to think it through, to wrestle with this possible intelligence, to demand explanation and understanding of those wars, deaths, pain. Now there was only the moment; she had a source to explain the petroglyphs to her. Only a slip of thought, in the home-speech: *I* will *remember . . . and so will others. You have my word.*

Presence grew within her, welling up like water so pure she was certain she would never thirst again. With presence came understanding. Staring at the petroglyphs, Brenna knew their meaning, tried to verbalize their prophecy. It was like the echo of a voice whispering from the past. . . .

After the clans reach their final home, the time will come when they will be conquered by a strange people. They will be forced to pattern their land and lives after these strangers, or be punished horribly. They are not to resist, for a deliverer will come. Their lost white brother, Pahana, will bring them the missing corner of the Fire Clan tablet, deliver them from their conquerors, and point the way toward a universal brotherhood of mankind. Until that coming, to leave the Hopi way will bring evil upon the tribes, and then the Bear Clan leader must be beheaded to dispel the evil.

The land between the two rivers is yours. Other tales . . . Brenna suddenly came back from the shadows, the ancient, quivering voice of a clan leader fading into the silence. She had *seen* the fire, the fire that had blackened the ceiling above her, the great man giving the tablets to the clan leaders, the making of prayer sticks and the chanting. The youths carving the story on the walls, copying the tablets. Tears had crept down her cheeks sometime during her trance; idly she brushed at the dusty tracks with the back of one hand. *Ah, Duncan, I will save this cave for you. . . . I will remember it.*

Preoccupied, Brenna rose to her feet, lifting the black box in passing. With any luck there would be enough evidence from the lab tests to narrow the dates, confirm her vision, give the Hopi back their sacred chamber—

Slanting sunlight drew her out of her thoughts. It was getting late; she would have to— And then Brenna was outside, and she forgot what she was going to do. The two Coyote Clan *Qaletaqa* still stood guard, but Pamösi, their leader, was waiting at the foot of the path. He gestured for Brenna to follow him.

Momentarily she held her ground. Other visions had told her that the people of peace had shed blood in the past, when they felt their way of life threatened. Then she moved to the clan leader's side.

Old Pamösi did not speak as they walked up the trail, his gait the equal of any man in his prime. Several times he stopped to let Brenna rest, but he offered no information, not even to explain David's absence. When they neared the top, Pamösi let her walk ahead of him, moderating his pace.

A silent crowd was waiting for them. Brenna slowed, confused, when she realized that four lines of cornmeal had been drawn across the trail. Pamösi had halted also; he waited quietly behind her. Searching the weathered faces of the gathering, Brenna realized that the village elders made up the majority of those present. She recognized David standing on the fringe of the group, his warm eyes reassuring. The elderly Bear Clan leader stood in the front; last of his line, spokesman of his people. Bright eyes peered at her from a wrinkled face; the man's withered hand did not shake as he extended it, palm up, to the young woman.

Brenna fought to control her trembling. David had the carved rock fragment—what else did the leader expect? She stood motionless while the sun went down into a sea of sharp flame and the air grew cold. Even the cave spirit held back, waiting.

Tragedy in their past . . . but in the beginning they were people of peace. Ah, well . . . she'd always been a creature of intuition. Brenna extended her hand palm-down to clasp the aged leader's hand.

A murmuring grew, like the roar of a seashell in her ears. The old man still held her hand, and Brenna could see his eyes fill with tears. David was suddenly beside them.

"I—don't understand," she started softly.

David's answer was laughter ringed in warmth. "You think too much, Brenna! You hold in your hand the *nakwach*. You are Pahana, bringing universal brotherhood to the people of peace."

"I am the Pahána? David—" her voice dropped to a hiss. "The Pahána is a white *man*—"

"Oh, I know," he said, his smile contagious. "The clan leaders had trouble with that, too. But you have fulfilled their prophecies, Brenna. They cannot deny you!"

In the midst of the crowd's excitement, a man behind them cried out something in Hopi, and all voices ceased, snuffed out like a torch. Brenna and David turned to face Pamösi and the breathless young man beside him. The youth continued speaking, his face strained and his words trembling.

David grew very still. "The warhead has dropped from orbit. It landed in India." Turning to the Bear Clan leader, he whispered something, even as Brenna looked away from the gathering, unwilling to face the Hopi as mass destruction mocked the advent of their universal brotherhood.

"Asbin's receiver is stronger than ours," David said softly. "Let us see what he has picked up on satellite."

The clan leaders began to descend to the desert floor.

It was hard for Brenna in the darkness, doubly bitter when she saw the shuttle lift off. It was Pamösi who picked her up when she faltered, carrying her like a small child.

Silence reigned on the flats, broken only by the shout of the young Coyote guard who still waited by the empty cave. The camp had been stripped; only the urethane tents and Asbin's headquarters remained. At first they thought Brenna alone had been left behind, until they approached the cinder-block building. They could hear weeping within.

The electronic eye was broken. Brenna knew there had to be an emergency switch, and tripped the lock with a swing of her arm; the panel responded, sliding open. Static and garbled voices struck them like a gust of wind. Ling A-Ttavitt huddled near the doorway, sobbing hysterically, oblivious to their arrival. Asbin's seated profile was just visible in the gloom beyond. David started toward the man, speaking his name. It seemed unreal to Brenna, who focused on A-Ttavitt, pulling her to one side while a village elder stepped over them and adjusted the delicate tuning of the receiver.

"He is dead," came a voice. Brenna looked up, and wished that she had not. Despite the growing darkness, she could see a dark spot on Asbin's forehead. Self-inflicted? Was this the cause of A-Ttavitt's frenzy? The result? Why didn't the soldiers take A-Ttavitt and the body? Was this because of the warhead, or their abandonment, or . . . Brenna held the tiny woman close, willing herself not to think.

Everyone seated themselves on the floor, listening to the babble of languages coming in over the airwaves. The Bear Clan leader flipped the dial at will, seeking the strongest signals. Some of the voices were calm, islands of tranquillity in the face of disaster. Others were edging hysteria, as reports continued to flow in. It had not stopped with the orbiting warhead. For the first time, Brenna truly understood the word "escalation."

She listened with little comprehension, drawing meaning from inflection as the night wore on. Myriad stars appeared in the night sky, a glittering wall of obsidian beyond the open door. David sat down next to her, although she did not remember him leaving Asbin. No one stirred; their entire existence was bound up in sound.

" 'Beloved,' " Brenna said at one point, and David shifted beside her. "Your name means 'beloved.' " He did not speak.

At last the broadcasts began to thin. Brenna first noticed the absence of the squeaky-voiced announcer. Signing off, their transmissions cut off? One strong signal vanished literally between one word and the next, and Brenna wondered if a satellite had been destroyed. How long to launch another one . . . ? Other signals faded—losing power, afraid to provide a target, allowing EBS to kick in?

Then the Bear Clan leader flipped the communicator switch, silencing the gibbering machine. Stillness wrapped itself around the group, weaving among them like a physical force. Even Ling A-Ttavitt had ceased to weep.

Momentarily, Brenna thought of protesting the man's action; only a moment. Then she noticed the silence . . . and the presence beyond the waiting. She began to wonder if the Hopi, like herself, could hear stone speak.

The group waited awhile, but the night offered no other messages; finally the clan leaders began exiting the blockhouse, supporting the steps of the eldest among them. Brenna waited until most of them had left before she helped A-Ttavitt stand. Sighing, she turned to David, trying to think of something to say, but gentle fingers to her lips stopped her. Only Pamösi waited with them.

David reached over and took Ling A-Ttavitt's arm. Together they helped the woman out the doorway. Behind them, Pamösi raised his arm, closing the door.

The flames rose higher, licking, curling at the ceiling—collapsing on themselves as Brenna came back to herself. A gust of cold wind rounded the corner, tickling her feet. With a sigh she shook back her silver hair, smoothing the warm woolen dress over her exposed, wrinkled hands. This time she had seen the Coyote-Swallow race at Sikyatki, the legendary home of the migrating Coyote Clan. She glanced at the entranceway; the light was dim. It was late, and she was tired. . . .

"Grana!" The clear voice echoed against the chamber walls, and the fire leapt in response.

Smiling, Brenna shouted: "Who are you? Come in!"

A hesitant youth slid into the outer corridor, barely discernible behind the flames. "It is Chöviohóya, Grana. Chief-father has prepared our dinner, and asks that you bid the spirits farewell for a time. Tonight is satellite night, remember." The boy began to back out.

"Young Deer!" she said softly in the home tongue, and he paused; he was one of the few who had learned it, and would deny her nothing when she spoke it. "Don't you like my cave?"

"Of course, Grana."

"Then why do you leave so swiftly? Do you fear it?"

"I fear nothing!" he said adamantly, taking one step back inside.

"Not even the sky falling? Even the bravest warriors of all feared the wrath of the gods. I think it is not the cave that you fear, but what is inside yourself." Silence. Brenna held tightly to her smile, controlling the corners of her mouth. "I can help you face it, young man. You can learn much from listening to the Great Spirit, and always return to walk in the light of day." Slowly the boy slipped into the first chamber, studying his grandmother with no small amount of awe. He had David's face, but her own father's broad shoulders and long legs. Shooting up like the corn . . . "Sit by me."

David would be wondering about them. But, after a bit, he would understand, and rejoice.

"What can you teach me, Grana?" the youth asked, his voice hushed.

"What would you know first? You are born of three great heritages, Chöviohóya. What would you know?"

"Will you tell me of the beginning, when the guardian spirit Másaw gave the sacred tablets to our people? And about the white warriors, who feared nothing but the sky falling?"

"That part is past, child," she said gently, "for I have seen the sky fall, and I do not fear it anymore." Brenna cleared her throat. *"After the clans reached their final home—"*

AFTERWORD

This is one of those stories that began as a dream, of a thin man with sunken features chiseling away at petroglyphs on a wall. The symbols were in vertical rows, as if they were a language, and I was filled with grief at their loss.

Stories with threads into myth always make me think of Roger, so it's no surprise I asked him about an earlier incarnation of this piece. He counseled cutting a subplot and a few characters, and encouraged me to stick with it. And so, like one particular Zelazny character, I toss this story like a jewel into the darkness, and hope that it will sparkle with the colors of life.

"Forever" is a relative concept. Sometimes knowing an ending will come can create a special kind of eternity.

■

KI'RIN AND THE BLUE AND WHITE TIGER
Jane M. Lindskold

THEY MEET ONCE EVERY ONE HUNDRED YEARS. ONE COMES FROM the sea, churning white foam and salt water, parting both with his terrible head and fang-heavy jaws, raising sleek striped flanks and iridescent claws.

The other comes running through the sky cloaked in storm cloud and sheeting rain, her spiraling horn parting mist and ringing thunder. Her head is dragonlike, horselike, her silver and onyx coat neither silken fur nor shimmering scales but something impossibly both.

On delicate polished hooves that chime against the rocks, she lands before the other, from whose coat seawater still runs in quantities enough to feed rivers.

They study each other, sea creature, sky creature, and, as one, in mutual deference, they bow. The spiral horn of the ki'rin cuts a crescent in the sand. The curling whiskers of the blue and white tiger sweep a dozen dozen delicate swaths across the crescent, completing rather than obliterating.

"Come and run with me through the meadows beneath the sea," the blue and white tiger says.

"Come and romp with me over moon-kissed mountains of cloud and mist," the ki'rin responds.

"Wait!" The third voice is shrill, breaking and quaking in fear. "Wait, noble kami, I have a boon to beg of you."

They turn and look then, bright, unblinking eyes the only thing alike about them, though those of the tiger are blue and those of the ki'rin pearl.

The woman who staggers out to meet them prostrates herself before the look in those eyes. She is young, barely more than a girl. Her shining black hair is loose like a girl's, but she is a woman and a mother and her baby waves tiny fists in protest from the cradle-board on her back. His feeble whimper gives her courage and she raises herself, folding her hands respectfully before her face, her eyes still downcast.

The ki'rin and the blue and white tiger wait patiently, for though they have only this one day every one hundred years, each one has forever and that does make a difference.

Voice still trembling, the woman addresses her words to the shadows the rising sun casts before the ki'rin and the blue and white tiger.

"My baby is ill with a wasting sickness that turns his bowels to water and turns my milk sour in his belly so that what he does not spit out makes him even more ill."

There is no answer, but the single-horned shadow of the ki'rin turns and the heavy jowled head of the blue and white tiger meets its gaze. Encouraged, if not emboldened, the woman continues.

"My great-grandmother, who is the wisest person in all our valley, says that the forces of the ki'rin and the blue and white tiger, when met in the shrine at the heart of this island, can defeat any ill. She says that her mother brought her before you a century ago and that you healed her so that even today she is hale and strong beyond her years."

"Child," says the rain-shower voice of the ki'rin, her accents rich with pity, "your great-grandmother recalls well but not entirely correctly."

"No, daughter," comes the wave rumble voice of the blue and white tiger. "The force of either the ki'rin or the blue and white tiger can defeat any ill. The other may be bane not blessing."

"Oh!" the woman sobs, the little storm of her tears making streamlets in the sand. "Oh, my baby! Oh, my soul! O-sensei, great kami, I beg you, teach me what I must do!"

"You must choose," the rain-voice, wave-voice say as one. "You must choose and that one will be your champion. The other will oppose."

"But how will I know to choose rightly?" the woman cries,

forgetting, in her fear for her baby, to look down and facing the creatures before her.

"That we cannot tell," the blue and white tiger says. "Nor can you hurry home to ask your great-grandmother what to do," the ki'rin says, "for only one day in every one hundred years do we meet."

The woman slides the cradle-board from her back and stares with desperate love at her baby boy. How can she decide and how can she not decide? To decide wrong will be inviting agony. To refuse to choose and thus know that her fear of choosing wrong has failed her boy would be more than she can bear.

But which could she choose? One would be champion and companion—the other enemy and opponent. The tiger's fur seems thick and soft. His blue eyes hold the ocean's depths. Is he the healer? She looks at the curving white fangs in his heavy jaws, at the iridescent claws that peek from his paws, and feels doubt.

As the rising sun touches her with wings of flame, the ki'rin's pearly eyes offer no answer. The single horn on her broad brow is formidable, but her cloven hooves are not weighted with claws, nor her jaws with fangs. She would be the more comfortable companion, but is she the healer? Can she oppose the might of the blue and white tiger?

As the woman stares and studies, Baby opens his rheumy eyes and holds out hands that should be plump, but are shriveled and yellowing. Impulsively, she snatches him from the cradle-board and holds him before the waiting kami.

"Choose your champion, my baby!" she cries, feeling how frail he is, silently praying for mercy and justice to guide him.

The baby's hands wave wildly. Then, with a chortle of amusement, he reaches for the glint of sunlight imprisoned within the ki'rin's horn. For a moment he is suffused with a ruddy glow—purification or fever?—the mother does not know. Gently, the ki'rin dips the horn's needle-point away from the baby's hands.

"Champion, I," says the storm voice.

"And enemy, I," says the wave roar. "I give you an hour. The game ends at sunset."

With a bound of great paws and a lashing of his tail, the tiger is gone, the forest swallowing his blue and white into green and shadow. The ki'rin raises her head to watch him depart and her flanks shudder with a sigh. Her pearl eyes are without an expression the woman can read as she lowers her head again.

"Since we are to be companions," the ki'rin asks, "what shall I call you, woman?"

"Yuki," she says and the ki'rin bobs her head and Yuki feels that the kami is smiling behind her eyes of pearl.

"Come then, Yuki. Take your baby and climb upon my back. The forest is deep and the shrine is far and I can run more swiftly than you."

Yuki carefully straps Baby onto his cradle-board and then mounts the ki'rin. Where the ki'rin's mane is fullest, she grasps a double handful and wraps it about her fists.

Even as Yuki decides that she is secure, the ki'rin begins to run. The gait is so smooth that Yuki can hardly believe that they are moving, but the pace is so great that roses blossom on her cheeks. For the first time since Baby fell ill, she actually smiles.

Beneath fruiting cherry and ripening plum, through solemn avenues of bamboo so tall that the rising sun does not penetrate, the ki'rin carries Yuki and her son. Though Yuki was born on this island and believed that she knew all of its haunts, she does not know these forests and realizes that they run in realms apart from those of humankind, where kami, kappa, and oni are the inhabitants. She shudders then and the ki'rin answers without slowing.

"Listen carefully, Yuki. Right or wrong, I am your champion and if you and your baby hope to return to your home, you must trust and obey me."

"I hear you, Ki'rin."

"The blue and white tiger will seek to keep us from the shrine, but do not mistake yourself about him. He may seem all fang and claw and terrible strength, but he is a creature of ancient guile and older magic."

Yuki wonders, unjustly perhaps, if she has chosen the wrong champion, for the ki'rin seems much in awe of the blue and white tiger. Still, she holds her tongue.

"You must obey me in all things," the ki'rin continues, "and, if you do, I will not fail to get you and the baby to the shrine before the day's end."

"I hear you," Yuki says, "and I will obey you."

But she continues to wonder, for the ki'rin has only promised to carry them to the shrine, not to heal the baby.

They run on and the running is like flying, the cloven hooves of the ki'rin never marking the earth over which she speeds.

After a time, Yuki hears a new sound, the heavy thudding of feet. The sounds come from two feet, not four. Nor could such slapping come from the velveted paws of the blue and white tiger, but nevertheless, Yuki is afraid. The ki'rin increases her pace, but their pursuer is not slowed by the weight of a mother and child. Soon Yuki sees what follows.

"An oni!" she shrieks.

The ki'rin nods, her horn slicing clear the path for them.

"Describe it for me," she says, and Yuki hears her panting beneath the words.

"He is so tall that he seems to brush the sky, and his skin is muddy blue," Yuki says. "His body is tufted with coarse hair but his head is bald as an egg—though not as shapely. Terribly, he has three eyes and tusks that twist out from his lower jaw. He wears little but a rag about his hips, but the mallet in his hand is spiked with iron."

"Ah," pants the ki'rin, "I know him. He is strong but foolish. Hold on."

Yuki does so, glancing fearfully over her shoulder as the oni grows closer. He begins to bellow threats that are lewd and mocking. Yuki's ears burn with shame, but the ki'rin does not pause.

And then it seems that disaster must come, for glancing ahead Yuki sees before them a lake of deep blue water interrupted only by lily pads, each bedecked with yellow or pink or white lilies. Horribly, the ki'rin is slowing, turning, facing the oni at last. Her flanks are heaving and her shimmering fur is dewed with sweat.

"Back away, oni!" she challenges. "Back or I will gore you!"

"Hah!" the oni guffaws. "Gore me? You would never get by my hammer!"

"You could never get close enough to use it!" the ki'rin taunts in return.

His answer is an angry bellow. Waving his hammer, the oni runs faster. Not panting now, the ki'rin spins and runs, her cloven hooves barely grazing the lily pads as she races across the lake. Yuki looks back in terror and sees the oni make a tremendous leap onto a lily pad. There is a terrific splash and he sinks in an upwelling of mud and water.

Laughter shakes the ki'rin's flanks. "May all of the blue and white tiger's allies be so foolish! I fear that they will not be, and the way is yet long."

She runs on then, through fields of golden daisies and purple asters, and over rising hills. The day is clear but not hot. Yuki is grateful. Baby sleeps, but his sleep is restless and punctuated with little cries. His wrappings smell foul and feel damp.

On a hillcrest, beneath a ruined arch, ghosts cry out to them—promising miracles. Yuki longs to turn, but the ki'rin runs on.

From a swampy pool beneath a weeping willow tree, a kappa wrinkles its green monkey-face and begs them to pause for a game of finger-pull. Yuki brightens, for kappa give magical gifts to those who defeat them, but the ki'rin runs on.

In a valley ringed with bamboo, the ki'rin finally pauses.

"I wish to rest," she says. "Watch until the sun touches the tip of the lone pine on that ridge. Wake me then or sooner if anything troubles you."

Yuki nods and dismounts. The ki'rin kneels then and folds her legs beneath her. Horn resting on the ground, she falls quickly to sleep.

Washing baby with water from a spring and freshening his reeking wraps keeps Yuki busy. Repeatedly, she checks the sun in relation to the pine. She rinses her own face and combs her wind-tangled hair with the tortoise-shell comb of her grandmother. When she finishes plaiting her hair, she checks the sun again.

Surely it should have moved further by now. Is this a trick of the spirit land—that the sun moves more slowly?

She glances at the ki'rin, then again at the sun. This time she sees something, a trembling in the bamboo and a faint flash of blue and white. She checks again. The pine tree has moved!

Anxiously, she shakes the ki'rin awake.

"Oh, Ki'rin!" she cries, "I have been fooled!"

Quickly, she explains. The ki'rin snorts in anger and admiration.

"He is clever, the blue and white tiger is. He must have heard my instructions to you. Climb on my back and we will run again. This time, your sharp eyes have saved us!"

If Yuki believed they flew before, now she learns what flying is. The ki'rin leaps on the wind. The speed of her passage scorches the air and tiny flames lick her coat. Yuki unwraps one hand from her grip on the ki'rin's mane and pats out the flames that threaten her and Baby.

Thunder rumbles from behind them and lightning flashes.

"As I feared," the ki'rin calls, "the blue and white tiger has set storm spirits after us. They could not find us on the ground, but here I am too visible. We must descend and go more slowly or they may harm you and Baby."

Yuki pats the silken neck in understanding. She begrudges the loss of speed, but the storm spirits are close now. She can see their gaping mouths and the clapping hands from which lightning spurts.

"How much further must we go, ki'rin?" she asks when again they are traveling over the earth.

"A far distance," the ki'rin replies. "The shrine is atop that snow-peaked crest. Were we to fly, we could be there swiftly, but the ground between is craggy and bad-tempered."

Yuki studies the snowy crest as the ki'rin runs. Is that a splash of blue and white on the slope? She keeps her fears to herself. Then the rain begins.

It is a slick rain, icy rain, rain that tastes of salt and sea. She does not need to be a ki'rin to know that this is more of the blue and white tiger's magic. Taking Baby from her back, she cradles him in her arms and bears the storm's fury on her bowed back and head. In time, her tears add to the salt storm's force.

Despite the rain, they continue on and then, unbelievably, the ki'rin stumbles, tries to recover, then falls, her horn plowing through the mud. Her knees smash into the wet earth and she lets out a tiny wail of pain.

Jolted, Yuki is thrown forward, only her arms entangled in the ki'rin's mane saving her from falling to the ground. From the cradle-board, Baby shrills more in anger than in fear.

Yuki slides to the muddy ground and strokes the ki'rin's head.

"O-sensei, how badly are you hurt?"

The ki'rin blinks, her pearl eyes washed with red. She weeps tears that look like blood.

"I hurt terribly, Yuki. My front legs ache like fire in the bones."

"Will you . . . will you die?"

"I cannot die. I am immortal." The ki'rin staggers to her cloven hooves. "But I cannot run. Certainly, I cannot run with a burden."

"Then we will walk," Yuki says bravely.

"That we must," the ki'rin agrees. "Perhaps we can outwalk this storm."

They struggle on. The ki'rin limps, favoring her forelegs, right over left. Yuki holds Baby, who grows increasingly still as he becomes colder and wetter.

Then, like a beacon through the rain, they see a cottage. It is small with a thatched roof, and mud and daub walls. A thin but steady stream of smoke comes from the cobblestone chimney.

Ahead the cloud cover is thinning and the sun can be seen, past apex now.

"Let us rest here," Yuki begs, when the ki'rin would have limped onward. "Baby is cold and miserable. So am I."

"And so am I," the ki'rin admits, "but Baby will stay ill if we do not get to the shrine before sunset."

Yuki brightens. "Does that mean that you are the Healer?"

The ki'rin shakes the rain from her mane. "I cannot say, Yuki. All I am saying is that there is no chance for Baby to be healed if we do not reach the shrine."

Baby sneezes.

"Please, o-sensei. Let us rest, just for a short time!"

"As you wish, Yuki," the ki'rin sighs.

Yuki hurries forward and raps on the door. It opens almost as soon as the sound dies off. A monk stands there, dressed in a robe of white belted with blue. He steps back and bows deeply.

"Come to my fire, travelers. I have tea, seaweed cakes, and rice to warm you."

Yuki bows as deeply as she can with the baby in her arms. The ki'rin also bows, although more slowly, tracing a crescent on the floor with her horn. Then she limps into the cottage.

"Tea, ladies?"

"Thank you," Yuki says, "and may I have some hot water for the baby?"

"Of course."

The monk busies himself serving tea, pouring a deep, shallow bowl for the ki'rin and heaping seaweed cakes on a flat tray that he sets by her head.

"You appear to be wounded," he says softly, "ki'rin."

"I am," she glances down to her bruised legs.

"I have a salve. Let me anoint your wounds."

She looks into the monk's eyes. They are blue.

"Very well. I would be appreciative."

The monk fetches a carved soapstone jar filled with a sweet-scented unguent. Dipping two fingers into the unguent he rubs it into the ki'rin's bruises. Her eyes lose their pinkness; then her eyelids grow heavy and she drifts to sleep.

Yuki watches with a mixture of fear and relief. Baby drowses now, his wet clothing steaming in front of the fire.

"The rainstorm is moving on," the monk says, standing at the window and looking out.

"How long until the ki'rin awakes?"

"You can awaken her now," the monk replies, "but let her sleep. She is in pain."

"But I need her to take me to the shrine at the mountain's crest before sunset," Yuki says, "and the sun is setting."

"Why do you need to go there?"

"Baby is ill and the ki'rin is helping me take her to the shrine— she is my champion against his illness."

"Have you chosen the correct champion?"

"I hope so," Yuki says softly. "It is too late to change."

"Is it?" the monk asks. "As you can see, I have the gift of healing. Why risk your son further? And can you trust the ki'rin? Hasn't her behavior been peculiar at times?"

"Peculiar?"

"The ki'rin can fly. Why didn't she simply fly you to the shrine? You could have been there in minutes."

Yuki frowns. "Ki'rin seemed to fear the storm spirits."

"She is a storm spirit—among other things. Why would she fear storm spirits?" The monk's voice is gently persuasive.

Yuki reaches for Baby's clothing and begins to dress him.

"The ki'rin is my champion. I will stay with her for the rest of the journey if she is strong enough to go on." She touches the ki'rin on one shoulder. "Wake, Ki'rin. Wake."

The pearl eyes blink open and the ki'rin staggers to her trembling legs. Shaking out her mane of black iron and silver, she bows to the monk.

"Thank you for the tea."

Outside the cottage, the ki'rin leads the way up the path to the shrine. The rain has stopped, but the trail is still slick with salty mud. Above, the sun is nearing a reddening horizon.

"How are your legs, Ki'rin?" Yuki asks timidly. "Did the monk's salve heal them?"

"It did not heal them, but the pain is somewhat numbed."

Yuki struggles on for a few more steps. "The monk—he was the blue and white tiger, was he not?"

"He was." The ki'rin's reply is a whisper.

"He helped us," Yuki says. "He gave us rest and medicine and made the rain stop. Why did he help if he is your enemy?"

"Perhaps he meant to delay us," the ki'rin says. "Even with rest and medicine, I cannot run for more than a short distance. I doubt that we will reach the shrine. Perhaps his charity was in reality the last move in a battle."

Yuki reflects, remembering what the monk had said, the temptations he had offered.

"No," she says at last. "He was worried about you. What is there between you? Why do you meet once every one hundred years? The blue and white tiger may be your opponent in this game, but he is not your enemy."

The ki'rin stops then and her eyes of pearl meet the dark brown eyes of the young woman. Carefully, she touches her with the tip of her spiraling horn. Yuki feels the tiny crescent caress before the ki'rin sighs and begins to climb again. As she climbs, she hesitantly speaks, choosing the words with as much care as she chooses where to place her injured hooves.

"Long ago, before even the gods had names, long before Amaterasu retreated into her cave or Susano slew the eight-headed dragon of Isumo, long ago when Izanagi and Izanami were populating the islands, both the blue and white tiger and I were born.

"We fell in love in those long ago days when all was new. Together we ran beneath the sea and through the clouds. We loved each other until the day that we learned that all who love must fade and die."

"Is that so terrible?" Yuki asks. "No one wishes to die, but death is a part of living—the fit end to a good life. Death is only terrible when it comes for one who has not yet lived."

Here she hugs Baby to her breasts.

"Maybe," the ki'rin says, "but I could not bear that because of my love someday the world would no longer know the terrible beauty of the blue and white tiger, that someday the waves would no longer resound with his roar or carry in their tossing the blue and white of his coat. And he . . ."

The ki'rin's voice becomes zephyr soft. "And he could not bear that the storm clouds would not flash with my passing or the cloud mountains part at my flight. So we resolved to part from each other and meet on one day each one hundred years. On that day, we would seek to learn if we still loved and try to learn to be enemies. In that way, each would live forever."

"So my boon and the cure for Baby's illness—is this nothing more than a game for you?" Yuki's voice cracks in anger.

"Oh, no, little human," the ki'rin says. "We care, for only a competition for life and death could drive us apart, only that reminds us why we have forsaken our love."

She pauses and in the setting sun Yuki sees that the ki'rin's eyes are red with tears.

"Can we reach the shrine before sunset?" Yuki asks.

The ki'rin sags, beaten.

"No, Yuki. My legs are so sore I could only bear you twenty places at a run. I cannot run to the mountain crest."

Yuki remembers the words of the monk who was the blue and white tiger. "But you can fly, Ki'rin. Fly us to the shrine!"

The ki'rin straightens, raising her horned head high. She studies Yuki and the tears are vanished from her pearly eyes.

"I would need to leap off the mountain to gain the air. I cannot run to embrace the wind as I did before. Can you trust me?"

"I can."

"I would need to fly so fast that my fur would be fringed with flames and even the scales below would be burning hot. Can you brave that?"

"I can!"

"We will be pursued by oni of the air, far more terrible than the ones of the land. If they catch us, they will eat Baby as a treat and drink sake from his skull. You they will dismember, feasting on your limbs as they rape your body. Can you dare this?"

"I can!" Yuki cries, but she shudders as she promises.

"Then climb on my back and hold Baby tightly. We run for the wind and fly for the shrine!"

Then the ki'rin, stumbling some on limbs still numb, charges for the mountain edge. She leaps into the emptiness and Yuki's screams tear her throat raw as they plummet toward the jagged rocks below.

She can see the rocks' polished points and scent the dirt before the ki'rin paws the heating air with her cloven hooves and turns them upward.

"We are flying!" Yuki cheers.

"We are," the ki'rin gasps, "but if I am to reach the top before the sun sets, I must burn the air. Hold fast, for if you let go, I will never be able to catch you!"

And she flies, and if before the air had burned hot, now it burns hotter, singeing Yuki's hair, even her brows, and scorching her throat and eyes. She bends over Baby to save him from the worst, but she knows she offers scant protection.

Then from behind she hears the threats of the oni of the air. Their voices grow louder and their lewd words more distinct until Yuki cannot tell if she burns from shame or from heat.

The ki'rin flies on unfaltering, but Yuki can feel her heart pounding beneath the scales and hear the rasp of breath that tears from the ki'rin's dilated nostrils.

Suddenly, there is a jolt. Motion ceases and Yuki fears that the oni have grabbed the ki'rin by her tail and even now are pulling them toward them. She struggles not to scream.

Then, wonderfully, the harsh voices wail in defeat and fade into the distance. Coolness soothes her burning skin and the wind voice of the ki'rin speaks.

"Brave Yuki, we are here. Open your eyes and look about. The shrine is before you and the sun is only touching her rest."

Yuki sits upright, then slides to the ground, Baby blinking sleepily in her arms. The shrine lies ahead, a simple place with a curving roof, fronted by a deep pool of dark water. Pine needles carpet the ground and snow nestles in the trees above and ices the curl of the pagoda roof.

"Are you the Healer?" Yuki asks, her voice soft with dread that his last challenge will mean her loss.

"For you, I am," the ki'rin says, "but so is the blue and white tiger, for without him I would not make this run nor be on the shore to hear your boon."

The blue and white tiger rises from the pool then and pads over to join them. Nose to nose, he greets the ki'rin and laps her legs with his coarse blue tongue. Instantly, the bruises vanish, her exhaustion fades, and she is again filled with the power of the wind, the power of the storm and the clouds.

"Hold out your baby," the blue and white tiger rumbles.

The young mother trembles at placing her son before the heavy jaws, but she obeys. The tiger rasps out with his tongue and Yuki can see the illness scoured away in one stroke. A second lick gives back flesh and color, and a third gives humor and health.

Baby chortles as she hugs him to her. The ki'rin and the blue and white tiger laugh their storm cloud, sea wind laughs with him. In perfect certainty, Yuki knows that baby will live and be strong.

With luck he will go on to his hundredth year and in turn tell the tale of the ki'rin and the blue and white tiger to his descendants as her great-grandmother had to her.

"And what will you do?" Yuki asks the kami. "The sun is nearly set and your one day of every one hundred years is nearly gone."

The blue and white tiger bows before the ki'rin.

"Come and run with me through the meadows beneath the sea."

The ki'rin studies first him, then Yuki, and bows in turn.

"Come and romp with me over moon-kissed mountains of cloud and mist."

"I would," the blue and white tiger growls, "but all things that love must die and I could not be your death."

"Perhaps there is more to life than merely not dying," the ki'rin responds. "I would not rob the world of your glory, but . . ."

"Oh, do it!" Yuki cries. "Run and romp—you're dead alive now, living only to preserve what you are. I promise that the sea and sky will always hold your memories. I will keep them and give them to Baby and he will pass them on to his children."

There is silence then, broken only by the waiting of the drifting snow in the pines. Then the ki'rin bows and etches a crescent in the snow with her horn. The blue and white tiger embellishes her mark with a dozen dozen delicate whisker swaths.

"We should take Yuki and the baby home before the night comes on," the ki'rin says. "Their family will miss them."

"Yes," growls the blue and white tiger, "and then?"

"I will come and run with you through meadows beneath the sea."

"And I will come and romp with you over moon-kissed mountains of cloud and mist."

"Forever?"

"Forever."

AFTERWORD

Unlike some of the authors in this anthology, I didn't meet Roger Zelazny until the final stage of his life. So, I never really knew the shy poet or the man awkwardly dealing with the acclaim that accompanied even his earliest efforts. (Everyone knows that Roger won a Hugo and two Nebulas in 1966. Did you know that in 1966 and 1967 his own novelettes competed against each other on the Hugo ballot?)

The Roger I met was the multiple award-winner, the man secure in his fame, content with his profession, and anticipating years of writing to come. He was still shy, but he had learned how to compensate for that shyness by becoming a polished public speaker, a man gently patient with his fans.

With people like me.

We met first through a letter I wrote, kept in touch with six months of brief notes, and finally met in person at Lunacon in New York in 1989. It was the beginning of a friendship that would grow stronger and more important to us both. In a strange way, even though he is gone, our friendship continues because of the impact he had on so many areas of my life.

The most obvious area was in writing. When we met, I was just finishing a Ph.D. in English Literature and planning to turn some of the mad energy I had focused on graduate work to writing fiction. Roger read my early efforts, provided gentle criticism, and, most importantly, introduced me to the intricacies of the business. He let me make my own mistakes, never strove to turn me into a carbon copy of himself (even when that might have meant I would have published more quickly), and rejoiced with me over my little successes.

He lived to see his belief in my abilities confirmed. We celebrated the acceptance for publication of my first four novels, collaborated on several projects, and discovered in each other the friend and playmate we'd been missing.

"Ki'rin and the Blue and White Tiger" was written before Roger's death. It was his favorite of my short pieces. (We even had a bet about it; he lost—twice.) For me, it was one of those stories written in a flurry of inspiration. The title came one day; the rest was written in the two days that followed.

Not until after Roger's death did I realize that I had written the story in response to my own awareness that, no matter how hard both of us were trying to prevent it, the cancer was probably going to kill him. It's a story that confronts the reality that when you love someone, you accept along with the joy the eventual sorrow— the pain, the loss, the incredible loneliness. It's a rare couple that faces death together. Usually, someone is left behind.

I think Roger knew what I was facing before I did and I suspect that's why he loved the story. I don't have the chance to ask him if I'm right or to ask any of the other questions I've wanted to ask since June 14, 1995. Still, I'm glad for the questions I did get to ask, for the answers that I have.

It's worth it all, even in the end, even for the one left behind.

*As in his three collaborations with Roger, Bob Sheckley's story
is wild, flip, and cynical, packing a fine sarcastic punch.*

THE ERYX
Robert Sheckley

I WOKE UP AND LOOKED AROUND. EVERYTHING WAS JUST ABOUT
the same.

"Hey, Julie," I said. "You up yct?"

Julie didn't answer. She couldn't. She was my imaginary playmate. Maybe I was crazy, but at least I knew Julie was someone
I'd made up.

I got out of bed, showered, dressed. It was all the same as it
always was. And yet, I had the feeling something had changed.

I didn't know what annoyed me the most about the setup. I had
given up being annoyed. I had one room and a bathroom. Outside
of my room was a glassed-in porch. I could walk out on the porch
and sun myself. They seemed to have the sun going all day long,
every day. I wondered what had happened to the rainy days I'd
known back in my youth. Or maybe there were rainy days but I just
wasn't seeing them. I had suspected for a long time that my room
and its glassed-in enclosure were inside some other sort of a building,
a really big building where they controlled the light and the climate,
made it just like they wanted it. Evidently the way they wanted it
was with hazy sunlight all day long. I couldn't see the sun even when
I was outside. Just a white sky and light glaring from it. It could
come from klieg lights, for all I knew. They didn't let me see much.

I had spotted the cameras, however. They were little units, Sonys, I suspected, and their tiny black matte heads rotated all of the time, keeping me in sight. There were cameras inside my one room, too, up in the corners, behind steel netting that I couldn't tear away even if I wanted to, which I didn't, and cameras even in my bathroom. I hated that. During my first days here, I'd screamed at the walls, "Hey, what's it with you guys, don't you got any sense of privacy? Can't a guy even take a dump without you watching?" But nobody ever answered me. No one ever talked to me. I'd been here seventy-three days, I made notches on the plastic table to keep count. But sometimes I forgot, and I wouldn't be surprised if it turned out to be a lot longer than that. They'd allowed me writing materials, too, but no computer. Were they afraid of what I might do with a computer? I didn't have any idea. They gave me reading material, too. Old stuff. *Moll Flanders. Idylls of the King. The Iliad* and *Odyssey*. Stuff like that. Good stuff, but not exactly up to date. And they never showed themselves.

Why was that? I couldn't figure it out. I didn't even know what they looked like. They'd grabbed me back then, seventy-three days ago. Stuff had still been happening back then. I'd been home. I'd received an urgent fax. Office of the President. "We need you urgently." I'd come. In fact, they'd sent men to bring me to this place. Men who didn't answer any of my questions. I'd tried to find out. What's this all about? They'll tell you more inside, that's all they'd told me.

And then I'd been inside. They'd given me a suite of rooms, told me to get some rest, there'd be a meeting soon. I'd gone to sleep that first night, and been awakened by sounds of shooting. I'd gone to the door. It was locked. I could hear men shouting, struggling out in the hall. And then there'd been silence. And the silence had gone on and on.

At first I'd thought I was pretty well off. The others had gotten killed, I suspected. Those blank-faced men who'd brought me here. All dead, I was sure of it. I was the only one remaining. But what for? What did they want me for?

I'd heard noises outside my suite of rooms. Sounded like someone was building something. What they were doing was cutting down my mobility. Reducing my three-room suite to a room, a bathroom, and a glassed-in outside area. Why had they done that? What was it all about?

The hell of it was, I had a feeling about what it was all about. I thought I knew. But I didn't want to admit it to myself.

The time of the tests had come. That had been a few weeks ago. They had poked instruments down through the ceiling. Stuff that looked at me, stuff on the end of wires that recorded me. I'd gone a little crazy during that time. I knew they'd gassed me a couple of times. When I came to, I found cuts and injection marks on my body. Bruises. They'd been experimenting with me. Trying to find out something. Using me as a guinea pig. But for what? Just because I'd started the whole mess? That wasn't fair. They'd no right to do that. It hadn't been my fault.

I invented an imaginary playmate after a while. Someone to talk to. They must have thought I was crazy. But I needed someone to talk to. I just couldn't go on talking in my head all the time.

"So listen, Julie, the way I figure it, it all began back then when Gomez and I went out to Alquemar. I don't think I ever told you about Alquemar, did I?"

I had, of course. But Julie was always obliging.

"No, you never mentioned it. What's Alquemar?"

"It's this planet. It's quite some distance from Earth. A long way. But I went there. Gomez and I. That's where we found the discovery that changed everything."

"What did you find?" Julie asked.

"Well, let me bring you back to those faraway days. . . ."

I was hanging out in this bar in Taos when I ran into Gomez over a bowl of hard-boiled eggs. We started to talk, as strangers will on a sleepy morning in a sleepy little town in New Mexico with nothing much to do with the long day ahead but drink a lot of beer and dream a lot of dreams.

Gomez was a short, barrel-chested guy from Santa Fe. A painter. He'd come to Taos to sketch tourists, make a few bucks. He'd taken a degree in art history at the University of New Mexico. But his interest was in alien artifacts.

"Is that a fact?" I said. "I'm interested in that stuff myself."

You gotta remember how it was back in those days. Exploration of space was brand spanking new. It had begun with the Dykstra Drive, the faster-than-light drive that made space exploration possible. You used the Dykstra only between the stars, out in deep space. When you got in close, you used the ion engines for maneuvering. That's where you burned up the fuel. And fuel cost money.

So the search was on. For intelligent life. Yes, that was the big one. But that was on a level above the one I was operating on. Or wanted to be operating on. I wanted to make some money in artifacts. It was a big market. Especially in the first ten years or so of the rush to space, when everybody was crazy to own some piece of shit from an alien planet. Put it up on the mantel. "See that doohickey? It came from Arcturus V. I've got papers to prove it."

Humans are crazy about conversation pieces. The fad ran down after a while, but there was still plenty of demand. By the time I got into the racket, collectors had become a whole lot more discriminating. The stuff you brought in had to be of artistic merit, as they phrased it. How do you judge artistic merit? I don't. That's why I had Gomez along. If Gomez, with his credentials, said it was good, dealers were apt to believe him.

I was qualified. I'd pushed ships for NASA for a couple of years, until a difference of opinion with my superior put me out of work. I was looking for a way to get back in. Gomez was a couple of years younger than me, but he had similar ideas.

Gomez was young, wanted to travel, and he was more than willing to sell his services cheap for the privilege of going out into deep space. An appraiser is important on a scavenging expedition. You need someone who has an idea of the current market, has some idea what dealers will pay for "genuine alien artifacts." You also need a guy to prepare and sign the provenance, the statement that gives whatever is known about the origin of the article. Although he was young, Gomez's reputation in the field was excellent. If Gomez swore it was real alien goods, dealers would know they weren't buying something faked in a factory in Calcutta or Jersey City.

That was the scavenging aspect. Of course, the main push was to find the folks who had left that stuff. But those guys just didn't seem to be around anymore. What happened to the vanished civilizations of the galaxy? That was a question that interested a lot of people. You know how much interest there is on Earth in vanished peoples. You don't, Julie? Take my word for it. Folks find it romantic.

Although the first buying spree was over, alien artifacts was still a pretty good racket. Even though there were a lot of people out there working it, the ruins scattered around the galaxy were a long way from being picked over. Just too many planets, too many ruins. And too few spaceships.

So Gomez and I talked about this stuff, there in the hazy cigarette smoke and beer smell, among Indians and tourists and farmers. After a while Gomez said, "You know, Dalton, we could make a good team. You're a spaceship jockey, and I've got the art-appraisal skills we'd need."

"I agree," I told him. "But we lack just one thing. A ship. And some backers."

Investing in spaceships to go scavengering in was a popular speculation in those days. You'd be surprised how many people were able to get their hands on a spaceship. For a while, every country in the world felt it needed at least one spaceship for national prestige. There was a time when there were more working ships than qualified men to run them. I had the know-how, and I had the right attitude. I mean, I was no pure-science freak. I liked to make a profit.

"I could maybe help us find something," Gomez said. "I know some people, did some art appraising for them last year. They were pleased with the results. I heard them talking about going into deep-space exploration."

"Sounds like a natural to me," I said. "Fifty-fifty between us, OK? Where do we see these guys?"

"Let me make a phone calls," Gomez said.

He went away, came back in a few minutes.

"I talked with Mr. Rahman in Houston. He's interested. We've got a meeting with him day after tomorrow."

"Rahman? What kind of name is that? Arab?"

"He's Indonesian."

Rahman had a suite at the Star of Texas. He was in town doing an oil deal with some Texas wildcatters. He was a little skinny guy, colored a medium brown, a shade darker than Gomez. Little mustache. He didn't wear no native clothes. Italian silk suit, must have cost thousands. He was a Moslem, but there was no silly stuff about not drinking alcohol. He poured us some Jim Bean Reserve and had one himself.

We talked, casual stuff for a while, and I got the definite impression that this Rahman and his people had a lot of money they didn't really know what to do with. A little birdie told me it might have been drug money. Not that I thought Rahman was a dealer. But he was an advance man for an Indonesian investment group, and their cash flow seemed a little heavy to be accounted for entirely from oil. But what do I know? Just an impression, and his willingness to do business with Gomez and me, a couple of unknowns.

First he went over my credentials. They were pretty good if I do say so myself. I'd worked ships for NASA for a couple of years until I got into a dispute with my superior and found myself out of a job. After that I'd gotten work for a private company pushing a supply ship between Earth and the L-5 colony. That went fine until L-5 went bust and I was out of work again. I had the papers and newspaper clippings to document everything.

"Your credentials look good to me, Mr. Dalton," Rahman said.

"I already know Mr. Gomez's work. We'd be willing to make an arrangement with you. Salary plus ten percent of the profits on whatever you find, to be split between you and Mr. Gomez. What do you think?"

"I'd like it a lot better if you could make that ten percent for each of us. It's not a deal-breaker, but it would be nice."

Rahman thought for a while. I guess he was thinking that this from his point of view was mainly a way to sock away some hot money. Profit was secondary. Rahman's group was making theirs right here on Earth.

"I suppose we could accommodate you," Rahman said. "Come to Djakarta with me and take a look at our ship. If you approve, we'll draw up papers. How soon can you begin?"

"We've started right now," I said, looking at Gomez. He nodded.

The *City of Djakarta* was a pretty good ship. German manufacture, Indonesian ownership. The Krauts made pretty good ships back in those days. We signed a contract, loaded supplies, I made a few phone calls, picked up some information, and in a month we were on our way.

The first planet we checked out, Alquemar IV in Boötes, circled an O-type star in the Borodin cluster, which is a dense region of a couple thousand stars, two-thirds of them with planets. I paid a lot for the information. I got it from a technician attached to a British star-mapping expedition. He hadn't been against earning a little on the side. There are channels where you can pick up that sort of information. I'm good with a spaceship, but I'm even better at working the channels and making a deal. This info cost a lot, but it looked like it was going to be worth it. My guy said he thought Alquemar IV had ruins, though his group hadn't gotten close enough to be sure. When Gomez and I got there, we agreed at once that we'd struck pay dirt. Now was the time to put down and let Gomez do his thing.

When I checked it out, I found Alquemar IV had enough oxygen for us, and gravity nine-tenths that of Earth. And so we went down hoping for a big strike, like Lefkowitz had when he discovered the Manupta friezes on Elgin XII, and sold them for a bundle direct to the Museum of Modern Art in New York. In fact, I knew this had to be good, or I was in trouble. I was using up a lot of fuel. It's costly to maneuver at sublight speeds in the area of planets.

It was a yellowish-brown planet with some green patches. Those patches showed where there was water and vegetation. We did an aerial recon of the largest patches, and found a section that looked good enough for us to go to the expense of putting the ship down on the ground. It's more economical to put the ship in orbit and go back and forth by orbiter, but it also takes more equipment, to say nothing of the cost of an orbiter. We didn't have one. When something good came up, we wanted the ship right down there with us.

There were ruins, all right. They were spread out over several hundred acres, circular ruins in a jungle. They were surrounded by what had once been a wall. The atmosphere checked out OK, no noxious stuff, so we unpacked our dirt bikes and rode into the area. The first couple days were spent just getting a feel of the place.

It took us almost a week before we hit on an area that looked worth examining closely. It was deep in the jungle, and it appeared to be the remains of a circular building. A temple, maybe. We'd call it that on the report, anyway. We went in slowly, filming everything, because film of these expeditions is worth some money, too. We were looking for just about anything. Household stuff is always good. Furniture, household items, cups, bowls, armor, weapons—anything that might look good hanging on a wall or sitting on a table in a museum or some rich guy's house. Trouble is, it's almost impossible to find stuff like that. The disappeared aliens don't leave you much. It's a mystery. Hell, everything's a mystery.

We came across a broken staircase leading down into the ground. This was a very good sign. In most ruins, you don't even find this much. I gave Gomez a wink. "This one's going to make us rich, partner."

Gomez shrugged. "Don't be too sure. Explorers have been disappointed before."

"I got a feeling about this one," I told him.

The steps led down a long ways, and into a big underground chamber. It was a spooky place: low, domed ceiling, protruding rocks casting weird shadows. There were some metal objects lying around on the ground. I picked up a couple of them and showed them to Gomez. He shook his head. "That stuff doesn't look alien enough."

That's a problem in this line of work. People have pretty firm ideas about what they think alien ought to look like. Something alien ought to look like something you couldn't find on Earth. Something that nobody ever thought of making. Something that gave off an air of mystery. And that's asking a lot of a pot or a chair. Just about everything you found on an alien planet was alien only by definition. But the few pots and cups that had been found could just as easily have been made on Earth. Not even a letter stating where and when the object had been found would give them any real value. The stuff people paid cash money for had to look alien, not just be alien. It had to fit people's idea of alien. It presented a challenge.

There was another chamber after the first one. We went into it, our floodlights sweeping the place with white light. And it was there we saw it. The object that came to be called the Eryx.

Now listen, Julie, don't carry this beautiful but dumb act too far. Everyone on Earth has heard of the Eryx. You've got to have heard of it. Maybe in your circle they called it the alien gizmo. Does that ring a bell?

It rested on a piece of shiny cloth with marks on it. It was sitting on a low stone pillar with fluted sides. The object seemed to be shiny metal, though no one has ever discovered what its made of. It was about the size of a child's head. It was carved or cast or worked into shapes I'd never seen before, nor had Gomez. The shapes looked random and chaotic at first, but when you sat down and studied them, you could see there was a logic at work there.

The thing glowed. It glistened. Its shapes and angles seemed to be curved. But it was difficult to say whether they were convex curves or concave ones. Sometimes it looked like one thing, sometimes another. Nor were all the planes identical. Optical effect, a triumph of the eye. Staring at it was like staring into a cubistic candle whose surfaces and facets were unfamiliar but fascinating, which held the eye, drawing it ever deeper.

"Man, we've got it," Gomez said. "The big one. This has to be the art find of the century. And the hell of it is, I can't tell if it was manufactured or grown, or if it's a natural form."

We didn't speak for a long time, Gomez and me. But we were thinking the same thoughts. Or at least I think we were. I was thinking, this is it, the big one, the pot at the end of the rainbow. This is the mother of all alien objects. It doesn't look like anything anyone has ever seen before, and it's small enough to fit on the mantel of the richest man in the world. It was the ultimate desirable object. You couldn't do better than that.

After gawking at it for a while, we went back to the ship and brought back equipment for carrying it to the ship. We didn't touch it with our hands. We used a neutral-surface manipulator to lift it and place it, every so gently, into a padded container. We didn't know if this thing was fragile or what. We just knew it was important not to break our egg on the way to market. Gomez even made a joke about it.

"We're putting all our egg into one basket," he said, as we got it back to the ship and stowed it away in the cargo hold. It was going to be Gomez's last joke for a while.

We decided to spend no more time on Alquemar. This one find was going to make our fortunes, and we decided to get right onto it. I cranked up the ship's engine and that's where we had our first indication that things weren't going to be quite as simple as we'd expected.

The engine wouldn't start.

Now, Julie, take my word for it, when your spaceship engine won't turn over, it's not a simple matter of changing spark plugs or adding gas. These engines aren't meant to be fooled with by the likes of me or Gomez. It takes a full maintainence crew working in a factory facility to do anything with one of those things. All we could do was run the diagnostics. All they told us was that the thing wasn't working. We knew that ourselves. What we didn't know was why, or what to do about it.

We didn't give up as easily as that. I went through the whole drill. Reran the diagnostics. Ran diagnostics on the diagnostics. Tried to get a signal to the home office back on Earth. That was futile, of course. Modern spaceship travel leaves you in the curious position of being able to reach a place faster than light can do it, and a hell of a lot faster than any form of signal transmission. It looked like we were stuck. And the hell of it was, there wasn't anyone who might come out to see what had gone wrong with us. We were like the pioneers trekking across the Rockies to California. Or like Cortés and his conquistadores slogging across unknown lands in search of Aztec riches. If a conquistador's horses broke down, Spain didn't send an expedition out to rescue him. They just wrote him off. And that's what would would happen with us. No one had asked us to come out here. Our Indonesian sponsors didn't a give damn if we got back or not. Not as long as they kept the insurance paid up.

We didn't panic. Gomez and I had always known this was one of the risks of this deal. We sat around and hoped maybe the engine would come back on line all by itself. It's been known to happen. We played chess, we read books, we ate our supplies, and at last we decided to take the Eryx out of storage and take a look at it again. If we had to go, at least we could go in what Gomez called an aesthetic manner.

I guess I haven't told you why we called it the Eryx. It was because of what we found on that piece of cloth the thing had been sitting on. That cloth was covered with marks and doodles. We thought it was just a design. But it turned out to be the first bit of alien writing anyone had discovered. And it was the only one until a year or so later. Clayton Ross came across the inscribed rock that they called the Space Age Rosetta Stone during his expedition to Ophiuchus II. One part was in an ancient variation of

Sanskrit, the rest in three alien languages, one of which corresponded to the writing on the Eryx cloth. Gomez and I had come up with the first writing ever discovered in an alien language.

But we didn't know that at the time. It took experts to point out that what we had thought was just a decorative pattern was in fact language. As for why we named the gizmo Eryx—follow me on this, Julie. At the top of the cloth, or what we figured was the top, there were four marks larger than the others in what turned out to be the text. We couldn't read them, of course. But the four largest characters looked like the English letters E-R-Y-X. So we called our gizmo the Eryx. The name caught on. Everybody called it that, right from the start.

As you've doubt surmised, being the clever little lady you are, we didn't die on Alquemar. We got off. What happened, you see, is that we brought the Eryx out of the hold and into the main cabin. So we could look at what might be costing us our lives. This put it not only close to us, but also to the engines. When we tried to start up again, something happened. We never did figure out what or why. But suddenly everything was in the green and our engine was working again.

Coincidence? We thought it might have been. But we weren't so filled with the spirit of scientific experimentation that we were ready to move the Eryx back to the hold just to see if the engine died again. That would be carrying the spirit of experimentation too far. We got the hell out of Alquemar while we could. Got back to Earth.

Rahman met us in the Disneyland Hotel in Jogjakarta. He thought the Eryx was pretty. But you could tell he wasn't impressed. Or maybe it was because he had a lot of other stuff on his mind. I only learned later that the CIA and local narcotics feds had become very interested in Rahman and his partners. I guess Rahman saw trouble coming. Because he said, "I'm sure we could sell this and realize a fine profit. But I have a better idea. I've consulted with my partners. We're going to give this object to a big American research company, to hold in the public trust, to study for the benefit of all mankind."

"That's very civic-minded of you," I said. "But why would you want to do that?"

"We'd like to stay on the good side of the Americans," Rahman said. "It could be useful later."

"But you won't make any money this way."

"Sometimes goodwill is more important than money."

"Not to us it isn't!"

Rahman smiled and muttered something in the local dialect. The local equivalent of "tough shit," no doubt.

I wasn't quite ready to give up. "But we'd agreed to sell any artifacts we found and split the profits!"

"That is not correct," Rahman said, rather coldly. "If you read your contract, you'll see that you participate in the sale of artifacts only if we do in fact decide to sell. But the decision is entirely up to us."

He was right about the wording of the contract. But who could have guessed that they wouldn't sell?

I realized the wisdom of Rahman's move—from his point of view—about a year later, after the CIA, working with the Indonesian authorities, busted him for the international dope trafficking. The fix must have been in. He got off with a fine.

Gomez and I followed orders and brought the Eryx to Microsoft-IBM in Seattle, the biggest private research facility in the States. We told them about the engine, said that if our inference was correct, this thing had indeed influenced its operation.

Well, at Microsoft-IBM, the guys in white coats ran tests from here to hell and back on the thing, and the more they saw the more excited they got, and they called in bigshot scientists from universities all around the world, and Microsoft-IBM was glad to pay for it because it gave them publicity like you couldn't believe, and besides, soon enough the government began funding it.

Gomez and I were superfluous. After taking our statement, nobody needed anything else from us. The Indonesian group went out of the spaceship business; it was save your ass time, and they were going to be busy for a long time. They gave us a pretty good bonus, however. I was already negotiating for new backers and a new ship and a better deal, and between us we had just enough money to swing it.

And then Gomez got himself killed in a traffic accident in Gallup, New Mexico, of all places, and his family were his heirs and I was in legal stuff up to the giggie. The court never believed that Gomez had verbally deeded his share to me, and it cost me a fortune in lawyers to finally not be able to prove it and have half of what was supposed to be our seed money go to some uncle Gomez had never even met down in Oaxaca, Mexico.

So I was on my own, and in what they call straitened circumstances. I managed to make a deal with some South African diamond people and took a new ship, the *Witwatersrand,* back to Alquemar to look for more stuff. That was when Stebbins, the company man the South Africans had forced on me, got killed in a cave collapse, and I got blamed. It was really unfair. I'd been sitting in the ship playing solitaire when he went out without authorization to the site, trying to make something on the side for himself, I doubt not. But they trumped up a case of negligence against me in Johannesburg and I lost my license.

So I came up empty on that one and suddenly people didn't want to hire me anymore for anything. So what with one thing and another I wasn't around when the white coats were making some of their most important discoveries about the Eryx. During that period I was doing six months in Lunaville on a trumped-up charge of embezzlement. So I had my hands full with my own problems when Guillot at the Sorbonne, working with Clayton Ross's New Rosetta stone, came up with a translation of the writing on the Eryx paper. And got promptly suppressed by court injunction while the Microsoft-IBM people sought corroborating evidence before releasing it. I heard about it while I was in jail. Everybody on Earth heard about it. (Except for you, my adorable Julie, caught up in your larcenous dreams.)

I got out on good behavior (I'm no troublemaker) and drifted around Luna City for a while, working as a dishwasher. My spaceship piloting career seemed to be dead. No license, and no one would have hired me if I'd had one.

But you can't keep a good man down. A change of administration on Luna gave me the opportunity to regain a pilot's license restricted to the inner solar system. This was accomplished by my employer at the time, Edgar Duarte, the owner of Luna Tours, who thought to use my fame or notoriety to enhance his tourist business. And so I got a job taking day trippers out to the asteroid belt, a far fall indeed for one who had discovered the Eryx.

I took it with equanimity, however: I've long known that fortune's a whore and life itself a kind of stupid muddle. I am not a religious man. Far from it. I hold, if anything, a belief which I believe was once ascribed to the Gnostics: that Satan won out over God, not the other way around, and the Dark Prince runs things in the dismal and disastrous way that suits his nature. I knew that everything was just chance and bad luck, in a universe in which things were stacked against us and even our ruling deity hated us.

But since it's all chance, good things happen from time to time, and, lo and behold, my time seemed to come around. I was running my tourists out to these stupid asteroids, sleeping in a flophouse since Duarte paid me next to nothing, bored out of my mind, when one day I got a letter from Earth.

This letter was written on genuine paper, not this insubstantial email stuff, but on stiff parchmentlike paper. It was from something that proclaimed itself "The First Church of the Eryx, Universal Pontifex of Everything and All."

The letter was not humor, as I had at first supposed, but a serious message from a group that had formed a church for the worship of the Eryx.

The Eryx was a suprahuman principle, they wrote me, which had revealed itself to those who could see as divinely alien in form and in essence, and this coming had been prophesied long ago because of the self-evident nature of man's fallen soul.

In the letter they pointed out how the Eryx was now in a citadel in the Seattle Space Needle which had been acquired for it by Microsoft-IBM. Thousands of people passed in front of it daily, looking for cures to what ailed them. And the Eryx helped many of them. The Eryx had literally thousands of miracles to its credit. Not only could and would it cure any and all human ailments, everything went better in the presence of the Eryx, from machinery (which I had been the first to observe) to the workings of the human mind (of which the writer of the letter was an example, I suppose).

After quite a bit more of this, the writer, a Mr. Charles Ehrenzveig, got to the point. It had recently come to the Church's attention (he didn't say how) that I was the person who had discovered the Body of the Deity and brought it to mankind. For this I was to be honored. It had been some years since I had had any contact with the Source. I had been denied my rightful fame, ignored where I ought to have been praised (my feelings exactly), and forced to live meanly far from Earth, whereas by rights I should take my place as The Discoverer of the Eryx. The letter also implied that there was something holy about me by association and by primogeniture.

Ehrenzveig closed by saying that they had bought a ticket for me, a passage to Earth. It was waiting in American Express in Luna City. They would be very pleased if I would come to Seattle as their guest, all expenses paid. They promised to reimburse me handsomely if I would come and talk to them about the circumstances of my expedition to Alquemar, my discovery of the Eryx, my feelings during my time of association with it, and so on and so forth.

Would I come? You bet I would. Luna City had been a drag for quite a while, and I'd had enough of tourists and asteroids to last me a very long time. With great pleasure I told Duarte where he could stick his job, and shortly after that I was on my way to the home planet.

A few weeks later, I was there.

Julie, I won't bore you with my impressions of Earth after an absence of almost ten years. All of that and a lot more is part of my standard lecture. It's available now both as a book and a CD. If you want, you can look it up for yourself. (But I know you, my darling. Not interested in anyone but yourself, are you?)

"Dalton! How good that you could come!" That was Ehrenzveig, a big, corpulent man, greeting me literally with open arms. He had a couple of other guys with him. They were all dressed in white. That was one of the marks of the cult, I later found out.

I was brought by limousine to Eryx House, their own church and residence on a private island in Puget Sound. I was wined and dined. They made much of me. It was very pleasant. Except that there was a strange undertone to everything Ehrenzveig and the others said. What the psych people might call a subtext. They knew something that I and the rest of the human race didn't know, and they felt very smug about that.

The next day they brought me to the Space Needle for the Viewing, as they called it. The way it worked for the peasants, they got a ticket (free from the Eryx foundation, but you had to have one), then were searched for weapons, then were allowed to form on the line that went all the way up to the viewing room, which they called the Citadel. I didn't have to do this. But Ehrenzveig thought I might like to see how it was done.

I was more than a little surprised at the numbers of sick and crippled people on that line. There were blind folks, people with cancer, and just about everything else. They were all hoping for a miracle cure. A lot of them, Ehrenzveig assured me, were going to get it.

I must have looked skeptical, because Ehrenzveig said, "Oh, it's real enough. It's not a matter of faith; it simply works. The other religions don't know what to do with us. The Eryx—actually performs miracles. All of the time. Every day. This is a stage that our prophets have written about. We call it the Grace of the Last Days."

"The Last Days? What's that supposed to mean?" I asked him.

He looked sly. "I'm afraid I can't discuss the inner doctrine with you."

"Why not? I thought you considered me a founder."

"A founder, yes, but not a member of our religion. You discovered the Eryx, Mr. Dalton, and for that we will always honor you. But you do not believe in its supernatural message. And because of that, we will not open our hearts and minds to you."

I shrugged. What are you going to say when a guy lays a rap like that on you? And anyhow, I didn't tell that to Ehrenzveig.

The guy was my meal ticket, and I didn't want to get him sore at me. Not yet. Not until I had something going for myself.

You see, Julie, and I'm sure you'll appreciate this point, I had gotten a free trip to Earth and I was being put up in what amounted to a fancy resort hotel. But there's been no talk of money. Scratch. The mojo. The stuff that makes it all go around.

I didn't bring this up, however. Not at that time. I was kinda sure Ehrenzveig and his people were going to make me an offer of some kind. After all, without me they wouldn't have had a religion.

I spent quite some time in the little room viewing the Eryx through glass. They had it on the cylinder of stone I'd found it on. I hadn't bothered to bring the cylinder back. They'd made a special expedition to Alquemar to fetch it. The room was designed to look just like the cave in which Gomez and I had made our discovery. Even the lighting was the same. And they'd replaced the cloth the Eryx had rested on. The Eryx was sitting on it again, looking pretty as a picture, the very last word in high-class alien artifacts.

"I thought somebody was studying that cloth," I remarked.

"Guillot, yes. But our foundation was able to suppress his translation and reclaim the cloth. It belongs with the Eryx, you understand. It is part of its substance."

"Do you know what thing says?"

"We have our surmises."

"So?"

"If you think I am going to tell you, Mr. Dalton, you are very mistaken. That knowledge will be made public when the time is right."

"And when will that be?"

"The Eryx itself will give us the indication."

So we stood around for a while watching guys throw away their crutches, and other guys shout, "I can see!" and all the rest of the bullshit. And then they took me back to Eryx House for a really first-rate banquet in my honor. It was after that dinner that Ehrenzveig made the proposition I'd been expecting.

We were sitting with cigars and brandy in this superluxurious sitting room down the hall from the main dining room. At first it was a bunch of us, me and Ehrenzveig and about ten others who were pretty obviously bigwigs in the organization. Then the others left as if on signal, and Ehrenzveig said, "You're probably wondering by now what this could possibly have to do with you, Mr. Dalton."

"The question did cross my mind," I said.

"If I have not read your character amiss," Ehrenzveig said, "I believe you would like money. Quite a large amount of money. Or am I being too direct?"

"Not at all. I'm all for plain speaking and high living."

"Excellent. We can give you both."

"High living," I mused. "Does that translate into actual cash of the realm, or do I get paid in religious points in the organization?"

Ehrenzveig smiled. "We are well aware that you are not a believer. That's fine. You're not required to be. Would it make you uncomfortable to know that we'd like to use you as a shill?"

"Not if there's any money in it."

"Excellent! I appreciate your candor."

"You don't mind, then, that I think your religion of the Eryx is a lot of bullshit, to put it bluntly?"

"I don't mind at all. These are modern times. Mr. Dalton, and the test of a modern religion resides in how it performs, not in what it promises. And in a religion such as ours, there's certainly no moral or ethical code. Such matters have nothing to do with a diety such as ours. The Eryx, whom some call the Great Satan, couldn't care less about right or wrong, good or bad. He's here for one thing and one thing only."

"And that thing is?"

"It will be plain to you in good time," Ehrenzveig said. "I predict that you will become a believer. An that'll be a pity, because we'll have lost ourselves a jovial and cynical rogue."

"Flattery will get you nowhere," I said, "unless you accompany it with large sums of money. Don't worry about supplying me with dancing girls. I'll take care of details like that myself."

"The money, yes," Ehrenzveig said. "How admirably direct you are. But I came prepared for you."

Ehrenzveig took a billfold out of an inner pocket and counted out ten thousand-dollar bills. He riffled them and handed them to me.

"Is this what I'm being paid?"

"Certainly not. This is just a little walking-around money. We're going to pay you a lot more than this, Mr. Dalton."

"And what am I supposed to do for it?"

"Just talk to people."

"You mean, give lectures?"

"Whatever you want to call them."

"What do you want me to tell them?"

"Whatever you wish. You might talk about how you discovered the Eryx. But you need not confine yourself to that. Tell them about yourself. Your life. Your opinions."

"Why should anyone be interested in my life?"

"Whatever you care to say will be of interest. In our religion, Mr. Dalton, you hold a very significant place."

"I told you I'm not religious."

"Important figures in religion frequently are not. Religious people come afterwards. They were the interpreters. But the original cast, the ones who were there in the beginning, they are not necessarily religious. Often they are quite the contrary."

"I've got a place in your religion? Like Judas, maybe?"

"Equal in importance, but nothing like him. We refer to you, Mr. Dalton, as the Last Adam."

Talking has never been any problem for me, and I didn't care if they called me the Last Adam or the First Charley. Or the Sixteenth Llewellyn, for that matter. A name is just another container for the waling pile of shit that is a man. If you'll pardon my French. But you've heard language like this all your life, haven't you, Julie? It's the way your father talked, and your mother, and all your friends. They all were a bunch of blasphemers, weren't they, doll? And you knew right from the start, right from the get-go, that the only thing to do in this world was to look out for number one, live high and leave a good-looking corpse. You and I are so alike, Julie. That's why you love me so.

I guess, as I went on giving my talks in Seattle, I started talking more about you, Julie girl. People started asking me, who is this Julie you're always raving about? And I'd always tell them, she's my dream girl, and she knows the way things really are. I told that to the ladies who kept me company during this time. There were a lot of them. I was famous, you see. I was Dalton, the guy who had found the Eryx.

Thanks to Ehrenzveig and his people, others began to see how important I was. They paid me a lot. They gave me respect.

"We're going to fulfill your dreams of avarice, John," Ehrenzveig said one day. It was a joke, I think, but he made it true. He kept on piling money on me, and I kept on buying things, and people, and more things. I had me a time, let me tell you. It was going so good for me that I didn't even notice for quite a while that a lot of people were dying.

When you're going good, like I was, you sort of overlook what other people are up to. I mean, let's face it, who gives a damn about other people when there's number one to be fed and pleasured? And as good as things might get, there's always room for improvement, right? So I took little notice of the bad stuff that was going on. The die-off, I mean. It was all very tragic. But I couldn't help thinking that it was for the best, in a weird sort of way, because it freed up a lot of real estate. And of course I wasn't very interested in why it was happening.

A lot of people were blaming it on the Eryx. That's people for you. Always ready to blame something. There were even scientists around eager to get their names in the papers, saying that the Eryx was a living organism, of a type never before seen. Long dormant. Now coming into activity. According to those guys, the Eryx had been releasing viruses since the day I found it. These viruses had traveled around the world, lodging in people's bodies, not doing any harm, not calling any attention to themselves, the sly little buggers. But this wasn't out of good nature. This was because this Eryx virus was waiting, waiting until it had spread to the whole Earth, infected everyone. Then it took off like a timed-release capsule.

It got pretty bad, this die-off thing. And I guess I went out of my way not to notice it. Because if you're going to die anyway, why depress yourself in advance with bad news? And anyhow, I figured some of those scientists they got out there would do something about it. And if not, not.

It was Ehrenzveig who finally clued me in to what was going on. To where it was all leading. He came to visit me one morning. Frankly, he looked like hell—red-eyed, and his hands were shaking. It occurred to me that he'd caught this disease, and I had a little tremor of fear. If he got it, and him so high up in the Church of the Eryx, then I could get it, too.

"You look like death warmed over," I told him. No sense kidding around.

"Yes. I've got it. Eryx Fever. I don't have long."

"Hasn't your god come up with a cure?"

Ehrenzveig shook his head. "That's not his way."

"Then what's the advantage of being in his church?"

"Some of us think knowledge is worth anything."

"Not me," I told him.

Ehrenzveig spent a while coughing. Quite pathetic it was. Finally he was able to speak again.

"I've come to tell you the translation of the cloth that was found with the Eryx."

"I'm all ears."

"It was a warning. It was written by one of the last beings to come across the Eryx."

"Let's cut to the chase. What did it say?"

"It said, 'The Eryx hates human life. It hates alien life. It tolerates no life but its own. When you find the Eryx, it is the beginning of the end of your species.' I'm translating very freely, you understand."

"No problem," I said. "It sounds like one of those old Egyptian curses."

"Yes, very similar. In this case, it happens to be true."

"That's great," I said, sarcastically, because of course Ehrenzveig was reading my own death sentence as well as his. But hey, I never thought I'd go on forever.

"So what happens now? Masque of the Red Death on a whole-world scale?"

"That's about the size of it," Ehrenzveig said.

"How long have you known?"

"For quite a while. All of us in the religion of the Eryx have known. The Eryx told us."

"How'd it do that? Send out thoughts?"

"Dreams. Prophetic dreams. And we accepted what it told us, and found it good. It is only right, you see, that the Eryx can tolerate no other life than its own."

"That's understandable," I said. "I like a little elbow room, too."

Ehrenzveig bowed his head and didn't speak.

Finally I asked him, "So what happens now?"

"I die," Ehrenzveig said. "Everyone dies."

"That's obvious, dummy. I mean what happens to me?"

"Ah," Ehrenczveig said, "the Eryx has plans for you. You're the Last Adam."

"What sort of plans?"

"You'll see. Come with me."

"On whose orders?"

"The Eryx wants to get a look at you."

Well, I didn't like the sound of that one bit. I decided it was about time to quit the organization, get away from the Earth, find something else. But Ehrenzveig wasn't having it that way. He had a bunch of his buddies outside my door. They escorted me—under protest, I can assure you—to this place where I live now.

The followers of the Eryx bustled around me for the next few weeks, setting me up in my little apartment, installing the cameras, arranging for food. There were fewer of them every day, and finally I was here all alone. Locked in.

But even if I could get out, where would I go? I've got a feeling everybody's gone now. I saw my last human face weeks, months ago. Frankly, I don't miss people one bit. They were a bad lot and to hell with them. I'm glad they're gone and I won't be sorry when I'm gone, too.

I've never seen the Eryx, but I suspect he's taken some form other than that in which I found him. He's studying me, I think. Maybe he studies the last specimen of each race he annihilates. Just out of curiosity, I suppose. That's what I'd do. Maybe the Eryx and I aren't so different. Except for our circumstances. He's got the world. The galaxy, I suppose. And I have one room and a bathroom and a glassed-in enclosure. And you, Julie.

AFTERWORD

I only knew Roger Zelazny through our three novel collaborations. We met in the flesh only a few times. Working with Roger was one of the great pleasures of my life. Roger was a great combination of intuitive genius, fantasy dreamer, and careful, punctilious story plotter. He was one of the great ones. I greatly regret not having had the opportunity to know him better. But I can't tell you how pleased I am at having had the privilege of working with him. Collaboration tells you a lot about a person, and about yourself.

Although it did not get as much acclaim as his stylized prose and fine sense of drama, Roger's writing often exhibited an element of wry, even low, humor. "The fit hit the Shan" broke into the otherwise poetic prose of Lord of Light. *The Hugo Award-winning "Unicorn Variation" introduced beer-drinking unicorns and sasquatches. The part of Roger that reveled in that humor would certainly take great delight in Jay Haldeman's irreverent look at fairyland tale.*

■

SOUTHERN DISCOMFORT
Jack C. Haldeman II

ETHEL WAS BORN TO TROUBLE. SHE HAD A MEAN STREAK THAT FLAT wouldn't quit. Getting exiled from the Enchanted Forest was the best thing that ever happened to her.

Being stuck in real-time Earth was supposed to be the ultimate punishment among the fairy community, but that was not Ethel's read on the situation. Let the do-gooders have their pixie dust and magic wands; Ethel would take a cold beer and a thrown rod any day of the week. Besides, she *liked* smelly bait; the riper it was, the better she liked it.

Ethel had lost her wings over a variety of infractions, minor and major. From short-sheeting the Queen Fairy's bed to tromping down the flowers in Tranquil Garden, she had been in hot water from the time she was a mere tad of a fairy. Getting the boot had only been a matter of time.

She blamed her parents. Not for the mutation in her fairy genes,

121

but for her name. *Ethel!* What the hell kind of a name was that for a fairy? Fairies were supposed to have cute, perky names like Trixie or Trina. Either that or something classical like Titania or Hypotenuse. *Ethel!* It sounded like some sort of a petroleum by-product. No wonder she turned out so sorry and deranged. She'd been marked at birth. Marked bad.

Ethel shrugged and sniffed the squid. Even for bait, it was wonderfully past its prime. She threw a spare tentacle to Luther, who snarled once and darted a dirty gray paw out from the shadows behind the jukebox to grab it. This, of course, woke up Diablo, whose untrimmed toenails clicked against the concrete floor of the bait and beer store as he came over to check things out.

Diablo was the ugliest and meanest-looking pit bull Ethel had ever seen. She'd won him in a poker game in a most dishonest fashion. Only a few of Ethel's fairy powers remained and they included manipulating games of chance, causing vehicle difficulties, and capsizing boats. All very handy powers when running a bait shop in this godforsaken Florida swamp. She tossed a rotten tentacle to Diablo, who caught it on the fly with a resounding snap of his powerful jaws.

Later he would probably go out and eat grass and throw up on the floor like he always did. Ethel scratched his ugly head and whapped him on the nose.

"Good dog," she said, bending the truth.

The screen door creaked open and a brief hint of light crept into the dark store. Slow-moving and looking every one of his sixty-four years, Bayport Bob shuffled past the warped pool table and somehow managed to find his way to a stool.

"Morning, Ethel," he muttered.

"The usual?" she asked.

He nodded. Ethel cracked a can of Budweiser and set it front of the old man. She dug out a bag of frozen chicken necks and set it beside the beer.

Diablo gave Bayport Bob's left boot a cursory sniff and went back to settle down on top of a stack of old newspapers by the wood stove. The old guy wasn't much interesting to Diablo, being a regular who came in every morning for a beer and a bag of chicken necks.

Bayport Bob was a crabber of sorts. He had a few traps he ran from his john boat in the salt marsh that surrounded Ethel's Bait and Beer. Bob was not a successful crabber. On a good day he might make enough to pay for his beer and have a few coins left over to supplement his Social Security.

Once a month, if the crabbing had been good, Bob and his wife Darlene would drive into town and have a real sit-down dinner at

Pete's Barbecue. They were simple people, and it was their only extravagance.

Ethel pulled the floaters out of the live bait tanks while Bob sipped his breakfast. She made a small pile of the dead shrimp and shiners, their bloated bodies already starting to rot. She wrapped them in tinfoil and put them in the beer cooler next to the Coors. They'd make dandy snacks for Luther, doled out at irregular intervals during the day.

A group of loud college students came in and bought a case of beer and some snacks. Party time. Diablo snarled at them and so did Ethel. Their laughter and youthful energy being out of place on such a wonderfully gloomy morning—grated on her nerves. She short-changed them and slipped a smelly squid-soaked napkin in the bottom of their bag of groceries, but it wasn't enough.

As they were walking out, Ethel felt the familiar tingling in the area of her shoulder blades where her wings had been. It was time to use one of her powers.

She closed her eyes and visualized the college students standing by the side of the road, shaking their heads at their car, hood up, steam billowing out. Yep. Radiator trouble, that's the ticket. She grinned. Done deal.

"Later, Ethel," said Bayport Bob, making his arthritic way out. His bag of chicken necks—crab bait—dripped blood in his unsteady wake.

Ethel grunted goodbye. Then she started on her morning tasks.

First she stopped up all the bathroom sinks with wads of toilet paper. Nothing like a wet bathroom floor to make patrons a bit edgy. Then she loosened the toilet seats so that they wobbled precariously and might even fall off if one was not balanced precisely upon the porcelain throne. She stuck a bent quarter in the tampon machine, effectively jamming it and rendering it useless. She checked the cartons of milk to make sure their expiration dates were ancient history. The butter and cooking oil passed her sniff test for the proper level of rancid aroma.

It helped that she was stuck here at the armpit of nowhere, at the end of about thirty miles of axle-breaking limerock road. Her customers, such as they were, had no other choice.

The meat cooler was running about fifteen degrees above safe temperature and there were mosquitoes breeding in the mop bucket. A one-legged chicken sat on the pool table, shedding feathers.

Ethel smiled as she wrapped tainted day-old tuna fish sandwiches. Real-time earth was one fine place. She had no complaints. It beat the hell out of namby-pamby land.

The morning passed quickly enough. Mostly regulars coming in for an early beer or people wanting bait, directions, or free advice.

Ethel took liberties with the free advice part, figuring people got what they paid for. She gave one tourist couple directions to Mosquito Lagoon, telling them it was a secret bass fishing spot. They'd be eaten alive by the nasty buggers and lucky if they caught anything but malaria. She got a kick out of that one.

For Ethel had a nasty streak about six lanes wide that ran through the Interstate Highway of her soul, and she loved every bit of potholed pavement. Exile was freedom, pure and simple. Her life as a merry prankster could not be broken unless she performed an unselfish and totally altruistic act of kindness to relieve someone's suffering. Fat chance. Ethel was looking forward to a long and productive stay. She cackled to herself as she tapped a keg of flat beer and tossed Luther a shrimp head which he caught from the shadows with a snap and a snarl.

Lunch was always fun, because she had a captive clientele. There simply wasn't anyplace else around for people to eat. Her specialty was fried fish sandwiches on stale buns. It was amazing what people would eat if you smeared enough tartar sauce on it. Once in a while someone would complain about the feathers or a piece of turtle shell in their fried fish sandwich, but all they'd get in return was car trouble down the road.

"Born lucky, that's me," said Scratch, washing a fish sandwich down with a warm beer. "Always have been."

"You so lucky, how come you ain't rich?" cackled Martha, who was having her usual lunch fare, two bags of chips and three beers.

Scratch ignored her. He was prone to ignore things that didn't feature him prominently. "Only last night, I won twenty dollars and a fine horse playing poker at Bert's."

"Horse," laughed Fred, who wore a set of grease-covered overalls with *Sam* stitched above the left pocket. "That horse was a mule. An old one, too. A sorrier animal I've never seen."

"Luck will out," said Scratch, looking real proud of himself.

"So how about a lottery ticket?" said Ethel. "This week's jackpot's up to sixteen million."

"I believe I will," said Scratch, pulling a wrinkled dollar bill out of his pocket and putting it on the bar. "Give me one of those quick picks."

Ethel punched the machine. Her shoulders tingled as it coughed out a supposedly random number, but one that would be one digit off all six winning numbers on Saturday's drawing.

"I'm off to catch me some speeders," said Gus, a deputy sheriff who loved pork rinds, Dr Pepper, and throwing his considerable weight around.

It was next to impossible that anyone could speed on the pothole-infested roads around Ethel's Bait and Beer. Gus just liked to give people a hard time. He was prone to calling everyone he came into contact with *suspect,* and giving poor people broke down with car trouble even more trouble.

Gus had a blown head gasket in his future. In his *real near* future.

It started to rain after lunch, and the place filled up with construction workers looking to kill some time. Ethel stayed busy and before she knew it, the day had slid into night.

The regulars were in place and Ethyl was so busy cracking beers she almost didn't notice Bayport Bob come in. But she did see him, and he looked awful. He was soaked and slumped. He sighed as he took the end stool at the dark end of the bar and started counting out nickels, dimes, and pennies.

It was rare to see Bayport Bob in at night. His usual was to have one beer during the day when he got his bait. Ethel walked over.

"Bad day?" she asked, setting a beer in front of him.

Bob nodded, adding two more pennies to the collection in front of him to make it right and pushing the pile toward Ethel. "Dirt in my gas line," he said. "Boat quit on me out by Miller's Pass in the storm. Ten crabs. I ain't never gonna make no money this way."

"At least you got Darlene to go home to," said Ethyl.

"Not this week," sighed Bob. "She's up in Atlanta for the tests."

Ethel looked at him.

"They say they can fix it with an operation, but we can't afford it. We done sold everything we got to pay for the doctors already. All I got left is that damn boat and it don't run now."

Larry called for another round and Ethel left Bayport Bob to take care of the rowdy group. On her way to get clean glasses she punched the lotto machine.

After Larry, she stopped to explain to Bertha for the millionth time that she didn't serve no drinks with umbrellas in them, then she moved down the bar to pop five quick beers and cleaned up where Diablo had piddled on the leg of a bar stool. On her way back to Bayport Bob, she palmed the ticket out of the lotto machine.

"Customer left this," she said, putting the ticket in front of him. "Might as well take it."

"Think it's lucky?" asked Bob, holding the ticket up to the light.

"Yes, I do," said Ethel, tossing some dead squid to the cat and feeling a hot burn across her shoulder.

Damn. She'd done it.

An unselfish act of kindness was about to suck her back to the

Enchanted Forest. All that sweetness and light. She could hardy bear the thought.

Well, at least there would still be flowers to trample in the Tranquil Garden and the Queen Fairy could always use a tweak or two. Ethel had always been one to make the best of a bad situation.

AFTERWORD

I first met Roger in Baltimore in the sixties. For over thirty years we were friends. Thirty years is a long time for most things, but this thirty years was far too short. He was a good friend and I miss him terribly.

I was a fan when we met, attracted to the science fiction world because of my love for the literature and the companionship of like-minded people. And to be truthful, the beer and all-night parties didn't hurt.

When I started writing professionally, Roger lived a few blocks away. He read most of what I wrote and was very supportive. It helped a lot.

A quiet man by nature, Roger had a great sense of humor. I fondly remember his laugh and the wry amusement he could find in all things human.

He enjoyed the short, humorous stories I occasionally wrote. Roger followed them closely, and would call or write me about a particular story or character of mine that caught his eye.

When he was putting together the anthology *Warriors of Blood and Dream,* he called me and asked for one of my short funny pieces to balance out the book. Actually, he asked for two of them, one for another collection, but I only had time for one.

The story was "True Grits," about a backwoods Southern redneck whose "martial arts" specialty was bashing people on the head with a tire iron. Roger liked the story a lot. He died as the book was coming out.

So "Southern Discomfort" is another short Southern humor piece. Maybe it was the one I didn't have time for.

The one that neither of us had enough time for.

Sometimes surrender is only the beginning of the battle.

■

SUICIDE KINGS
John J. Miller

i.

THE DEATH OF HER CAT GAVE KARIN THE IDEA.

Faffy was seventeen years old. Karin had had him for three-quarters of her life and he was the only creature in the world who loved her. Her mother had died when Karin was very young. Karin's older sister, prettier, smarter, and much more successful than Karin had ever dreamed to be, told her once that their mother had been an alcoholic. One night she'd fallen in a drunken stupor and hit her head on the corner of the coffee table and bled to death from the resultant gash. Her father was still alive, but he never took much of an interest in Karin—or, to be fair, her sister. He was a scientist, a metallurgist whose specialty was malleable memory-retentive metals. Karin suspected that human beings were beyond his interest because he couldn't hammer them into the shape he preferred and make them retain it.

Karin lived with Faffy in a tiny walk-up apartment, the only thing she could afford on her store-clerk salary. One day Karin noticed that Faffy was drinking a lot more water than he usually did, but it was summertime, hot, and she didn't worry about him until she found him wandering around one morning on wobbly legs, dazed and obviously confused.

She took him right away to the vet's. They told Karin that Faffy

127

was dehydrated, put him on an I.V., and took a blood sample for tests. The results weren't good. It was complete renal failure.

The last thing Karin wanted was for Faffy to suffer. When she went to see him that night, she'd already made the awful decision to put him to sleep. But when he saw her, Faffy looked up and meowed. He held up his taped paw to show her the I.V., then purred when Karin touched his head. She couldn't do it.

The doctor told Karin she'd thought that Faffy was going to die that night, but gradually the cat got better. Karin kept him in the hospital for five days, practically wiping out her savings account, until the doctor told her it was safe to take him home. He wasn't cured, however; he'd just survived the current crisis. Karin asked how much time he had left, days, weeks, or months, but the doctor couldn't or wouldn't say.

It turned out to be three months, then the poisons overwhelmed his system, and Karin had to take him to the vet's again. This time, she came home alone.

Karin realized, after an eternity of an afternoon in her suddenly empty apartment, that Faffy had escaped the pain of life, and she could, too.

She considered, then rejected, a gun, a razor, and a leap from a tall building. She wanted to escape her pain, not create more for herself, no matter how transitory. She couldn't gas herself because her oven was electric, and she didn't own a car. Poisons were ghastly, and besides, she just didn't know enough about them.

In the end it came down to sleeping pills, something she was an expert on anyway. It'd been three years since she'd been able to sleep without them. She had an impressive collection garnered from the prescriptions of the half dozen doctors and therapists she'd seen those three years. She didn't know how many to take to ensure she'd never wake up, so she took them all.

She washed them down a handful at a time with the quart of orange juice she had in the refrigerator. Torn by pain, crushed by loneliness, she huddled in a pathetic bundle in the corner of her sofa, and closed her eyes.

ii.

Karin opened her eyes.

She was in a soft bed in a white room. The sheets were delightfully cool and the air smelled subtly of violets, one of her favorite fragrances. She was the only one in the room. As she glanced around, more bewildered than anything else, the door opened and a man came in with a clipboard in his hand and a smile on his face.

He was the most beautiful man Karin had ever seen. Tall, but not excessively so, broad-shouldered, narrow-hipped, with the unlined forehead of a god and the brown, thick-lashed eyes of a deer. He had high cheekbones and a full, sensual mouth with even white teeth.

He smiled at Karin and held out his hand for her to shake. Even his hands were beautiful. His grip was warm and powerful, comforting without undue pressure.

"How are you doing today, Karin?" His rich, deep voice made her feel as if she were the only woman in the world.

I'm in love, she thought, but managed to say in a quiet, timid voice, "I'm okay. I—I didn't die?"

He laughed, creating a sound that could heal the world.

"No talk of that," he said, eyes twinkling. "I'm Dr. Chamberlain. We're going to take care of you here."

"Just where am I?"

"Don't worry about that. Just worry about getting better."

He stifled any more questions by taking her right hand again. He put two fingers on her wrist and looked at the watch on his other hand.

The touch of his flesh was electric. The warmth of his hand spread into her wrist, ran up her forearm and shoulder. She could feel her face blush and her nipples stiffen. She was shocked to realize that she wanted him very badly. She had never felt remotely like this before.

He smiled again and released her hand. "Well, your pulse seems normal enough."

Does it? Karin thought. It was racing like a set of electronic drums programmed for speed.

"I'll be back to check on you later," Dr. Chamberlain said.

Karin wanted to call out to him, to beg him to stay with her forever, but with a smile and a flourish of his lab coat, he was gone, striding out of the room into the hallway beyond.

"Wow," Karin said aloud as she sank back onto the soothingly cool pillow. "Get a hold of yourself."

She could still feel her heart pounding, could still feel the overwhelming desire that she'd never felt before. It wasn't as if she'd never been in love. There'd been a few schoolgirl crushes, of course, but also two men she'd truly loved. Her sister had taken both men from her, used them up, then discarded them when she was tired of them. But Karin had never felt this instant, magnetic, almost magmatic attraction. It was as if—

The room's other door, which led, Karin had assumed, to the bathroom, suddenly swung open.

"Who in the world are you?" Karin asked, more bewildered than frightened.

Not that she was totally without fear. It wasn't every day that a man lurked in your bathroom. She probably would have been more afraid if he didn't look so, well, innocuous.

He was good-looking in an unassuming, homespun, kind of way. Maybe cute was the better word. He was young, about Karin's age, with a round face, buck teeth, and the mildest blue eyes Karin had ever seen. He was rather small and lightly-built. He wore worn jeans and a faded blue workshirt.

"Call me Billy, ma'am," he said as he approached her bed. "We'd best be leaving now."

Karin gripped the sheet and shrank back against the softness of the bed. "Leaving? I don't understand."

"You will, ma'am. Let's—"

The door to the corridor flew open again and Dr. Chamberlain stood in the entrance, looking heroically angry.

"How did you get here so quickly?" he ground out between clenched teeth.

Billy smiled. "I have my ways, Doc. Bye-bye."

He reached behind his back and pulled out a gun that must have been stuck in his belt. It was big and clunky looking. He pointed it at Dr. Chamberlain and pulled the trigger. The shots sounded like explosions in the enclosed room. He fired so fast that Karin had only started to scream when he'd emptied all the gun's cylinders.

He was a good shot, too. The first bullet took Dr. Chamberlain in the center of the chest. The next five were grouped in a palm-sized cluster around the first. The force of the multiple impacts blew the doctor out of the room and into the corridor beyond as Karin let go of her first scream.

Things happened so quickly that she was only drawing breath for her second scream when Billy stuck the gun into the waistband of his jeans, reached down, and scooped her into his arms. He raced toward the window and crashed through the glass, turning shoulder first to shield Karin from most of the flying shards.

As they fell Karin really screamed. Her abductor twisted in mid-air, so he took the brunt of the collision when they smashed into the ground. Despite being so insulated, Karin felt her whole skeleton rattle. Billy made an agonized, wordless sound beneath her, then took a deep breath and sort of sighed.

"Okay, ma'am," he said. "We'd best be going now."

She stared at him, her faces inches from his. "You're—you're not hurt?"

"Course not," Billy said. "Not much, anyway."

"How . . ." She couldn't finish the question.

"Well, ma'am, I'm dead. We all are, you know."

Karin shook her head.

"No," she said. "That's impossible. Dr. Chamberlain . . ."

She remembered again the explosions erupting from Billy's gun, the close spacing of the bullets as they struck the doctor in the chest, hurling him backward like a doll tossed against a playroom wall by an angry child. She looked at Billy, fear in her eyes. She jumped up and ran.

Billy stood, but made no move to follow. Karin heard him call out, but could scarcely understand his words in the face of the overwhelming terror that had seized her mind.

"There's no use in running away, ma'am. There never is."

iii.

The city was like no other Karin had ever seen.

At first glance it was just another faceless urban monolith like the one where Karin had spent most of her life. Buildings, streets, cars, 7-Elevens, taxis, pedestrians.

The differences were subtle. There was little trash. The buildings all looked new with none of the unavoidable buildup of grime that plagued all urban areas. The air was fresher than it had any right to be. Its smell reminded Karin of the few times she'd been in the country. It was clean, cool, somehow soothing.

The major difference between this city and the others she knew was the total lack of urgency in those she passed on the street. People moved slowly, not in a dream, but as if they were deep in thought, as if they were taking stock of their surroundings or themselves, as if they had questions on their mind that needed sorting, as if they had somehow lost track of things and were trying to figure out who they really were.

Since she'd woken up—at least since Billy had come out of her bathroom—nothing made sense. Nothing. Maybe Billy was right and she was dead. If he was, Heaven sure wasn't paradise. It was a nuthouse.

If this was Heaven.

That thought stopped her cold. Karin had never done anything to send her to Hell. She'd always been a good girl, quiet and shy. She'd never hurt anyone. Only herself, when she tried to kill herself. But even then she hadn't succeeded. Even then . . .

Karin suddenly realized that she wasn't alone.

They stood before her, beside her, behind her. They were all younger than her. Some were just children, but all looked fierce and feral. Among them were enough leather to decimate a herd of cows, enough chains to supply a slave ship, enough hate and anger to fuel the return of the Third Reich.

She thought she'd been afraid before, but that was only the barest taste of what she felt now, the barest hint of the terror gripping her like the hand of a cruel giant. Her knees went so weak that they couldn't support her and she folded down on the sidewalk while those watching snickered and grinned.

Two stood slightly apart from the pack, and Karin realized that they were the leaders. One was a man, white, with the size and appearance of a malignant dwarf. He looked almost as broad as he was tall, with a deep chest, thick shoulders, and hugely muscled arms left bare by the sleeveless T-shirt that he wore. His hair was shaved down to a sixteenth of an inch. His forehead had the word HATE tattooed in big letters across it, and there was a swastika between his deep-set eyes. The other was a woman, black, tall and slim, almost elegant in her dark leather. She had a face that once had been beautiful, but was crisscrossed by scars from a bad slashing. Whoever had fixed her face had botched it, so that she looked like a patchwork girl whose pieces barely matched.

"What's this?" she asked the tattooed dwarf.

"New meat," he said.

"She shines," a voice said from within the pack. It was a little girl speaking. She was a beautiful blond thing with a dirty stuffed bear half her size. "She has a bright rainbow all around her."

The leaders of the pack glanced at each other, then back at Karin.

"I don't know how the brat does it," the black woman said, "but she's always right."

"She's a clever little brat," the dwarf agreed.

They looked at Karin again, and the black woman nodded. "Look at her eyes. She's a weak bitch. Suicide."

"Young," the dwarf said. "Could have plenty of juice left."

The black woman smiled and iron glinted in her mouth. Her teeth were filed and reinforced with shining metal. Karin pictured them closing on her flesh and tearing out a bloody chunk.

She closed her eyes in despair. Dr. Chamberlain would help her, she thought, if that killer hadn't shot him down. He felt the heat when he touched me . . . the need . . .

Karin heard a hundred rustling sounds, a hundred clankings as they closed upon her. She was overcome with despair so deep she knew that it would last forever. Or at least until the pack reached her.

A big, meaty hand grasped her shoulder and she would have fainted if she knew how to, but it wasn't as easy to turn off her consciousness as it was for the heroines in all those romances she'd read.

The dwarf pulled her upright and she heard the black woman say, "On your feet, bitch," and then there was the sound like an angry lion roaring. She opened her eyes to a frozen tableau that was as bewildering as anything she'd encountered since waking.

She was stunned to see Dr. Chamberlain in the outskirts of the pack. He wasn't dead. He didn't even look like he'd been hurt. He'd changed out of his hospital whites to a beautiful custom-tailored suit that fit him like a king's robe. He loomed above the pack, his anger cowing many of them into immediate submission, his wordless shout of command opening a path to Karin, the hateful dwarf, and the black woman.

Dr. Chamberlain, was all Karin could think. He's come to rescue me.

He grabbed the dwarf's thick forearm and squeezed, and the malignant creature let go of her shoulder and dropped to his knees with closed eyes and clenched jaws.

"You dare!" Dr. Chamberlain roared, and shook him as if he were a frail child.

Karin was astonished at the doctor's strength and the awesome wrath he expended in her cause. No one had ever stood up for her before. No one had ever taken her part with such fierceness. She felt the heat burning in her. She wanted him more than she'd ever wanted anyone or anything.

The dwarf cried out, mewing like a cat in pain.

"No—no—we was just holdin' her, like—"

The doctor threw him away contemptuously. He hit the sidewalk hard and lay there like a kicked dog. Chamberlain turned and looked right at Karin. His eyes were wide with anger and strange, exultant power, and something else she couldn't read, but didn't exactly like.

She forgot all that when he reached for her and swept her into his arms. The connection between them was so strong that it felt like a living thing. He smiled, his teeth white and even and beautiful, his eyes wide and bright with laughter.

Then, in his hand was a scalpel, shining in the sunlight. Karin stiffened as he showed it to her. She tried to pull away, but he was far too strong. He plunged it into her stomach and ripped sideways and she felt an explosion of pain like she'd never felt before.

Her mouth opened to scream and he closed his own upon it. She could feel him suck her life away as his hand moved around inside of her.

The pain was intense but she still couldn't faint. The kiss went on and on and in a way was more painful than the knife ripping her stomach and the hand rooting around inside. It was taking something from her, what she didn't know, but all her strength was draining away.

Finally he took his mouth from hers and looked at her with a wild, exultant expression. He pushed her away. She stumbled, but managed to remain on her feet.

He looked past her, to the tall black woman.

"Take her back to the hospital," he said. "But first you may have some of her. Some. Remember—she's mine."

The pack cheered and shouted in voices only vaguely human as they crowded around like starving dogs. The black woman reached her first, her smile all sharp, pointed teeth.

"Come on, meat," the woman said, fastening her teeth on the flesh of Karin's shoulder.

She fell to the pavement as they overwhelmed her. The last thing she remembered was Chamberlain's awful laughter, the press of bodies struggling to reach her, and the sight of the little girl, watching, hugging her pathetic stuffed bear to her chest.

Mercifully, then, she discovered that she could faint, after all.

iv.

Karin was surprised when she woke up, and even more surprised to find that she was whole. There was no sign of the gash Chamberlain had made in her stomach, no trace of teeth marks on her shoulder, no remains of the various bruises, welts, and abrasions she should have had from the pack's beating.

It was a miracle, she thought. All right. It was just what she needed. She would change her life. She closed her eyes and made a deal with God.

You've given me another chance, she told Him, and I won't let it slip away. I won't foul up this time. Just let me open my eyes and let this dream be over and let me be safe in my apartment again and I'll keep my end of the bargain. I'll do better from now on, really, I'll do better.

She opened her eyes and looked around to see that nothing had changed.

She was still in what seemed to be the hospital room where she'd first awoken. At least it seemed like the same room—the configuration and dimensions were the same and the same window was broken where the crazy man had grabbed her and leaped from the building. But everything else about it had changed terribly. It had been transformed into a trashed out, foul-smelling nightmare from a junkie's worst trip.

The bed she was lying on was a mass of twisted, rusty metal. The mattress was torn and stained and stank of unguessable fluids. The walls were spattered with graffiti and blood and garbage was scattered all over the floor.

The door to the outside lay broken off its hinges in the corridor, but Karin, stunned that God had refused her bargain and that her nightmare still continued, made no move to escape. She had no-where to escape to, nowhere to go where it'd be any better.

The sound of footsteps echoing down the corridor drew her eyes to the open doorway. She stared hopelessly, not knowing what to expect, half-wishing, half-fearing that it was Chamberlain.

But it wasn't the doctor. It was the little girl, her shadow looming like a monster ready to pounce, her dirty toy bear clutched to her chest. She stared at Karin with no emotion at all in her little girl's eyes, no expression on her tight face.

"What's your name?" the girl asked after a long moment.

"Karin," she said, and asked the reflexive question, "What's yours?"

"My name is Krystal. Mommy named me after the star of her favorite TV show. My Daddy didn't like it, though. He didn't like much, except hitting me and Mommy."

Karin was vaguely aware of *Dynasty*. It had gone off the air when Karin was just a little girl, too little to remember much of it. And Krystal was at least fifteen years younger than she.

"Krystal," she half-whispered, "what is this place?"

"You don't know much, do you?" the little girl asked.

Karin shook her head. "No. No I don't."

Krystal made a sweeping gesture with her hand, encompassing the room, the building, and all that was outside.

"This is the Dead Place. Everyone goes here when they're dead. I asked Billy if this was Hell, on account of my Daddy always said I was such a bad girl I was sure to go to Hell when I died, and when he killed me and I woke up here I thought I was in Hell. But Billy's been here a long time and he says, No, this ain't Hell. This is just the Dead Place where people go when they die."

"But I'm not dead," Karin said.

"Don't be stupid. If you wasn't dead you wouldn't be here. I'm dead. Billy's dead. The Doctor's dead. Only Bearry isn't dead, and he's stuffed."

Sudden anger flared through Karin. "What is this, God's idea of a cruel joke?"

When she killed herself—there, she admitted it—it had been out of desperation to end her pain. But she'd also thought, mostly subconsciously, that maybe she'd be going to someplace better, someplace where she needn't be alone. Maybe her mother would be there . . . maybe even Faffy. But this—this was a thousand times worse. She felt a great anger rising that she knew was beyond her control. It surprised and also frightened her, at the same time.

Krystal shrugged. "I don't know. Maybe Billy does."

"Billy." The man with the gun. The man who'd tried to get her away from Chamberlain in the first place. "Who is this Billy?"

"He's my friend," Krystal said. She held out her disreputable bear. "Bearry was my best friend ever when I was alive and Billy found him for me again. Do you want to see him?"

"I see him," Karin muttered.

"Not *Bearry*. *Bearry's* right here." Krystal cast her eyes upward. "I mean Billy." She leaned forward confidingly. "His name's really Henry, you know. He told me. But he likes to be called Billy."

"Yes." She would like to see him. He might be able to answer some questions about the bizarre happenings in this horrifying asylum. "Can you take me to him?"

"Sure. He's right down the hall."

That was unexpected, but what wasn't in this place?

They went out the door and down the corridor together. As Krystal had said, Billy was just a few doors down. His room was just as trashed as Karin's. The only difference was that Chamberlain and his minions had not simply left Billy in the room. He was shackled to a wall, arms upstretched, his toes dangling an inch from the floor. His face looked tired and pained, his clothing was torn as if he'd been beaten, but there were no marks on his lean body.

He managed a smile as Krystal and Karin came into the room. "Hello, little darlin'."

Karin was about to make an angry retort when she realized that Billy had spoken to Krystal, not her. The girl ran to him and, tucking Bearry into the crook of one arm, hugged him tightly around the waist, burying her face against his stomach. Billy smiled fondly at her, then looked up at Karin.

"How're you doing, ma'am?"

"I've been better."

"I can say the same myself," Billy said. "How'm I doing, Krystal?"

The little girl released him and took a step back. She looked at him critically for a moment, then shook her head.

"Not so good, Billy."

"I was afraid of that. How about the lady over there?"

Krystal glanced at her.

"Oh, she's still pretty bright. The Doctor took some of her color, then the pack took a little more. But she had plenty to start with." She made a serious face. "Too bad she's not smarter."

"Hey!"

Billy smiled gently. Karin had the sense that he would have reached out and tousled Krystal's hair if he hadn't been manacled to the wall.

"Now, you know how confusin' this place can be, little darlin'. Remember when you first came here."

"I remember—"

"Just what," Karin interrupted, "are you two talking about? What's this 'color' business? What is this place, anyway? And just *who the hell are you?*"

She didn't mean to shout, but the anger had taken control of her again. She was mad at everyone and everything. At Faffy, for dying and leaving her alone. At her mother, for dying when she was so young. At her father, so absorbed in his work that he never seemed to notice her, never cared what was happening in her life, never even bothered to ask. At her sister, older, smarter, much more beautiful, who only took from Karin and otherwise treated her as if she never existed. She was mad at the world, at the universe, at the entity who'd created such an awful place and left her alone and defenseless, sad and lonely, until she couldn't take it anymore and killed herself to escape, only to find in this madhouse inhabited by evil creatures worse things than any she'd ever encountered in the real world.

"Well, ma'am," Billy said in his slow, unflappable drawl, "you may find this kind of hard to believe, but my name—at least the name I go by—is Billy Bonney. People called me the Kid."

"Hard to believe?" Karin said. She laughed, long and hard, and realized that she was teetering on the edge of insanity. "Hard to believe? Jesus Christ, why the hell shouldn't I believe you? So who's the Doctor?"

"Well, ma'am," Billy said, "he was a doctor in life, but he used an alias, too, when he was out and about on his private business. He called himself Jack the Ripper. Still does, in fact."

Karin's laughter shut off like a valve turned tight.

"Oh my God." She shot a glance Krystal. "And her?"

"Just a little girl," Billy said tenderly. "Beaten an' brutalized an' finally killed by her no-good Pa."

"What is this place?" Karin whispered.

"I call it the Dead Place," Billy said. "The place where people go after they die, before they get all sorted out and move on."

She looked at him. "But you died . . ." She thought about it, and realized that she didn't know when he'd died. ". . . a long time ago. Why are you still here?"

"People have various reasons for staying on, ma'am. Some people, takes them a long time to figure out their ultimate destination. Some others like it here. They prey upon newcomers, set themselves up like kings, especially 'cause of folks like you. Then some others stay on because they have a job or two to do."

"Some prey on others because of people like me?"

"Yes, ma'am. Suicides."

"I don't understand."

"It works like this. When they're born everyone has a certain amount of, I guess you'd call it energy, that they use to live life. When it's gone, they're dead. Simple as that. Some people get sickly and they use up their share faster than others. Some get killed by accident or design. They get to use what's left, so to speak, when they move on.

"But suicides—well, suicides are special. They have energy, but they don't want it no more. They reject the gift. When they move on, there's people like Chamberlain who can take it from them, suck it away and use it for their own purposes. They like people you, 'specially young ones. You probably had, what, forty, fifty years left."

"At least fifty," Krystal put in.

Billy glanced down at her. "The young'un here is 'specially talented. She's tuned into the energy. She can see things, among which is the colors shining about you like a rainbow halo all over your body. That's why the Doctor likes to have her around."

"I . . ." Much of what Billy said didn't bear thinking about, at least not now. To keep from thinking she asked more questions. "How about you?"

"Me?" The Kid tried to shrug. "Like I said, some folks stay on 'cause they have a job to do. Now me, I wasn't much like folks later made me out to be. I didn't kill no twenty, thirty men. I killed, sure. Maybe I killed unwisely. Maybe I've got something of a score I have to settle before I move on. Maybe I just can't plain stand scum like the Doctor and I stick around to make sure he don't bully everybody and live like a devil king off of others. Maybe he treats Krystal a little better 'cause he knows I'm around and while my guns can't blow the bastard to Hell where he belongs, they can sure hurt him enough to make him scared of me."

Karin remembered the agony of the Doctor's scalpel ripping through her flesh, and she knew that there was indeed still pain in this world.

"But what happened?" she asked. "Why are you here?"

The Kid looked rueful. "Well, after we went out the window and I was watching you run off, the Doctor and his gang got the jump on me. And here I am."

"Can he hurt you—I mean, I know he can hurt you. But can he, well . . ." She didn't know how to ask it.

"Kill him?" a voice asked.

Karin jerked around to see Chamberlain standing in the open doorway, the pack crowding on his heels.

"Close enough," the Doctor said. For the first time she saw him as he really was. He'd abandoned the glamour that he'd cast to fool her and capture her. He was a small man, with dark, greasy hair and the face of an insane rodent. His eyes were wild, his yellow teeth crooked and sharp. His clothes were dirty and smelled of blood and gore. "I can make him suffer hugely. I can cut him and gut him and feast on his entrails so that it will be a long, long time before my Billy boy bothers me again."

He approached slowly, the sliver of steel shining in his hand like a piece of painful, inescapable death.

V.

Karin felt totally, completely overwhelmed.

The Ripper stalked by her without even a glance, marking her as beneath notice. A smile was fixed on his face and a line of drool ran down the left corner of his mouth. He advanced slowly on Billy, who hung placidly from his chains, as if awaiting the inevitable.

Krystal moved, stepping between them, holding her bear tight against her chest like a shield. Her face was screwed up in fear and it looked as if she were going to cry as she planted herself between the Ripper and the gunslinger.

"Don't you hurt Billy," she said. "He's my friend."

Karin realized that it took an immense amount of courage for the little girl to act. Perhaps it was the first time in her entire life, before and after her death, that she'd stood up for anyone, including herself. The Ripper looked at her, faintly surprised, and then he slashed with his scalpel in a motion almost too quick to see. It bit deep and cut long and Bearry's head flopped to one side, stuffing leaking from him like wads of cottony blood.

"You hurt Bearry!" the little girl screamed. She dropped her bear and quick as a thought threw herself at the Ripper, crying and screaming as she pummeled him with her little fists.

Chamberlain laughed, and something broke in Karin.

The anger she'd felt before returned, multiplied by a factor near infinity. She shouted, drenched in an instant sweat. Her body felt super-hot. Her mind was devoid of conscious thought, except for her undeniable need to help Krystal vanquish the monster threatening her.

Krystal squeaked like a mouse and stopped pummeling the Ripper. The laughter died in the killer's throat as he stared at the little girl's face, and his own expression twisted at what he saw there. He shouted a wordless cry, and reached out to slice Krystal's throat with his bright-bladed scalpel.

But fast as he was, and as strong, the little girl was even faster and stronger. She caught his knife wrist with a grip as unbreakable as a promise made with love.

"You're a bad man," she said serenely. "It's time for you to go where you'll never hurt anyone again."

The Ripper tried to yank away, but couldn't break the grip of her tiny fist. There was the sound of meat sizzling, like, Karin thought dizzily, fajitas brought to your table at a Mexican restaurant. It was the Ripper. He was burning at Krystal's touch.

He screamed in pain and shook himself like a rat trying to break free from a terrier, but Krystal wouldn't let him go. A terrible odor speared the air. It was more than the stench of burning flesh. It was as if something old and evil, something that had been steeped in rottenness for a long time, had suddenly caught fire. In moments the Ripper was covered with flame. He fell to his knees, face to face with Krystal.

"Please," he begged before the fire ate his lips and tongue. "Please."

Unaffected, Krystal wrinkled her nose. "You stink," she said, and as they watched the Ripper burned to a pile of greasy, foul-smelling ashes.

The pack looked at each other. The dwarf took a single step forward, then Krystal fixed him with her stare.

"You better not try to hurt anyone," she said, and then they all looked at each other again, and ran from the room.

"Help me with Billy," Krystal said.

Karin shook her head, coming out of her astonished stupor, and realized that the anger had burned out of her with the Ripper's demise. She felt awfully tired and almost fell when she helped Krystal let Billy's chains play out so he could put his feet on the floor.

"How did you do that?" she asked Krystal as they unhooked the chains from their wall sockets.

"You gave me your power."

"I did?"

Billy nodded. "It was a gift of strength freely given. Krystal used it." He tousled her hair, then snapped the manacle on his left wrist with little effort.

Karin frowned. "You could have done that anytime, couldn't you?"

"Maybe," Billy smiled. "Maybe I figured the two of you should have a chance to sort things out by yourselves. You both had things to learn and decisions to make."

Krystal nodded seriously. She picked up Bearry and looked at him. Magically, his head joined back to his shoulders and suddenly he was clean and bright and fresh looking. She hugged him closely.

"I'm glad," she told Billy.

"So am I."

"I'm tired," Karin said. "Tired and sad . . . and still more than a little mystified."

"Take your time, ma'am. Plenty of time here to figure things out."

"I gave some of my energy to Krystal, didn't I?"

The others nodded.

"Krystal has a talent for using it, like the Ripper had," Billy said.

"What about the rest of it?"

"You've still got a lot," Krystal told her. "You were awful young when you killed yourself."

She sat down, suddenly too tired to stand. "What should I do with it?" she asked quietly.

Billy shrugged. "If it feels like too much of a burden, give it away."

She looked at him. "To you?"

Billy shook his head. "There's plenty of folk still living who could use it. Sick folk, fighting for their lives, desperate to stay in the world. It's the best use of a suicide's energy. Helps balance the accounts, so to speak."

"I can do that? I can help someone that way?"

"Sure," Billy said. He nodded to Krystal. "Take her hand."

Krystal smiled at her and they held hands. Her tiny hand was strong for its size, and still warm, pleasantly warm, no longer burning. They looked at each other, then there was a moment of almost intolerable dislocation. Karin felt pain and suffering all around her and grief that was almost too much to bear, but the warm presence of the little girl steadied her. She didn't know what to do so she just gave, and she felt her gift accepted all around her. Then they were back in the room and she was leaning on Billy and Krystal to keep from slipping to the floor.

"You'll be all right in a moment," Billy told her. "Giving like that takes a lot out of you. But you'll be fine."

"Did it work?" she asked. "Did I save someone?"

Billy nodded. "A man in New Mexico. A fine man, dying too soon of cancer. He was a writer, much admired. Now he'll have another twenty-five, maybe thirty years. He'll write a lot of fine books, help a lot of others along the way. He'll live to see his grandchildren born and grow and the Earth will be a better place for his continued presence."

"I'm glad," Karin said.

"How about you?" Billy asked. "What do you want?"

She was tired and sad, whether from giving up her energy or just because she was tired and sad, she didn't know. She shook her head.

"I know," Krystal said.

Karin felt a familiar rubbing sensation on her legs and looked down. Faffy looked up at her and meowed. He wasn't an old, tired cat, wasted by disease, but sleek and beautiful, as he'd been in his prime.

"Oh," Karin said, and she went down to her knees as Faffy rose up on his hind legs to meet her embrace. She gathered her friend to her and Faffy purred loudly, love and contentment on his face. He licked the tears that ran down Karin's cheek and rubbed his head against her chin.

"If you want," Billy said, "you can see your mother soon. Some people just have too much put on them, and she's in a place where she's been resting and recovering." He looked down at Krystal and smiled. "Ole Krys, here, will go somewhere's where she can just be a kid for a while, but I suspect I'll see her again."

Krystal hugged her bear and smiled delightfully. "You sure will, Billy."

Karin stood, cradling her cat to her breast. She smiled through her tears.

"I'm not totally useless," she said, "I mean, since I've given all my energy away?"

Billy rubbed Faffy's head and Faffy meowed at him.

"I should say not, ma'am. We can always use another hand around the place."

Karin smiled, happy for the first time in a long time, content for maybe the first time in her life. She hoped she had a long, long time left.

AFTERWORD

I first read Roger's work around 1970. In fact, *Lord of Light* was the first great novel that I ever read. There was also *This Immortal, Creatures of Light and Darkness,* the Amber books, and many, many other fine novels, short stories, and novelettes. I moved to New Mexico in 1976, and once I'd met Roger, it didn't take long for me to realize that he was a fine a man as he was a writer. It was a true honor to work with him on the *Wild Cards* series. I regret more than I can say that I had cause to write this story. I'll miss him forever.

In some small way, "Suicide Kings" is also my farewell to Fafhrd, our seventeen-year-old cat who died during the writing of this story. We miss her, too.

Necessity can make unlikely allies.

■

CHANGING OF THE GUARD
Robert Wayne McCoy and Thomas F. Monteleone

IF I STARTED OUT BY TELLING YOU MY REAL NAME WAS THOR AND I'd spent the previous evening in a wrestling match with Jesus, you probably wouldn't believe me.

I doubted my old college roommate, Jay Leshinsky, would either. So when he asked me how I was feeling, I eased into my story by way of an elaborate retelling of a dream I'd been having with alarming frequency.

About once a month Jay and I would get together with a couple of other professors at Middlebury College for a few hours of poker, microbrews, and conversation banal and profane. Afterwards, Jay and I would usually stop at this all-night diner on Route 7 for some coffee and cheesecake before I drove back up to my house in Burlington. The last two months hadn't been much fun for me because I was still trying to get used to the idea that, yes, my father had really died, and another door had been closed in my life. The old man had been living with me and Margaret ever since he'd retired from the carpentry business at the age of eighty-two. A couple of years of sitting there with a remote control in his hand didn't seem to excite a guy who'd been extremely active all his life, so I guess he kind of let go of things, just let himself wear out.

But I missed him terribly, and Jay had made himself available to listen to my regrets and reminiscences. As we sat there in the booth at the diner, the only people other than Susan, the third-shift waitress, and a plaid-capped trucker at the counter, I sipped my coffee from a thick, dinged-up, porcelain mug.

"It's this dream I keep having," I said.

"About your father?" said Jay.

I shrugged. "Not that I can tell. It's just *weird*, that's all. Listen . . ."

I walk along a path that twists through absolute darkness like a silvery ribbon of satin that has been Möbiused though time and space. I am striding boldly toward a point that feels familiar, as though I've been there many times, yet it also appears alien and unknown. The night writhes about me in lively anticipation, the air around me feels charged. It is an invigorating sensation, and my breath escapes me in rapid bursts of frosted air.

I'm carrying a really huge hammer made of some dense metal, and I know the hammer has a name: *Mjolnir.* It feels like a weapon, a comfortable and familiar one. I speak its name and it begins to glow as if just raised from a blacksmith's forge. As I walk forward, I begin the Summoning. It's an ancient ritual that I know by heart, but I have no idea how I know it. I have a feeling that I am moving toward a confrontation, but I feel no fear, no anticipation. I am on some kind of mission, I can sense this, in the tradition of my father. Don't ask me how I know this; it just seems to be a part of who I am.

Which is a pretty big, muscular guy. I look down at my broad chest, feel it pushing against some polished body-armor, and even I am impressed. I feel powerful, confident, driven. The twisting path through darkness begins to fan out in front of me and it transforms into a vast, snow-blanketed plane. It appears endless, and a hideous silence holds the place in its eternal grip.

Taking a breath, I inhale the salty tang of the sea, the lingering scent of a thousand ancient tales. I close my eyes and call my allies; icy winds skim across dark waters like razors. The winds come to me like faithful pets, surrounding me, whirling about me, carrying the detritus of their passage, full of discontent.

Something bad was going to happen, I could tell that much, but nothing more than that.

As I stood there at the edge of the endless place, I watched a cold, yellow fog roll inexorably toward me. It is the stuff of distortion, its essence obscuring the world about me, sculpting phantoms and specters. Tricks of the eye . . . or maybe not.

It is time to call forth the rest of my elements, my soldiers and allies. I know this, and the simple thought brings it into being. I beckon an incredible torrent of rain and roiling thunder, torn like sheets from the darkness that enfolds me. And then the lightning dances around me, nocked like arrows and ready to be unleashed. All these things come to me, surrounding me protectively, like the powerful embrace of a friend long lost.

The ground shakes and ripples, sending out great waves along the solid plane ahead of me. The earth screams, hurling out volcanic gouts of fire like pillars to hold up a dead sky.

I watch as the ground in front of me splits open, like a seal being broken. An unholy enemy comes forth; the first wave bubbles forth from the fissures like lava, out and into the world.

And I meet them with uncompromising fury on what I suddenly know is the longest of all nights. I know I have relived this night many times, but I am still amazed by the sheer spectacle of the macabre unfolding before me.

They were the creatures of the pit, born of sin and pain and hellfire. Bloody claws, rotted teeth, some with sleek, knotted muscle, coiled and wound like springs, others immensely bloated and diseased. Insane features grafted onto familiar ones. Beasts both natural and of nightmare. My enemies drip acid and slime from pores and maws, hate form eyes of fire. Like crabs on a beach, they scuttle toward me, their bodies of hard bone, spiked and horned, mandibles clicking. Others fly, slither, lurch, and shamble. A flood of all that is loathsome and evil, and I seem to be the only thing standing between them and the world they seek to devour.

But this didn't seem to bother me.

Raising my mighty hammer, I notice it is now glowing like something radioactive: white hot, pulsing like a living thing. With a single arc of my hammer, I will my rampaging rain and arctic winds against the dark horde, and it surges over the blanket of bodies with titanic force. Back into the pit, the millions of creatures collapse into a spiraling mass of flesh and bone. They are washed away like the dirty water at the bottom of a drain, and I know they cannot best me.

I simply stand and watch, knowing this was but the first wave and they the lesser of my foe.

But I do not wait long before an immense serpent rises from the pit, carried on wings which look like they could cover a lot of football fields. It scales are black and iridescent; and liquid fire drips from its mouth, sizzling loudly on. It looks at me with emerald eyes, bulging like giant blisters from its streamlined head. It is a gaze designed to paralyze me with fear as it dips to swallow me with a single snap of its open-scooped jaw.

I smile and unleash my lightning like arrows from a phalanx of longbows.

The dark vault of the endless night above me suddenly pales under the fusillade of white heat. The vault cracks as jagged pieces of light converge on the serpent. On impact, the creature shudders, ravaged by bolt upon countless bolt. It staggers back like a heavy-weight stumbling under the savage assault of a master. Its great eyes go slack and pale, and its black scales grow dull as they begin to smolder. The great head swings past me like a pendulum and I see my reflection for the briefest instant in the mirror of its already-dead eyes.

I am smiling.

But there is a final wave. This I know. There always is a final onslaught of the ebon legions, a final clash of my power against hordes of the broken seal. They flow the pit like lava once again, and I raise my weapon to redirect my energy. The rain and wind and lightning batter the advancing columns of evil, but this time, it is different. They do not fall back, or even stagger against my power.

For the first time, I feel . . . unsure, even a bit anxious.

And then, from behind me, a tremendous blast of light rushes past me like a burst from a nuclear bomb as its shock and heat waves ripple outward from ground zero. I watch as the demon armies are withered in the devastating wash of radiation. This time they do not so much reel from the deadly blow they receive as they are simply crisped into papery ash and blown away in the single blink of an eye.

It is suddenly over. I lower my hammer and the raging storms whirling around me like a force field abruptly dissipate. The keening, humming sound runs down, as if someone pulled the plug on a giant generator.

"Nice try," says a voice behind me.

It catches me off-guard and I spin automatically at the sound, raising Mjolnir high above my head.

"What?" I say, admittedly confused.

I am surprised to see a man approaching me with a casual, fearless gait. A subtle nimbus of light precedes him, dispelling the heavy cloak of dread that has weighted down this place.

"I figured I'd better give you a little help," he says. "Before things got out of control."

He is of average size and looks vaguely familiar, but I can't place him. He favors no protective gear, and looks slightly effeminate in the pale caftan he wears. But I stand in respect because of what I've just seen him do.

"What do you know of my mission?" I say.

The man shrugs. "Enough to know you won't be need to do it any longer. Excuse me for a second. . . ."

I watch as he holds up a single index finger for an instant, then turns to the open crevasse of the pit, looking like an unhealing wound.

"In the name of my Father, I cast you demons of hell from this place, and close the seal for all eternity." His voice was gentle, but still seethed with power.

I watch: the earth groans as the entrance to the pit seals over and is gone. I know somehow it will never open again.

"Who are you?" I asked of him, boldness filling my voice.

"I am the new defender of the light. I am the truth, and whomever comes by me comes to the All Father." He smiled.

"Odin is the father."

He walked toward me, arms outstretched. I could see there were nail holes in his palms, but they were scarred and seemed to cause him no pain. "Well, yes, he is . . . but Odin has a Father as well."

"No! This cannot be." But even as I say these words, I know they are hollow. Having just witnessed the power of this man, I am already half-convinced.

"Sorry," he says. "But I'm afraid it is. . . ."

"What does this mean?" I ask sincerely, because I truly do not understand what our meeting portends.

"Thor," he says gently. "You've done a good job. A great job, really. But it's time to let someone else take their turn."

"But there is no 'time' for me," I say. "There never has been."

"Oh, yes, there was," he says. "You just never knew it."

"Your words are like a paradox." I shake my head, step back to regard him more fully. I must admit that despite his simple appearance, I am afraid of him.

"Only because you choose to hear them as such." He extends a hand. "Come on with me. I will find you plenty of good work to do with the new regime."

I hesitate, holding my great hammer in front of me.

"You know," I say slowly, "I want to go along with what you say, but it seems to go against my . . . purpose, my nature."

The man smiles. "How about if we settle this the easiest way—a little wrestling match."

"What?!" I am truly surprised by his words. "Are you kidding?"

"Serious as cancer, my friend."

"But why? To what end?"

"When I win, you'll work for me and my father."

I study him for a moment, regarding his frail frame. Anybody betting on us wouldn't give him a chance against me.

I nod. "Okay, let's do it. . . ."

I set Mjolnir aside and move to grapple with him. He steps forward into the embrace of my attempt for a quick takedown. I close down on him and I am surprised by the tensile strength of his lean arms and shoulders. He is built like tightly wrapped steel cable, but offers little resistance. I make the mistake of assuming this is a lack of ability or power. Planting my thick legs, I prepare for a body-lift and slam—

—but he twists deftly, turns, and tilts me over his hip. It is one of those arcane, subtle, martial arts moves that I have never understood and appreciated even less.

Large error, that.

In an instant, I am hurtling through the air, my own massive bulk allied with gravity against me. I slam onto the ancient pathway like a safe falling from a loft.

Looking up, I see him smiling at me. "Too bad," he says. "You want to try two out of three?"

This pisses me off and I leap upward, lunging for him with an embarrassing grunt. Stepping aside with the grace of a matador, he avoids my charge, and barely touches my arm at the elbow and wrist. Using the force of my own forward momentum and his own keen sense of leverage and balance, I am again sent hurtling into the air on a very short flight.

When I impact on my back, I am again looking up at him. Smiling, he offers me his hand.

"That's okay," he says. "No hard feelings, my friend. No big deal, you'll just be working for my father and me."

"Doing what?" I say.

"Well, your job specs are going to change, but we will need you eventually."

"When?"

He shrugs. "Not sure yet. You know how it is with something as bothersome as time."

I nod. He was right about that.

"So let's do it like this," he says. "For now, you won't remember any of this. You'll have a kind of 'secret identity,' a regular life, probably a whole series of them, just like your father did."

"My father?"

He waves off my question. "Too much explaining for right now. You'll understand everything eventually. But for now, it's better if you don't remember any of this."

And I didn't . . .

* * *

". . . until these dreams started. And I keep having this feeling that they're really memories of my past reality."

Jay grinned. "That's a nice touch—wrestling with Jesus."

"Do you think I'm crazy?" I said.

"Of course not. Freud would say you are experiencing some great resentment toward your father, or a latent reverse-Oedipus complex, or something like that. Who knows?"

"Is that all it means?" I sipped the last of my coffee.

"Even if it is true, and you are, or were Thor, so what?" Jay looked at me sagely, like a philosopher. "You're Bob Schaller these days, and doing a real good job of it."

"Do you believe in God?" I said.

Jay shrugged. "Some days I might say yes, and some days no. But remember, I used to believe in Santa Claus, the Easter Bunny, and the American Dream. Maybe if we're lucky, part of us never stops. . . ."

"Easy for you to be so casual about it, Jay. But to tell you the truth, it's got me kind of scared. I'm even afraid to tell Margaret about it."

My friend nodded. "Well, if you *are* some ancient god, then so be it. It's something out of your control. Or, on the other hand, if your dream is just a dream laced with symbolism relevant to real events in your life, then that's okay too."

"That seems so existential," I said.

"Well, it is. The point is there's *nothing* you can do about it, no reason to fret over it, I mean. Don't let it bug you. I'll always be here if you want to talk about it. But you're not crazy, that's for sure."

Just about then, Susan came but to check the levels in our coffee cups, but we both waved her off. I paid the tab, and we headed out to the parking lot and our cars. I thanked Jay for listening, and he told me to stop worrying. We shook hands in the hardy, muscular way of true male bonding, and retreated to the safe harbors of our vehicles before things got too sappy.

As I headed north toward Burlington, rethinking our conversation and my crazy dream, I figured out what I would do, as soon I got home.

Down in the basement, under my workbench, lay dad's old grease- and paint-spattered tool box. I thought it might be a good idea if could take out that carpenter's hammer Dad said I should keep, even after he was gone.

I'm going to hold it in my hands, and speak its name.

After that, well, we'll just have to wait and see. . . .

AFTERWORD
by Robert Wayne McCoy

I never had the honor of meeting Roger Zelazny, though I feel as if I knew him as a friend. I never sat and held a conversation with him, but yet I can say with assurance he has talked to me.

I first became acquainted with Roger several years ago at the urgings of a friend, Steve S. We were both role players since childhood and he introduced me to a diceless role-playing game called Amber. I was hooked, not only on Amber; there was an insatiable need to read everything Roger had written, knowing that this was just a starting point to his wonderful, imaginative mind and fiction. Before it was even considered a style, Roger brought to life the science fantasy genre.

I showed my cousin, Tom Monteleone, some of the stories I had written. He told me that I had what it took to be a writer and described the journey. Tom became my mentor, showing me the business. Most importantly, he became my friend. He also knew Roger, from when they both lived in Baltimore. I was floored. Roger's works had been my classroom, he the silent teacher.

My journey is not complete, but my dream of being a full-time writer is in sight. I would never say that "Changing of the Guard" is representational of Roger's work. If anything, it is an approximation, a mere shadow of his grace and craft. In this tribute, I do not say goodbye. I will keep walking the wasteland until I reach my goal. I am comforted to know in some way, I don't travel alone. When it is late at night and I lie curled up rereading one of his master works, I will learn something new, I will hear another voiceless whisper from a friend.

Thanks, Roger.

AFTERWORD
by Thomas F. Monteleone

I try not to think about it too often—that he's really *gone*—because it bothers me to know that a mind so clever, so incredibly bright and curious, has been shut down.

I respected Roger Zelazny as a writer and a thinker and an inspiration, but most importantly as a friend. When I met him, in 1971, he was enjoying a peak of critical popularity and just entering a period of work that would ensure him a decent level of commercial success as well. At the time, genre publishing was in a kind of mini-boom phase, gearing up (even though they didn't know it) for the day Luke would zap the Death Star and change everything.

I was working on my master's degree in English (with the idea that I could teach college) but I really wanted to be a writer, a *science fiction* writer, and I had selected several writers whose work I wanted to emulate because of their originality and their literate approach to the genre.[1] One of them was Roger Zelazny. And the funny part was that I had no idea back then that he, like me, lived in Baltimore and was less than fifteen minutes' drive from my house.

After I met him at a convention in Washington, D.C., he gave me his phone number and said I could call him any time for advice or encouragement regarding my writing and the whole business of becoming a writer. I was reluctant to take him up on it because I didn't want to bug him. So we remained acquaintances, and didn't really become friends until I asked him if he'd like to be the subject of my master's thesis (!).

Yeah, I agree—what a surprise.

Thinking back on it, I'm sure he was kind of stunned that his work might be placed under the dusty lens of a microscope forged in the groves of academe, but he graciously agreed, and opened himself up to about six months of intensive and (I realize now) invasive interviews, discussions, and bull sessions. It was during that time, meeting with Roger for hours at a clip, my cheesy tape recorder grinding on, that I discovered several important things about Roger Zelazny: he was one of the smartest people I'd ever met; he was easily the most gentle and kind man I'd ever met; and that I couldn't imagine ever having a friend as genuine and undemanding as he.

I also learned to appreciate what good writing was all about. In forcing myself to analyze Roger's stories, taking them apart and spreading all the pinions and gears across my desktop, I learned how a true craftsman works. His short fiction of the sixties and seventies had a magical, lyrical quality, containing just the right amounts of emotion, humor, and intellect to make them soar above the rest of us. In fact, I'm not going to preach to the converted here. If you're reading this pale tribute to Roger, you already *know* what a fine writer he was.

[1] And as far as the story I wrote for this anthology with Bob McCoy, I can't say that it reads like a "Zelazny story," but I must hope that it at least conveys the spirit of his work—his mordant and often playful interpretation of classic myths and philosophical or religious themes. The style of the story is at best a pale approximation of Roger's clean, yet poetic, lines, but again, we hope imitation serves as the finest form of flattery.

Better if I tried to tell you something you might not know about him.

Like:

When he moved to Santa Fe, we would correspond erratically, and his letters (which still reside in one of my many file cabinets) were always single-spaced, never less than seven or eight pages, and *impeccably* typed. I was always knocked out by the content of his letters—a heady mix of local/family news, writing projects, and wonderfully tangential observations and philosophizings in that same jeweled style that made his prose sing so. But I was almost equally impressed by the typescripts themselves—they were, as I said, always *perfectly* typed. Never a misspelling, a typo, any errant mark or scratch-out. I used to marvel at how he could just sit down at his typewriter and just *glide* across the keys without a single hitch. He was stylish and elegant even in the way he typed, but it was an indicator of a mind so sharp and clean and always in control. He always knew what he wanted to say and how to say it, and he never missed a stroke. Incredible when you think about it.

Or the night we were sitting in his living room smoking pipes (a period when we had both tried them as an interim bridge to quitting nicotine) and he said: "I'm going to tell you something I've never told anyone, ever, not even my wife." And I sat there feeling honored and special, and a little scared, as he told me about a thing in his life that frightened him and drove him, and that he eventually conquered. I never shared what he told me, and I won't now. But I can tell you it was a night when I witnessed a side of Roger few ever did, and felt ever more his solid friend for it.

Or another night that we were driving back to Baltimore from the University of Maryland after he had been there to give a talk and a reading. He told me about this weird recurring dream he had: in which it was apparent that everything he'd ever done was a fraud, and that sooner or later, people would be "on" to him, and he would be discovered to be a complete and utter fake. I can remember being so shaken by what he said and the *way* he talked about it that I found I couldn't really comment without sounding like a fool. I was still in my twenties back then, and hadn't been living off my imagination as long or as well as Roger had; and so I really wasn't equipped to understand what his dream meant or why it hounded him so. I think, now, I know more about what he spoke that night. A lot more.

He was trying to tell me that writing is perhaps the strangest of professions. We who do it for any lasting amount of time are most likely *driven* to do it. We probably couldn't live *without* writing. But at the same time, we live in fear of the day when there might be nothing left to write, nothing left to say. The scariest thing for any of us is to stare into the dark pool that is the reflection of our soul and admit we're starting to repeat ourselves, allowing ourselves to get fat and lazy and use the same trick or plot device, or the same kind of character.

Because what does that really mean?

Are we running out of ideas, or something far worse? Do we ever reach a point when we stop seeing the world through the eyes of the star-gazing twelve-year-old when he *almost* comprehends the limitless complexity of universe? Can our own personal vision, our sense of wonder, ever just seize up like an old truck engine and *stop?*

Sure, I guess it can. But not for the best of us.

So, I think I know what Roger was trying to articulate that night as we rode through the darkness between the cities. If I'd better understood the process back then, I'd have told him he had nothing to worry about.

He still doesn't.

*In his short story "And I Only Am Escaped to Tell Thee,"
Roger took a wry look at the tale of the Flying Dutchman. In
his piece, John Varley returns to the fertile waters of that legend
for a story that any air traveler will read with a shudder.*

■

THE FLYING DUTCHMAN
John Varley

IT WAS DARK WHEN THE PLANE REACHED O'HARE, THREE HOURS
late. Snow swirled in white tornadoes over the frozen field. The
plowing crews had kept just one runway clear. Planes were stacked
up back to New Jersey. Flights were being diverted to St. Louis,
Cleveland, Dayton, and other places people didn't really want to
go when they *intended* to go there.

The 727 hit the icy tarmac like a fat lady on skates, slewed to
the left, then straightened out as the nose came down and the
thrust reversers engaged. Then the plane taxied for thirty minutes.

When the jetway finally reached them and the FASTEN SEAT BELTS
sign went off, Peter Meers stood up. He was immediately bumped
back into his seat by a large man across the aisle. Somebody
stepped on his foot.

He struggled to his feet again, reached for his carry-on bag under
the seat. When he jerked on the handle, it snagged on something.
He pushed at it with his foot, being jostled from behind and almost
falling into the man from Seat B, waiting for Meers to get out. He
yanked again, and heard a sound that meant there was a new,
deep scratch on the expensive leather.

154

He looked up in time to have a filthy duffel bag fall from the overhead compartment into his face. A filthier hand appeared and yanked on the canvas strap, and the bag vanished into the press of bodies. Meers glimpsed a ragged man with a beard. How had such a man got aboard an airplane? he wondered. Could you buy airline tickets with food stamps?

Retrieving his briefcase and his laptop computer, he slung everything over his shoulders. It was another ten minutes of shuffling before he reached the closet at the front of the plane where a harried flight attendant was helping people reclaim their garment bags. He found his, grabbed it, and slung it over his shoulder. Then he waddled sideways toward the door and the jetway. On the way out he barked his shin against a folded golf cart leaning against the exit door. Then he was trudging up the jetway into O'Hare.

O'Hare. ORD. On a snowy night with one runway operating, an inner circle of Hell. Meers shuffled down the concourse with several million other lost souls, all looking to make a connection. Those who had abandoned all hope—at least for the night—slumped in chairs or against walls or just stood, asleep on their feet.

At O'Hare, connections were made not on shadowy street corners, cash for tiny baggies, but at the ends of infinite queues shaped, twisted, and redoubled by yellow canvas bands strung between stainless steel poles, under lights as warm and homey as an operating theater. Meers found the right line and stood at the end of it. In ten minutes, he shoved his garment bag, his carry-on, his briefcase, and his laptop forward three feet with the tip of his shoe. Ten minutes later, he did it again. He was hungry.

When he reached the ticket counter the agent told him he had missed his connecting flight for home, and that there would be no more flights that night.

"However," she said, frowning at her computer screen, "I have one seat available on a flight to Atlanta. You ought to be able to make a connection from there in the morning." She looked up at him and smiled.

Meers took the rewritten ticket. The departure gate was a good three miles from where he stood. He shouldered his burdens and went off in search of food.

Everything was closed except one snack bar near his gate. Airport unions were on strike. The menu on the wall had been covered with a sheet of butcher paper, hand lettered: HOT DOGS $4. COKES $2. NO COFFEE. Behind the counter were two harried workers, a fiftyish woman with gray wisps of hair straggling from her paper cap, and a Hispanic man in his twenties with mustard and ketchup stains all over his apron.

When Meers was still a good distance away, the counterman

suddenly threw down his hot dog tongs, snatched the hat from his head and crumpled it into a ball.

"I'm through with this shit!" he shouted. "I quit. *¡No más!*" He continued to scream in Spanish as he ran through a door in the back. The woman was shouting his name, which was Eduardo, but the man paid no attention. He hit the red emergency bar on a fire door and an alarm sounded as he scrambled down stairs outside.

Meers could see a little through the glass. The Hispanic man was short and stocky, but a good runner. He charged away from the building. From somewhere beneath, two uniformed security guards charged out, guns in their hands. Eduardo was nowhere to be seen. The guards kept going. There was a flash of light. Gunfire? There was too much noise from jet engines for Meers to be sure. He shivered, and turned back toward the snack counter.

He was still ten people back in line when they announced his flight to Atlanta. He was three back when they made the second announcement. The gray-haired women, still distracted by the flight of Eduardo, slapped a hot dog into his hand and spilled a third of his Coke on the counter as another call came over the public address. Meers hurried to a stand-up counter. There were no onions, no relish. He squeezed some mustard out of a plastic packet, half of it squirting cleverly onto his tan overcoat. Cursing, dabbing at the mustard, Meers took a bite. It was lukewarm on one end, cold on the other.

Gulping Coke and choking down cold wienie and stale bun, Meers hurried to the boarding area. Down the jetway and into the 727. Most of the passengers were seated except a few struggling with crammed overhead compartments. He sidled down to seat 28B. In 28C was a woman who had to be three hundred pounds, most of it in the hips. In 28A was a man who was more like three-fifty, his face shiny with sweat. Meers looked around desperately, but he already knew this was the last, the absolute last seat on the plane.

The woman glared at him as she stood. Meers got his carry-on under the seat, then popped the overhead rack. There was about enough space to store a wallet. The next one was just as full. A flight attendant took his briefcase and laptop and hurried away.

He wedged himself into the seat. The lady wedged herself into hers. He felt his ribs compressing. From his right came gusts of a sickening lilac perfume. From the left, waves of stale terror.

"My first flight," the fat man confided.

"Oh, really?" Meers said.

"I'm real scared."

"No need to be." The fat lady scrambled in her purse for a box of tissue, then blew her nose loud enough to frighten a walrus. She crumpled the noisome tissue and dropped it on Meers's shoe.

They were pushed back, they taxied, they waited two hours and taxied some more, they were deiced and waited another hour. All of which took much longer than it takes to tell about it. Then they were in the air. The fat man promptly threw up into the little white bag.

Atlanta. ATL. They landed under a thick pall of black smoke. Somewhere to the west, a large part of Georgia was tinder-dry and burning. Hartsfield International sweltered in hundred-degree heat, and soot swirled across the runways. It was dark as night.

The fat man had filled barf bags all through the flight. In spite of this, he had eaten like a starving hyena. Meers had been unable to eat. He could barely get his hands to his mouth. He had stared at the meal on his tray table, as immobilized as if bound to his seat, until the stewardess took it away.

Just before reaching the gate the flight attendant arrived for the fat man's latest delivery. Meers eyed the bulging bottom of the bag in horror as it passed over his lap, but it didn't break.

The heat slammed him as he left the plane. It didn't abate when he entered the terminal. The air was thick, hot syrup. The forest fires had downed power lines, and the air conditioning was off. So were the lights. So were the computers and telephones.

Somehow the ticketing staff were still working, though Meers couldn't imagine how. He joined the endless line and began shuffling forward. He shuffled for five hours. At the end of that time, nearing starvation, the agent told him he hadn't a hope of a connection to his home, but he could put Meers on a flight to Dallas–Fort Worth where his chances would be better. The flight would leave in nine hours.

Meers roamed the ovenlike interior of the airport. None of the restaurants and snack bars were open. With no refrigeration and no electricity to run the stoves, there was no point. The bars were open and serving warm beer, but had not so much as a pretzel. People sat wilted in their chairs, stunned by the heat, looking out over the ashen landscape. A nuclear holocaust might look a lot like this, Meers thought.

A few profiteers were selling ice water at five dollars a bottle. The lines were enormous. Meers found a clear space against a wall and sat down on his luggage. When he leaned forward sweat dripped off his nose.

He heard a commotion, and saw a man approaching with boxes on a hand truck. He was the pied piper of Atlanta, trailed by a mob of jostling people.

He stopped at an empty vending machine. When he opened the front someone in the crowd started pulling at a box. Someone else grabbed the other end. The box burst and spilled Snickers bars on the floor. In moments all the boxes had been torn open. When the tide ebbed away, the delivery man sat on the floor, feeling himself cautiously, amazed he hadn't been ripped to shreds. He got up and wandered away.

Meers had snagged a bag of peanuts and a Three Musketeers. He ate every bite, then made himself as comfortable as possible against the wall and nodded off.

A lost soul was screaming. Meers opened his eyes, found himself curled up over his possessions, a rope of drool coming from his mouth. He wiped it away and sat up. Across the concourse a man in the remains of a suit and tie had gone berserk.

"Air!" he shrieked. "I gotta have air!" His shirt was torn at the neck, his coat on the floor. He swung a fire ax at a plate glass window. The ax bounced off and he swung it again, shattering the glass. He leaned out the window and tried to breathe the smoke outside. He shouted again and began struggling with his pants. His hands were spouting blood, deeply slashed on the jagged sill, but he didn't seem to notice.

Off he ran, naked but for his pants trailing from one ankle and a blue silk tie like a noose around his neck.

Half a dozen security guards converged on him. They hit the man with their nightsticks and sprayed pepper in his face. They zapped him with tasers until he flopped around like a fish slick with his own blood. Then they cuffed and hogtied him and carried him away.

The flight to Dallas was another 727. Half the passengers were under ten years old, in Atlanta for a Peewee beauty contest. The boys were in tuxedos and the girls in evening gowns, or what was left of them after twenty-four hours living rough at the airport with no luggage. Some of them were cranky and some were playful, and all were spoiled rotten, so they either sat in their seats and screamed, or turned the aisle into a rough-and-tumble racetrack. Supervision consisted of the occasional fistfight between fathers when a child's nose was bloodied.

Meers had a window seat, next to a father who spent the whole flight carping about the judging. His son had not made the finals. The son, who Meers felt should have been left out for wolves to devour along with the afterbirth, sat on the aisle and spent his time tripping running children.

There was no meal. The catering services had been just as crippled as the snack bars at the airport. Meers was given a pack of salted peanuts.

Dallas–Fort Worth. DFW. It had been raining forty days and forty nights when the 727 landed. The runways were invisible under sheets of water. The mud between the taxiways was so deep and thick it swallowed jetliners like mammoths in a tar pit. Meers saw three planes mired to the wingtips. Passengers were deplaning into knee-deep muck, slogging toward buses unable to get any closer lest they sink and never be seen again.

The airport was almost empty. DFW was operating in spite of the weather, but flights were not arriving from other major hubs. Meers made it to the ticket counter where the small line moved at glacial speed because only one agent had made it through the floods. When his turn came he was told all flights to his home had been canceled, but he could board a flight to Denver in six hours, where a connection could be made. It was on another airline, so he would have to take the automated tram to another terminal.

On the way to the tram he stopped at a phone booth. There was no dial tone. The one next to it was dead, too. All the public telephones in the airport were dead. The flood had washed them out. He knew his wife must be very worried by now. There had been no time for a call from O'Hare, and Atlanta and now Dallas were cut off. But surely the situation would be on the news. She would know he was stranded somewhere. It would be great to get back home to Annie. Annie and his two lovely daughters, Kimberly and . . .

He stopped walking, seized by panic. His heart was hammering. He couldn't recall the name of his youngest daughter. The airport was spinning around him, about to fly into a million pieces.

Megan! Her name was Megan. God, I must be punchy, he thought. Well, who wouldn't be? The hunger had made him lightheaded. He breathed deeply and moved off toward the tram.

The door had closed behind him before he noticed the man lying on the floor at the other end of the car. There was no one else on board.

The man was curled up in a pool of vomit and spilled purple wine. He wore a filthy short jacket and had a canvas duffel bag at his feet. He looked like the man Meers had seen on arrival in Chicago, though that hardly seemed likely.

The tram made a few automated announcements, then pulled away from the concourse and out into the rain. It was pitch black. The rain pounded on the roof. There were flashes of distant lightening and a high, whistling wind. The tram pulled into the next concourse and the doors opened.

Three security guards in khaki uniforms stormed aboard. Without warning, one of them kicked the sleeping vagrant in the face. The man cried out, and the guards began battering him with their batons and boots. Blood and rotten teeth fountained from the man's mouth and nose. Peter Meers sat very still, his feet and knees drawn together protectively.

One of the security men took a handful of the screaming man's hair and another grabbed the seat of his pants, and they dragged him through the rear door of the tram and onto the platform. The third looked over at Meers. He smiled, touched the brim of his hat with his nightstick, and followed the others.

The door closed and the tram moved away. Meers could see the three still beating the man as the car moved out into the night.

Just short of the next concourse the lights flickered and went out, and the tram car stopped. Rain hammered down relentlessly. It gushed in rivers over the windows. Meers got up and paced his end of the car. He was careful not to walk as far as the stain of wine, urine, and blood at the other end, which looked black in the light of distant street lamps. He thought about what he had seen, and about his family waiting for him back home. He had never wanted so badly to get home.

After a few hours the lights came back on and the tram delivered him to the right concourse. He had to hurry to make the flight on time.

This time he was on a wide-bodied aircraft, a DC-10. There were not many passengers. He was assigned an aisle seat. The takeoff was a little bumpy, but once at altitude the plane rode smooth as a Cadillac on a showroom floor. This late at night he was given a box containing a tuna sandwich, a package of cookies, and some grapes. He ate it all, and was grateful. By the window was an old man wearing an overcoat and a fedora.

"All those lights down there," the old man said, gesturing toward the window. "All those little towns, little lives. Makes you wonder, huh?"

"About what?" Meers said.

"You don't feel a part of the world when you're up here," the man said, "Those people down there, going about their lives. Us up here, disconnected. They look up, see a few flashing lights. That's us."

Meers had no idea what the codger was getting at, but he nodded.

"Used to be the same feeling, in my day. Trains back then. Night trains. When you're traveling, you're out of your life. Going from somewhere to somewhere else, not really knowing where you are. You could lie there in your berth and look out the window at the night. Moonlight, starlight. Hear the crossing signals as you passed them, see the trucks waiting. Who was driving them? More lost souls." He fell silent, looking out at the lights below. Meers hoped that was the end of it.

"I always wear a hat now," the old man went on. "Had a little haberdasher shop in Oklahoma City, opened it right after the war. Not far from where that building blew up. Got into the haberdashery business just in time for men to stop wearing hats." He chuckled. "One day it's nineteen forty-nine, everybody wears hats. Then it's nineteen fifty, suddenly all the hats are gone. Some say it was Eisenhower. Ike didn't wear hats much. Well, I did okay. Sold a lot of cuff links. Men's hosiery, silk handkerchiefs. Now I travel. Mostly at night."

Meers smiled pleasantly and nodded.

"You ever feel that way? Cut off? Trapped in something you don't understand?" He didn't give Meers time to answer.

"I recall the first time I thought of it. Got my discharge in New Jersey, nineteen and forty-six. I took the train under the river. Came out where that World Trade Center is now. Say, they bombed that, too, didn't they? Anyway, I thought I'd see Times Square. I went to the subway token booth. Not much bigger than a phone booth, and there's this little . . . gnome in there. Dirty window, bars in front, a dip in the wooden counter so money could slide under the window, back and forth, money in, tokens out. It looked like that dip had been worn in the wood. Over the years, over the centuries. Like a glacier cutting through solid rock. I slid over my nickel and he slid back a token, and I asked him how to get to Times Square. He mumbled something. I had to ask him to repeat it, and he mumbled again. This time I got it, and I took my token. All that time he never looked at me, never looked up from that worn dip in the wood. I watched him for a while, and he never looked up. He answered more questions, and I thought he probably knew the route and schedule of every train in that system, where to get off, where to transfer.

"And I got the funniest thought. I was convinced he never left that booth. That he was a prisoner in there, a creature of the night, a troll down in the underground darkness where it was never daytime. That he'd long ago resigned himself to his lot, which was to sell tokens." The old man fell quiet, looking out the window and nodding to himself.

"Well," Meers said, reluctantly. "The night shift comes to an end, you know."

"It does?"

"Sure. The sun comes up. Somebody comes to relieve the guy. He goes home to his wife and children."

"Used to, maybe," the old man said. "Used to. Now he's trapped. Something happened—I don't know what—and he came loose from our world where the sun eventually does come up. But does it have to?"

"Well, of course it does."

"Does it? Seems to me it's been a long time since I've seen the sun. Seems I've been on this airplane ever so long, and I have no way of telling that it's actually getting anywhere. Maybe it isn't. Maybe the plane will never land, it'll just keep on its way from somewhere to somewhere else. Just like that train, a long time ago."

Meers didn't like the conversation. He was about to say something to the old man when he was touched lightly on the shoulder. He looked up to see a stewardess leaning toward him.

"Sir, the Captain would like to speak to you in the cockpit."

For a moment the words simply didn't register. Captain? Cockpit?

"Sir, if you'd just come this way . . . ?"

Meers got up, glanced at the old man, who smiled and waved.

At first he could see little in the darkened cockpit. In front of the plane was clear night, stars, the twinkling lights of small towns. Then he saw the empty flight engineer's seat to his right. As he moved forward, he kicked empty cans. The cabin smelled of beer and cigar smoke. The captain turned around and gestured.

"Clear the crap off that and siddown," he said, around the cigar clamped in his teeth. Meers moved a pizza box with stale crusts off the copilot's chair, and slid into it. The pilot unfastened his harness and got up.

"If I don't take a crap in thirty seconds, I'm gonna do it in my drawers," he said, and started toward the rear. "Just hold 'er steady."

"Hey! Wait a goddamn minute!"

"You got a problem with that?"

"Problem? I don't know how to fly an airplane!"

"What's to know?" The pilot was dancing up and down, but pointed to the instruments. "That's your compass. Keep her right where she is, three one zero. This here's your altimeter. Thirty-two thousand feet."

"But don't you have an autopilot?"

"Packed it in, weeks ago," the pilot muttered, and banged hard with his fist on an area with dials that weren't lit up. "Bastard. Look, I really gotta go."

And Meers was alone in the cockpit.

He had a wild notion to just get up, pretend this never happened. Return to his seat. Surely the pilot would come back. It had to be some sort of joke.

The plane seemed level and steady. He touched the column lightly, felt the plane nose down the tiniest bit, saw the altimeter move slowly. He pulled and the big bird settled back at thirty-two thousand.

He quickly learned the biggest problem a pilot faced on a long night flight: boredom. There was nothing to do but glance at the two dials from time to time. His mind wandered, back to what the old man had been saying. And it just didn't add up. Well, of course the plane was getting somewhere. He could see the lights moving beneath him. Those brighter lights at the horizon; could that be Denver? As for the sun not rising, that was just ridiculous. The world turned. One moment followed another. Eventually it was day.

The pilot came back in a cloud of cigar smoke. He reached into an open cooler near his seat and got out a can of beer, popped the top, and drained it into one gulp. He belched, crushed the can, and tossed it over his shoulder.

"Looks like I fucked up," he said, with no apparent concern. "Sent for the wrong guy. Sorry about that, pardner." He laughed.

"What do you mean?"

"Thought you was in the know. Looks like it was that old guy. Somebody wrote down the wrong seat number. Who's runnin' this fucking airline, anyway?"

Meers would have liked to know the same thing.

"Don't you have a copilot? What do you mean, 'in the know'?"

"Copilot had him a little accident. Night cops. They broke his fuckin' arm for him. He's in the hospital." The man shuddered. "Could be three, four months yet till he gets out."

"For a broken arm?"

The pilot gave him a tired look. He jerked his thumb back toward the cabin.

"Screw, why don'cha? Get outta here. You'll get it, one of these days."

Meers stared at him, then got up.

"He's dead, anyway," the pilot said.

"Who's dead?" The pilot ignored him.

Meers made his way down the aisle. The old man seemed asleep. His eyes were slightly open, and so was his mouth. Meers reached over and lightly touched the old man's hand. It was cold.

A big fly with a metallic blue back crawled out of the old man's nostril and stood there, rubbing its hideous forelegs together.

Meers was out of his seat like a shot. He hurried five rows

forward and collapsed into an empty seat. He was breathing hard. He couldn't work up any spit.

Later, he saw the stewardess put a blue blanket over the old man.

Denver. DEN. Tonight, it made Chicago seem like Bermuda. The sky was hard and fuming as dry ice, and the color of a hollow-point bullet. Temperature a few degrees below zero, but add in the wind chill and it was cold enough to freeze rubber to the runway.

The huge plate-glass windows rattled and bulged as Meers lurched down the concourse, his luggage caroming off his hips, ribs, and knees. A chill reached right through the floor and swept around his feet. He hurried into the men's room and set his bags down on the floor. He ran water in the sink and splashed it on his face. The room echoed with each drop of water.

He couldn't bear to look at himself in the mirror.

He had to find the airline ticket counter. Had to get his boarding pass. Needed to find the gate, board the plane, make his connection. He had to get home.

Something told him to get out. Leave everything. Go.

He walked quickly through the nearly deserted departure area, slammed through the doors and out onto the frozen sidewalk. He hurried to the front of a rank of taxis. It was an old yellow Checker, a big, boxy, friendly sort of car. He got in the back.

"Where to, Mac?"

"Downtown. A good hotel."

"You got it." The cab driver put his car in gear and carefully pulled out onto the packed snow and ice. Soon they were moving down the wide road away from the airport. Meers looked out the back window. The Denver airport was like a cubist prairie schooner, a big, horribly expensive tent to house modern transients.

"One ugly mother, ain't she?" the cabbie said.

Meers saw the cab driver in profile as the man looked in the rearview mirror. Bushy eyebrows under an old-fashioned yellow Checker Cab hat with a shiny black brim. A wide face, chin covered with stubble. Big hands on the wheel. The name on the cab medallion was v. KRZYWCZ. A New York medallion.

"Krizz-wozz," the man provided. "Virgil Krzywcz. Us Polacks, we sold all our vowels to the frogs. Now we use all the consonants the Russians didn't have no use for." He chuckled.

"Aren't you a little far from home?" Meers ventured.

"Let me tell you a little story," Krzywcz said. "Once upon a time, a thousand years ago for all I know, I was takin' this fare in from LaGuardia. To the Marriott, Times Square. I figure, that time of night, the Triborough, down the Roosevelt, there you are. But this guy'd looked at a map, it's gotta be the BQE, then the midtown tunnel. Okay, I sez, it's your money. And whattaya know, we make pretty good time. Only coming outta the tunnel what do I see? Not the Empire State, but the fuckin' bitch of a terminal building. I'm in Denver. I never been ta Denver. So I looks back over my shoulder," Krzywcz suited the action to his words, and Meers got a whiff of truly terrible breath, "and no tunnel, just a lotta cars honkin' at me, me bein' stopped in my tracks. And that's the way it's been ever since."

Krzywcz accelerated through a yellow light and up onto an icy freeway. Meers saw a green sign indicating DOWNTOWN. Straight ahead, just above the horizon, was a full moon. Traffic was light, not surprising since the roadway was frozen hard. It didn't bother the cabbie, and the old Checker was steady as a rock.

"So you decided to stay out here?" Meers asked.

"Decided didn't have nothin' to do with it. You figure I went on a bender, drove here in a blackout, something like that?" Krzywcz looked over his shoulder at Meers. In a sweep of streetlamp light Meers saw the left side of the driver's face was black and swollen. His left eye was shut. There was a long, scabbed-over wound on his cheek, a slash that had not been stitched. "Well, suit yourself. Fact is, none of these roads go to New York. And believe me, buddy, I've tried 'em all."

Meers didn't know what to make of that statement.

"What happened to your face?" he asked.

"This? Had a little run-in with the night cops. A headlight out, would you believe it? I got lucky. One whack upside the head and they let me go. Hell, I've had a lot worse. A lot worse."

Hadn't the pilot said something about night cops? They had sent his copilot to the hospital. Something was very wrong here.

"What do you mean, these roads don't go to New York? It's an Interstate highway. They all connect."

"You're trying to make sense," Krzywcz said. "You'd better learn to stop that."

"What are you trying to tell me?" Meers asked, feeling his frustration rise. "What's going on?"

"You mean, are we in the fuckin' Twilight Zone, or something?" Krzywcz looked at Meers again, then back to the road, shaking his head. "You got me, pal. I think we're in Denver, all right: Only it's like Denver is all twisted up, or something."

"We're in hell," a voice said over the radio.

"Aw, shut the fuck up, Moskowitz, you stupid kike."

"It's the only thing that makes sense," the voice of Moskowitz said.

"It don't make no damn sense to me," Krzywcz shouted into

his mike. " Look around you. You see any guys with pitchforks? Horns? You seen any burnin' pits fulla . . . fulla—"

"Brimstone?" Meers suggested.

"There you go. Brimstone." He gestured with the mike. "Moskowitz, my dispatcher," he explained to Meers. "You seen any lost souls screamin'?"

"I've heard plenty of screamin' souls over the radio," Moskowitz said. "I scream sometimes, myself. And I sure as shit am lost."

"Listen to him," Krzywcz said, with a chuckle. "I gotta listen to this shit every night."

"Why do ya think it's gotta be guys with horns?" Moskowitz went on. "That guy, that Dante, you think everything he said was right?"

"Moskowitz reads books," the cabby said over his shoulder.

"Why do you figure hell has to stay the same? You think they don't remodel? Look how many people there are today. Where they gonna put 'em? In the new suburbs, that's where. Hell useta have boats and horse wagons. Now it's got jet airplanes and cabs."

"And night cops, and hospitals, don't forget that."

"Shut your mouth, you dumb hunky!" Moskowitz shouted. "You know I don't want nobody to talk about that over my radio."

"Sorry, sorry." Krzywcz smirked over his shoulder and shrugged. *Hey, what can you do?* Meers smiled back weakly.

"It don't make sense any other way," Moskowitz went on. "My life is hell. Your life is hell. Everybody you get in that freakin' cab is livin' in hell. We died and gone to hell."

Krzywcz was furious again.

"Died, is it? You remember dyin'? Huh, Moskowitz? You sit in that stinking office livin' on pizza and 7-Up, nothin' happens for *months* in that shithole. You'd think you'd notice a thing like dyin'."

"Heart attack," Moskowitz shouted back. "I musta had a heart attack. And I floated outta my body, and they put me *here*. Right where I was before, only now it's *forever,* and now *I can't leave!* Either it's hell, or limbo."

"Aw, limbo up a rope. What's a Jew know about limbo? Or hell?" He switched off the radio, glanced again at Meers. "I think he means purgatory. You wanna know from hell, you ask a Catholic Polack. We know hell."

Meers had finally had enough.

"I think you're both crazy," he said, defiantly.

"Yeah," Krzywcz agreed. "We oughta be, we been here long enough." He studied Meers in his mirror. "But you don't know, buddy. I could tell soon as you got in my cab. You're one a those airplane pukes. Round and round ya go, schleppin' your Gucci suitcases, cost what I make in a month. In and out of airports, off planes, onto planes. Round and round, and you think things are still makin' sense. You still think tomorrow comes after today and all roads go everywhere. You think that 'cause the sun went down, it's gonna come up again. You think two plus two is always gonna equal three."

"Four," Meers said.

"Huh?"

"Two plus two equals four."

"Well, pal, two plus two, sometimes it equals you can't get there from here. Sometimes two plus two equals a kick in the balls and a nightstick upside the head and a tunnel that don't go to Manhattan no more. Don't ask me why 'cause I don't know. If this is hell, then I guess we was bad, right? But I'm not that bad a guy. I went to mass, I didn't commit no crimes. But here I am. I got no home but this cab. I eat outta drive-thru's and I piss in beer bottles. I slipped offa something somewheres, I fell outta the world where you could go home after your shift. I turned inta one of the night people, like you."

Meers was not going to protest that he wasn't one of the "night people," whatever they were. He was a little afraid of the mad cabbie. But he couldn't follow the logic of it, and that made him stubborn.

"So we're in a different world, that's what you're saying?"

"Naw, we're still inna world. We're right *here,* we've always been here, night people, only nobody don't notice us, that we're in a box. The hooker on the stroll, they think she goes home when the sun comes up, with her pimp in the purple Caddy. Only they don't never go home. The street they're on, it don't lead home. That lonely DJ you hear on the radio. The subway motorman, it's night there alla time. The guy drivin' the long-haul truck. Janitors. Night watchmen."

"All of them?"

"How do I know all of 'em? I'm gonna drive my cab inna office building, ask the cleaning crew? 'Hey, you stuck in purgatory, like me?' "

"Not me."

"Yeah, you airplane pukes. Most of us, we *know.* Oh, some of 'em, they gone bugfuck. Nothin' left of 'em but eyeballs like gopher holes. But you been here long enough, you stop thinkin' you're gonna find that tunnel back home, you know? Except you 'passengers.' Like they sez in the program. In . . ."

"Denial."

"In denial. You said it. Look ahead there."

Meers looked out the windshield and there it was, just below the yellow moon. The sprawling canopy of the Denver Airport, like some exotic, poison rain-forest caterpillar. He stared at it as the cab eased down an off-ramp.

"Always a full moon in Denver," Krzywcz cackled. "Makes it nice for the werewolves. And all roads lead to the airport, which is bad news for airplane pukes."

Meers threw open the cab door and spilled out onto the frozen roadway. He scrambled to his feet, hearing the shouts of the driver. He clambered up an embankment and onto the freeway, where he dodged six lanes of traffic and tumbled down the other side. There were a lot of closed businesses there, warehouses, car lots, and one that was open, a Circle-K market. He ran toward it, certain it would vanish like a mirage, but when he hit the door it was wonderfully prosaic and solid. Inside it was warm. Two clerks, a tall black youth and a teenage white girl, stood behind the counter.

He paced up and down the abbreviated aisles, hoping he looked like someone who belonged there. When he heard the door security buzzer, he picked up a box of cereal and pretended to study it.

He saw two police officers walk past the counter. They've come for me, he thought.

But the cops walked toward the back of the store. One opened the beer cooler, while the other took a box and loaded it with donuts.

Both officers passed within ten feet of him. One had two six-packs of Coors hooked in a black-gloved hand and he cradled a huge black weapon that had a shotgun bore but a fat round magazine like a tommy gun. The other wore two automatic pistols on her belt. She glanced at Meers, and gave him a smile both insolent and sexual. She wore bright red lipstick.

They strolled past the clerks, who were very busy with other things, things that puts their backs to the police officers. They went out the door. There was a moment of silence, then a huge explosion.

Meers saw a plate-glass window shatter. Beyond it, the male cop was firing his shotgun into the store as fast as he could pump it. His partner had a gun in each hand.

He hit the floor in a snowstorm of corn flakes and shredded toilet paper. Both cops were emptying their weapons, and they had a lot of ammunition. But finally it was over. In the silence, he heard the police laughing, then opening their car doors. He got to his knees and peeked over the ruined display counter.

The patrol car was backing out. He caught a glimpse of the woman drinking from a beer can as the cruiser pulled out on the road. In a second, a yellow Checker cab pulled into the lot, the battered face of Krzywcz behind the wheel. He saw Meers and motioned frantically.

Shattered glass and raisin bran crunched under his feet as Meers walked down the aisle. Behind the counter the black man was crouched down near the safe. The girl was lying on her back in a pool of blood, holding her gut and moaning. Meers hesitated, then Krzywcz leaned on the horn. He turned his back on the girl and pushed out through the aluminum door frame, empty now of glass.

Krzywcz took it slow and careful out of the lot. Parked off to the left was the police car, headlights turned off, facing them. Meers couldn't breathe, but Krzywcz turned the other way and the police car did not move.

"They'll be piggin' out on beer and sinkers for a while," the cabbie said.

"That girl . . . she—"

"She'll be all right." Krzywcz pointed ahead at flashing red lights. In a moment an ambulance rushed by in the other direction. He hunched down in his seat until it had gone by. "Eventually."

"What is it with the hospital?" Meers asked. "Moskowitz didn't even—"

"Hospitals is where you get hurt," Krzywcz said. "There's diseases in hospitals. Your wounds, they get infected. They give you the wrong pills, make you puke your guts up. All kinds of things can go wrong. Then you hear about the 'experiments.' " He shook his head. "Better to stay out. Them night doctors and night nurses, they ain't human."

Meers asked, but Krzywcz would say no more about "experiments."

The cab pulled up to the terminal building and Meers got out. He ran.

They fired at him, but he kept running. They chased him, but he was pretty sure now they had lost him. He was out on the runways. A fog had moved in; the terminal was no longer visible.

This was no place for a human being, even on a summer night. He kept moving, avoiding the lumbering, shrieking silver whales that taxied through the darkness. He stopped by a low, poisonous blue strobe light that drove cold icepicks into his eyeballs every time it flashed. He had no idea where he was, no idea where to go.

". . . help me . . ."

It was more whimper than word. It came from just beyond the range of the light.

". . . for the love of God . . ."

Something was crawling toward him. It moved slowly into the

light, a human figure pulling itself along with bloody hands. Meers fell back a step.

". . . please help me . . ."

It was Eduardo, from the O'Hare snack bar. His white shirt was a few blood-soaked scraps, black in the alien light. His pants were gone. One of his legs was gone, too. Torn off. Shattered white thighbone protruded.

Meers became aware of others. Like beasts hovering beyond the range of the campfire, figures were suggested by a blue-steel glint, a patch of pale cheek. They were darkened patches against the black of night. They wore fighter-pilot black visors, black helmets, Terminator sunglasses. Shiny black boots. Belts and jackets creaked like motorcycle cops. Somewhere out there were ranks of black Harleys, he was sure of it. He smelled gun oil and old leather.

There were other shapes, other beasts. These were black, too, with fangs snarling blue in the night. They strained at their leashes, silently.

Meers began to back away. If he didn't make a sudden movement they might not come after him. Perhaps they hadn't even seen him.

Soon the shapes were swallowed back into the fog. Not once had he seen a distinct human figure.

Something brushed against his leg. He did not look down, but kept backing. Dark areas on the ground, seen peripherally, resembled body parts. But they were moving.

He heard a distant siren, saw flashing red and blue lights. A boxy white ambulance pulled up, a big orange stripe on its side with the words EMERGENCY RESCUE. The rear doors flew open. The light inside was dim and reddish. The angle was wrong for Meers to see very far inside. A black cloud of flies exploded into the air. He could hear them buzzing. A thick, black fluid seeped over the floor and ran over the bumper to pool on the frozen ground, steaming. Meers understood that in white light the stuff would be dark and red.

From the far side of the ambulance men and women appeared, clad in crisp whites or baggy surgical blues. They all wore gauze masks. The masks, their rubber-gloved hands, and their clothing were all spattered with gore. None of them had horns or carried pitchforks. Their attitude was efficient and workmanlike.

The doctors and nurses lifted Eduardo and tossed him into the open ambulance doors like a sack of laundry. One nurse loomed out of the fog with Eduardo's leg. The leg was twitching. She tossed it after Eduardo.

Meers was going backward at a walking pace now. A man in

blue surgical scrubs looked in his direction. All the rest did, too. He turned and ran.

The world began to spin again, and this time it did not stop. He felt himself flying apart, and when he came back together, not everything fit in just the way it had before. He felt much better. He was smiling.

He had found the terminal building again. He stood there on the sidewalk for a moment, getting his breathing under control. A big man with a battered face stood leaning against a taxi painted bright yellow with a checkerboard stripe down the side. The man held up a thumb. When Meers stared at him blankly, the cabbie switched to his middle finger and muttered something about "airplane pukes." Meers brushed snow and ice from his overcoat and ran his hands through his unruly hair. He entered the terminal.

Inside were Christmas lights, tinsel and holly. It was jammed with a sea of humanity, few of them showing any Christmas spirit.

He glanced to his left, and there was his luggage, sitting neatly against the wall. Meers hefted his possessions. Someone had put a strip of silver duct tape over the gash in his carry-on.

Meers was still smiling after three hours in line. The harried ticket agent smiled back at him, and told him there was no chance of reaching his home that night.

"You won't get home for Christmas morning," she said, "but I can get you on a flight to Chicago that's leaving in a few minutes."

"That'll be fine," Meers said, smiling. She wrote out the ticket.

"Happy holidays," she said.

"And a Merry Christmas to you," Meers said.

They were already announcing his flight. ". . . to Chicago, with stops at Amarillo, Oklahoma City, Topeka, Omaha, Rapid City, Fargo, Duluth, and Des Moines."

Christmas, Meers thought. Everyone trying to go somewhere at once. Pity the poor business traveler caught in the middle of it. Puddle-jumping through most of the medium-sized cities on the Great Plains. It sounded like air-travel hell. But he took heart. Soon he would be home with his family. Home with his sweet wife . . . and his lovely children . . . he was sure he'd think of their names in a moment.

He shouldered his burdens like Marley's Ghost shouldered the chains he had forged in life, and shuffled along with the slow crowd toward his boarding gate. He would be home in no time. No time at all.

As in Creatures of Light and Darkness, *William Sanders's tale demonstrates the power that the ancient Egyptian gods still hold for us, long past the days when their kingdoms became dust.*

■

NINEKILLER AND THE NETERW
William Sanders

JESSE NINEKILLER WAS FIVE THOUSAND FEET ABOVE THE EGYPTIAN desert when his grandfather spoke to him. He was startled but not absolutely astonished, even though his grandfather had been dead for almost thirty years. This wasn't the first time this had happened.

The first time had been way back in '72, near Cu Chi, where a brand-new Warrant Officer Ninekiller had been about to put a not-so-new Bell HU-1 into its descent toward a seemingly quiet landing zone. He had just begun to apply downward pressure on the collective pitch stick when the voice had sounded in his ear, cutting clear through the engine racket and the heavy *wop-wop-wop* of the rotor:

"Jagasesdesdi, sgilisi! You don't want to go down there right now."

Actually it was only later, thinking back, that Jesse recalled the words and put them together. It was a few seconds before he even realized it had been Grandfather's voice. At the moment it was simply the shock of hearing a voice inside his helmet speaking Oklahoma Cherokee that froze his hands on the controls. But that was enough; by the time he got unstuck and resumed the descent, the other three Hueys in the flight were already dropping rapidly

earthward, leaving Jesse well above and behind, clumsy with embarrassment and manhandling the Huey like a first-week trainee as
he struggled to catch up. Badly shaken, too; he didn't think he'd
been in Nam long enough to be hearing voices. . . .

Then the tree line at the edge of the LZ exploded with gunfire
and the first two Hueys went up in great balls of orange flame
and the third flopped sideways into the ground like a huge dying
hummingbird, and only Jesse, still out of range of the worst of the
metal, was able to haul his ship clear. And all the way back to
base the copilot kept asking, "How did you know, man? How did
you *know?*"

That was the first time, and the only time for a good many
years; and eventually Jesse convinced himself it had all been his
imagination. But then there came a day when Jesse, now flying
for an offshore oil outfit out of east Texas, got into a lively after-
nooner with a red-headed woman at her home on the outskirts of
Corpus Christi; and finally she got up and headed for the bathroom, and Jesse, after enjoying the sight of her naked white bottom
disappearing across the hall, decided what he needed now was a
little nap.

And had just dropped off into pleasantly exhausted sleep when
the voice woke him, sharp and urgent: "Wake up, *chooch!* Grab
your things and get out of there, *nula!*"

He sat up, blinking and confused. He was still blinking when he
heard the car pull into the driveway; but he got a lot less confused,
became highly alert in fact, when the redhead called from the bathroom, "That'll be my husband. Don't worry, he's cool."

Not buying that for a second, Jesse was already out of bed and
snatching up his scattered clothes. He sprinted ballocky-bare-assed
down the hall and out the back door and across the scrubby lawn,
while an angry shout behind him, followed by a metallic *clack-clack*
and then an unreasonably loud bang, indicated that the husband
wasn't being even a little bit cool. There were more bangs and
something popped past Jesse's head as he made it to his car,
and after he got back to his own place he discovered a couple of
neat holes, say about forty-five hundredths of an inch in diameter,
in the Camaro's right rear fender.

In the years that followed there were other incidents, not quite
so wild but just as intense. Like the time Grandfather's voice woke
him in the middle of the night in time to escape from a burning
hotel in Bangkok, or when it stopped him from going into a Beirut
café a couple of minutes before a Hezbollah bomb blew the place
to rubble. So even though Grandfather's little visitations never got

to be very frequent, when they did happen Jesse tended to pay attention.

As in the present instance, which bore an uneasy similarity to the first. The helicopter now was a Hughes 500D, smaller than the old Huey and a hell of a lot less work to drive, and Egypt definitely didn't look a bit like Nam, but it was still close enough to make the hairs on Jesse's neck come smartly to attention when that scratchy old voice in his ear (his left ear, for some reason it was always the left one) said, *"Ni, sgilisi!* This thing's about to quit on you."

Jesse's eyes dropped instantly to the row of warning lights at the top of the instrument panel, then to the dial gauges below. Transmission oil pressure and temperature, fuel level, battery temperature, engine and rotor rpm, turbine outlet temperature, engine oil pressure and temperature—there really were a hell of a lot of things that could go wrong with a helicopter, when you thought about it—everything seemed normal, all the little red and amber squares dark, all the needles where they were supposed to be. Overhead, the five-bladed rotor fluttered steadily, and there was no funny feedback from the controls.

Beside him, in the right seat, the man who called himself Bradley and who was supposed to be some kind of archaeologist said, "Something the matter?"

Jesse shrugged. Grandfather's voice said, "Screw him. Listen. Make about a quarter turn to the right. See that big brown rock outcrop, off yonder to the north, looks sort of like a fist? Take a line on that."

Jesse didn't hesitate, even though the lights and needles still swore there was nothing wrong. He pressed gently on the cyclic stick and toed the right tail-rotor pedal to bring the nose around. As the Hughes wheeled to the right the man called Bradley said sharply, "What do you think you're doing? No course changes till I say—"

Just like that, just as Jesse neutralized the controls to steady the Hughes on its new course, the engine stopped. There was no preliminary loss of power or change of sound: one second the Allison turbine was howling away back there and the next it wasn't. Just in case nobody had noticed, the red engine-out light began blinking, while the warning horn at the top of the instrument console burst into a pulsating, irritating hoot.

Immediately Jesse shoved the collective all the way down, letting the main rotor go into autorotation. Under his breath he said, "Damn, *eduda,* how come you always cut it so close?"

"What? What the hell?" Bradley sounded more pissed off than seriously scared. "What's happening, Ninekiller?"

Jesse didn't bother answering. He was watching the airspeed needle and easing back on the cyclic, slowing the Hughes to its optimum speed for maximum power-off gliding range. When the needle settled to eighty knots and the upper tach showed a safe 410 rotor rpm he exhaled, not loudly, and glanced at Bradley. "Hey," he said, and pointed one-fingered at the radio without taking his hand off the cyclic grip. "Call it in?"

"Negative." Bradley didn't hesitate. "No distress calls. Maintain radio silence."

Right, Jesse thought. And that flight plan we filed was bogus as a tribal election, too. Archaeologist my Native American ass.

But there was no time to waste thinking about spooky passengers. Jesse studied the desert floor, which was rising to meet them at a distressing rate. It looked pretty much like the rest of Egypt, which seemed to consist of miles and miles and *miles* of simple doodly-squat, covered with rocks and grayish-yellow sand. At least this part didn't have those big ripply dunes, which might look neat but would certainly make a forced landing almost unbearably fascinating.

"Get set," he told Bradley. "This might be a little rough."

For a minute there it seemed the warning had been unnecessary. Jesse made a school-perfect landing, flaring out at seventy-five feet with smooth aft pressure on the cyclic, leveling off at about twenty and bringing the collective back up to cushion the final descent. As the skids touched down he thought: *damn,* I'm good.

Then the left skid sank into a pocket of amazingly soft sand and the Hughes tilted irresistibly, not all the way onto its side but far enough for the still-moving rotor blades to beat themselves to death against the ground; and things did get a little rough.

When the lurching and slamming and banging finally stopped Bradley said, "Great landing, Ninekiller." He began undoing his safety harness. "Oh, well, any landing you can walk away from is a good one. Isn't that what you pilots say?"

Jesse, already out of his own harness and busy flipping switches off—there was no reason to do that now, but fixed habits were what kept you alive—thought of a couple of things one pilot would like to say. But he kept his mouth shut and waited while Bradley got the right door open, his own being jammed against the ground. They clambered out and stood for a moment looking at the Hughes and then at their surroundings.

"Walk away is what we get to do, I guess," Bradley observed. He took off his mesh-back cap and rubbed his head, which was bald except for a couple of patches around the ears. Maybe to compensate, he wore a bristly mustache that, combined with a snubby nose and big tombstone teeth, made him look a little like

Teddy Roosevelt. His skin was reddish-pink and looked as if it would burn easily. Jesse wondered how long he was going to last in the desert sun.

He climbed back into the Hughes—Jesse started to warn him about the risk of fire but decided what the hell—and rummaged around in back, emerging a few minutes later with a green nylon duffel bag, which he slung over his shoulder. "Well," he said, jumping down, "guess we better look at the map."

Grandfather's voice said, "Keep going the way you were. Few miles on, over that rise where the rock sticks out, there's water."

Jesse said, *"Wado, eduda,"* and then, as Bradley looked strangely at him, "Come on. This way."

Bradley snorted. "Long way from home, aren't you, to be pulling that Indian crap? I mean, it's not like you're an Arab." But then, when Jesse started walking away without looking back, "Oh, Christ, why not? Lead on, Tonto."

Grandfather's few miles turned out to be very long ones, and, despite the apparent flatness of the desert, uphill all the way. The ground was hard as concrete and littered with sharp rocks. Stretches of yielding sand slowed their feet and filled their shoes. It was almost three hours before they reached the stony crest of the rise and saw the place.

Or *a* place; it didn't look at all as Jesse had expected. Somehow he had pictured a movie-set oasis, a little island of green in the middle of this sandy nowhere, with palm trees and a pool of cool clear water. Maybe even some friendly Arabs, tents and camels and accommodating belly dancers . . . okay, he didn't really expect that last part, but surely there ought to be *something* besides more God-damned rocks and sand. Which, at first, was all he could see.

Bradley, however, let out a dry-lipped whistle. "How did you know, Ninekiller? Hate to admit it, but I'm impressed."

He started down the slope toward what had looked like a lot of crumbling rock formations and sand hillocks, but which Jesse now realized had too many straight lines and right angles to be natural. Ruined buildings, buried by sand? Jesse said, "Does this do us a lot of good? Looks like nobody lives here any more."

"Yeah, but there's only one reason anybody would build anything out here."

"Water?"

"Got to be." Bradley nodded. "This is a funny desert. Almost no rain at all, but the limestone bedrock holds water like a sponge. Quite a few wells scattered around, some of them pretty old."

"Maybe this one went dry," Jesse suggested. They were getting in among the ruins now, though it was hard to tell where they began. "Maybe that's why the people left."

"Could be. But hey, it's the best shot we've got." Bradley glanced back and grinned. "Right, guy?"

He stepped over what had to be the remains of a wall—not much, now, but a long low heap of loose stone blocks, worn almost round by sand and wind. The whole place appeared to be in about the same condition; Jesse saw nothing more substantial than a few knee-high fragments of standing masonry, and most of the ruins consisted merely of low humps in the sand that vaguely suggested the outlines of small buildings. These ruins were certainly, well, ruined.

But Bradley seemed fascinated; he continued to grin as they picked their way toward the center of the village or whatever it had been, and to look about him. Now he stopped and bent down. "Son of a bitch," he said, very softly, and whistled again, this time on a higher note. "Look at this, Ninekiller."

Jesse saw a big block of stone half buried in the sand at Bradley's feet. Looking more closely, he saw that the upturned surface was covered with faint, almost worn-away shapes and figures cut into the stone.

"Hieroglyphics," Bradley said. "My God, this place is Egyptian."

Egyptian, Jesse thought, well, of *course* it's Egyptian, you white asshole, this is *Egypt.* No, wait. "You mean ancient Egypt? Like with the pyramids?"

Bradley chuckled. "I doubt if these ruins are contemporaneous with the pyramids, guy. Though it's not impossible." He straightened up and gazed around at the ruins. "But yes, basically, those Egyptians. I'd hate to have to guess how old this site is. Anywhere from two to four thousand years, maybe more."

"Holy shit," Jesse said, genuinely awed. "What were they doing out here? I thought they hung out back along the Nile."

"Right. But there was a considerable trade with the Libyans for a long time. They had regular caravan routes across the desert. If there was a first-class well here, it would have been worth maintaining a small outpost to guard the place from marauding desert tribes."

He flashed the big front teeth again. "Kind of like Fort Apache, huh? Probably a detachment of Nubian mercenaries under Egyptian command, with a force of slaves for labor and housekeeping. They often sent prisoners of war to places like this. And, usually, worked them to death."

He took off his cap and wiped his sweaty scalp. "But we're

going to be mummies ourselves if we don't find some water. Let's
have a look around."

The well turned out to be square in the center of the ruined
village, a round black hole fifteen feet or so across and so deep
Jesse couldn't see if there was water at the bottom or not. Hell's
own job, he thought, sinking a shaft like that in limestone bedrock,
with hand tools and in this heat. He kicked a loose stone into the
well and was rewarded with a deep muffled splash.

"All *right*," Bradley said. "I've got a roll of nylon cord in my
bag, and a plastic bottle we can lower, so at least we're okay
for water."

Jesse was studying the ground. "Somebody's been here. Not too
long ago."

"Oh, shit," Bradley said crankily, "are you going to start with
that Indian routine again?" Then he said, *"Hah!"*

Next to the well, lying there in plain sight, was a cigarette butt.

"Should have known," Bradley said after a moment. "No doubt
the nomadic tribes and caravan guides know about this place.
Good thing, in fact, because the well would have filled up with
sand long ago if people hadn't kept it cleaned out."

"Bunch of tracks there." Jesse pointed. "These desert Arabs, do
they go in for wearing combat boots?"

"Could be." Bradley was starting to sound unhappy. "We better
check this out, though."

It didn't take an expert tracker to follow the trail away from the
well and through the ruined village. There had been a good deal
of booted traffic to and from the well, and the boot wearers had
been pretty messy, leaving more butts and other assorted litter
along the way. "Hasn't been long," Bradley said. "Tracks disappear fast in all this sand and wind. You're right, Ninekiller." He
stopped, looking uneasily around. By now they were at the western
edge of the ruins, where the ground began to turn upward in a
long rock-strewn slope. "Somebody's been here recently."

A few yards away, Jesse said, "Somebody's still here."

On the ground, in the sliver of black shade next to a low bit of
crumbling wall, lay a man. He was dressed in desert-camo military
fatigues, without insignia. A tan Arab headcloth had been pulled
down to cover his face. He wasn't moving and Jesse was pretty
sure he wasn't going to.

"Jesus," Bradley said.

The dead man wasn't a pleasant sight. There had been little
decomposition in the dry desert air, but the right leg was black and
enormously swollen. The camo pants had been slashed clear up to

the hip and what looked like a bootlace had been tied just above the knee. It hadn't helped.

"Snakebite," Bradley declared. "Sand viper, maybe. Or even a cobra."

"More tracks over here," Jesse reported. "Somebody was with him. Somebody didn't stick around."

The footprints climbed a little way up the slope and then ended. In their place was a very clear set of tire tracks—a Jeep, Jesse figured, or possibly a Land Rover—leading off across the slope and disappearing out into the desert. The driver had thrown a lot of gravel when he left. Lost his nerve, Jesse guessed. Found himself out here in the empty with no company but a dead man and at least one poisonous snake, and hauled ass.

A large camouflage net, lying loose on the ground beside the tire tracks as if tossed there in a hurry, raised interesting questions. Jesse was about to remark on this when he realized that Bradley was no longer standing beside him, but had moved on up the slope and was now looking at something else, something hidden by a pile of rocks and masonry fragments. "Come look," he called.

Jesse scrambled up to join him and saw another hole, this one about the size and proportions of an ordinary doorway. A rectangular shaft, very straight-sided and neatly cut, led downward into the ground at about a forty-five-degree angle. Some kind of mine? Then he remembered this was Egypt, and then he remembered that movie. "A tomb?" he asked Bradley. "Like where they put those mummies?"

"Might be." Bradley was scrabbling around in his duffel bag, looking excited. "It just might be—ah." He pulled out a big flashlight, the kind cops carry. "Watch your step, guy," he said, stepping into the hole. "You don't want to be the next snakebite fatality."

Bradley seemed to assume Jesse was coming along. That wasn't a very sound assumption; screwing around with any kind of grave was very high on the list of things Indians didn't do.

And yet, without knowing why, he climbed over the heap of scree and rubble and stepped down into the shaft after Bradley.

Bradley was standing halfway down the stone steps that formed the floor of the shaft. He was shining his flashlight here and there on the walls, which were covered with colored pictures. The paint was faded and flaking, but it was easy to make out lively scenes of people eating and paddling boats and playing musical instruments—some naked dancing girls in one panel, complete with very candid little black triangles where their legs joined—as well as other activities Jesse couldn't identify. Animals, too, cats and baboons, crocodiles and hippos and snakes; and, in among the pictures, lines of hieroglyphic writing.

There were also some extremely weird figures, human bodies with bird or animal heads. "What are they," Jesse asked, pointing, "spirits?"

"Gods," Bradley said. *"Neterw,* they were called. The one with the jackal head, for example, is Anubis, god of burials and the dead."

"This one's got a boner."

"Oh, yes. Ithyphallic figures weren't unusual." Bradley headed down the steps, swinging his flashlight. "But we can look at the art later. Let's see what we've got down here."

The shaft leveled off into a narrow passageway. The walls here were covered with murals too, but Bradley barely spared them a glance as he strode down the corridor. "Ah," he said as the hall suddenly opened into a larger and very dark space. "Now this is—oh, my God."

Behind him, Jesse couldn't see at first what Bradley was ohing his God about. He looked over Bradley's shoulder into a low-ceilinged chamber, about the size of a cheap motel room. The flashlight beam showed more paintings on the walls and ceiling. It also showed a stack of wooden boxes against the back wall.

Bradley crossed the room fast and began yanking at one of the boxes. The lid came off and thudded to the stone floor. "Shit!" Bradley cried, shining his light into the box. He reached in and hauled out what Jesse instantly recognized as an AK-47 assault rifle. Kalashnikov's products tend to make an indelible impression on anyone who has ever been shot at with them.

Bradley leaned the rifle against the wall and opened another box. This time it was a grenade he held up. "Bastards," he said, almost in a whisper.

Another corridor led off to the rear. Bradley charged down it, cursing to himself, and Jesse hurried after him, disinclined to wait alone in the dark. The corridor was a short one, ending in another room about the size of the first. It contained an even bigger stack of boxes and crates, piled to the ceiling. Some wore red DANGER—EXPLOSIVES markings in Arabic and English. There were also a number of plastic jerricans full of gasoline. No wonder they went outside to do their smoking, Jesse thought. What the hell was this all about?

Bradley ripped off the top of a cardboard box. "Great," he said sourly, and pulled out a small oblong packet. "U.S. Army field rations. Good old Meals, Ready to Eat. Possibly the most lethal item down here. Wonder where they got them?"

He flashed the light around the room. This chamber was fancier than the other one. Somebody had even painted fake columns along the walls.

"Bastards," he said again. "A priceless treasure of art and knowledge, and they used it for a God-damned terrorist supply dump."

"What do you suppose they did with the mummy?" Jesse asked, thinking about those stories about the mummy's curse. And that snake-bit guy lying outside.

"Oh, that was probably disposed of centuries ago, along with any portable valuables. Tomb robbing is a very ancient tradition in this country." Bradley made a disgusted sound in his throat. "Here." He tossed the MRE packet to Jesse and fished out another. "We better do lunch. We've got a burial detail waiting for us, and I don't think we'll have much appetite afterwards."

They buried the dead man in a shallow grave, using a couple of shovels that they found in the outer chamber of the tomb, piling rocks on top. "Rest in peace," Bradley said. "You poor evil little son of a bitch." He wiped his forehead with his hand. The heat was incredible. "Let's get out of this sun," he said. "Back to the tomb."

Back in the outer chamber, he tossed his shovel into a corner and sat down on a crate. He took off his cap and hoisted the water bottle and poured the contents over his head. "Needed that," he said. "I'll go get a refill in a minute."

"Don't bother," Jesse told him. "There's a big plastic jug of water over here, nearly full." He was poking around in a clutter of odds and ends by the front wall. "You can save your flashlight, too." He picked up a big battery lantern and switched it on.

"Sons of bitches made themselves at home, didn't they?" Bradley clicked his flashlight off. "Ninekiller, I'm about to commit a major breach of security. But the situation's pretty unusual, and there's no way to keep you out of it, so you'd better know the score."

He leaned back against the wall, his head resting just beneath a painting of an archer taking aim from a horse-drawn chariot. "Does the name Nolan mean anything to you?"

"Isn't he the American . . . renegade, I guess you'd say, supposed to be working for the Libyans? Running some kind of commando operation?" Jesse sat down on the floor next to the entrance. "I heard a few rumors, nothing solid. They say he's hiring pilots."

"Yes. Quite a few Americans are working for Gadhafi now," Bradley said, "fliers mostly, young soldier-of-fortune types gone bad. But Nolan is an entirely different, higher-level breed of turncoat. It's not easy to impress people in this part of the world when it comes to terrorism, sabotage, and assassination, but Nolan is right up there with the best native talent. The Colonel values his services very highly."

A circuit closed in Jesse's head. "So that's what this business was all about. Archaeology hell, you were hunting Nolan."

"A preliminary reconnaissance," Bradley said. "Word was he had something going on in this area. You wouldn't have been involved in any real action."

"Nice to know this was such a safe job," Jesse said dryly. "Why not just let the Egyptians do it?" Another realization hit him. "That's right, I remember what I heard. Nolan's a rogue CIA officer, isn't he? You guys want him out of the way without any international embarrassment."

"That, of course, I couldn't tell you," Bradley said calmly. "Your need to know extends only to the immediate situation."

He picked up one of the AK-47s from the open box. "Sooner or later, somebody is going to show up here. Too much to hope that it'll be Nolan himself, but at least it'll be somebody from his outfit. If the odds aren't too bad, and we make the right moves, we'll have a handle on Nolan *and* a ride out of here." He hefted the AK-47. "Know how to use one of these?"

"The hell," Jesse said angrily. "I'm a pilot, not a gunfighter. Do your own bushwhacking. You're the one who works for the CIA."

"Oh? Who do you think owns Mideast Air Charter and Transfer Services?" Bradley paused, letting that sink in. "You're a pilot? Okay, I'm an archaeologist. No shit," he said, and glanced around the tomb chamber. "Got my degree from the University of Pennsylvania, did my field work over at Wadi Gharbi. That's where they recruited me . . . and there was a time I'd have given a leg and a nut to find something like this. Well, as it turns out, I've made myself a valuable discovery of a different kind."

He looked at Jesse. The Teddy Roosevelt grin didn't even try to make it to his eyes. "But you're welcome to sit on your ass and play conscientious objector while I take the bastards on alone. Then if they kill me you can tell them all about what an innocent bystander you are. I'm sure they'll believe you."

"Son of a bitch."

"So I've been told." He got up and walked over and held out the AK-47. "Take it, Ninekiller. It's the only way either of us is going to get out of this place alive. Or even dead."

Bradley insisted they maintain a constant watch, taking turns up at the crest of the rise, hunkering in the inadequate shade of the fist-shaped rock outcrop and staring out over the empty desert. "Have to, guy," he said. "Can't risk getting caught down in that tomb when the bad guys arrive."

When the sun finally went down, in the usual excessively spectacular style of tropical sunsets, Jesse assumed they'd drop the sentry-duty nonsense for the night. Bradley, however, was unyielding. "Remember who these people are," he pointed out, "and what they're up to. Moving by night would make good sense."

He thumbed his watch, turning on the little face light. It was getting really dark now. "I'll go below and catch a few Zs, let you take the evening watch. You wake me up at midnight and I'll take over for the graveyard shift. That okay with you, guy?"

Jesse didn't argue. He hardly ever turned in before midnight anyway. Besides, he didn't mind spending a few hours away from Bradley and the God-damned tomb. Both were starting to get on his nerves.

Alone, he slung the AK-47 over his shoulder and walked up the slope, taking his time and enjoying the cool breeze. It wasn't so bad now the sun was down. The stars were huge and white and a fat half-moon was climbing into the black sky. In the silvery soft light the desert looked almost pretty.

A dry voice in his left ear said, " 'Siyo, chooch."

Jesse groaned. " 'Siyo, eduda. What's about to happen now?"

There was a dusty chuckle. "Don't worry, chooch. No warnings this time. Turn around—and keep your hands off that war gun."

Jesse turned. And found himself face to face with Wile E. Coyote.

That was who it looked like at first, anyway: the same long pointy muzzle, the same big bat ears and goofy little eyes. But that was just the head; from the neck down, Jesse saw now, the body was that of a man about his own size.

Jesse said, "Uh."

Grandfather's voice said, "This is Anpu. Anpu, my grandson Jesse."

"Hi," Coyote said.

That's it, Jesse thought dazedly. Too much time out in the sun today, God *damn* that Bradley. Talking coyotes—no, hell, no coyotes in Egypt, must be a jackal. Sure looks like a coyote, though. Then memory kicked in and Jesse said, "Anubis. You're Anubis."

"Anpu." The jackal ears twitched. "The Greeks screwed the name up."

"Anpu wants you to meet some friends of his," Grandfather said.

"This way," Anpu said. "The way you were going, actually."

He walked past Jesse and headed up the slope, not looking back. Grandfather's voice said, "Don't just stand there, chooch. Follow him."

"I don't know, *eduda,*" Jesse said as he started after the jackal-headed figure. "This is getting too weird. How did you get hooked up with this character?"

"He's the god of the dead, in these parts. And, in case you've forgotten," Grandfather pointed out, "I'm dead."

Anpu was standing at the base of the fist-shaped rock outcrop. "Here," he said, pointing.

Jesse saw nothing but a big cleft in the rock, black in the moonlight. He'd seen it dozens of times during the day. "So?" he said, a little irritably.

Anpu stepped into the cleft and disappeared, feet first. His head popped back out long enough to say, "Watch your step. It's pretty tricky."

Jesse bent and stuck his arm down into the crack. His fingers found an oval shaft, just big enough for a man's body, angling steeply down into the rock. It was so well camouflaged that even now he knew it was there, he couldn't really see it.

"It's all right, *chooch,*" Grandfather said. "Go on."

Jesse stuck a cautious foot into the hole. There were notches cut into the wall of the shaft for footholds, but they weren't very deep. Gritting his teeth, he let himself down into the darkness.

He couldn't tell how far down the shaft went, but the absolute blackness and the scariness of the climb made it feel endless. The rock seemed to press in on him from all sides; he gasped for breath, and might have quit except that going back up would be just as bad. The tunnel bent to one side and then there was nothing under his feet. He probed with one toe, lost his grip, and plummeted helplessly out of the shaft and into open space. Off balance, he hit cross-footed and fell on his ass onto very hard flat stone.

He opened his eyes—he didn't know when he'd closed them—and saw immediately that he was in another tomb. Or another underground chamber, anyway, complete with artwork on the walls and ceiling. This one was filled with a soft, slightly yellowish light; he couldn't see the source.

Anpu was standing over him, reaching down a hand. "Are you all right?" the jackal-headed god asked anxiously. "I should have warned you about that last bit. Sorry."

Jesse took the hand and pulled himself to his feet. Suddenly a tall, beautiful woman in a flowing white dress came rushing up, shoving Anpu out of the way and putting her arms around Jesse's neck. "Oh, poor man," she cried, pulling Jesse's head down and pressing his face against her bosom. It was one *hell* of a bosom. "Did you hurt yourself? Do you want to lie down?"

"This is Hathor," Anpu said. His voice sounded muffled; Jesse's ears were wonderfully obstructed for the moment.

"Goddess of love and motherhood," Grandfather's voice said. "Get loose, *chooch,* there's others to meet. Later for the hot stuff."

Jesse managed to mumble something reassuring and Hathor reluctantly let him go. As she stepped back he realized she had horns. Not just little ones, either, like the ones on the Devil in the old pictures. These were big, curving horns like a buffalo's, white as ivory and tipped with little gold balls.

A deeper voice said, "Nasty bit of work, that access tunnel. We don't like it either. But the main entrance shaft is sealed, and buried by sand as well."

The speaker was another animal-faced figure, this one with the head of a shaggy gray baboon atop a short, skinny human body. He looked a little like Jesse's high school principal. "I am Thoth," he added.

"God of wisdom and knowledge," Grandfather explained in Jesse's left ear.

"And this," Anpu said, waving a hand at a fourth individual, "is Sobek."

Jesse would just as soon have missed meeting Sobek. From the shoulders down he looked like a normal man—though built like a pro wrestler—but above that grinned the head of a crocodile. The long jaws opened, revealing rows of sharp teeth, and a voice like rusty iron said, "Yo."

"I still don't get what he does," Grandfather admitted. "Got a feeling I don't want to know."

"Sorry we can't offer refreshments," Anpu apologized. "We didn't come prepared for social occasions."

"Excuse me," Jesse said, "but where did you all learn English?"

"Your grandfather taught us," Thoth replied. "This afternoon, in fact."

"That fast?" Talk about quick studies.

"Of course," Thoth said stiffly. "Simple brain-scan. I mean, we *are* gods."

"Yeah," Grandfather's voice said, "but I tried first to teach them Cherokee and they couldn't get it worth a damn."

Jesse looked around the chamber. It was larger than the ones the Arabs had been using, and finer. The ceiling was cut in an arching vault shape, and the pictures on the wall had been carved in low relief as well as painted. "Nice place," he remarked politely. "Somebody loot this one too? I don't see any mummies."

"As a matter of fact," Thoth said, "this tomb was never used. It was built for the last commander of this outpost, a nobleman named Neferhotep—"

"He screwed up bad back in Thebes," Sobek croaked, "and Pharaoh sent him to this shit-hole."

"—who was killed," Thoth went on, glaring at Sobek, "in a clash with Libyan raiders. His body was never recovered. Soon afterward the outpost was abandoned."

"So what are you, uh, gods doing here now?" Jesse was trying not to stare at Hathor. That gown was so thin you could see right through it, and she wasn't wearing a damn thing underneath. For that matter none of the *neterw* had exactly overdressed; the others wore only short skirts and assorted jewelry.

"A mistake," Anpu said. "Strange business. You see, the dead man, the one you buried today, happened to be a very distant but direct descendant of the Pharaoh Ramses the Great. Though of course it's unlikely he knew it."

"The death of one of royal blood," Thoth said, "so near an unused tomb, somehow resulted in a false reading in the House of the Dead."

"Osiris stepped on his dick," Sobek growled. "Old Green-Face is losing it."

"Even Osiris," Anpu protested, "could hardly have predicted such an improbable coincidence."

"Oh, I don't know." Thoth looked thoughtful. "Perhaps not such a farfetched chance as it might seem—"

He produced a polished wooden box, bound in gold, about the size and shape of an attaché case. Sitting cross-legged on the floor, he flipped a jeweled catch and the box opened into two sections. The lower half, which rested flat on his lap, contained a long ebony panel with rows of carved ivory pegs. The upper section was entirely filled by a smooth rectangle of some dark crystalline stone. Thoth tapped his fingertips over the pegs and a row of hieroglyphics appeared on the surface of the crystal, glowing with a faint greenish light.

"Let's see," Thoth mused. "Ramses the Second lived thirty-two centuries ago. He had over one hundred known offspring by his various wives. Now assuming an average number of progeny—"

"At any rate," Hathor sighed, "the four of us were sent, and here we are." She gave Jesse a smile that would have given the Sphinx an erection. "Well, perhaps things could be worse."

"—and a conservative estimate of three point five generations per century—" Thoth's fingers were dancing on the pegs. The crystal was covered with hieroglyphics.

"But," Jesse said, "if it was all a mistake, why are you still here?"

"—allowing a reasonable factor for infertility and infant mortality—"

Anpu shrugged. "Come on. I'll show you."

He led the way to an arched doorway at the rear of the chamber. Hathor and Sobek followed behind Jesse. As they left the room Thoth was staring at the crystal and scratching his head with one finger. "That can't be right," he muttered.

"At the rear of this tomb," Anpu explained as they made their way down a long hallway, "is what you might call a portal. Every burial center in Egypt has at least one. It's—" He stopped and looked back at Jesse. "I can't really explain it to you. It's a place where we can pass back and forth between this world and ours. Mortals can't even see it, let alone penetrate it."

"Except when they die," Hathor added, "and we come and get them."

"Which hasn't happened for a long time," Anpu said, nodding. "It's been almost two thousand of your years since anyone was interred with the necessary procedures. We were really disappointed to find out this was a false alarm. We had hoped the people were returning to the old ways."

He turned and started walking again. Only a few paces along the corridor, he stopped again. "There," he said. "You see the problem."

A huge slab of stone, apparently fallen from the ceiling, totally blocked the passageway. It was as big as a U-Haul trailer.

"It happened just after we arrived," Anpu said. "Evidently, when the other man drove away, the vibration caused the fall. Of course it must have been badly cracked already."

"And now you can't get back? To—wherever you came from?"

Anpu shook his head. "The nearest other portals are off in the Nile valley. I'm not sure we could make the journey." He looked at the great stone slab and his ears drooped a little. "But we may have to try."

"Never," Hathor declared. "That sun, that wind. My skin. No."

Jesse noticed a strange, impractical-looking contrivance lying on the floor, an assemblage of improvised ropes and levers. He recognized a couple of machine-gun barrels, and twisted-together rifle slings. He said, "What's this?"

"Something Anpu invented," Sobek grunted. "He calls it an *akh-me*. Doesn't work for shit."

"It seemed worth a try." Anpu kicked dispiritedly at the device. He looked at Jesse. "Can you help us? Your grandfather says you know about machinery."

Jesse studied the barrier. "I don't know. It's not in my usual line—" He felt Hathor's eyes upon him. "Maybe," he said. "I'll think about it. Let me sleep on it."

They went back up the corridor. As they entered the burial chamber Thoth looked up. "It's right here, I tell you." He touched a fingertip to the glowing crystal. "There's no arguing with the numbers. Everyone in the world is a descendant of Ramses the Second."

*   *   *

At midnight Jesse walked back down to the other tomb to wake Bradley. Anpu walked with him, for no apparent reason but sociability. Halfway down the slope they met Bradley coming the other way, lugging his rifle. "Hey, guy," he said cheerfully. "Get some sleep, now. I'll wake you at daybreak."

He went on up toward the big rock. Anpu chuckled. "Your friend can't see me. Not if I don't want him to, anyway."

"He's not my friend," Jesse said, more emphatically than he meant to.

Anpu looked curiously around as they entered the tomb. "I haven't really taken the time to look at the other tombs around here," he remarked as Jesse switched on the battery lantern. "This one isn't bad, actually."

Jesse leaned his AK-47 against the wall by the door. "Other tombs?"

"Oh, yes. Quite a few nearby—all sealed and hidden, of course. You'd never find them if you didn't know where to look."

He leaned forward, examining a hieroglyphic inscription on the wall. Jesse said, "What's that say, anyway?"

Anpu tilted his head to one side. "A free translation," he said after a moment, "might be: 'There once was a goddess named Isis, whose breasts were of different sizes. One was dainty and small, almost no breast at all, but the other was huge and won prizes.' "

"Get out of here."

"All right," Anpu said. "Have a pleasant night, Jesse."

When he was gone Jesse looked around briefly and then picked up the battery lantern and went down the corridor to the rear chamber. The air felt cooler there and the floor was cleaner. He took a gray military blanket from a stack in one corner and made himself a pallet on the floor, rolling up another blanket for a pillow. Lying down and switching off the lantern, he wondered if he would be able to sleep in this place; but he did, almost immediately, and without dreams.

When he awoke—he didn't know how long he had been asleep; later, he thought it couldn't have been long—it was with the distinct feeling that he was no longer alone in the burial chamber. That might have been because somebody was trying to take his clothes off.

He said, "Wha," and fumbled for the battery lantern and switched it on.

Hathor was crouching over him, tugging at the waistband of his pants. "You must help me," she said urgently. "I don't understand these strange garments."

Jesse blinked and shook his head. "Well, that is, ah—"

"Don't worry, *chooch*," said the voice in his left ear. "She's not out to steal your soul or anything like that. She just wants to get laid. It's been a long time since she did it with anybody who wasn't at least a couple thousand years old."

Hathor was now yanking his shoes off. Jesse skinned his sweaty T-shirt up over his head and reached to undo his belt buckle. Grandfather's voice said, "I'll leave you two alone now."

As Jesse got rid of his briefs—wishing he'd worn a better pair—Hathor rose to her feet and undid a clasp at her shoulder, letting the white gown fall away, leaving her naked except for wide gold bracelets on her wrists. "I shall give you love," she announced. "I shall serve you a feast of divine pleasure."

Throbbingly ithyphallic, Jesse watched as she put a foot on either side of him. The horns, he decided, weren't so bad once you got over the first shock of seeing them. In fact they were kind of sexy.

She knelt, straddling him. "Yes," she said, bending forward, mashing those astonishing breasts against his chest, "impale me with the burning spear of your desire." Clasping with arms and thighs, she rolled onto her back, pulling him on top of her, heels spurring him. "Oh, fill my loins with your mighty obelisk," she cried, "come into me with the Nile of your passion. Do me like a hot baboon, big boy!"

Well, Jesse thought, you always did like horny women with big ones. . . .

He awoke again to disturbing dreams of Vietnam; sounds of gunfire and rotors rattled in his ears. The room was still dark but his watch showed almost eight o'clock. Hastily he dressed, pausing as he felt the bracelet on his right wrist. Hathor's. She must have put it there as he slept. Memories of the night came rushing back, and he stood for a moment grinning foolishly to himself.

Then he heard it again, faint but unmistakeable: a rapid snapping, like popcorn in a microwave.

He jerked his shoes on, not bothering with socks, and ran down the corridor to the front chamber. He was halfway across the room, going for the gun he had left there, when a man appeared in the doorway: no more than a vague dark shape in the poor light that came down the entrance corridor, but Jesse knew immediately that it wasn't Bradley. He saw a dull glint that had to be a gun barrel.

Without hesitation he threw his arms in the air as high as they would go. "Don't shoot!" he yelled, wishing he knew how to say it in Arabic. "See? No gun. *Salaam aleykum,*" he added somewhat desperately. "Friendly Indian. Okay?"

The gun swung his way and his insides went loose. But either the man got the idea or, more likely, he realized it wasn't a good idea to fire shots inside a room full of munitions. A harsh voice hawked up several syllables in what sounded like Arabic, and then, in a loud shout, *"No-lan! No-lan!"*

An answering shout came from outside. The man jerked his weapon at Jesse and said, *"Yalla.* You come. Quick."

He backed slowly up the corridor, keeping Jesse covered. Jesse followed, hands still in the air, sphincter clenched. The sunlight blinded him as he reached the foot of the stone steps and he stumbled, and was yelled at. At the top of the steps the gunman said, "Stop."

Jesse stopped, blinking against the glare, trying to focus on the three backlit figures standing before him. A big booming voice, American by accent and cadence, said, "Well, what have we got here? Speak English, fella?"

Jesse thought about replying in Cherokee, just to confuse matters, but he didn't think that would do any good. He nodded. "Sure."

He could see all right now. The man who had found him stood four or five feet away, a dark, skinny little bastard dressed in desert camo, like the snakebite victim they had buried yesterday. A face that was mostly nose and bad teeth stared unpleasantly at Jesse from the shade of a sand-tan headcloth. To his left stood another who was virtually his twin in build, ugliness, and attitude. Both men held AK-47s, pointed at Jesse's belt buckle.

It was the third man, the one who had just spoken, who got and held Jesse's attention. He wore the same unmarked camo-and-headcloth outfit as the others, but if he was an Arab Jesse was Princess Leia. He was taller than Jesse, six feet at least, with broad shoulders and a big beefy face. A rifle dangled casually from his right hand.

"Nolan," Jesse said without thinking.

The big man fixed him with bright blue eyes. "Do we know each other?"

"Everybody's heard of you." Shovel a little, never hurts. "All the pilots around this part of the world, anyway."

"Pilots? Ah." Nolan nodded. "You'll be the one who piled up that Hughes, down yonder beyond the ridge."

Before Jesse could reply a fourth man came down the slope, feet sliding in the loose rocks and sand. "Hey, Nolan," he began, and then stopped, seeing Jesse. "What the hell?" he said. "Who's this?"

"One of your professional colleagues," Nolan told him. "Apparently he was flying that Hughes."

The new arrival was about Jesse's height and rather slight of build, with small sharp pretty-boy features. He wore light-blue coveralls and a baseball cap. His hands were empty but a shoulder-holstered pistol bulged beneath his left armpit.

"No shit?" The accent was Southern. "How'd you do that, man?"

"Engine failure," Jesse said.

Looking past the Southerner, Jesse saw that there was another helicopter sitting on the ground on the far right side of the rise. He could just see the tail and part of the main rotor. It looked like a French Alouette but he wasn't sure.

What he couldn't see, anywhere, was Bradley. That might be good. Probably it wasn't.

Nolan said, "Well, I wish you'd had it somewhere else. That wreck is liable to draw all sorts of attention. Can't believe it hasn't been spotted already." He gave Jesse a speculative look. "Just what were you doing around here, anyway?"

Jesse shrugged. "Flying this guy around." Play it dumb, that shouldn't be much of a reach. "He said he was an archaeologist."

The pilot, if that was what he was, laughed. Nolan grimaced. "Maybe he should have been. He wasn't worth a damn at what he was trying to do."

"Is he all right?" Jesse asked innocently.

"Not so you'd notice," the pilot said. "In fact he's pretty damn dead."

"He tried to ambush us," Nolan told Jesse. "It was a stupid business. The odds were impossible and he didn't have a clue what he was doing."

Jesse felt sick. He hadn't liked Bradley but still . . . why hadn't the damn fool called him when he saw the helicopter coming? Maybe he had. Maybe he hadn't realized how little Jesse could hear, down in that tomb. Or maybe he'd just decided he was John Wayne.

One of the gunmen said something in Arabic. Nolan said, "He wants to know if you buried the man who was here."

Jesse nodded. "We didn't kill him. Looked like a snake got him."

"We know," Nolan said. "It's why we're here. That worthless punk who was with him took off and tried to make the border, only he happened to run into some of our people. They interrogated him and sent a message. I came at first light."

He jerked his head at the Arab who had spoken. "Gamal only wanted to thank you for burying his cousin. Don't be misled. He'll kill you just as quickly if you make a mistake."

"So," the pilot said, "what now?"

"Shut the place down," Nolan said. "We've got to assume it's been compromised. Why else would a CIA agent be sniffing around?" He rubbed his chin and sighed. "God, what a mess. . . . I'll take Gamal and Zaal and set some charges."

"Going to blow it all up?" The pilot sounded slightly shocked.

"Yes. Damn shame, after all the effort and risk that went into bringing all that material here. But it's not as if there weren't plenty where it came from." He looked at Jesse. "You better keep an eye on this joker till we're done."

The pilot nodded and reached for his pistol. "Gonna take him back with us?"

"Oh, sure," Nolan said. "Major Hamid can ask him some questions—"

Suddenly the man called Gamal let out a high excited screech and grabbed Jesse's right arm. *"Shoof, shoof!"* he cried. "No-lan, *shoof!"*

The other Arab joined in, shouting and squawking, pushing for a better look. Nolan barked something short and pungent and both men fell silent. Then everybody stood and stared at the gold band on Jesse's wrist.

Nolan took the arm away from Gamal and bent his head, studying the bracelet closely. "Where did you get this?" he asked softly.

Jesse said, "Well, there was this old Egyptian lady—"

Nolan sighed again, straightened, and hit Jesse hard in the stomach with his fist. Jesse doubled up and fell to his knees, retching and fighting for air. "Now," Nolan said patiently, "stop being silly and tell me where you got that bracelet. Did you find it around here?"

Unable to speak, Jesse nodded. The pilot said, "What's going on, Nolan?"

"Look at it," Nolan said. "That gold, that workmanship. You've never seen anything like it outside the museum in Cairo."

"Old, huh?" The pilot whistled, like Bradley. "Worth money?"

"Worth a great deal, even by itself. If there's more around here—"

"God *damn,"* the pilot said. "All right, bud. Where'd you find it?"

Still on his knees, clutching his midriff and trying to breathe, Jesse looked past the two renegades and up the slope. A dark prick-eared head had popped up out of the hole in the fist-shaped rock. Silhouetted against the bright sky, Anpu looked even more like that cartoon coyote.

"If Gamal and Zaal have to get it out of you," Nolan said, "you won't like it."

Anpu wiggled his ears. A skinny arm came up and waved. Anpu pointed with exaggerated motions at the backs of Nolan and his men. Then he jabbed his finger downwards, toward the rock. He grinned and disappeared.

Jesse raised a hand. "Okay," he said weakly. "Let me up. I'll show you."

He got to his feet and started up the slope. "Be careful," Nolan warned, falling in behind him. "This better not be a trick."

Up by the rock outcrop Jesse stopped. The pilot said, "Shit, there ain't anything here."

"Over here." Jesse showed them the hole. Nolan bent down and felt around with one hand. His eyebrows went up. "It goes down to this tomb," Jesse said. "Lots of interesting stuff down there."

"I'll be damned." Nolan's voice was almost a whisper. "Ray, have you got a flashlight?"

"Sure." The pilot unclipped a small black cylinder from his belt and passed it over. "Not real big, but she's brighter than she looks."

"Come on, then." Nolan handed his AK-47 to the man called Zaal. He stepped into the shaft and began working his way downward. When he had vanished from sight the pilot, looking very dubious, climbed down after him.

That left Jesse and the two Arabs, who were still eyeing him and fingering their weapons. He stood still and didn't eye back. Inside his head he was trying to replay the climb down the shaft. By now they should be about halfway down. Now Nolan would have reached the bend in the tunnel. Big as he was, he'd have a tight time of it. Now he should be almost there. Now—

The scream that came up the shaft was like nothing Jesse had ever heard. Or ever wanted to hear again, but almost immediately there was another one just like it.

Both Arabs made exclamations of surprise. Zaal ran over, still clutching his own AK-47 and Nolan's, and stared down the shaft. Gamal simply stood there with his mouth open and his eyes huge.

That was about as good as it was likely to get. Jesse put his hands together in a double fist and clubbed Gamal as hard as he could on the side of the neck. The AK-47 came loose easily as Gamal's fingers went limp. Jesse turned and put a long burst into Zaal, who seemed to have gotten confused to find himself holding two rifles. He swung the AK-47 back and shot Gamal in the chest a couple of times, just in case he hadn't hit him hard enough. Then he went and looked down the tunnel, keeping the gun ready but not expecting to have to use it.

Sure enough, Anpu stuck his head out of the hole. "Are you all right?" he asked. "Well," he said, seeing the two bodies, "not bad. Your grandfather said you could take care of yourself."

Some muffled nightmare sounds floated up the shaft. Anpu cocked his head and winced. "That Sobek," he murmured. "Good at what he does, but so *crude. . . .*"

He looked at Jesse and cleared his throat. "I realize this isn't a good time," he said apologetically, "but about that matter we discussed—?"

"I'll see what I can do," Jesse said. "Looks like I owe you."

A couple of hours later, standing by the rock outcrop, Jesse said, "Now you're certain this is going to work?"

"Hey, *chooch.*" Grandfather sounded hurt. "Don't question an elder about his medicine. Have I ever let you down?"

Jesse snorted. "Where were you this morning?"

"You mean why didn't I wake you up, so you could run out and get yourself killed along with that white fool? He didn't have a chance," Grandfather said, "and you wouldn't have either. Be glad you were in the back room, where you couldn't hear till it was too late."

Jesse nodded reluctantly. "I guess you're right," he said. "Let's do it."

He looked around one more time. The *neterw* were standing there, as they had been for an hour or so, watching him with expressions of polite patience. Hathor raised a hand and wiggled white fingers and smiled. Sobek fingered something out of his back teeth and belched. None of them spoke.

Jesse picked up the little black box from between his feet, being careful not to foul the two wires that ran down into the tunnel. "Fire in the hole," he called, and thumbed the red button.

The noise was much less than he expected, just a dull quick *boomp.* The ground jumped slightly underfoot. That was all.

Anpu was already moving past him, sliding feet-first into the shaft, ignoring the smoke and fumes pouring out of the hole. "You'd better stay here," he said to Jesse. "It might be hard for you to breathe down there."

He dropped out of sight. Grandfather said, "Like I say, this is my medicine. Ought to be, after three years in the Seabees and eight in that mine in Colorado. Not to mention the Southern Pacific—"

A high-pitched yipping came up the tunnel. Anpu sounded happy.

"One thing I know," Grandfather finished, "is how to shoot rock."

"Then why didn't you just tell them how to do it?" Jesse wanted to know. "Why bring me in?"

"Trust those four with explosives? I may be dead but I'm not *stupid*. The thing about gods," Grandfather said, "they got a lot of power, but when you get right down to it they're not very smart. I remember once—"

Anpu's head and shoulders emerged from the hole. He was grinning widely. His tongue hung out on one side.

"It worked," he said cheerfully. "It was perfect. Shattered the rock into small fragments without damaging anything else. As soon as we clear away the rubble—nothing Sobek can't handle—we can reach the portal and be on our way."

He went back down the shaft. Thoth was right behind him, then Sobek. Hathor paused and touched Jesse's cheek.. "Call me," she said, and stepped gracefully into the hole.

"How about that," Grandfather said. "It worked."

"For God's sake," Jesse said, "you weren't sure? I thought you said—"

"Listen," Grandfather said defensively, "it's been a long time. And that funny plastic explosive those A-rabs had, I never used anything like that before."

Jesse shook his head. He walked around the rock outcrop and started down the side of the rise, toward Nolan's helicopter. An Alouette, all right. He'd never even ridden in one. This was going to be interesting.

Grandfather said, "Can you drive that thing, *chooch?*"

"Sure," Jesse said dryly. "It's my medicine."

It took three tries to get the Alouette started and off the ground. Lifting clear at last, struggling with unfamiliar controls, Jesse heard: "You got it, *chooch?* I'm cutting out now."

"You're staying here, *eduda?*" The Alouette kept trying to swing to the left. Maybe it wanted to go home to Libya.

"Going back to the spirit world," Grandfather said. "That portal of theirs is a lot easier than the regular route."

Jesse got the Alouette steadied at last, heading northward, and let out his breath. What next? Try to make the coast, ditch the Alouette in a salt marsh, walk to the coastal highway and try to hitch a ride to the nearest town. He had a little cash, and if he could get to Alexandria he knew people who would be good for a no-questions one-way trip out of this country. If things got tight that gold bracelet ought to buy a good deal of co-operation. It wasn't going to be easy, but the alternative was to land at some airfield, tell his story to the authorities, and spend the next lengthy piece of his life in an Egyptian prison.

"Take care, *sgilisi,*" Grandfather said. "I'll be around."

Like that, he was gone. Jesse almost felt him leave.

After a minute Jesse sighed and settled back in the seat. Feeding in more throttle, pressing cautiously against the cyclic, he watched the airspeed needle climb. Below him, the Alouette's shadow flitted across the sand and the rocks, hurrying over Egypt.

AFTERWORD

I met Roger in the mid-sixties at a Baltimore establishment notable for its overpriced drinks and underpaid entertainers. On weekends the latter item was me, just back from Asia with a bad-conduct discharge, a new guitar, and not a clue.

The clientele was mostly pretty awful. You could have had Jesus Christ playing jazz therein with Emily Dickinson on vocals and few of these precious proto-yuppies would have paused in their posing to listen. But there was one skinny, long-nosed guy who did listen, and even made requests—usually for "Waltzing Matilda."

One of the waitresses, with whom I was hotly involved, said his name was Roger. She reported that he tipped well and never tried to grope her. That was all we knew; he was just one of those shy guys you find in any bar in the world.

Later things went bad for me. I lost the job, the lover, and the guitar, in that order, and next year found myself in Omaha, sweating a couple of California felony warrants. One night I picked up a new paperback titled *Lord of Light* and read it straight through, pausing only to exclaim "Holy shit!" and the like. The fast-moving prose, the excruciating gags, the use of ancient mythic figures in modern fantasy fiction—I'd never read anything like it before. But it never occurred to me to connect this "Roger Zelazny" with the bony table-sitter who had loved the Antipodean national ballad.

It was a couple of decades before our paths crossed again. By then I was a Promising First Novelist; Roger contributed a cover quote. (Roger's cover quotes were legendary. No one was quicker to help a struggling newcomer with a blurb.) I called to thank him and at some point in the conversation a circuit closed: "You mean you're the guy who—" "Yeah, and you—" "Hey, remember when—"

We stayed in touch; we became, well, friends. Roger had an extremely rare quality: he *listened*. During one especially low time in my personal life, he was an authentic lifeline. No matter how late it was, how drunk I was, or how depressing my latest tale, he never brushed me off or hung up on me.

On the professional side, it was Roger who got me back into the sf&f field after a long bitter absence, and who first suggested I try writing modern fantasies based on American Indian themes. Without Roger's encouragement and guidance I would have dropped out of the game years ago.

When I heard that he was dead I wandered about the house crying helplessly for hours; and then late that night I got very, very drunk, and at last got out my current guitar and played "Waltzing Matilda" over and over again in the dark.

The novel published as This Immortal *first appeared under the title . . .* And Call Me Conrad. *It won Roger his first Hugo. In the following tale, Robert Silverberg's Titan discovers, as did Conrad, that nothing ever goes quite as one plans.*

■

CALL ME TITAN

In Memoriam: RZ

"HOW DID *YOU* GET LOOSE?" THE WOMAN WHO WAS APHRODITE asked me.

"It happened. Here I am."

"Yes," she said. "You. Of all of them, you. In this lovely place." She waved at the shining sun-bright sea, the glittering white stripe of the beach, the whitewashed houses, the bare brown hills. A lovely place, yes, this isle of Mykonos. "And what are you going to do now?"

"What I was created to do," I told her. *"You* know."

She considered that. We were drinking ouzo on the rocks, on the hotel patio, beneath a hanging array of fisherman's nets. After a moment she laughed, that irresistible tinkling laugh of hers, and clinked her glass against mine.

"Lots of luck," she said.

That was Greece. Before that was Sicily, and the mountain, and the eruption. . . .

198

The mountain had trembled and shaken and belched, and the red streams of molten fire began to flow downward from the ashen top, and in the first ten minutes of the eruption six little towns around the slopes were wiped out. It happened just that fast. They shouldn't have been there, but they were, and then they weren't. Too bad for them. But it's always a mistake to buy real estate on Mount Etna.

The lava was really rolling. It would reach the city of Catania in a couple of hours and take out its whole northeastern quarter, and all of Sicily would be in mourning the next day. Some eruption. The biggest of all time, on this island where big eruptions have been making the news since the dinosaur days.

As for me, I couldn't be sure what was happening up there at the summit, not yet. I was still down deep, way down, three miles from sunlight.

But in my jail cell down there beneath the roots of the giant volcano that is called Mount Etna I could tell from the shaking and the noise and the heat that this one was something special. That the prophesied Hour of Liberation had come round at last for me, after five hundred centuries as the prisoner of Zeus.

I stretched and turned and rolled over, and sat up for the first time in fifty thousand years.

Nothing was pressing down on me.

Ugly limping Hephaestus, my jailer, had set up his forge right on top of me long ago, his heavy anvils on my back. And had merrily hammered bronze and iron all day and all night for all he was worth, that clomp-legged old master craftsman. Where was Hephaestus now? Where were his anvils?

Not on me. Not any longer.

That was *good,* that feeling of nothing pressing down.

I wriggled my shoulders. That took time. You have a lot of shoulders to wriggle, when you have a hundred heads, give or take three or four.

"Hephaestus?" I yelled, yelling it out of a hundred mouths at once. I felt the mountain shivering and convulsing above me, and I knew that my voice alone was enough to make great slabs of it fall off and go tumbling down, down, down.

No answer from Hephaestus. No clangor of his forge, either. He just wasn't there any more.

I tried again, a different, greater name.

"Zeus?"

Silence.

"You hear me, Zeus?"

No reply.

"Where the hell are you? Where is everybody?"

All was silence, except for the hellish roaring of the volcano.

Well, okay, *don't* answer me. Slowly I got to my feet, extending myself to my full considerable height. The fabric of the mountain gave way for me. I have that little trick.

Another good feeling, that was, rising to an upright position. Do you know what it's like, not being allowed to stand, not even once, for fifty thousand years? But of course you don't, little ones. How could you?

One more try. *"ZEUS???"*

All my hundred voices crying his name at once, fortissimo fortissimo. A chorus of booming echoes. Every one of my heads had grown back, over the years. I was healed of all that Zeus had done to me. That was especially good, knowing that I was healed. Things had looked really bad, for a while.

Well, no sense just standing there caterwauling, if nobody was going to answer me back. This was the Hour of Liberation, after all. I was free—my chains fallen magically away, my heads all sprouted again. Time to get out of here. I started to move.

Upward. Outward.

I moved up through the mountain's bulk as though it was so much air. The rock was nothing to me. Unimpeded I rose past the coiling internal chambers through which the lava was racing up toward the summit vent, and came out into the sunlight, and clambered up the snow-kissed slopes of the mountain to the ash-choked summit itself, and stood there right in the very center of the eruption as the volcano puked its blazing guts out. I grinned a hundred big grins on my hundred faces, with hot fierce winds swirling like swords around my head and torrents of lava flowing down all around me. The view from up there was terrific. And what a fine feeling that was, just looking around at the world again after all that time underground.

There below me off to the east was the fish-swarming sea. Over there behind me, the serried tree-thickened hills. Above me, the fire-hearted sun.

What beautiful sights they all were!

"Hoo-*ha!*" I cried.

My jubilant roar went forth from that lofty mountaintop in Sicily like a hundred hurricanes at once. The noise of it broke windows in Rome and flattened farmhouses in Sardinia and knocked over ten mosques deep in the Tunisian Sahara. But the real blast was aimed eastward across the water, over toward Greece, and it went across that peninsula like a scythe, taking out half the treetops from Agios Nikolaus on the Ionian side to Athens over on the Aegean, and kept on going clear into Turkey.

It was a little signal, so to speak. I was heading that way myself, with some very ancient scores to settle.

I started down the mountainside, fast. The lava surging all around my thudding feet meant nothing to me.

Call me Typhoeus. Call me Titan.

I suppose I might have attracted a bit of attention as I made my way down those fiery slopes and past all the elegant seaside resorts that now were going crazy with hysteria over the eruption, and went striding into the sea midway between Fiumefreddo and Taormina. I am, after all, something of a monster, by your standards: four hundred feet high, let us say, with all those heads, dragon heads at that, and eyes that spurt flame, and thick black bristles everywhere on my body and swarms of coiling vipers sprouting from my thighs. The gods themselves have been known to turn and run at the mere sight of me. Some of them, once upon a time, fled all the way to Egypt when I yelled "Boo!"

But perhaps the eruption and the associated earthquakes kept the people of eastern Sicily so very preoccupied just then that they didn't take time to notice what sort of being it was that was walking down the side of Mount Etna and perambulating off toward the sea. Or maybe they didn't believe their eyes. Or it could be that they simply nodded and said, "Sure. Why not?"

I hit the water running and put my heads down and swam swiftly Greeceward across the cool blue sea without even bothering to come up for breath. What would have been the point? The air behind me smelled of fire and brimstone. And I was in a hurry.

Zeus, I thought. *I'm coming to get you, you bastard!*

As I said, I'm a Titan. It's the family name, not a description. We Titans were the race of Elder Gods—the first drafts, so to speak, for the deities that you people would eventually worship— the ones that Zeus walloped into oblivion long before Bill Gates came down from Mount Sinai with MS-DOS. Long before Homer sang. Long before the Flood. Long before, as a matter of fact, anything that might mean anything to you.

Gaea was our mother. The Earth, in other words. The mother of us all, really.

In the early days of the world broad-bosomed Gaea brought forth all sorts of gods and giants and monsters. Out of her came far-seeing Uranus, the sky, and then he and Gaea created the first dozen Titans, Oceanus and Cronus and Rhea and that bunch.

The original twelve Titans spawned a lot of others: Atlas, who now holds up the world; and tricky Prometheus, who taught humans how to use fire and got himself the world's worst case of cirrhosis for his trouble, and silly scatterbrained Epimetheus, who had that thing with Pandora, and so on. There were snake-limbed giants like Porphyrion and Alcyoneus, and hundred-armed fifteen-headed beauties like Briareus and Cottus and Gyes, and other over-sized folk like the three one-eyed Cyclopes, Arges of the storms and Brontes of the thunder and Steropes of the lightning, and so on. Oh, what a crowd we were!

The universe was our oyster, so I'm told. It must have been good times for all and sundry. I hadn't been born yet, in that era when Uranus was king.

But very early on there was that nasty business between Uranus and his son Cronus, which ended very badly for Uranus, the bloody little deal with the sharp sickle, and Cronus became the top god for a while, until he made the mistake of letting Zeus get born. That was it, for Cronus. In this business you have to watch out for overambitious sons. Cronus tried—he swallowed each of his children as they were born, to keep them from doing to him what he had done to Uranus—but Zeus, the last-born, eluded him. Very unfortunate for Cronus.

Family history. Dirty linen.

As for Zeus, who as you can see showed up on the scene quite late but eventually came to be in charge of things, he's my half-sister Rhea's son, so I suppose you'd call him my nephew. I call him my nemesis.

After Zeus had finished off Cronus he mopped up the rest of the Titans in a series of wild wars, thunderbolts ricocheting all over the place, the seas boiling, whole continents going up in flame. Some of us stayed neutral and some of us, I understand, actually allied themselves with him, but none of that made any difference. When all the shouting was over the whole pack of Titans were all prisoners in various disagreeable places, such as, for example, deep down underneath Mount Etna with the forge of Hephaestus sitting on your back; and Zeus and his outfit, Hades and Poseidon and Apollo and Aphrodite and the rest, ruled the roost.

I was Gaea's final experiment in maternity, the youngest of the Titans, born very late in the war with Zeus. Her final monster, some would say, because of my unusual looks and size. Tartarus was my father: the Underworld, he is. I was born restless. Danger-ous, too. My job was to avenge the family against the outrages Zeus had perpetrated on the rest of us. I came pretty close, too.

And now I was looking for my second chance.

Greece had changed a lot since I last had seen it. Something called civilization had happened in the meanwhile. Highways, gas stations, telephone poles, billboards, high-rise hotels, all those nice things.

Still and all, it didn't look so very bad. That killer blue sky with the golden blink in it, the bright sparkle of the low rolling surf, the white-walled cubes of houses climbing up the brown knifeblade hillsides: a handsome land, all things considered.

I came ashore at the island of Zakynthos on the Peloponnesian coast. There was a pleasant waterfront town there with an old fortress on a hilltop and groves of olives and cypresses all around. The geological disturbances connected with my escape from my prison cell beneath Mount Etna did not appear to have done much damage here.

I decided that it was probably not a great idea to let myself be seen in my actual form, considering how monstrous I would look to mortal eyes and the complications that that would create for me. And so, as I approached the land, I acquired a human body that I found swimming a short way off shore at one of the beachfront hotels.

It was a serviceable, athletic he-body, a lean, trim one, not young but full of energy, craggy-faced, a long jaw and a long sharp nose and a high forehead. I checked out his mind. Bright, sharp, observant. And packed with data, both standard and quirkily esoteric. All that stuff about Bill Gates and Homer and high rises and telephone poles: I got that from him. And how to behave like a human being. And a whole lot more, all of which I suspected would be useful to acquire.

A questing, creative mind. A good person. I liked him. I decided to use him.

In half a wink I transformed myself into a simulacrum of him and went on up the beach into town, leaving him behind just as he had been, all unknowing. The duplication wouldn't matter. Nobody was likely to care that there were two of him wandering around Greece at the same time, unless they saw both of us at the same moment, which wasn't going to happen.

I did a little further prowling behind his forehead and learned that he was a foreigner in Greece, a tourist. Married, three children, a house on a hillside in a dry country that looked a little like Greece, but was far away. Spoke a language called English, knew a smattering of other tongues. Not much Greek. That would be okay: I have my ways of communicating.

To get around the countryside properly, I discovered, I was going to need land-clothing, money, and a passport. I took care of these matters. Details like those don't pose problems for such as we.

Then I went rummaging in his mind to see whether he had any information in there about the present whereabouts of Zeus.

It was a very orderly mind. He had Zeus filed under "Greek Mythology."

Mythology?

Yes. Yes! He knew about Gaea, and Uranus, and the overthrow of Uranus by Cronus. He knew about the other Titans, at any rate some of them—Prometheus, Rhea, Hyperion, Iapetus. He knew some details about a few of the giants and miscellaneous hundred-armed monsters, and about the war between Zeus and the Titans and the Titans' total downfall, and the takeover by the big guy and his associates, Poseidon and Apollo and Ares & Company. But these were all stories to him. Fables. *Mythology.*

I confess I looked in his well-stocked mental archives for myself, Typhoeus—even a Titan has some vanity, you know—but all I found was a reference that said, "Typhon, child of Hera, is often confused with the earlier Titan Typhoeus, son of Gaea and Tartarus."

Well, yes. The names are similar; but Typhon was the bloated she-dragon that Apollo slew at Delphi, and what does that have to do with me?

That was bad, very bad, to show up in this copiously furnished mind only as a correction of an erroneous reference to someone else. Humiliating, you might actually say. I am not as important as Cronus or Uranus in the scheme of things, I suppose, but I did have my hour of glory, that time I went up against Zeus single-handed and came very close to defeating him. But what was even worse than such neglect, far worse, was to have the whole splendid swaggering tribe of us, from the great mother Gaea and her heavenly consort down to the merest satyr and wood-nymph, tucked away in there as so much mythology.

What had happened to the world, and to its gods, while I lay writhing under Etna?

Mount Olympus seemed a reasonable first place for me to go to look for some answers.

I was at the absolute wrong end of Greece for that: down in the southwestern corner, whereas Olympus is far up in the northeast. All decked out in my new human body and its new human clothes, I caught a hydrofoil ferry to Patra, on the mainland, and another ferry across the Gulf of Corinth to Nafpaktos, and then, by train and bus, made my way up toward Thessaly, where Olympus is. None of these places except Olympus itself had been there last time I was in Greece, nor were there such things as trains or ferries or buses then. But I'm adaptable. I am, after all, an immortal god. A sort of a god, anyway.

It was interesting, sitting among you mortals in those buses and trains. I had never paid much attention to you in the old days, any more than I would give close attention to ants or bumblebees or cockroaches. Back there in the early ages of the world, humans were few and far between, inconsequential experimental wildlife.

Prometheus made you, you know, for some obscure reason of his own: made you out of assorted dirt and slime, and breathed life into you, and turned you loose to decorate the landscape. You certainly did a job of decorating it, didn't you?

Sitting there among you in those crowded garlicky trains, breathing your exhalations and smelling your sweat, I couldn't help admiring the persistence and zeal with which you people had covered so much of the world with your houses, your highways, your shopping malls, your amusement parks, your stadiums, your power-transmission lines, and your garbage. Especially your garbage. Very few of these things could be considered any sort of an improvement over the basic virgin terrain, but I had to give you credit for effort, anyway. Prometheus, wherever he might be now, would surely be proud of you.

But where *was* Prometheus? Still chained up on that mountain-top, with Zeus's eagle gnawing away on his liver?

I roamed the minds of my traveling companions, but they weren't educated people like the one I had chanced upon at that beach, and they knew zero about Prometheus. Or anybody else of my own era, for that matter, with the exception of Zeus and Apollo and Athena and a few of the other latecomer gods. Who also were mere mythology to them. Greece had different gods these days, it seemed. Someone called Christos had taken over here. Along with his father and his mother, and assorted lesser deities whose relation to the top ones was hard to figure out.

Who were these new gods? Where had they come from? I was pleased by the thought that Zeus had been pushed aside by this Christos the way he had nudged old Cronus off the throne, but how had it happened? When?

Would I find Christos living on top of Mount Olympus in Zeus's old palace?

Well, no. I very shortly discovered that nobody was living on top of Olympus at all.

The place had lost none of its beauty, infested though modern-day Greece is by you and your kind. The enormous plateau on which the mountain stands is still unspoiled; and Olympus itself rises as ever in that great soaring sweep above the wild, desolate valley, the various summits forming a spectacular natural amphitheater and the upper tiers of rock splendidly shrouded by veils of cloud.

There are some roads going up, now. In the foothills I hired a car and a driver to take me through the forests of chestnut and fir to a refuge hut two thirds of the way up that is used by climbers, and there I left my driver, telling him I would go the rest of the way myself. He gave me a peculiar look, I suppose because I was

wearing the wrong kind of clothing for climbing, and had no moun-
taineering equipment with me.

When he was gone, I shed my borrowed human form and rose
up once again taller than the tallest tree in the world, and gave
myself a set of gorgeous black-feathered wings as well, and went
wafting up into that region of clean, pure air where Zeus had once
had his throne.

No throne. No Zeus.

My cousins the giants Otus and Ephialtes had piled Mount Pel-
ion on top of Mount Ossa to get up here during the war of the
gods, and were flung right back down again. But I had the place
to myself, unchallenged. I hovered over the jagged fleece-kissed
peaks of the ultimate summit, spiraling down through the puffs of
white cloud, ready for battle, but no battle was offered me.

"Zeus? Zeus?"

Once I had stood against him hissing terror from my grim jaws,
and my eyes flaring gorgon lightning that had sent his fellow gods
packing in piss-pants terror. But Zeus had withstood me, then. He
blasted me with sizzling thunderbolts and seared me to an ash, and
hurled me to rack and ruin; and jammed what was left of me
down under Mount Etna amid rivers of fire, with the craftsman
god Hephaestus piling the tools of his workshop all over me to
hold me down, and there I lay for those fifty thousand years, muttering to myself, until I had healed enough to come forth.

I was forth now, all right, and looking for a rematch. Etna had
vomited rivers of fire all over the fair plains of Sicily, and I was
loose upon the world; but where was my adversary?

"Zeus!" I cried, into the emptiness.

I tried the name of Christos, too, just to see if the new god
would answer. No go. He wasn't there either. Olympus was as
stunning as ever, but nobody godly seemed to have any use for it
these days.

I flew back down to the Alpine Club shelter and turned myself
back into the lean-shanked American tourist with the high forehead
and the long nose. I think three hikers may have seen me make
the transformation, for as I started down the slope I came upon
them standing slack-jawed and goggle-eyed, as motionless as
though Medusa had smitten them into stone.

"Hi, there, fellas," I called to them. "Have a nice day!"

They just gaped. I descended the fir-darkened mountainside to
the deep-breasted valley, and just like any hungry mortal I ate
dolmades and keftedes and moussaka in a little taverna I found
down there, washing it down with a few kilos of retsina. And then,
not so much like any mortal, I walked halfway across the country
to Athens. It took me a goodly number of days, resting only a few

hours every night. The body I had copied was a fundamentally sturdy one, and of course I had bolstered it a little.

A long walk, yes. But I was beginning to comprehend that there was no need for me to hurry, and I wanted to see the sights.

Athens was a horror. It was the kingdom of Hades risen up to the surface of the world. Noise, congestion, all-around general grittiness, indescribable ugliness, everything in a miserable state of disrepair, and the air so thick with foul vapor that you could scratch your initials in it with your fingernails, if you had initials, if you had fingernails.

I knew right away I wasn't going to find any members of the old pantheon in *this* town. No deity in his right mind would want to spend ten minutes here. But Athens is the city of Athena, and Athena is the goddess of knowledge, and I thought there might be a possibility that somewhere here in her city that I would be able to learn how and why and when the assorted divinities of Greece had made the transition from omnipotence to mythology, and where I might find them (or at least the one I was looking for) now.

I prowled the nightmare streets. Dust and sand and random blocks of concrete everywhere, rusting metal girders standing piled for no particular reason by the side of the road, crumbling buildings. Traffic, frantic and fierce: what a mistake giving up the ox-cart had been! Cheap, tacky shops. Skinny long-legged cats hissed at me. They knew what I was. I hissed right back. We understood each other, at least.

Up on the hilltop in the middle of everything, a bunch of ruined marble temples. The Acropolis, that hilltop is, the highest and holiest place in town. The temples aren't bad, as mortal buildings go, but in terrible shape, fallen columns scattered hither and yon, caryatids eroded to blurs by the air pollution. Why are you people such dreadful custodians of your own best works?

I went up there to look around, thinking I might find some lurking god or demigod in town on a visit. I stood by the best of the tumbledown temples, the one called the Parthenon, and listened to a little man with big eyeglasses who was telling a group of people who looked exactly like him how the building had looked when it was new and Athena was still in town. He spoke a language that my host body didn't understand at all, but I made a few adjustments and comprehended. So many languages, you mortals! *We* all spoke the same language, and that was good enough for us; but we were only gods, I suppose.

When he was through lecturing them about the Parthenon, the tour guide said, "Now we will visit the Sanctuary of Zeus. This way, please."

The Sanctuary of Zeus was just back of the Parthenon, but there really wasn't very much left of it. The tour guide did a little routine about Zeus as father of the gods, getting six facts out of every five wrong.

"Let me tell you a few things about Zeus," I wanted to say, but I didn't. "How he used to cheat at cards, for instance. And the way he couldn't keep his hands off young girls. Or, maybe, the way he bellowed and moaned the first time he and I fought, when I tangled him in the coils of my snakes and laid him low, and cut the tendons of his hands and feet to keep him from getting rambunctious, and locked him up in that cave in Cilicia."

I kept all that to myself. These people didn't look like they'd care to hear any commentary from a stranger. Anyway, if I told that story I'd feel honor bound to go on and explain how that miserable sneak Hermes crept into the cave when I wasn't looking and patched Zeus up—and then how, once Zeus was on his feet again, he came after me and let me have it with such a blast of lightning bolts that I was fried halfway to a crisp and wound up spending the next few epochs as a prisoner down there under Etna.

A dispiriting place, the Acropolis.

I went slinking down and over to the Plaka, which is the neighborhood in back of it, for some lunch. Human bodies need to be fed again and again, all day long. Swordfish grilled on skewers with onions and tomatoes; more retsina; fruit and cheese. All right. Not bad. Then to the National Museum, a two-hour walk, sweatsticky and dusty. Where I looked at broken statues and bought a guidebook that told me about the gods whose statues these were. Not even close to the actualities, any of them. Did they seriously think that brawny guy with the beard was Poseidon? And the woman with the tin hat, Athena? And that blowhard—Zeus? Don't make me laugh. Please. My laughter destroys whole cities.

Nowhere in the whole museum were there any representations of Titans. Just Zeus, Apollo, Aphrodite, Poseidon, and the rest of them, the junior varsity, the whole mob of supplanters, over and over and over. It was as if we didn't count at all in the historical record.

That hurt. I was in one hell of a sour mood when I left the museum.

There was a Temple of Olympian Zeus in town, the guidebook said, somewhere back in the vicinity of the Acropolis. I kept hoping that I would find some clue to Zeus's present place of residence at one of the sites that once had been sacred to him. A vestige, a lingering whiff of divinity.

But the Temple of Olympian Zeus was nothing but an incomplete set of ruined columns, and the only whiff I picked up there was the whiff of mortality and decay. And now it was getting dark and the body I was inhabiting was hungry again. Back to the Plaka; grilled meat, wine, a sweet pudding.

Afterwards, as I roamed the winding streets leading down to the newer part of the city with no special purpose in mind, a feeble voice out of a narrow alley said, in the native language of my host body, "Help! Oh, please, help!"

I was not put into this world for the purpose of helping anyone. But the body I had duplicated in order to get around in modern Greece was evidently the body of a kindly and responsible person, because his reflexes took over instantly, and I found myself heading into that alleyway to see what aid I could render the person who was so piteously crying out.

Deep in the shadows I saw someone—a woman, I realized— lying on the ground in what looked like a pool of blood. I went to her side and knelt by her, and she began to mutter something in a bleary way about being attacked and robbed.

"Can you sit up?" I said, slipping my arm around her back. "It'll be easier for me to carry you if—"

Then I felt a pair of hands grasping me by the shoulders, not gently, and something hard and sharp pressing against the middle of my back, and the supposedly bloodied and battered woman I was trying to help rolled deftly out of my grasp and stepped back without any trouble at all, and a disagreeable rasping voice at my left ear said quietly, "Just give us your wristwatch and your wallet and you won't get hurt at all."

I was puzzled for a moment. I was still far from accustomed to human ways, and it was often necessary to peer into my host-mind to find out what was going on.

Quickly, though, I came to understand that there was such a thing as crime in your world, and that some of it was being tried on me at this very moment. The woman in the alley was bait; I was the prey; two accomplices had been lurking in the shadows.

I suppose I could have given them my wristwatch and wallet without protest, and let them make their escape. What did a wristwatch mean to me? And I could create a thousand new wallets just like the one I had, which I had created also, after all. As for harm, they could do me none with their little knife. I had survived even the lightnings of Zeus. Perhaps I should have reacted with godlike indifference to their little attempt at mugging me.

But it had been a long dreary discouraging day, and a hot one, too. The air was close and vile-smelling. Maybe I had allowed my host body to drink a little too much retsina with dinner. In any event, godlike indifference was not what I displayed just then. Mortal petulance was more like the appropriate term.

"Behold me, fools," I said.

I let them see my true form.

There I was before them, sky-high, mountainous, a horrendous gigantic figure of many heads and fiery eyes and thick black bristles and writhing viperish excrescences, a sight to make even gods quail.

Of course, inasmuch as I'm taller than the tallest tree and appropriately wide, manifesting myself in such a narrow alleyway might have posed certain operational problems. But I have access to dimensions unavailable to you, and I made room for myself there with the proper interpenetrational configurations. Not that it mattered to the three muggers, because they were dead of shock the moment they saw me towering before them.

I raised my foot and ground them into the pavement like noxious vermin.

Then, in the twinkling of an eye, I was once more a slender, lithe middle-aged American tourist with thinning hair and a kindly smile, and there were three dark spots on the pavement of the alley, and that was that.

It was, I admit, overkill.

But I had had a trying day. In fact, I had had a trying fifty thousand years.

Athens had been so hellish that it put me in mind of the authentic kingdom of Hades, and so that was my next destination, for I thought I might get some answers down there among the dead. It wasn't much of a trip, not for me. I opened a vortex for myself and slipped downward and there right in front of me were the black poplars and willows of the Grove of Persephone, with Hades' Gate just behind it.

"Cerberus?" I called. "Here, doggy doggy doggy! Good Cerberus! Come say hello to Daddy!"

Where was he, my lovely dog, my own sweet child? For I myself was the progenitor of the three-headed guardian of the gate of Hell, by virtue of my mating with my sister, Tartarus and Gaea's scaly-tailed daughter Echidna. We made the Harpies too, did Echidna and I, and the Chimera, and Scylla, and also the Hydra, a whole gaudy gorgeous brood of monsters. But of all my children I was always most fond of Cerberus, for his loyalty. How I loved to see him come running toward me when I called! What pleasure I took in his serpent-bristled body, his voice like clanging bronze, his slavering jaws that dripped black venom!

This day, though, I wandered dogless through the Underworld. There was no sign of Cerberus anywhere, no trace even of his glittering turds. Hell's Gate stood open and the place was deserted. I saw nothing of Charon the boatman of the Styx, nor Hades and

Queen Persephone, nor any members of their court, nor the spirits of the dead who should have been in residence here. An abandoned warehouse, dusty and empty. Quickly I fled toward the sunshine.

The island of Delos was where I went next, looking for Apollo. Delos is, or was, his special island, and Apollo had always struck me as the coolest, most level-headed member of the Zeus bunch. Perhaps he had survived whatever astounding debacle it was that had swept the Olympian gods away. And, if so, maybe he could give me a clue to Zeus's current location.

Big surprise! I went to Delos, but no Apollo.

It was yet another dismal disillusioning journey through the tumbledown sadness that is Greece. This time I flew; not on handsome black-feathered wings, but on a clever machine, a metal tube called an airplane, full of travelers looking more or less like me in my present form. It rose up out of Athens in a welter of sound and fury and took up a course high above the good old wine-dark sea, speckled with tawny archipelagoes, and in very short order came down on a small dry island to the south. This island was called Mykonos, and there I could buy myself passage in one of the boats that made outings several times a day to nearby Delos.

Delos was a dry rubble-field, strewn with fragments of temples, their columns mostly broken off close to the ground. Some marble lions were still intact, lean and vigilant, crouching on their hind legs. They looked hungry. But there wasn't much else to see. The place had the parched gloom of death about it, the bleak aura of extinction.

I returned to Mykonos on the lunchtime boat, and found myself lodgings in a hillside hotel a short distance outside the pretty little narrow-streeted shorefront town. I ordered me some more mortal food and drank mortal drink. My borrowed body needed such things.

It was on Mykonos that I met Aphrodite.

Or, rather, she met me.

I was sitting by myself, minding my own business, in the hotel's outdoor bar, which was situated on a cobblestoned patio bedecked with mosaics and hung with nets and oars and other purported fishing artifacts. I was on my third ouzo of the hour, which possibly was a bit much for the capacities of the body I was using, and I was staring down the hillside pensively at, well, what I have to call the wine-dark sea. (Greece brings out the clichés in anyone. Why should I resist?)

A magnificent long-legged full-bodied blond woman came over to me and said, in a wonderfully throaty, husky voice, "New in town, sailor?"

I stared at her, astounded.

There was the unmistakable radiance of divinity about her. My Geiger counter of godliness was going clickity-clack, full blast. How could I have failed to pick up her emanations the moment I arrived on Mykonos? But I hadn't, not until she was standing right next to me. She had picked up mine, though.

"Who are you?" I blurted.

"Won't you ask a lady to sit down, even?"

I jumped to my feet like a nervous schoolboy, hauled a deck chair scrapingly across and positioned it next to mine, and bowed her into it. Then I wigwagged for a waiter. "What do you want to drink?" I rasped. My throat was dry. Nervous schoolboy, yes, indeed.

"I'll have what you're having."

"*Parakolo,* ouzo on the rocks," I told the waiter.

She had showers of golden hair tumbling to shoulder length, and catlike yellow eyes, and full ripe lips that broke naturally into the warmest of smiles. The aroma that came from her was one of young wine and green fields at sunrise and swift-coursing streams, but also of lavender and summer heat, of night rain, of surging waves, of midnight winds.

I knew I was consorting with the enemy. I didn't care.

"Which one are you?" I said again.

"Guess."

"Aphrodite would be too obvious. You're probably Ares, or Hephaestus, or Poseidon."

She laughed, a melodic cadenza of merriment that ran right through the scale and into the infra-voluptuous. "You give me too much credit for deviousness. But I like your way of thinking. Ares in drag, really? Poseidon with a close shave? Hephaestus with a blond wig?" She leaned close. The fragrance of her took on hurricane intensity. "You were right the first time."

"Aphrodite."

"None other. I live in Los Angeles now. Taking a little holiday in the mother country. And you? You're one of the old ones, aren't you?"

"How can you tell?"

"The archaic emanation you give off. Something out of the pre-Olympian past." She clinked the ice cubes thoughtfully in her glass, took a long pull of the ouzo, stared me straight in the eyes. "Prometheus? Tethys?" I shook my head. "Someone of that clan, though. I thought all of you old ones were done for a long time ago. But there's definitely a Titan vibe about you. Which one, I wonder? Most likely one of the really strange ones. Thaumas? Phorcys?"

"Stranger than those," I said.

She took a few more guesses. Not even close.

"Typhoeus," I told her finally.

We walked into town for dinner. People turned to look at us in the narrow streets. At her, I mean. She was wearing a filmy orange sun dress with nothing under it and when you were east of her on a westbound street you got quite a show.

"You really don't think that I'm going to find Zeus?" I asked her.

"Let's say you have your work cut out for you."

"Well, so be it. I *have* to find him."

"Why is that?"

"It's my job," I said. "There's nothing personal about it. I'm the designated avenger. It's my sole purpose in existence: to punish Zeus for his war against the children of Gaea. You know that."

"The war's been over a long time, Typhoeus. You might as well let bygones be bygones. Anyway, it's not as though Zeus got to enjoy his victory for long." We were in the middle of the maze of narrow winding streets that is Mykonos Town. She pointed to a cheerful little restaurant called Catherine's. "Let's go in here. I ate here last night and it was pretty good."

We ordered a bottle of white wine. "I like the body you found for yourself," she said. "Not particularly handsome, no, but *pleasing*. The eyes are especially nice. Warm and trustworthy, but also keen, penetrating."

I would not be drawn away from the main theme. "What happened to the Olympians?" I asked.

"Died off, most of them. One by one. Of neglect. Starvation."

"Immortal gods don't die."

"Some do, some don't. You know that. Didn't Argus of the Hundred Eyes kill your very own Echidna? And did she come back to life?"

"But the major gods—"

"Even if they don't die, they can be forgotten, and the effect's pretty much the same. While you were locked up under Etna, new gods came in. There wasn't even a battle. They just moved in, and we had to move along. We disappeared entirely."

"So I've noticed."

"Yes. Totally out of business. You've seen the shape our temples are in? Have you seen anybody putting out burnt offerings to us? No, no, it's all over for us, the worship, the sacrifices. Has been for a long time. We went into exile, the whole kit and kaboodle of us, scattered across the world. I'm sure a lot of us simply died, despite that theoretical immortality of ours. Some hung on, I suppose. But it's a thousand years since the last time I saw any of them."

"Which ones did you see then?"

"Apollo—he was getting gray and paunchy. And I caught sight of Hermes, once—I think it was Hermes—slow and short-winded, and limping like Hephaestus."

"And Zeus?" I asked. "You never ran into him anywhere, after you all left Olympus?"

"No. Never even once."

I pondered that. "So how did *you* manage to stay so healthy?"

"I'm Aphrodite. The life-force. Beauty. Passion. Those things don't go out of fashion for long. I've done all right for myself, over the years."

"Ah. Yes. Obviously you have."

The waitress fluttered around us. I was boiling with questions to ask Aphrodite, but it was time to order, and that was what we did. The usual Greek things, stuffed grape leaves, grilled fish, over-cooked vegetables. Another bottle of wine. My head was pulsating. The restaurant was small, crowded, a whirlpool of noise. The near-ness of Aphrodite was overwhelming. I felt dizzy. It was a surpris-ingly pleasant sensation.

I said, after a time, "I'm convinced that Zeus is still around somewhere. I'm going to find him and this time I'm going to whip his ass and put *him* under Mount Etna."

"It's amazing how much like a small boy an immortal being can be. Even one as huge and frightful as you."

My face turned hot. I said nothing.

"Forget Zeus," she urged. "Forget Typhoeus, too. Stay human. Eat, drink, be merry." Her eyes were glistening. I felt as if I were falling forward, tumbling into the sweet chasm between her breasts. "We could take a trip together. I'd teach you how to enjoy your-self. How to enjoy me, too. Tell me: have you ever been in love?"

"Echidna and I—"

"Echidna! Yes! You and she got together and made a bunch of hideous monsters like yourselves, with too many heads and drool-ing fangs. I don't mean Echidna. This is Earth, here and now. I'm a woman now and you're a man."

"But Zeus—"

"*Zeus*," she said scornfully. She made the name of the Lord of Olympus sound like an obscenity.

We finished eating and I paid the check and we went outside into the mild, breezy Mykonos night, strolling for fifteen or twenty minutes, winding up finally in a dark, deserted part of the town, a warehouse district down by the water, where the street was no more than five feet wide and empty shuttered buildings with white-washed walls bordered us on both sides.

She turned to me there and pulled me abruptly up against her. Her eyes were bright with mischief. Her lips sought mine. With a little hissing sound she nudged me backward until I was leaning against a wall, and she was pressing me tight, and currents of energy that could have fired a continent were passing between us. I think there could have been no one, not man nor god, who would not have wanted to trade places with me just then.

"Quickly! The hotel!" she whispered.

"The hotel, yes."

We didn't bother to walk. That would have taken too long. In a flash we vanished ourselves from that incomprehensible tangle of mazelike streets and reappeared in her room at our hotel, and from then to dawn she and I generated such a delirium of erotic force that the entire island shook and shivered with the glorious Sturm und Drang of it. We heaved and thrust and moaned and groaned, and rivers of sweat ran from our bodies and our hearts pounded and thundered and our eyes rolled in our heads from giddy exhaustion, for we allowed ourselves the luxury of mortal limitations for the sake of the mortal joy of transcending those limitations. But because we *weren't* mortal we also had the option of renewing our strength whenever we had depleted it, and we exercised that option many a time before rosy-fingered dawn came tiptoeing up over the high-palisaded eastern walls.

Naked, invisible to prying eyes, Aphrodite and I walked then hand in hand along the morning-shimmering strand of the fish-swarming sea, and she murmured to me of the places we would go, the things we would experience.

"The Taj Mahal," she said. "And the summer palace at Udaipur. Persepolis and Isfahan in springtime. Baalbek. Paris, of course. Carcassonne. Iguaçú Falls, and the Blue Mosque, and the Fountains of the Blue Nile. We'll make love in the Villa of Tiberius on Capri—and between the paws of the Sphinx—and in the snow on top of Mount Everest—"

"Yes," I said. "Yes. Yes. Yes. Yes."

And what I was thinking was, *Zeus. Zeus. Zeus. Zeus.*

And so we travel about the world together, Aphrodite and I, seeing the things in it that are beautiful, and there are many of those; and so she distracts me from my true task. For the time being. It is very pleasant, traveling with Aphrodite; and so I permit myself to be distracted this way.

But I have not forgotten my purpose. And this is my warning to the world.

I am a restless being, a mighty thrusting force. I was created that way. My adversary doesn't seem currently to be around. But Zeus is here somewhere. I know he is. He wears a mask. He disguises himself as a mortal, either because it amuses him to do so, or because he has no choice, for there is something in the world of which he is afraid, something from which he must hide himself, some god greater even than Zeus, as Zeus was greater than Cronus and Cronus was greater than Uranus.

But I will find him. And when I do, I will drop this body and take on my own form again. I will stand mountain-high, and you will see my hundred heads, and my fires will flash and range. And Zeus and I will enter into combat once more, and this time I will surely win.

It will happen.

I promise you that, O small ones. I warn you. It will happen.

You will tremble then. I'm sorry for that. The mind that came with this body I wear now has taught me something about compassion; and so I regret the destruction I will inevitably visit upon you, because it cannot be avoided, when Zeus and I enter into our struggle. You have my sincerest apologies, in advance. Protect yourselves as best you can. But for me there can be no turning away from my task.

Zeus? This is Typhoeus the Titan who calls you!

Zeus, where are you?

AFTERWORD

He wrote a lot of magnificent, unforgettable science fiction, sure, but so did my late and still lamented friends X, Y, and Z, and yet their deaths didn't have the kick-in-the-belly impact of Roger's. For one thing, it came so soon. Fifty-eight isn't an appropriate age for dying—especially when you're as youthful and vigorous and full of life and creative energy as Roger still was. But I lament him also because he was such a sweet and completely lovable man. I knew him almost thirty years, and I had hoped to know him thirty years more, and now that is not to be. In all those three decades I never heard him utter an unkind word about anyone. (Nor did I ever hear anybody utter an unkind word about *him*.) He was a man of great patience, high good humor, and warm goodwill, as I learned when the inordinately punctual Robert Silverberg showed up an hour late for dinner with him two times running, for a different silly reason each time. In all senses of the word he was a joyous man to know.

So I'm going to miss the author of "A Rose for Ecclesiastes" and ". . . And Call Me Conrad" and all the rest of those wonderful stories, sure. We'll never know now what marvels of inventiveness were about to emerge from his fertile mind. But most of all I'll miss my friend Roger. If you live long enough, you're going to outlive a lot of your friends, and you come to expect that after a time, although you don't ever quite get used to the frequency and inevitability of the losses. This one, though, is a particularly hard one to accept.

Sometimes, there are things that one must do—even at the risk of all one holds dear.

■

THE OUTLING
Andre Norton

HERTA PULLED IMPATIENTLY AT THE HOOD THE WILD WIND AT-tempted to take from her head. Facing this was like trying to bore her body, sturdy as it was, into a wall. The dusk was awaking shadows one did not like to see if only in a glimpse from eye corner. She shifted her healer's bag and tried to hold in mind the thought of her own hearth fire, a simmering pot of stew, and a waiting mug of her own private herb restorative.

The wind hollowed and within her hood Herta grinned. Let the Dark go its way, this eve it held no newborn in its nets. Gustava, the woodsman's wife, had a new son safe at her breast and a strong boy he was.

Then she slowed her fight against the wind, actually pushed aside a bit of hood to hear the better. No, there was no mistaking that whimper—pain, fear, both fed it.

In the near field there was a rickety structure Ranfer had once slovenly built for a sheep shelter, though all flocks would be safely bedded this night. She had not been mistaken—that was a lonesome cry, wailed as if no help could be expected.

Herta bundled up thick skirts, gave a hitch to her bag, to push laboriously through the nearest gap in the rotting fence. She did allow herself a regretful sigh. There was pain and she was a healer; for such there was no turning aside.

218

She tore a grasping thorn away from her cloak and rounded the end of the leanto. Then she halted again almost in mid-step, and her white breath puffed forth in a gasp.

There was a form stretched on the remains of rotting straw, yes. Great green eyes which yet had a hint of gold in them were on her. The body which twisted now as if to relieve some intolerable pain was—furred. Yet it was womankind in all its contours.

Herta dropped her cloak and strove to pull it over brush and crumbling wood to give some shelter. Light—not even a candle lantern. But she had the years behind her to tell her what lay here—a thing of legend—yet it lived and was in birth throes.

White fangs showed between pale lips as Herta went to her knees beside that twisting figure.

"I would help," the healer got out. She was already pulling at her bag. But there was no fire to warm any potion and half her hard-learned skills depended upon such.

She shook off mittens and into the palm of one hand shook a mixture. As she leaned closer the thing she would tend swept out a long pale tongue to wipe her flesh clean.

Having turned back her sleeves, Herta placed her hands on that budge of mid-body. "Down come." She recited words which might not be understood by her patient but were the ritual. "Come down and out into this world, without lingering."

She never knew how long she kept up that struggle, so hampered by the lack of near all that was necessary for a proper birthing. But at last there was a gush of pale blood and a small wet thing in her hands. While she who had yielded it up at last cried aloud a mournful cry—or was it a howl?

Though Herta held now, wrapping in her apron, what was undoubtedly a female child, large to be sure but still recognizable for what it was, the body which had delivered it once more writhing. Foam dripped from the jaws and a strong animal smell arose. But the eyes went from Herta to the babe and back again. And in them, as if it were shouted aloud, there was a plea.

Without knowing why, except that somehow this was a part of her innermost being, Herta nodded. "Safe as I can, I shall hold."

Her breath caught as she realized what she had just promised. But that it was a true oath she had no doubt. The eyes held to hers; then came a dimness and the figure twisted for the last time. Herta squatted, a wailing baby in her arms. But at her feet there was now, stiffening and stark, the body of a silver white wolf.

Herta's hand started to move in the traditional farewell to those passing beyond and then stopped. All living things in the world she had always known paid homage to That Beyond, but did an

Outling come within that shelter? Who was she to judge? She
finished the short ritual with the proper words almost definitely.

"Sleep well, sister. May your day dawn warm and clear."

Stiffly she got to her near-benumbed feet. The babe whimpered,
and she sheltered it with a flap of cloak. Night was closing in. She
did not know how or why the Outling had come to the fringe of
human habitation, but either those of her kind would find her or
else, like the wood creatures whose blood she was said to share,
she would lie quiet here to become part of the earth again.

Heavy dusk was on Herta when she reached her cottage at the
outer edge of the village street. Lanterns were agleam above the doorways after the Law and she must set hers also. But luckily she
seemed to have the village street to herself at the moment. It was
the time for day's-end eating and all were at their tables.

Inside she laid the baby, still bundled in her apron, on her bed
and then saw to the lantern and gave a very vigorous poking to
the embers on the hearth, feeding them well from her store. She
even went to the extravagance of lighting a candle in its grease-
dripped holder.

To swing a pot of water over the awakening fire took but a
moment or so, and she rummaged quickly through her supplies of
castoffs, which she kept ready for those too poor to have prepared
much for birthings.

Once it was washed and clad she would have vowed that this
was a human child—healthy of body—born with a thick thatch of
silver fair hair—but human as the one she had earlier brought into
the world.

She hushed a hungry wail by a rag sopping with goat's milk to
suck. It's eyes opened and Herta would always swear that they
looked up at her with strange knowledge and recognition.

Briary, she named her find, and the name seemed to fit. And
she had her story ready, too: a beggar woman taken by her time
in the forest, who died leaving one there was none to claim.

Briary was accepted by the village with shrugs and some mutterings. If Herta wished to burden herself with an extra mouth
during the lean months, the care of a stranger's offthrow—that
was her business. Too many owed life and health to the healer to
raise questions.

As time passed, though, Herta was hard put to explain some
things. Why her charge grew so quickly and showed wits and
strengths village children of near age did not. Yet, though she
watched carefully, especially on the full moon nights, she saw no
sign of any Outling change.

Briary early advanced from a creeping stage to walking, and she
was always a shadow to Herta. She seldom spoke and then only

in answer to a direct question, but when Herta sat by the fire of an evening, a warm posset in her mug, stretching her feet to the fire's warm, she would feel a small hand stroking her arm and then her cheek and she would gather up the child to hold. Perhaps it was because she had lived alone for so long herself that she felt the need for speech, and so she first told Briary of her own childhood, and then tales of older times. But she never spoke of Outlings nor such legends. Instead she repeated the names of herbs and plants and most of the lore of her trade, even those the child she held on her lap could not understand. Yet Briary seemed to find all Herta's speech a comfort, for when the healer would take her to bed she would ask in her soft voice for more.

When spring came Briary grew restless, pacing to the door of the house and fingering the latch bar, looking to Herta. At first the healer was reluctant to let her out. There were two reasons—the Outling blood in her, which Herta tried hard to forget, and the fact that she was so forward for her age that surely the village women would gossip about it.

But at length she yielded and allowed Briary to go into the garden, which must be carefully tended, and even, walking, with one hand grasping Herta's skirt, to the mill for a packet of meal, standing quietly, sometimes with a forefinger in her mouth, listening while Herta exchanged greetings and small talk with her neighbors.

If Briary did not hunt out the children of the village, they were quick to spy her. To the older ones she was but a baby, but there were others who shyly offered flowers or a May apple. At length she became accepted; all differences denied that she was a stranger. She could outrun even Evison, who had always been fleetest of foot. And as the years passed Herta also forgot her wariness and looked no more for what she suspected might come.

Somehow the villagers came to accept though they sometimes commented on her rapid growth of both mind and body. She became a second pair of hands for Herta, learning to grind, to measure, to spread for drying, to measure drop by drop liquids from the clay bottles on the shelves. It was she who stopped the lifeblood flow when Karl misswung an axe until Herta could come. And Lesa swore that Briary only touched the ugly wart rising on her chin and it grew the less and vanished. Herta was given credit for training so good an apprentice.

When summers reached the height of sticky weather and one sweated and slapped at the flies, hunting shade at noontide, Briary was made free of another of the children's secrets. For she had early learned that there were some things one did not blab about. This was one mainly known to the boys until Briary had fol-

lowed them. And, seeing her watching, they somehow could not
send her away.

Among the ancient stories Herta had shared with her was one
of the village itself. There had been a mighty lady, such as had
never been hereabouts before, who had come with workmen and
had built a stone house which stood now fields apart from the
village. Before it was dug a pool as the lady ordered, and a spring
had burst to fill it, nor had the water ever failed. Then she had
built across the upper end of the pool, nearest to the building, a
screen of stone.

Once that had been done she dismissed the workpeople, offering
land to those wanting to stay. Later came others, odd-looking in
queer garments. They, too, worked, for one could hear the ring of
their hammers throughout the day and sometimes on nights when
the moons were full.

Whatever they wrought was also finished at last, and they left
very quickly between dawn and dusk of a single day. The native
villagers took an aversion to the building. Of the lady they never
saw anything again, and it was thought she must have gone with
the last workpeople.

However, in time the boys used to dare each other to try the
pool and, nothing ill happening, it became a place of recreation
for the village in the high heat of summer. But no one ventured
beyond the screen or tried to explore what stood there.

Briary seemed able to swim as easily as one already tutored,
though the other girls squealed and splashed and floundered into
some manner of propulsion—though some gave up more than just
the splashing.

It seemed that life flowed as smoothly as always, one day melting
into another one, until the coming of the peddler. He arrived on
a day for rejoicing for the crops, for the last of the harvest had
been brought in and there was a table set up in the middle of the
street whereon each housewife set a dish or platter of her best and
most closely guarded recipe. They were just about to explore these
delights when Evison came running to say there was a stranger on
the road from the south.

Perhaps twice or three times a year such a thing might happen.
It meant news to be talked over for months and sometimes things
to be learned. To have this happen on the day of Harvest Home
was a double event which near aroused the younger members of
the village to a frenzy.

He came slowly, the peddler, with one hand on the pack frame
of his mule, as if he in some manner needed support, and his face
was near as red as a field poppy.

Johan, the smith, hurried to meet him, a brimming tankard of

Harvest Mix in his hand. The man gave him a nod of the head and drank as if he had been in a desert for days. When he came up for air he pulled his dusty hand across his wet chin.

"Now that's a fair greeting." His voice had a cracked note as if some of the dust had plagued him to that point. "I be Igorof, trader. May all your days be sunny and your crops grow tall, good people."

"Let us help your beast, trader." Johan already had a hand on his shoulder and was pulling him toward the table. "Good feasting, Igorof." He placed him on the nearest bench while the women crowded forward with this dish or that full of the best for him to make choice.

Evison had taken the donkey to the nearby field, where two of the other boys helped him lift off the heavily laden pack frame while another brought a pail of water for the thirsty animal.

"Feast, let us feast!" Johan hammered the hilt of his knife on the table.

Briary had squeezed in beside Herta, but she noted, as she always was able, that the healer was eyeing the newcomer with a frown beginning to form between her eyes.

Feast well they did, with many toasts in the more potent drink offered the elders. Igorof's tankard was kept brimming and he emptied it nearly as quickly, though he did not seem as drawn to do more than taste what lay on his plate.

Herta leaned forward suddenly and asked, her voice loud enough to cut through the general noise, "How do those in Langlot, friend? You have come from there—what news do you bring?"

His eyes were watching her over the edge of the tankard.

"Well as one would wish, goodwife. There be three new babes and—" Suddenly he set down the tankard so its contents splashed and his mouth was drawn crooked in grimace.

What moved Briary arose inside her as one might suddenly come from a dark into light. She skidded under the table and caught the edge of Johan's smock, pulling him backwards with all her might, away from the stranger. He cried out in surprise and tripped.

The girl continued to face the stranger, flung out her arms and pushed against all those near him she could reach. "Away— away—" Her voice was shrill.

"What do you, brat!" Ill-tempered Trike aimed a slap at her.

Herta arose. "She saves your life!" she told Trike. "Stranger, what is the truth of what you have brought to us?"

He grimaced again, his eyes turning swiftly from side to side.

"No! Not the fire!" He had scrambled up from his seat. His shirt only loosely held together fell open to show red splotches on his chest. Herta's eyes widened, fear masked her face.

"Plague!"

One word, but enough to silence them all. Those nearest the trader strove to get away, and those beyond tried to elude them in turn. There had been no plague in many years, but when it struck, whole villages went to their deaths and only the wild creatures were ever seen in their streets.

Such was the role of deaths, it was said that those bearing the contagion were often hurled into fires, the living with the dead.

A wild scramble rolled along the street, each family seeking their own home, though one could not shelter with any bolt against this menace.

The man threw back his head and howled like a beast at the slaughter pen and then crumpled to the ground. Briary could see the heavy shudders that shook his body.

"Get away from him, fool!" Johan's wife showed her hatchet face at their cottage window.

Herta moved around the table to the stricken stranger. She did not look to Greta in the window, but her voice surely reached the woman, for the shutter was slammed shut again.

"I am healer sworn," Herta said, then she spoke to Briary.

"Bring me the packets from the drawer with the black spot on it." Briary ran as swiftly as in a race. But fear was cold within her. She knew the nature of those packets—they brought an end to great suffering—but also to life, and she who used them would take a great weight upon her inner self for every grain of the powder she dispensed. Yet it was said that the last moments of the plague brought pure torment and if that were lessened it was a boon well meant.

There were two sides always to the healer's craft. In her hands from time to time she held both life and death. Briary found the packets, thrust them deep into her apron pocket and returned to the wreckage of the feast.

Herta was on her knees by the still shuddering body of the trader. As Briary came up she grabbed a tankard from the edge of the table before her and there was an answering slosh of drink unconsumed. Then she spoke to Igorof.

"Brother, you are plague gripped. There is no cure—but your passing can be eased if you will it so."

His head turned so his sweating face could be seen, and it seemed that the shudders ran also across his features. His bitten lips, flecked with blood, twisted.

"Give—peace—" Somehow he grated out the words.

Calmly Herta held packet and tankard up to eye level and shook some grayish ashes into the tankard. Then she pushed the packet back to Briary.

As if the man had been stricken by an ordinary fever and lay in her own cottage, she slipped an arm about his shoulders and lifted him, setting the tankard to his lips.

"Thanks of all good be on you, healer," he grated out. "But you have doomed yourself thereby."

"That is as it may be," she said steadily as he drank what she offered.

To Briary's eyes his passing was quick, but the body he had left behind was as much a danger to the village as the living man had been.

Herta arose and faced down the street. And her voice came high and clear.

"Show your courage now. Those who were near to this poor soul and his belongings—already, as well you know, the taint may lie upon you. Away from those you cherish until you know you are clean. Come forth and give aid for what must be done."

There was silence, no other answer. Then a door was flung open and a youthful figure half fell, half flung himself into the street. There were screams and calls from behind him as he lurched to his feet, stood for a moment as if to get his full breath, and then came forward with visible reluctance. It was Evison, who had dealt with Igorof's pack and mule. He gulped twice and turned his head not to view the dead as he approached, and his face was gray beneath the summer's tan.

His coming might have been a key turned in a stubborn lock, for now other doors opened and the wailing from within the cottages mingled in a great cry of sorrow and loss. But they came— Johan, and the others who had drunk with the stranger, three women who had taken it upon themselves to fill his plate and so had been shoulder close to him.

Johan loosened one of the benches and they brought pitchforks and staffs, to roll the limp body on that surface, carrying it into the field where the trader's pack had been left. It was Stuben who smoothed the mule's neck and, looking into the animal's eyes, said in a shaking voice.

"What must be done, will be done." And with his butcher's practice brought down the heavy axe in the single needed blow.

There was movement again in the village, though those who had come forth stood carefully away from the known cottage while doors or windows were opened. Wood cut for the hearth, a roll or two of cloth, several jugs of oil were thrust into the street.

So Igorof came to the fire after all, though it was only his tortured husk which lay there in the lap of flames. And with him burned all his belongings, the frame on which those had ridden, and the mule.

It took hours and those who worked tottered with weariness as they pulled together more fuel for that fire. Also their eyes went slyly now and then from one to another, watching, Briary knew, for some sign of the sickness to show.

Herta oversaw the building of the pyre and then went to her cottage and began to sort out bottles and packets, Briary following her directions as to blending and stirring.

"What can be done, shall be. Gather all the cups and tankards left on the table, child, and have them ready."

The stink of the fire hung like a doom cloud over the whole village, and Briary could see those others still adding to its fury with whatever they could lay hands upon. She readied the cups and Herta came, a pot braced against her hip. The workers must have sighted her and taken her arrival as a signal, for they gathered again, singed, smoke darkened, though no one stood close to another.

"A Healer is granted only such knowledge as the Great Ones allow. I can promise you nothing. But here I have the master strength of many remedies, some akin to a lighter form of the plague. Drink and hope, for this is all which has been left to us, if we would not wipe out all who are kin to us."

Drink they did, with Herta watching that each might get his or her full share. When they had done, their weariness seemed to strike at them, and they settled on the bank of the stream. Two of the women wept, but the third wore a face of anger against fate and dug her belt knife again and again into the earth as if she would clean it well for some use; while the men, grim of face, looked now and then to the towering flag of flame.

Briary had first sought Herta, tagging at her heels as might a babe who had but shortly learned to walk and needed a skirt to cling to. Inside she felt strange and wanted comfort, but of what sort she could not tell, perhaps better than most, for she had learned of Herta's knowledge. Yet there grew in her a strange feeling that this thing was no threat to her, and that those sorrowing and damning fate upon the river bank were its prey—not she.

She still trod in Herta's footsteps as they returned to the healer's cottage. But on the very doorstep she halted as if a wall had risen past which she could not go. Yet all she could see was a string of drying herbs somehow fallen from its ceiling hook. The odor from it grew more pungent and she made a small sound in her throat—more like a whine than a true protest.

Herta swept around and stood staring at her as if she were some fragment of the plague broken loose. The healer sank down on her chair. Her lips moved as if she were speaking.

Briary heard no sound, but there came a tingling in her skin as if the briars which had been her birthing bed once more pricked at her. There seemed to be stronger smells, and some of them she found worse than those which had come from the fire.

Her hands itched and she rubbed them together and then looked down in startled horror, for skin did not touch smooth skin—rather hair. She looked to see a down appearing—gray as fire ash and certainly not true skin. Frantically she pushed up her sleeves to discover that that fluff continued, and then she tore apart the fastening of her bodice and looked down upon just the same growth.

The plague! And yet the trader had showed no such stigmata. Briary cried out her terror and from her throat there arose no true words, but rather a howl.

Despairing she held out one of those strangely gloved hands toward Herta and went to her knees, begging aid.

The healer had arisen from her seat, the twisted astonishment on her face fading. She wet her lips with her tongue tip and then enunciated slowly as if speaking to a small child who must be made to understand.

"You are—Outling!" Again she wet her lips with tongue tip. "Now you meet your true self. Why I do not know, unless what has happened this day has also a strange effect on those of your blood. But this I will tell you, daughterling: get you away. They," she gave a short nod in the direction of the rest of the village, "will wish for one on whom to blame disaster—they will remember how unlike their kin you are—the more so now!"

"But," Briary's voice was hardly more than a harsh rumble. "I— I smelled the evil—I wished to aid—"

"Truth spoken. But you have never been one to measure beside the other younglings. There have always been some who wondered and whispered. And now that black doom has descended upon us, their whispers will become shouts."

"You call me Outling." Tears gathered in the girl's eyes, matted in the fur on her cheeks. "Am I then of the night demon kind?"

Herta shook her head. "Your kind is old. Before the first of the human landseekers came down valley your people knew this land. But then you passed, as a fading race passes when pressed by a stronger, fresher planting. I do not know why your mother returned here, though her need must have been sore, for death companied her. I do not—"

Suddenly she paused, arose from her chair. "The shrine," she said. "Surely only the shrine could have drawn her hither, that she must have aid for some dire hurt!"

"The shrine—?"

"Yes, that which lies beyond the pool. None ever saw clearly the Great One who ordered its building, nor did any who worked upon it understand why it was set here—at least they answered no questions. But if it *is* a thing of power for your kind perhaps you can save yourself there—"

"But you—the plague—" faltered Briary.

"Listen, youngling, ends come to all living creatures, and the reason behind such we do not ever know. I am a healer; what I can do for these people, some I have known from their cradles, that I shall do. But I also know how fear twists minds, and I will not have you fall into their hands. Someone need only say 'Outling,' and point a finger—and the hunt would be swift and short. Perhaps your mother lost in just such a race. Go you to the shrine. You, I am sure, will find no barrier at the screen there. Go beyond and may all the blessings of seed and fruit, earth, and stream, be upon you. Go—I say—already they are on the move."

Briary glanced back over her shoulder. Those who had thrown themselves on the river bank no longer were apart but had drawn together, and Herta was right, in that their faces were turned toward the healer's cottage.

Though what Herta had said had not seemed possible to the girl, she was certain that the healer believed her own words, was moved by fear—

Perhaps—perhaps they would also hunt down Herta if they fastened on Briary as the one who had somehow attracted ill fortune. After all, she was Herta's fosterling from birth.

It was too quick, too much, Herta's words—

"Ayyha, Healer—" A man's voice, those by the river were standing now, moving in their direction.

"Go!" She could not withstand Herta's command after all these years of obedience. Briary turned and ran.

As she went her clothing seemed to impede her movements, her skirts twisted about her legs to bring her down—as if such were not for her wearing. But she was still fleet of foot and, though she heard voices baying behind her as if hounds had been loosed, she gained the upper slopes, cut across recently mown fields, and then the pool was before her. The pool—and the screen. What lay behind that—who knew? Though some of the more venturesome had dived in the past to discover that there was space yawning at its foot.

Now she struggled with clothes which were more and more of a hindrance, until she at last poised to dive, her small body still human in form but clad in fine gray fur.

Down she fought her way through the water, straining to reach that dark line of the screen's edge. And then one of her hands hit against it and she seized upon the edge to pull herself forward—

into what? Some crevice in which her aching lungs would betray her?

Fortune was with her: the screen was less than her struggling body in length. She was still in the water but she could fight her way up frantically, until her head burst from the pool and she could breathe again, tread water, and look about her.

On this side of the barrier the expanse of water was far less, and facing the screen was a series of bars set in the stone as if to provide handholds to draw oneself out. She swam toward the nearest and pulled her body waist high into the open, her feet finding niches below into which they fitted by instinct.

Then she was fully out and facing what lay before her, what the screen had guarded all these years. It was not a large building, rather tall and narrow, hardly wider than the open doorway that pierced its side directly before her.

There was no door—only darkness—darkness thick as a curtain. Briary, not really knowing what she did, flung back her dripping head and gave voice to a call which no human could have uttered.

There was something like an early morning fog which gathered to the right of that opening, gathered, thickened, as flesh upon bone. Then she fronted a being far stranger than her known world held.

A woman, yes, for it stood on two feet, and held before its furred body a spear. Though the jaw was somewhat elongated, and the eyes set at a slight angle in the skull, which was framed with large furred ears, it was still enough like those she had dwelt among.

"What clan, cubling?" the woman guard asked.

Briary still clung to the handhold she had above the pool.

"Lady," she quavered, "I know nothing of clans."

The woman thing leaned forward a little and looked at her more closely.

"Threb's get. We thought you long dead, cubling. Neither of the People or of the Wasters are in truth, since Threb broke hearth law and lay with a Wasters to conceive you. So the Wasters have at last thrown you out?"

"No! It was Herta—and the plague—she was afeared that they would fasten on me the cause of their deaths." Somehow Briary felt she must make this statuelike figure understand and believe her.

Quickly she spoke of the healer who had brought her life and how now her own presence might threaten with harsh judgment.

"Ever the Wasters look beyond their own follies and errors to set the consequences upon others. Stupid they are—look you!"

She turned a fraction and sent the point of her spear into that dark behind her. It split and light poured out upon them, streaming from a land beyond. In Briary arose a mighty longing to race, not from what lay behind but toward what lay ahead.

"Their plagues are borne of dirt, of their rooting in their own waste." The guardian was scornful. "This land was ours before they befouled it, and every secret it had it freely shared with us. See you this?" She stabbed forward again and then swung the spear toward Briary. Impaled on its sharp point was a thing which wriggled and squirmed and yet seemed more vine section than any animal.

"This they have torn from its rooting wherever they discovered it; for to them it was nothing, and it covered ground which they wanted for their own purposes. Yet it had its duty which it did well. As other growth struggles for water to live, so this struggles for refuse and filth. They need only leaves to lay upon their ailing and aid would come. But they are fools and worse. Now, your gate is open, cubling; I make you free to the world in which you rightfully should have been born."

But Briary's eyes were on the plant. She suddenly roused herself and made a half leap to catch the vine with one hand. It rolled itself about her arm, and it was as if she had stuck her hand into a fire. Yet still she held to it.

The woman's green eyes measured her. "There is a price," she said evenly.

Briary nodded. Of course, there would be a price. But there was Herta, who knew herbs as a mother knows her children, and in Herta's hands this might yet save the village.

"If you return to the waste world"—the woman's voice was cold—"you will turn from all which is yours, and you may well pay for it with your blood. Outlings are hunted when they are seen. And it cannot be promised this gate will open to you again."

Briary huddled on the edge of the pool, her head turned to what lay beyond that doorway—a clean land in which her kind had found refuge. But between those flowers, and distant trees, and the warm sweet wind which beckoned to her, stood the vision of a sturdy woman, her gray hair knotted at her neck, her shoulder a little crooked from the many years of carrying a healer's bag.

Perhaps it was that portion of human blood which anchored her, but Herta she could not abandon.

"For your grace, thanks, Lady." She raised the arm about which the vine still clung. "This I must take to her who brought me into life and dealt always kindly with me."

Fearing that perhaps the guard might strive to take it from her, she dived once more, heading for that passage to the world she knew.

She made the journey as quickly as she could, climbed from the outer pool, and reluctantly put on her skirt and bodice though they were quickly wet through from her fur.

It was approaching dusk; that would serve her. She slunk as fast as she could from shadow to shadow. Then she saw—the cottage door was open wide—strewn outward from it were smashed pots and bottles, torn-apart lengths of drying herbs.

"Herta!" Only fear moved her now as she leaped forward. And she found what she sought, a bundle of torn clothing about blood-ied and bruised flesh. But still living—still living!

Through the night she tended the healer, trying to find among the debris the nostrums she needed, not daring to strike a light, lest she draw some villager. Oddly enough her sight seemed unhindered by the lack of any lamp, and she worked swiftly with practiced hands.

It was breaking dawn when Herta roused. She stared at Briary and then her face became a mask of fear—

"Off with you! I would not have them gut you before my very eyes."

"Listen, Heart Held." Few times in her life had Briary used those words but she realized they had been with her forever. Swiftly she swung up her arm to which the vine still somehow clung and repeated what the guard had told her.

"Bindweed, rot guts." Herta looked at her offering in wonder. "Yes, it has always been rooted forth wherever found. Cattle eat of it and die, as do the fowl of the barnyard. And now you say that it, also, has its part and the folly has been ours. Well, enough, one can only try to do one's best."

She somehow got to her feet and Briary found that the vine slipped from her furred arms smoothly as metal. Looking at that she thought she knew its price which had never been fully stated.

"I shall go," she said in her new hoarse voice. "None shall see me with you. Certainly not all of those in the village have turned mad. You have been their ever-present aid for many seasons. Let the bindweed work but once and they shall know shame at their madness. But not if I remain."

"Where do you go?" There were seldom seen tears on Herta's cheeks.

"That lies in fortune's hands. But see it is nearly light and—" The girl shivered, "I hear voices."

Herta reached for her but she slid from the other's grasp, and somehow only the bulky clothing remained for Herta to hold. Then she was running free with the rising first wind of morning around her, up and back, up and back.

She was Outling with nothing now here to hold her unless she

was weak in purpose. The gate to her own place might indeed be
closed by her choice, but she had the right to go and see.

Reaching the side of the pool, Briary paused once to look down
to those about Herta's cottage as the morn's light made them clear.
And then she dove arrow quick and smooth into the water, down
and down, until the dark edge of the screen was before her. Nor
did she hesitate to see what her choice had cost her but swam on,
for this was the thing she had to do.

AFTERWORD

I first met Roger when we were both inhabitants of Cleveland in
the very dim days of the past. He was a warm and generous person,
someone one felt at home with at once. And while a great deal of
distance divided us in the following years, I had the pleasure of
looking forward to his next spectacular production in print. Such
as he leave an unfillable void behind—but also set goals for those
who followed.

In Eye of Cat *Roger presented one future for New Mexico's Indian people. Here Pati Nagle takes a wry look at a future that seems all too possible for the Land of Enchantment.*

■

ARROYO DE ORO
Pati Nagle

HE WAS BEAUTIFUL. AN ANGEL'S FACE—SOFT BROWN HAIR FRAMING chiseled cheeks, skin so fair it seemed never to have seen the sun, and the sweetest almost-smile on his lips—that was my first deader.

He was found at 10:47 A.M. in one of the less-frequented hallways of the Rainbow Man Hotel and Casino, right near the hologram of the Blue Corn Maiden. See, every morning at 11:00 the Maiden speaks—a recorded blurb about her role in pueblo religion—which is what the tourists who found him came to hear. But I doubt they caught a word.

By time I got there it was almost 11:30. I left the field office as soon as the call came in, but downtown Albuquerque is a long way from "Arroyo de Oro." That's what they call the strip. It runs right up the Sandia Reservation on the north edge of town, and it rivals Las Vegas for glitz.

I got on the freeway and headed north, feeling pretty unhappy about the assignment. I am not a cloak and dagger kind of girl. Numbers I can do; my background is in accounting, and I naturally expected my job with the FBI would entail investigating bank fraud and money laundering and that sort of thing. When they sent me to New Mexico after graduation I figured I might also have to handle some shady across-the-border deals, but murder investigations I was not expecting. This murder, however, had taken place on the reservation and was therefore under Federal jurisdiction, so I got tapped to help check it out.

The directions said to take the Tramway Exit and turn toward the mountains. Serious mountains, too—bare granite jutting up over the city—pretty stark for a girl used to wheat fields and rolling green hills. There was not much green here to speak of at all, and as if it wasn't enough that the land was brown, these people had to make most of their buildings brown, too. I had been in town all of two days, and was already wondering how soon I could transfer back east.

I reached the exit, turned toward this gigantic arch, all neon, that said "Welcome to Arroyo de Sandia," and drove under it. It was like entering another world.

Hotels lined the street, neon-traced towers crowding right up to the sidewalks, flashing and glittering even in midday. Hotel Sandia, Hotel Bien-Mur, Hotel Kokopeli, each with its own casino. Traffic crawled, blocked by herds of tourists on foot walking up and down in sneakers and shorts with big plastic cups in their hands. More tourists in rented cars sat gawking at the glitz and, OK, I did a little gawking myself, especially when I got to the Rainbow Man. Big, flashy entrance with a gigantic neon figure on the hotel tower above it. It was a kachina; I had learned that much, having seen bunches of kachina dolls in the airport.

Kachinas are sort of minor deities, only not exactly. This one's head was a mask, with black rectangles for eyes and some feathers and horns and things. The feet were pretty normal, but the body between them arced in an enormous rainbow that put head and feet on the same level. Gorgeous. I stared at it too long. The red Camaro behind me had to lean on his horn before I realized the light had changed.

I parked on a side street that was a box canyon of slab-sided casinos. All the glitz was out front on the Arroyo. I hurried back toward Rainbow Man's entrance and went into what I thought was the lobby, but it turned out to be the casino, and I immediately got lost. The place was a labyrinth; big rooms full of light and color and this incessant circus music. Took me a few minutes to realize it was the slot machines. Man, I don't know how anybody can stand that sound all day long.

I wandered around a while, thinking I had to be getting close, but every time I thought the crime scene should be around the next corner there was a restaurant instead, or a bank of elevators. I never saw so many little hallways and fountains and things. And everywhere—in corners and crannies, and odd little coves—were these holograms of kachinas. Life-sized, so lifelike they were scary. They bothered me, mostly because I knew that kachinas had some kind of religious meanings of which I was entirely ignorant.

Well, I broke down and asked for directions. Twice. By the time I finally found the crime scene I had lost a significant measure of my professional cool, and a crowd was already gathering. I had my hand clamped around my badge, and flashed it to the first cop-looking guy I saw—a huge man—Hispanic or Native American, I wasn't sure. He was wearing a gray wool suit, mildly rumpled, that looked pretty nice even on his bulk.

He took one look at me and said "More feds? We got Chase here already."

"I'm Agent Sandra Marsh," I said, pocketing my badge. "I'm here to assist Special Agent Chase."

"Armando Mora, BIA PD," he said, sounding bored. His face was a mask of stone. He glanced away and shouted "Arnold, get the damned spectators out of here, will you?"

Some men in brown Tribal Police uniforms started shepherding the crowd away, and the big guy went to help while I was still trying to remember what "BIA" stood for. That's when I spotted the yellow tape and the deader lying behind it on his back, his blood pooled around him like a mantle.

A woman was kneeling beside him, black "FBI" windbreaker proclaiming her an evidence tech. Standing over him was a hologram: the Blue Corn Maiden. She was wearing a black dress and moccasins, and a shawl, and a mask painted blue with black rectangles for the eyes. Her hair was black too, done up in a kind of Princess Leia do on the sides of her head, and she was holding a basket filled with ears of corn.

I ducked under the tape, and got up close to the deader. Man, he was gorgeous! Late twenties, very slender, dressed in silk trousers and a shirt that had to have been tailored: the model/actor type. His eyes were closed; unusual, perhaps done by the killer. I knelt beside him, and the tech glanced at me.

"Shot, or stabbed?" I asked.

"Stabbed, I think. Nobody reported a shot."

She picked up his hand—long delicate fingers—and began slipping a plastic bag over it. I looked at that serene face again, wondering who had destroyed such beauty, and why. I'm not ashamed to admit wishing I'd met him alive.

"Do we have an ID?" I asked.

"Alan Malone," said a rich, deep voice to my right.

I glanced up and found myself staring at the Blue Corn Maiden, but she couldn't have spoken in that masculine voice. Just past her a tall man in a worn leather jacket was leaning against the wall, taking an unhurried drag on a pipe. The coal glowed angry-hot as he pulled on it, at odds with the calm blue of his eyes. High forehead, big crooked nose, looked vaguely northern European. He was staring kind of absently at the body, jaw cocked a little to one side and a muscle or a vein pulsing on his temple underneath the thinning hair.

I stood up. "Special Agent Chase?"

He unfolded a lanky arm to shake my hand, then took the pipe from his mouth. "Welcome to New Mexico," he said. "I hear you've just arrived."

"Yes," I said, straightening my shoulders a little. Yeah, I was defensive. Every cop I met was giving me the cool treatment, and this guy was no different.

"You'll find Albuquerque is very different from Quantico. He's a singer," he said, gesturing toward the deader with the pipe. "Was, I mean. Worked here, in the Kachina Theater. Two shows a night, dark Tuesdays."

"Dark?"

"No show. It's their only day off."

It was Wednesday. "So he was killed coming in this morning?" I said.

"Probably. Except that this hallway is nowhere near the theater entrance."

"Between it and the parking lot?"

"Not really," said Chase. "There's an exit nearby, but there are closer ones to the theater."

The BIA guy came back from shooing off the gawkers, and walked up to Chase. "How soon can we get him out of here?" he said.

"Easy, Mondo," said Chase. "Did any of the staff see him alive?"

"Not so far. We're still talking to the buffet people. The manager's bitching—it's almost time for lunch to open."

Chase glanced past the Corn Maiden. "The line forms out there?"

"Right there," said the big cop, nodding his head. He got an extra chin with each downward thrust of his jaw.

Chase looked down the hallway, then back at Mondo, and got this gentle little smile. "Maybe you should find a screen, then," he said. He turned to me. "Shall we go look at the theater?"

"Sure," I said. I followed him back the way I'd come, walking fast to keep up with his long stride, knowing I would most likely get lost again trying to find my way through the casino alone. "Um, Special Agent—"

"Call me Chase," he said.

"OK. Do you happen to know where there's a restroom?"

"Should be one right over here." He led me past some craps tables to a bank of restrooms tucked in a corner, and said, "Meet you back here."

He was nowhere in sight, however, when I came out. I waited, looking across the casino, watching the tourists gamble, listening to the clatter of slots paying off.

"I am Buffalo," boomed a voice beside me.

"Jesus!" I said, jumping.

A hologram set off in a little alcove near the restrooms had come to life: a big guy in a huge furry headdress-robe thing that went all the way down his back. In one hand he held a rattle, which he started to shake. Distant drums throbbed.

"I am the gift of the Great Spirit," he said. "I give the blessings of my body to the people. . . ."

"All set?" said a voice behind me, and I jumped again. Chase had come out of nowhere. He hadn't been in the men's room, and he hadn't come across the casino, and the only thing behind me was a wall.

"Shit," I muttered. My heart was pounding.

"Sorry," said Chase. "Didn't mean to scare you."

He sucked on his pipe, and glanced at the hologram giving its spiel. Then, just as I was really beginning to wish I was back in Quantico, he turned those blue eyes on me and smiled.

It transformed him. Suddenly he wasn't just another tired cop, but a human being full of love and joy, sharing something fun with me, simply because I was a fellow human. Swear to god, his eyes actually twinkled. He grinned at me, and said, "They give me the willies, too!"

I managed a smile in return. Chase took off toward the casino again.

We passed more slots, poker tables, holograms of course, some kind of big wheel-of-fortune thingie, and still more slots. I followed Chase through an acre of blackjack and up a half-dozen steps to some closed banks of doors labeled "Kachina Theater" in orange and green neon. Two big holograms with antlers and bits of pine branches hanging off them stood on either side. Chase knocked at the center doors, knocked again, then pushed them open and we went in.

Dark. After all the noise and light of the casino, I felt like I'd stepped into some underground cavern. The doors fell shut with a muffled whump, sealing us off from light and life. I peered hard at nothing, trying to adjust my eyes.

A gust of wind hit my face with an audible "whoosh." In the distance something pale moved. My neck hairs prickled; I stared at it until I discerned a bird flying, flapping great, lazy wings, glowing white against the darkness, growing closer, larger. An eagle; no, an eagle kachina with long, feathered wings strapped to arms that filled the width of the room as it rose toward us, enormous, majestic and terrible. I could hear the flap of the great wings, feel their wind wash over me. It flew overhead and vanished, leaving me drenched in silence.

"Sorry to interrupt," said Chase pleasantly beside me, "but we need to talk to someone connected to the show."

"Tickets at the concierge desk," an irritated voice returned from the darkness. "Sorry, no visitors. You'll have to leave the theater."

I noticed a dim row of aisle markers on the floor. My eyes were adjusting. Chase was now a shadow nearby.

"We're not visitors," he said. "We're with the FBI. If you'll bring up some lights and talk with us, we'll try not to take up too much of your time."

Mutterings, indistinguishable. I glanced over my shoulder at the doors. The faint seam of light between them flickered; a silent shadow passing. My skin prickled with the sense of someone unexpectedly near, and I was still peering after the shadow when the lights came up hard, making me blink. There was no one there.

"Thank you," said Chase.

I followed him down the steps to where three men were sitting in a booth; two Native Americans and one Anglo. The natives both had that ageless, flat, round face that looked like it hid centuries of secrets; they stared at Chase with dark, watchful eyes. The white guy was around forty, with frizzy, graying hair in a ponytail and a pair of headphones around his neck. He looked pissed.

Chase flashed his badge. "Any of you know Alan Malone?"

"Yeah," said the white guy. "The little shit's late."

"Well, yes, as a matter of fact," said Chase gently. He was halfway through explaining before I noticed the pun. Cop humor. I gave him a look but he seemed not to notice, except that a corner of his mouth twitched a little. The others didn't have a clue.

"Oh, man!" said the Anglo, his eyebrows going up. "Oh, shit! Joe, call Ben and tell him to get down here!"

One of the natives nodded and started up the aisle at a jog. "Joe," I wrote in my pocket notebook, starting a list of people to interview.

"Can I have your name, sir?" I said.

"Huh? Oh, sure. Stauffer. Daniel. Jesus, when did he die?"

"We're not sure yet," said Chase. "When was the last time you saw him?"

"Monday night. Final performance of 'The Wild West.' "

Stauffer turned out to be the director for the Kachina Theater. He

alternated between puzzlement over Malone's death and dismay at
its impact on the upcoming premiere, and some kind of excitement
that I didn't fully understand.

A few other people connected with the show emerged from various parts of the theater. Most of them, to my surprise, were white,
not Native American. A couple were Hispanic. I took down names
while Chase encouraged Stauffer to chat about Malone and the
show. It sounded spectacular; from the way he was talking the
eagle we'd seen was nothing. Live performers interacting with holographic gods, acting out the legend of creation. State-of-the-art
physical simulation effects. When Stauffer offered Chase a pair of
tickets, I felt a stab of envy.

Stauffer glanced past me, and I turned to see Joe coming back.
I suppressed a shiver; hadn't heard the door.

"He's coming," said Joe.

"Good," said Stauffer. "Jesus. OK, let's set everything up for the
opening number again. Tom, recalibrate the soundtrack for Ben."

"Who's Ben?" Chase and I asked in unison.

"He's, um, Malone's understudy," said Stauffer.

"Hey, Danny," yelled a stagehand. "Somebody's made a mess
of the props!"

"Shit!" said Stauffer, pulling off the headphones and starting
down the aisle toward the stage.

"We'll get out of your way," said Chase.

Stauffer paused. "Yeah, I'm sorry—"

"So are we. We'll be in touch."

I followed Chase up the steps. As he opened the door the casino's noise struck me like thunder. I paused, gearing up to plunge
into that chaos of light and sound. I'd always been kind of curious
about Las Vegas or Atlantic City, but now I was beginning to lose
interest. The people sitting at the slots all had this kind of weary,
hope-against-hope expression as they fed the machines gold tokens
from their plastic cups. False gold, false hopes. Seemed everything
around here was false.

"Let's go talk to the manager," said Chase, raising his voice
over the circus music. "You should meet him."

"You know him?"

Chase nodded. "Been working pretty closely with all the managers in the Arroyo. Setting up good relations, so they'll cooperate
when there's a problem. Lets them know we're watching out for
trouble."

We passed several craps tables and some banks of blackjack tables I hadn't previously seen. "Are all the casinos like this?" I
asked.

"Like what?"

"Uh—this big, I guess."

"Pretty much," said Chase, heading up a half dozen steps. At their top the red carpet gave way to marble floors and velvet ropes. We were suddenly in the hotel lobby, and the noise of the slots diminished behind us as we crossed it. I sighed with relief. Chase led me past a bank of elevators and down a hall.

Another kachina stood a little way ahead. This one was male, wearing a green mask with feathers on top and a white kilt-thing. His bare torso was painted black with green and yellow designs.

"This way," said Chase's voice behind me.

Turning, I saw him standing at the foot of an escalator discreetly tucked into an alcove. I'd gone right past without even seeing it. We rode up to a floor blessedly silent: not a slot, not a video game, not a scrap of neon. Even the carpet was more subdued. A small brass sign pointed the way to Meeting Rooms.

Chase led me through a set of carved double doors into a plush reception area. I mean, seriously plush. Leather sofa and chairs. Bronze planters full of calla lilies. Expensive art on the walls.

"Good afternoon, Mr. Chase," said a smiling Native American receptionist.

"Hello, Sally. This is Agent Marsh. Is Kyler still in that meeting?"

"All day. Can Emily help you?" said the receptionist.

"Sure," said Chase. He sat down on the leather couch and invited me to join him. I did, feeling a flash of the little kid's trepidation at sitting on the grown-up furniture. Chase's fingers tapped the shiny brass of an ashtray standing next to the couch. The pristine sand had been shaped by some modern magic into a relief of the Rainbow Man's mask.

"Mr. Chase?" said a soft voice to our right.

A woman walked out of a side hall and up to us, a pretty Native American with a long waterfall of black hair spilling over the shoulders of her cream-colored suit. She looked vaguely familiar, I thought. Chase stood up and shook her hand.

"Ms. True-hee-oh," he said. (I learned later from Mondo that it's spelled "Trujillo.") "This is Agent Marsh."

She shook my hand with dry, warm fingers. "I'm Mr. Kyler's assistant. How can I help you?"

"Can you give us a room to conduct interviews?" said Chase. "We're investigating the death of Alan Malone."

Sally the Receptionist's eyebrows went up, and she glanced at Ms. Trujillo, whose face showed a flicker of pain. The latter opened one of the heavy doors and led us out into the empty hallway.

The escalator hummed quietly at our feet. Ms. Trujillo led us down a hall flanked on one side by meeting rooms and the other by a wall of glass. The windows overlooked the hotel's swimming pool, a huge affair with a waterfall, lots of landscaping, and a couple dozen tourists courting melanoma.

She took out a keychain and opened a door to a small room dominated by a conference table. Masks on the walls acted as sconces, light gleaming behind their eyes. I didn't like them; they made me feel like I was being watched.

"You can use this room for your interviews," she said.

"Fine," said Chase. "Have a seat, please. I just have a few questions."

Ms. Trujillo sat across the table from us. "I'm sorry," Chase added. "I understand that you and Malone were close."

"We were good friends," said Ms. Trujillo, her voice barely above a whisper.

"Not lovers?" Chase's voice was gentle, but his eyes watched. I was glad I wasn't the one being questioned.

"Friends," she said firmly.

"When did you see him last?"

Ms. Trujillo's eyes got faraway, and she didn't respond for a moment. Then she blinked, and sighed. "Sunday there was a Corn Dance at the pueblo. He always came to the public dances."

"Any trouble between you?"

Her eyelashes fell over her eyes—black slits—then she looked up at Chase. "No."

"No disagreements?"

"We understood each other. He was very interested in our ways. He studied them. He knew them well."

"Where were you this morning?"

"In my office. Sally can tell you."

"Thank you," said Chase. He leaned back in his chair. "Can you get us a list of everyone who works in the theater? I know they're having a rehearsal, but we need to start interviewing—"

"I'll have Sally make you a copy of the roster," said Ms. Trujillo. I suddenly realized why she seemed familiar. She reminded me of the Blue Corn Maiden.

"Ms. Trujillo, did you pose for any of the kachina holograms?" I asked on impulse.

A flash of scorn in her eyes surprised me, then her lids half-hid them and her face became a mask of calm. "Those are actors," she said flatly.

"Well, you might have done one for fun—"

"No," she said. "I didn't pose for them." She looked from me to Chase, then stood up. "I've got some calls to make," she said. "Is there anything else you need?"

"Just that list," said Chase.

"Sally will bring it to you. Would you like some coffee?"

"Yes, thanks," said Chase.

She left, sable hair swaying. I glanced at Chase, who gazed at the doorway long after she was out of sight. She *was* pretty. I suppose if I were a man I'd stare after her, too.

Chase took off to find out about the autopsy, leaving me to spend the rest of the afternoon interviewing Malone's coworkers with the masks glaring down like a row of judges. Mondo fetched dancers and stage crew and waiters for me to grill. Dark-eyed natives from catering looked in now and then, silently refilling water and coffee, and once leaving a plate of dull but nourishing sandwiches.

Through the interviews I began to build a picture of Malone. They all agreed he was talented, well-liked, and would be sorely missed. No one could think of any reason someone would want to kill him. No one could even think of anyone who disliked him. He had no ex-wives, estranged lovers, or creditors. His drug use was confined to an occasional joint backstage. He didn't gamble, drank moderately, never fought except for disagreements with Stauffer over staging and such. His family lived back east, and he spoke of them lovingly and infrequently. Yes, they'd been notified. The mother was flying in to claim her angel boy.

Chase called around five to tell me the ME's opinion: Malone had been stabbed several times in the back with a thin, straight-bladed knife, possibly a stiletto. The killer was right-handed and no taller than Malone. Time of death between 9:30 and 10:30 A.M., and how was I doing with the interviews? I told him fine, fine. Actually, I was pretty discouraged.

I hung up and looked at the list Sally had brought. Check marks ran down three quarters of the page, with gaps here and there where some folks had not yet come in to work. A number of those I'd interviewed had alibied each other, and I'd established that Malone had been alive and well when he left the hotel after Monday night's performance. Beyond that I hadn't learned much.

The door opened, and Mondo stuck his head in. "Got the director for you finally. And the understudy. Which one you want first?"

"Understudy," I said. I was getting ticked at the director, who'd been putting me off all afternoon, so now it was his turn to wait. "Hey, Mondo—did the victim's car turn up?"

He nodded. "In the parking garage. Nothing useful in it. Nothing in the apartment either."

"OK, thanks." Malone's life was too clean. This was not going to be easy.

Mondo let in a sharp-dressed, slick-haired stud whose every

move said "gay." He sat down across from me while I ran a finger down my list.

"Good afternoon, Mr. . . ."

"Hanes," he said. "Benjamin Hanes."

"Mr. Hanes. Where were you before nine this morning?"

"With my voice coach. Every Wednesday."

"All morning?"

"Till eleven. Then I had lunch with a friend, and then Joe paged me and I came down here. I guess I got here around one."

"You hadn't been here before that?"

"No, thank God! Poor Alan!"

"What was your relationship with Alan Malone?"

Hanes laughed. "Purely professional. Alan was depressingly straight. We all used to—"

"You were his understudy," I said.

"Yes."

"So you stood to gain from his death."

His cheerful mask slipped a little. "I resent that," he said with a laugh, but instead of sounding light he sounded sullen. "I would never hurt Alan."

"I see. Do you know of anyone who would?"

"I can't imagine. Everyone adored him. Even Miss T, and she doesn't much care for the rest of us."

"Why not?" I asked.

"Doesn't like the new show, on account of the kachinas. Doesn't like the holograms either."

Now that was interesting. Maybe Ms. Trujillo had wanted to stop the premiere.

"Did she argue about the show with Malone?"

"Not that I know of. He knew how she felt, and she knew he had to work."

So dies a promising lead. I felt like I'd reached for a door, only to have the handle melt away under my hand. I asked Hanes a few more questions and got nothing useful, so I freed him and called for the director. They passed in the doorway and exchanged a glance that told me something more about Hanes.

"Thank you for taking the time to come up, Mr. Stauffer," I said. "I know you've been rehearsing all day."

The director looked haggard and pissed as he sat down. Coming in he'd looked worried. It had been a long day and I didn't feel like pussyfooting around, so I said "You and Mr. Hanes are lovers, right?"

He frowned at me, then shrugged. "Yeah. You keeping a list of everybody Ben's slept with?"

"Not yet. Where were you this morning before nine?" I said.

He sighed. "In the theater, setting up for the premiere."

"When did you arrive?"

"I never left last night. I crashed upstairs."

I hadn't expected that. "In a hotel room?"

"Yeah. There's usually a couple free. Mr. Kyler lets us use 'em if we're crunched for time mounting a new show."

"Was anyone with you?"

"Ben went home. He wasn't anywhere near the place until this afternoon."

"That's not what I asked."

Stauffer's frown deepened a bit. "Steve Clay shared the room with me. He's on an errand right now, be back in about an hour."

"What's the errand?" I asked.

"Somebody dicked with our props, and there's one missing. He's getting a replacement."

A chill ran down my back. "What kind of prop?" A knife, perhaps?

"A rattle."

Oh.

"Did you like Alan Malone?" I asked, for lack of a better question.

"Sure, I liked him. He was a decent guy. Saw things his own way, of course. All actors do."

"But you're glad Ben has his part now, right?"

Stauffer sat back, as if he'd been waiting for that. "Listen, Ben's got a lot of talent"—he dropped his voice with a glance at the door—"but he's no Alan Malone. Yeah, I'm glad he's getting a shot, but if you think I'd kill Alan to give it to him, you're crazy."

There was not much more to say. I got the names of his alibis for the morning, and let him go back to the theater. It was almost six by now and Mondo was looking hungry, so I called it a day. With my notes under my arm I headed back down the escalator in search of dinner, grateful to be up and about even if it meant running the casino gauntlet again.

I swear they were moving the walls. The place never looked the same twice, except that it all looked more or less the same. Slots, slots, tables, slots, and holograms. I noticed one I'd seen before— a guy painted red all over with a big, snaggle-toothed snout on his mask—and made a mental note of the landmark. I was making progress; the casino still disoriented me, but it didn't seem quite so huge. I had almost gone past the Blue Corn Maiden before I recognized her and stopped.

The little hallway was empty. A damp area of recently shampooed carpet was the only sign of disturbance. I stared at it, feeling a crazy stab of loss. Blue Corn Maiden still stood guard over the spot where Alan Malone had died, but the casino had already forgotten him. Well, I wouldn't. Someone that handsome—and, apparently, that nice—deserved justice.

Looking up at the hologram, I had no idea why I'd thought she was like Ms. Trujillo. Her hair wasn't loose, and her face was a mask. I reached toward her, my hands passing through the air where she was and was not. My fingers seemed to disappear into her basket of corn.

"There you are," said Chase's voice behind me, making me jump again.

"Damn it," I said. "Quit sneaking up on mc like that!"

"Sorry. What were you doing with the hologram?"

I looked up at him, then on impulse I stepped into the hologram and turned to face him.

He shook his head. "Doesn't work. You're just blocking the projector. Watch."

I moved aside, and when Chase stepped into her place the Corn Maiden vanished. We found the projection equipment in the wall behind her, and played a little more with the image, figuring out how it worked. We concluded the hologram could hide a small object—my notebook disappeared nicely into her feet—but nothing as big as a person. Still, the back of my neck tingled, as if some dormant hunter's sense had awakened. I fumbled with the projectors, squinting to see past the bright beams of light, and spotted a small red button.

Flute music blasted out of the speaker in front of me. I jumped back, and the hologram flicked into existence, raising the basket of corn in her arms.

"I am the Blue Corn Maiden," she said. "I guard the seed of the sacred corn, and watch over the young plants as they grow. I am the keeper of our gift from the gods."

"What did you do?" said Chase, as the Corn Maiden gestured in different directions with her basket.

"Pushed a button," I said.

"You must have found a test mode."

The flute music subsided, and the Corn Maiden resumed her normal frozen stance.

"Chase . . . would you mind blocking the projectors again? I want to check something."

"Not now," he said softly. I turned and saw Ms. Trujillo coming toward us.

"Agent Chase, I'm glad I caught you," she said. "I had a note from Daniel Stauffer asking me to give you these," she said, handing him an envelope. He took it, and pulled out a pair of tickets.

"They're for the seven o'clock dinner show," said Ms. Trujillo. "Is that all right?"

"Fine," said Chase. "Want one?" he asked, turning to me and making me blush, because of course, yes I did.

Ms. Trujillo smiled briefly at us both, said, "Enjoy the show," and headed back into the depths of the casino.

Chase held out a ticket. I glanced up and saw him smiling. I guess I was more tired than I'd realized, because that smile hit me straight in the chest.

"Thanks," I said, taking the ticket and hoping he hadn't noticed how red I was getting.

"Be warned—I'm going to talk about work," he said.

Chase led the way back into the depths of the casino. I saw the Buffalo guy coming up, and noted that he was near a large bank of slots with a neon eagle above them. Across from him was a doorway.

Now, I was pretty sure that that was the same wall I'd been standing by earlier, and there had not been a door in it, and there had not been a hologram in front of it either, but now there was. I stared at the kachina, which had curving antennae and was painted head to toe in black and white stripes. He was wearing a black kilt and holding what looked like a handful of grass. How I could have missed him earlier I don't know.

Chase went through the doorway into a fern bar. He made a beeline for a table of executive types, one of who looked up and grinned.

"Chase! Pull up a chair! Who's your friend?"

"Agent Marsh. She's assisting me in the investigation," said Chase, turning to me with a nod. "This is Mr. Kyler."

"Agent Marsh," said a big, friendly rancher-type, standing up to shake my hand. "Pleased to meet you." His smile was the painted-on kind you see on politicians and other salesmen. He said names around the circle—they turned out to be the Rainbow Man's board of directors, every last one of them white—and offered to buy us a drink. We sat in padded leather chairs and I sipped at a beer while Chase settled into a glass of Irish whiskey.

"Terrible about Malone," said Kyler. "We were just discussing it. Terrible. He was a great draw."

"Maybe the new guy won't cost so much," said a silver-haired guy with a Texas twang. "You always used to gripe about how expensive this kid was."

"Yeah, but he was good," said Kyler. "Pulled in the crowds. Gotta keep those patrons coming in. You'll wind this thing up nice and quiet, won't you, Chase?"

Chase shrugged and sipped his liquor. "Do what I can. Murder is never tidy, though."

The talk turned to the casino and a new hotel Mr. Kyler was planning further up the Strip. Most of it was about negotiations to lease the land from the pueblo. Boring stuff. After a few minutes I excused myself, promising to meet Chase at the theater at quarter to seven. I went past the elevators and up the discreet escalator to businessland. There was something I wanted to check without Chase around.

I pushed against the heavy double doors, half expecting them to be locked, but they weren't. They creaked a little as I poked my head in. Sally the Receptionist looked up from her desk.

"Oh, hello," she said. "Did you need something?"

I came in, letting the doors fall shut behind me. "I just have a couple of questions, if you don't mind. Were you leaving?"

"In a few minutes. Have a seat."

I watched her tidy up some papers on her desk. She had a round face and short, curly black hair. Smiled easily. A mama type. "You're working late," I said.

"Because of the board meeting," said Sally. "I had to get tomorrow's agenda straightened out. Things got off schedule today."

"What time did Mr. Kyler get here this morning?" I asked.

"Around eight, I think," said Sally.

"Did you see him come in?"

"Yes. He and Mr. Parker came in together. They went out again, but I'm not sure when."

Parker was one of the guys I'd met in the lounge. I made a note.

"What time did you get here?"

"Mm—ten to eight, I guess."

"Was anyone else here who might have seen them?"

"Emily was in her office. She spent the whole morning on the phone."

"Ms. Trujillo? Is her office near his?"

"Yes—let me show you."

She got up and led me down a wide hallway. The plush carpet deadened our footsteps. Sally waved a hand toward an open doorway. "That's Emily's office, and this is Mr. Kyler's."

I didn't get to Kyler's. Behind the desk in the corner of Ms. Trujillo's office stood a kachina hologram. It was a woman, with a white mask and towering stairstep headdress—decked in feathers and carved wooden flowers—a red shawl, and a white skirt. I stared at her.

"That's the Butterfly Maiden," said Sally. "They did a pretty good job on that one. At least I think so. She's Hopi, so I'm not sure."

"What's she doing in Ms. Trujillo's office?"

"Mr. Kyler gave her to Emily. He pretty much gives her what she wants."

"She wanted this?"

Sally nodded. "She asked for it Monday. I'm not sure why—she doesn't really like them. Mr. Kyler wanted them because there was some unhappiness when this hotel was built. It's the only hotel in the Arroyo that's not Indian-owned."

"So he decided to add some Ind—some Native American culture."

Sally nodded. "Emily tried to talk him out of it, but he went ahead with it. The holograms were created by Dan Stauffer and his staff, using local actors. Some people got very angry."

"Does it make you angry?"

She hesitated. "They're not really kachinas," she said slowly. "They're more like the dolls—something you could use to teach about the kachinas—only these aren't very accurate. I guess I would like it better if they weren't here, but I want to keep my job, so I don't say anything."

How many others feel that way, I wondered? I reached through the image, skin tingling, and found the projector on the wall behind. As my hands blocked the light the image vanished, and I glanced at the floor. Nothing there.

"Are you and Ms. Trujillo from the same, uh—"

"Pueblo?" said Sally. (I'd been about to say "tribe.") "Yes, we're both from Sandia."

I looked through the doorway at Kyler's office across the hall, then back at the hologram. Butterfly Maiden bothered me.

"Tell me about Sandia," I said.

"We're one of the smallest pueblos. Less than five hundred. A big family, really."

"I heard something about a dance—"

"Oh, the Corn Dance. Yes, it was just a couple of days ago."

Corn Dance. Corn Maiden. A connection?

"Was Alan Malone there?" I asked, remembering something Ms. Trujillo had said.

"Oh, yes. He's been coming to all the dances this year. He likes to pick up the feel of them, for the new show."

"Did he have any enemies in Sandia?"

Sally's eyes widened a little. "No—everyone liked him. Even the elders. He's—he was—always very polite."

I stared at Sally's flat face, feeling like I was forgetting to ask some basic question. Something like, "Did you kill the guy?" I didn't think Sally was the murderer, though. Besides the fact that she and Ms. Trujillo had both been upstairs all morning, she was just too nice. She let me stand there a full minute before she started to fidget.

"This is Mr. Kyler's office," she said, stepping across the hall. I peered into a huge room with big picture windows. The late sun was slanting through orange anvil clouds outside, and the Arroyo was really beginning to sparkle. I could see a corner of the Cibola Hotel across the street, all gold-glitter glitz.

Kyler had a hologram too—the Rainbow Man, of course—along with other bits of expensive art and a desk made out of some huge gnarled tree trunk. On it sat a Rainbow Man kachina doll: foot-high, carved wood, like the ones I'd seen at the airport.

"Is there anything else you wanted to see?" Sally asked.

"Yeah," I said, giving up. "A photo of Alan Malone."

I followed her back to the foyer, and she dug up an eight-by-ten glossy and two show flyers, one for "The Wild West" and one for "Pageant of Creation."

"We'll have to redo that one, I guess," she said, handing them over.

"Thanks, Sally," I said. "You've been a big help."

I went down to the theater, which I found by a somewhat round-about but effective route of Buffalo-guy to neon eagle to Red Snout to black-with-rabbit-ears to antlers. The casino looked exactly as it had at midday—bright lights, lots of color, lots of noise—and I realized there were no windows and no clocks anywhere. Made sense, I guess. If you're a casino owner you don't want your customers thinking about how late it is.

The theater was open and I was promptly seated in a booth, one of the best seats in the house, for the simple reason that it faced the stage. The tiers above and below the booths were jammed with narrow tables perpendicular to the stage; people sitting there would have to turn their heads to see the show. Cram in the customers, make big bucks.

The stage was hidden behind a glittery blue curtain. In front of it a giant hologram hung in midair: the Rainbow Man's mask, with black rectangle eyes. I took out Alan Malone's black and white glossy, held it in both hands and stared at it long and hard. His eyes—which I had only seen closed—had been blue or gray or some other light color; they almost looked clear in the photo. His smile was intensely charming. Gorgeous boy, everyone's darling. Why did you die? And who closed your eyes against the night?

I looked at the "Wild West" flyer, dismissed it, and picked up the one for "Pageant of Creation." The eagle kachina we'd seen earlier was on the front page, along with a full-length photo of Alan Malone all in white. I opened the flyer, activating a snap-holo, the gimmicky kind you find in greeting cards. The eagle again, soaring across the page before winking out. Not a cheap flyer. Too bad they'd have to redo it. Alan Malone had clearly been the star attraction; his face and name were all over the brochure, along with slogans like "Discover Sandia's Ancient Mysteries" and "Journey through the Indian Myth of Creation." I wondered why Malone—obviously talented but undeniably white—was the star of a show about Native American mythology. Circumstance, maybe. Malone probably had a contract with the hotel, and the show had been designed to attract tourists. Plug star into show and you have an instant hit, right?

"Looking forward to the show?"

I looked up at Chase. He sat down across from me and leaned across the table. "What do you have?" he said.

I told him the results of my interviews. He nodded and said I'd done well, which was nice of him.

"No one has a clear motive," I said. "Did the weapon ever turn up?"

Chase shook his head. "Mondo's boys spent the day going through every trash can and Dumpster on the premises," he said. "They're starting on the neighboring hotels."

I sighed. "No weapon, no motive, no suspect. So far we don't have much of a case."

"It's early yet," said Chase. "And we have a potential suspect. You said Stauffer had motive."

"Yeah, and when I pointed it out he agreed, and then denied killing Malone. He's got three alibis for this morning, unless we can break them."

Chase took a thoughtful sip of his drink.

"There's another potential suspect," I said. "Mr. Kyler."

"Hm. I don't think Kyler would."

"Remember his partner saying he complained about how much he had to pay Malone?"

"Yes." Chase swirled the ice in the bottom of his glass, peering into it as if he saw something mystic in there. "It doesn't seem a strong enough motive."

"How about this? He gives his assistant expensive art for her office, but she was close to Malone."

Chase raised an eyebrow. "Love triangle? I don't think so. He's devoted to Marie. Mrs. Kyler. Besides, he has an alibi."

"We haven't established that yet—"

"Don't have to. It's me." He looked up at me. "I was here at eight-thirty. Kyler asked me to breakfast."

"Why didn't you say so?"

He sighed. "I should have. I'm sorry."

I watched him frown into his glass, and wondered how close a friend Kyler was. Our dinners arrived, and I remembered something I'd wanted to ask about. It was kind of an embarrassing question, but I figured what the hell.

"Chase—you know the lounge we had a drink in? Near the stripy guy?"

"Yeah?"

"It, ah—wasn't there earlier. This morning. I think."

Give him credit, he didn't laugh. He just cocked his head and gave me that intent, puzzled look. "Wasn't there?"

"There was a blank wall there—"

"Oh . . . that's a security feature," said Chase.

"Security?"

"It's a hologram. The hotel uses them to discourage people from entering areas that are closed—"

"Ladies and gentlemen," boomed a voice from the house speakers, "the Kachina Theater is proud to present 'Pageant of Creation,' starring Benjamin Hanes!"

The lights went out. The kachina mask glowed for a second, then faded and the place went pitch dark. Then I heard a "whoosh" that made my scalp tingle even though it was familiar. The pale speck of the eagle dancer began to grow in the black well of the stage. The audience gasped as it flew overhead.

The stage lit up with flying holograms of kachinas—I counted a dozen before I lost track—along with live performers dancing to the rhythm of a row of drummers in colorful garb. The music and the images increased in speed and intensity until they became a maelstrom of sound and color. Then the place went dark again, and another pale spot began to glow in the depths of the stage while the drums rumbled low and a voice began chanting. The image took form: a man, all in white, arms outstretched. It grew larger than life, and brighter, reaching out over the audience, and I gasped as I realized it was Alan Malone's ghost in the second before it vanished. Chase must have heard me, because he laid a hand on my arm. The stage lights came up on the singer—all in white, raising arms draped in a cape of white feathers—Benjamin Hanes.

"They didn't have time to rerecord the hologram," Chase said in my ear. I nodded, still feeling a weird shiver.

There were more holograms of Malone—he was inextricably part of the show, and I felt grimly privileged to watch his final performance. In one number Hanes sang a duet with Malone's hologram—something about twin brothers journeying to the sun—truly spooky. Hanes was good, but he didn't have Malone's charisma. This was only a ghost of the show it would have been.

Even so, I enjoyed the hell out of it. Lots of color, beautiful use of holography and sensory effects. When the lights came up for intermission I clapped till my hands ached.

Chase's applause was more reserved, so much so that I asked if he disliked the show. He frowned, and said, "The performance is fine. I'm just not sure about the content."

"What about it?" I asked.

"Well, it's a mish-mosh, and some of those Indian chants—"

"You mean Native American."

"I mean Indian. They call themselves Indians, so I do too."

I felt myself blushing. "I'd been given to understand 'Native American' was the accepted term."

"Maybe the eastern tribes prefer it. My friends would laugh if I called them Native Americans."

Our waiter brought us dessert, which was a scoop of something white (not ice cream) in a puddle of something brown (not chocolate). I took a bite, and pushed the rest away. It was like everything else in this place—a sham—not what it looked like.

"Not going to eat that?" said Chase. He had already inhaled his. He gestured toward my plate with his spoon, and I handed it over.

"Oh, hey," I said, watching him dig in. "There's something else we should check. May not mean anything, but Stauffer said somebody stole one of the props."

"A knife?" said Chase, eyes sharp.

"Nope. A rattle."

"Rattle? What kind?"

"I don't know." We'd seen dozens of rattles in the show.

Chase dropped his spoon on the empty plate and stood up. "Let's go ask."

"Ah—in the middle of the performance?"

"Why not?"

One thing about Chase, he didn't waste time. We went down the aisle and climbed a half-dozen steps at the side of the stage. Backstage was crammed with towering racks of lights and projectors. Chase found the props girl—a sharp-faced Hispanic I'd interviewed that afternoon—arranging things on a long table. He flashed his badge.

"Could you tell us about the missing rattle?" he said.

"How about after the show?" she said. "I'm kind of busy."

"Was it the same as these?" said Chase, picking up a rattle from the table.

"Hey! Put that down!"

Chase did. "Was the rattle that was stolen like this?"

"Yes, it was, only it wasn't stolen, it was broken."

"Broken?"

"Somebody rummaged through the props last night, and they broke one. So if you don't mind—"

"What's that one?" I said, pointing to a smaller rattle that we hadn't seen onstage. Unlike the others, it wasn't painted. A single white feather was tied to it with a leather thong.

"That's Alan's. I mean Ben's. Don't touch it, please," she said as Chase reached for it. "It's fragile."

"Lucky it wasn't broken, too," said Chase.

"It wasn't here. Alan asked me to keep it locked up."

Chase and I looked at each other. "Why?" I asked.

"He said it was special—Uncle Joe Vigil gave it to him."

"Who's—"

"Five minutes," said a guy in black, brushing past us.

The props girl gave me a pleading look. "I really can't talk now—"

"We'll come back after the performance," I said. "Please don't leave."

"Can't. There's another show at ten."

I pulled out my notebook and tried to scribble in the half-dark while I followed Chase. "What name did she say? Vee-heel?"

"Joe Vigil," said Chase. "He's about the oldest guy at Sandia Pueblo." He stopped. Dancers were pouring out of a bright doorway in a stream of colored feathers, heading for the stage to start the second act. When they'd cleared out Chase went on, but I stayed.

Down the hall, in an open doorway, Emily Trujillo was arguing with Benjamin Hanes. I got as close as I could without entering the hall, and heard Hanes say, "—didn't give it to me." Then he started toward me and I ducked back, and nearly tripped over one of the racks of lights. Hanes came out and went onstage. I waited for Trujillo, but she didn't appear, and I glanced back down the hall just in time to see her go into Hanes's dressing room.

"Chase!" I hissed. I couldn't see very far; figured he'd gone back to our table. The show was about to start again. The rational thing to do would be to go back to my seat. So I went down the hall and knocked at the dressing room door.

No answer. I waited, knocked again, then opened it.

The room was empty.

I stepped in and pushed the door closed behind me. I was getting pissed off. This whole place was a lie, and as soon as this damn case was over I was requesting that transfer.

"Ms. Trujillo?"

There were no other doors; not even a closet, just a rack of costumes in one corner, some of which I recognized. The feather cape was there, white plumes flickering slightly in the breeze.

Breeze?

No fan in the room. There was an air duct in the ceiling, but when I reached up toward it I felt nothing. I held my hand over the feather cape, and caught a whisper of air coming from behind the costume rack. I pulled it aside and reached a hand toward the bare wall behind it. It went through.

"Shit!"

I took a deep breath and stepped through the wall. Weird feeling—all my imagination, of course—but only ghosts and superheroes are supposed to walk through walls.

I was in a short, dark corridor. Light at the other end, and carpet that looked like some part of the casino, but no sign of Ms. Trujillo. I went toward the light, stepped out into it and stopped cold. Across the hall and down a few feet stood the Blue Corn Maiden.

"Jesus."

I turned around, and found myself facing a blank wall. Reached out, and through; another hologram. Security feature, Chase had said. I remembered my confusion over the lounge. They *were* moving the damn walls!

Things started clicking in my brain. Private entrance to the star's dressing room. Alan Malone had a perfectly good reason to be in the hall by the Blue Corn Maiden; he was on his way to the theater. The killer was someone who knew about the concealed corridor, maybe even hid there. Didn't look good for Daniel Stauffer. Then again, Kyler might have known it was there; his assistant certainly did. For someone who didn't like holograms, Ms. Trujillo sure knew a lot about them.

Oh.

I started through the casino, trying not to run. I crossed the lobby and passed the elevators, then hopped on the escalator and took the steps two at a time. The doors to the office were gone; a solid wall now stood at the top of the escalator. I put a hand through it and felt the carved doors behind. They were unlocked.

Dark. I felt around on the wall for a light switch, then gave up and started down the hallway. Arroyo-light from the picture windows in Kyler's office spilled across the carpet.

Kyler had an alibi. Stauffer had three alibis. And Sally the Receptionist said Trujillo had been on the phone all morning. On the phone, talking to no one. Just sitting at her desk.

I nearly tripped myself getting to Trujillo's office. Butterfly Maiden still stood in the corner, glowing in the dark room. It hadn't occurred to me before to wonder why Trujillo had put the hologram *behind* her desk, where she couldn't see it. I fumbled with the projectors, found the button, pushed it, stepped back.

Butterfly Maiden vanished. In her place, seated in a holographic desk chair and murmuring into a holographic phone, was Emily Trujillo in her pretty cream-colored suit.

"Holy shit!"

I stopped thinking at that point. All I knew was that Trujillo had killed her very dear friend, and that I had to find her. I tore out of there and back down to the casino, but of course she was nowhere in sight.

I headed for the theater, intending to get Chase. The maître d' let me in and I stood in the dark at the back of the house, waiting for my eyes to adjust so I wouldn't fall on my face on the steps.

The stage lights were low. Hanes was alone, kneeling in front of a holographic fire, chanting low and loud, unaccompanied. Some small movement to my right caught my eye; I saw a pale shape moving down the far aisle, and a shiver went down my back. I went toward it.

Hanes chanted louder and waved his arms over the fire as if casting some magic spell. A darker shape loomed between me and the pale blob, and my stomach lurched as I hurried toward them both, touching the backs of chairs and shoulders, whispering, "Sorry, sorry," and trying to keep half an eye on the stage.

Hanes reached into the false fire, brought out the little plain rattle I'd seen on the prop table, and raised it over his head. At the same time a pale arm was raised ahead of me, and I saw it was Emily Trujillo's arm, holding a gun. Then the shadow between us blocked it.

I screamed "No!" and the gun went off, and all hell broke loose. I ran the last few feet between me and Trujillo, barked my shin on something, cussed as I saw the shadow-shape crumple. The gun went off again, flash nearly blinding me, screams all around, not the least of which was Benjamin Hanes shrieking like a lunatic and blowing out the house speakers.

The Quantico boys would have been proud. More by feel than by sight I tackled Trujillo, sat on her and took the gun away.

The house lights came up. On the floor nearby Chase lay bleeding, looking very surprised. I stared down at Trujillo, and managed to refrain from smacking her. Her black eyes were narrowed to slits—like the rectangle eyes of the kachinas—then she closed them. She never gave in, even then.

She was charged with premeditated murder and assault with a deadly weapon. She hadn't hit Hanes, and I still think she never meant to. Her second shot shattered the rattle that Uncle Joe

Vigil—the oldest, and incidentally the most senile man in Sandia Pueblo—had given to Alan Malone.

Mondo told me it had been a ceremonial rattle, and it should never have been seen by a white man, much less taken from the pueblo. But Alan Malone was a charmer; he made his living making people like him, and he'd fooled even Emily Trujillo. She'd brought him to Sandia, and doubtless she felt responsible when he took the rattle. I wondered what he'd said when she asked for its return, and if he'd really realized what it meant to her and her people.

I went to her arraignment, which was really just the usual, but I'd promised Chase a full report. He was stuck in the hospital for a few days, and maybe another junior agent would have resented being sent to fetch chocolate and ice cream and jelly beans, but I had learned something. Of all the masks I'd encountered, Chase's was the easiest to see through if you bothered to look. His was just shyness, and underneath it was a wonderful being.

I stayed at the back of the courtroom, so Trujillo didn't see me until she was being led away. The eyes she turned on me were flat black, with no more emotion in them than the Blue Corn Maiden's black rectangles. She had her own mask. We all do.

It's my job to notice little things, though, and as she looked away, I saw the flicker of grief. Maybe for Malone, maybe for a deeper loss, or maybe more than one. No regret, though. She'd done what she felt was necessary to make things right. I went away sad, but satisfied. I had seen the gentle and determined soul who had taken Alan Malone's life, and then reached out to close his eyes.

AFTERWORD

This is the story of a story come full circle.

A few years ago, I heard about an anthology Roger Zelazny was editing, and I decided to try writing a story for it. The theme of the anthology was gambling, so I decided to write about gambling at cards, specifically bridge. At the time, Indian gaming in New Mexico consisted of only a couple of bingo halls, and I decided to set my story in the near future, in a casino on the Sandia Indian reservation.

Well, the story didn't work. It had some nice stuff in it, but overall it was awful, so awful that I didn't bother trying to fix it, and I never sent it to Roger.

I was honored, this year, to receive an invitation to pay tribute to Roger with a story. I immediately thought of that old failed attempt, and decided to make use of it. Nowadays there really is a casino on the Sandia reservation, so I decided to go it one better, and salvaged the good bits from that first try, and stuck them into "Arroyo de Oro."

So here's your story, Roger, at long last. Thanks for being your wonderful self.

Billy Blackhorse Singer of Eye of Cat *would certainly understand the conflicts faced by Will Jared in Bradley Sinor's tale.*

■

BACK IN "THE REAL WORLD"
Bradley H. Sinor

WILL JARED KNELT ON ONE KNEE NEXT TO THE REMAINS OF THE campfire. The cold ashes had been there three days, perhaps as many as five.

This late in October campers were not unknown in this part of northeast Oklahoma, just unusual. Most people preferred an electric blanket to a plastic ground sheet and a sleeping bag. Plus most campers who used Hyatt State Park registered with the park ranger's office. There were always a few who didn't bother.

A lean dark figure, dressed in leather flight jacket, black jeans and boots, the badge of an Oklahoma State Park ranger pinned on his shirt, Jared had spent a half hour studying the campsite. Ordinary park visitors probably, but there was always a chance of something else.

Jared was justly proud of his tracking skills. He'd learned from the best, his maternal grandfather, Marcus Conley, who was said to have been one of the best Cherokee hunting guides in decades. What Grandfather hadn't taught Jared, six years in the United States Army Rangers had.

He took a handful of ashes, rolling them between his palms. Then he gently blew, his breath and the ash lingering as mist in the cold night air.

It began slowly as it had so many times since his return to "The Real World," from Vietnam, three years before. The sounds of the forest became distant and faint, overlaid with other sounds, vague echoes that grew gradually into voices.

I know this isn't the sort of honeymoon that you expected. It's . . . just . . . that . . .
I don't care. I'm here, with you, we're together. That's all that counts. Us.

Honeymooners?! Of course, it made sense. Just people who wanted to be left alone. A sentiment that Jared could appreciate. Being alone was one of the main reasons he had taken the job as a park ranger.

There were more words, words that gradually faded into other sounds. Jared struggled to pull himself away from them. It was difficult not to let himself go, to let the echoing sounds of voices, the wind, the trees and the very soil itself just pull him into them.

He could feel a rightness about it. So easy, so very easy. Only not this way. Gradually that certainty brought him to himself, the odors of pine, grass and water growing around him.

Jared's hands were trembling as the gray ashes fell slowly between his fingers. A breeze brought the distant sound of an owl screeching.

When everything around him began to move, Jared grabbed the limb of a nearby sapling to balance himself. He pulled his flight jacket tighter. *Afterward* Jared always felt like he had been dumped in a freezer.

There were probably reasons to explain the reaction, there always were. Jared often suspected that they made as little sense to the people giving them as to the people hearing them.

But, Jared knew better than to mention this to the chief ranger, a bureaucrat from the word go. This was the sort of thing that would convince him that Will Jared had gone round the bend.

Once, Jared had tried to describe the experience to the doctors at the Veterans Administration hospital in Tulsa. They had listened, muttering phrases like "survivor's guilt," "delayed stress syndrome," and "fear trauma." Their answer had been yet another prescription, which, like the others, had disappeared into the waiting-room trash can.

When he told his grandfather about the voices, and the rest, Marcus Conley didn't say much. The old man had just sat on the porch, listening and puffing away on his pipe, surrounding himself with clouds of Jameson blend tobacco smoke.

"You're not crazy, boy. You just have to wait. You got the

potential to be something very special, for yourself, and for our people. But you've got demons you've got to face, inside yourself, like every one of us. Only yours are tougher, harder, more devious. And you can't pick the time to face them, they pick it, and you just have to do the best you can."

"Yeah, right," Jared said.

The wind came from the west, off the lake and into the narrow valley. The chill in it was a stark contrast to the last remnants of summer that had clung to the area until only a half a dozen days before.

Jared came down along the hillside, pausing here and there to look and listen. The nearest neighbors were a good three miles away, closer on the shoreline, near the park's edge.

He fumbled through his jacket pockets and pulled out a pack of Camels, along with a lighter. Its brass surface was scarred and bent, but not enough to obscure the engraving: KHE SANH 1969.

Thumbing the lighter to life, he sucked on the cigarette, its smoke burning harshly as he drew deep on it.

Jared smothered a cough in his sleeve, fought to hold himself up as it racked his body. He told himself that it was just the tag end of a summer cold, but it had held on for nearly two months. Maybe it wouldn't be such a bad idea to visit the tribal medical complex near Tahlequah, or maybe the V.A. Hospital for a checkup.

No, if he went to Tahlequah, that would mean the obligatory visit to his parents. It was never a pleasant task, not since the morning he had walked into the house and announced that he had enlisted in the Army.

Going back to the V.A. didn't appeal to him either. Not because of the doctors. No, that had been where he had his first flashback: one minute he'd been in Tulsa, the next in 'Nam. No, he shook his head, no V.A. Besides there were probably too many new forms to fill out if he went in.

Jared glanced across the clearing. Even knowing where to look, it was still hard to see the cabin in the dark. *All the better,* he told himself. *If I have trouble seeing it, others do too.*

The cabin seemed to fit here, as if it had always been a part of the forest. It was set against the side of a hill, and a dozen small ash trees surrounded it. In the years since they had planted them, the trees had grown much larger than anyone would have expected.

Lingering on the porch, Jared partially unzipped his flight jacket. His hand rested on the butt of the silver-gray Deutonics .45, waiting. When at last he was certain there was no one else around, Jared stepped inside.

Dropping his jacket on the couch, Jared drew a deep breath, savoring the warmth of the house. The cabin had three rooms: kitchen and living area combined, bedroom with bath, and a storage area. Small it might be, but that summer after graduation when he, Larry Sheppard, and Larry's father had sweated, struggled, and cursed to build it, the cabin had seemed as big as an Alpine A-frame. Originally they had intended it for an occasional getaway. Since Jared had come back from 'Nam, to "The Real World," it had been home and refuge for him.

That was when he remembered the ice cream. A half gallon of homemade chocolate chip, carefully packed and handed to him by his mother on his last visit to his parents' home. Yeah, that was exactly the prescription, the sort the V.A. doctors *should* be writing. He filled a big bowl, helping himself to several large bites in the process, then carried it into the living room.

Spooning a mouthful of ice cream, Jared found himself staring at the scar across the palm of his right hand. With the edge of a fingernail he carefully traced the line. That had come from a screwdriver slipping out of his grip. It had hurt but the memory didn't anymore.

That summer they had built the cabin had been special, very special for Larry and him. They had been best friends almost from the first day at the Cherokee boarding school near Lawton. That summer, nine years ago, they had become in formal ceremony what they were already in fact: brothers.

A blood brother was always there, always ready when you needed him.

Only when push came to shove, I wasn't there when Larry really needed me.

Jared repeated it over and over again in his mind, like a Gregorian chant.

I wasn't there. I wasn't there.

On the table next to the divan was a framed photo of the two of them in Class A uniforms, taken the week they had arrived in Vietnam, perfectly ironed shirts, spit-shined boots, a dream image as far from the reality as Jared wished he were now.

He picked up the picture, his slim brown fingers tightening around the metal. . . .

. . . tell the truth, you broke your ankle when her husband was coming home and you had to dive out the window.

Right! You know without me at point you couldn't find your way out of a one-room schoolhouse.

Sure! Just stay here, recuperate on the beach, with all these nice army nurses to look after you, while the real men are out working.

My friend, it's hard duty but that's what they pay me the big bucks for.

I'm sorry, Lt. Jared, they found what was left of the patrol. Charlie hit Sheppard and the rest of them hard, about five klicks from the LZ. . . . No survivors . . .

Jared *listened* for a long time, the sounds holding him tight, yanking the very breath out of his body. As swiftly as it had begun, everything ended in a wave of pain, like someone slamming a fist into his stomach. He rammed the photo down on the table, jarring the bowl of half-eaten ice cream onto the floor.

As his fingers parted from the metal, Jared found himself watching the whole scene with a disinterested eye, coldly picking out details that echoed loudly in his vision.

For a long time he just sat there, staring at the fire, the puddle of melting ice cream and broken glass. Struggling to his feet, Jared finally began to pick up the pieces; it just didn't seem right to leave them there.

The drumming awoke Jared. He had been aware of it for a long time, hoping the whole thing was part of a dream that would run its course and go on to something different.

Half-heartedly, Jared buried his face in the pillow, but he knew as he rolled to one side that it would do no good. He forced his eyes open, looking toward the digital display on the bedside clock.
3:45
"Damn!"

As he stepped onto the cabin's porch, a few moments later, the night chill cut through him. For a long time he just walked, boots lost in the knee-high ground fog.

The wind did sometimes play funny tricks in the hills. He could remember nights during the summer when you could hear sounds coming from the far side of the lake as easily as if they had been next door. Only tonight there wasn't any wind.

"Too much chocolate-chip ice cream will do it to you every time, kiddo." The voice came from just ahead of him, as did the drumming.

Sitting cross-legged on a lightning-blackened stump was an old man, dressed in jeans and a Grateful Dead T-shirt. He had a small drum on his lap. The man's shoulder-length gray hair was held in place by an ornately beaded hair tie, the kind that Jared had seen some of the tribal elders wear.

"Do you take requests?" Jared said.

The old man looked up and smiled, produced a Scottish pennywhistle, and began to play.

The tune was familiar.

"As Time Goes By."

After he finished, the old man looked at Jared, raising the whistle in a salute.

"I really don't think that anybody is going to mistake you for Dooley Wilson," Jared said.

The old man shrugged.

"Does this mean I should call you Sam?"

"Up to you. I answer to a lot of things."

And Jared knew him. He couldn't really say just what wild leap of logic suddenly told him just who "Sam" was, it just happened. "In this day and age it sounds a little more suitable than calling you Coyote."

Sam nodded, a look of satisfaction on his face. "Not bad, you're quicker on things than I'd been told." The fog began to move in slow circular motion around the two men.

That was when Sam changed. He was younger, closer to Jared's own age. A few white hairs streaked the man's otherwise ink-black hair. He now wore a gray sport jacket, sunglasses, purple shirt, and an outlandish paisley neckerchief. The drum was replaced by a saxophone.

Sam produced a white handkerchief from his jacket sleeve and began to polish the instrument. When he had finished Sam pulled the reed loose and held it up for a closer look. The edges were visibly cracked and worn. With a flourish he flung the reed off into the darkness, produced another one, and fit it into place.

"You know, boy, I'm sure beginning to wonder if you're really worth the amount of *my* time that you've taken up," he said.

"Well, excuse me! I don't seem to recall asking for your time or your attention. I think I was doing just fine without you sticking your nose into my affairs. And even if I did need help, I'm not sure I would want *yours*," Jared said.

Anger flared on Sam's face. "Look, boy, in spite of what you may have heard, I'm not nearly the interfering bastard that I've been played up as being over the years. Let's just say that I've gotten a lot of bad press and leave it at that." He began to play, this time a tune that Jared did not recognize.

"Would you mind doing your rehearsing somewhere else? There are a few people around here who want to sleep."

"Well, pardon me," Sam answered with mock indignation. At that moment he was once more the old man, though the saxophone was still gripped tightly in his hands. "Besides, that's not the way you were taught to address someone. Now was it?"

Jared suppressed a feeling if irritation. Sam was correct and that bothered him.

By tribal custom one should address an older man as either uncle or grandfather, whether you were related or not. It was just good manners, as well as a sign of respect; if he truly were Coyote, this Sam's age alone gave him claim to the title.

Jared turned to walk away, shivering, as Sam began playing again. The sound echoed around him, even louder than it had been. The sudden desire for a cigarette filled him. The problem was he realized almost at once that the cigarettes and his lighter were back in the cabin.

The fog had grown so heavy that Jared could barely see more than a half dozen steps in front of him. It was difficult to even make out the numbers on his watch.

3:48

Three minutes? That hardly seemed possible. It was getting more and more difficult to know what to believe standing there at the center of a moving whirlwind of fog, color, motion, and sound.

The smell of burning diesel and gas filled his lungs. People sped by on foot, in rickshas, on motorcycles and in cars; voices chattered in French, Vietnamese, Thai, American, a dozen dialects and a hundred combinations, all melding into one voice.

Saigon.

He knew where he was, although at that particular moment he would not have been willing to bet that the sun would rise in the east tomorrow morning.

Saigon.

Not the pale gray echo called Ho Chi Minh City. It could be no other place but Saigon, in all its decadence and glory.

Jared drew a breath, held it and then slowly exhaled. He wasn't sure if he wanted this to be a bizarre nightmare or an even more bizarre reality.

A small gray cat, missing a single fang, emerged from an alley and hopped up on packing crate in front of Jared. The animal eyed him for nearly a minute, seeming to dare Jared to walk past, then began ever so calmly to bathe itself.

"You here to tell me something? I'm open for suggestions." He felt kind of silly talking to the cat, but at the moment it seemed the thing to do.

"Would you listen if I did?" the cat said.

"That tears it," Jared mumbled. "I'm outta here."

Half walking, half jogging, Jared moved in and out among the constant flow of people and vehicles, moving from shadow to light and back again. After a half hour he found himself in more residential streets, where most of the houses reflected the architecture of thirty and forty years before.

That was when a trio of U.S. Army half-ton trucks came round the corner. The glare from their headlights made it impossible to see the drivers' faces as they passed.

The final one had no tailgate. On impulse Jared ran after it, boosting himself onto the back with no problem. Scooting inside he wrapped himself in the steamy darkness. The engine roared and the truck pulled ahead.

Just a place to rest, a chance to think, that was all he wanted. For a moment the image of himself wrapped in a straightjacket, screaming his throat raw in some V.A. padded cell, lingered in his mind, mixed with the quiet face of his grandfather.

A few moments later he was lost in sleep.

Jared was jolted awake when the truck hit a rut in the road. The stiffness in his shoulders and back were painful testimony to how much time had passed. The truck continued to barrel along at a good clip, as Jared crouched on the back edge before stepping off into the darkness. He barely managed to stay on his feet when he landed.

The sky was awash in stars. Around him the night sounds of the jungle abounded the darkness. Beads of sweat rolled down his neck to stain his shirt and the fur collar of his flight jacket.

Carefully he picked a path among the bushes and vines. As he walked, the jungle noises around him began to fade. Not quickly, but over a period of time, until there was nothing, no wind, no animal noises, no annoying buzz of insects. Nothing, except the sounds of his own steps.

Jared's foot was almost on top of the booby trap when he spotted the first Viet Cong.

A tripwire wrapped in vines had been strung about five inches above the ground, hooked to a claymore mine that would have peppered him with shrapnel if he had set it off.

"Just be a bit more careful. Somebody who's been in country all of thirty minutes would have spotted this," he told himself, stepping over the wire.

The guerrilla fighter, on the other hand, was a good twenty yards in front of Jared, with his back to him. Bent low, the man wore black homespun and clutched a Russian AK-47 in his hands. Jared's hand began to slowly loosen the heavy, hand-tooled belt he wore. Garroting someone with your cowboy belt might not have much style, but it would do in a pinch.

Only this guy didn't seem to notice Jared. As the young man got closer, the V.C. didn't look round, didn't move, and gave every appearance of being frozen solid. Jared moved up besides him and just stood there, staring. After several minutes, he thought he might have seen the other man's chest move, but couldn't be sure.

Just head and to his right Jared spotted more figures. Some were

V.C., the rest were North Vietnamese regulars. All standing as stone still as the first.

That was when he spotted Larry.

His blood brother had an M–16 balanced in the crook of his arm, freeing his hands up to examine a map. Next to him were two faces that Jared knew well, Cpls. Kelley Wilde and Hal Williams.

Like the VC and the North Vietnamese regulars they were frozen in mid-movement.

For several long minutes Jared just stared. This time he was sure he saw one of Wilde's arms move, ever so slightly. If they *could* see him he suspected all they would notice would be a shadow, a vague movement out of the corner of one eye.

Just to one side were the rest of the squad: Matt Charles, Jim Allen, Bill Gordon, Jonas Mason, Karl Tattershawl, and K.T. Dixon.

Gordon and Dixon were carrying a makeshift litter, with Charles stretched across it, a heavy bandage across the man's chest. All of the men bore wounds of some kind.

"They must have been in one hell of a firefight."

Something hit Jared hard, driving him to the ground. He managed to roll to one side, grabbing handfuls of grass as he did. Pulling to his feet, Jared found himself facing not a VC or NVA regular, but someone wearing American-issue combat fatigues. Dogtags glittered in the moonlight, hanging loose on the man's chest, and a bandanna covered most of his face.

"Hey, bro. I'm one of the good guys," Jared stammered.

The newcomer didn't hear or seem to care. Pulling a knife from his boot he advanced toward Jared.

Using his left hand Jared began to slowly whirl his belt around. Moving in concert with the other man, he never let his eyes lose contact with the stranger's.

They both struck at once, Jared driving the heavy metal buckle hard against the head of the other man, who skillfully jabbed the knife as he tried to duck away. The blade's razor-sharp edge slid across Jared's side, cutting leather, cloth and flesh.

He'd been cut before, but this was different. The pain stung like nothing he had ever experienced, tearing through every fiber of his body. The other man managed to land several good kicks that sent Jared collapsing into a crouch on the ground.

Reality began to fragment. Jared felt his body being pulled apart. Muscle and sinew rolled in waves, ripping and splitting and melding into a dozen, a hundred new forms. Every time he tried to scream his voice was lost in waves of pain that seemed like they would never end.

And it was over.

Jared pulled his hands up to his face; only what he saw weren't hands, but fur-covered paws. The claws of a great brown bear faced him. A bear's growl tore out of his throat.

Jared turned to face his opponent. From somewhere the man had produced an M–16 and had it at his shoulder ready to fire. With a single swipe of a huge paw the bear/Jared knocked it from the man's hand, sending his opponent flying onto the ground.

Then the bear was gone.

Jared felt his muscles and bones ripping and tearing, again, shifting in an intricate jigsaw puzzle. With the brushing of a wind across them, they began to re-form. Jared felt *himself* step away from his body. There was pain, but he accepted it, allowing the sensation to become something distant and not part of him.

A screaming falcon flapped its wings in anger above the prone form of Jared's enemy. It would have been so easy to let go, let the bird or the bear rip this man apart. So easy.

No!

The voice was enough to bring Jared back. The falcon faded, but did not disappear entirely. It merged into the background, standing with the bear. The part of him that was Will Jared had found a balance, an uneasy one, between the man, the animals, and the earth itself. He held on to it for all that he was worth.

Kneeling next to the other man Jared grabbed up the discarded knife, pushing it up against his throat.

"If you move, if you even blink wrong, I'll gut you like a fish. You understand?"

The man nodded.

Jared pulled the bandanna away. The face that stared back at him as covered in camouflage makeup and dirt. He knew the face, it was his own.

"Hi, guy!"

"I should kill you."

"Go ahead, but somehow I don't think you've got the guts."

"What are you?"

"Oh, give me a break. You know as well as I do. I'm you. Without all that crap and sentimental junk you've carried around for years. From your folks. From your grandfather. I wasn't born in Oklahoma. I was born right here in 'Nam, for one reason . . . to survive. And I'll kill anybody it takes to do it."

"Even me or Larry?"

"Of course you! I'd do it in a minute and laugh the whole time. Larry . . . that little piss-ant, I'd crush him under my boot. Why do you think I'm here? A little post-mission revenge. An idea that has crossed your mind more than once, though you haven't got the balls to do anything about it."

Revenge? For his own pain and guilt. Sure the thought had crossed Jared's mind, more often than he cared to admit. "Maybe. But I'm not the one flat on his back with a knife at his throat."

"Then just push it in and get this over with. You are beginning to bore me."

Jared pushed the blade a fraction of an inch. The single drop of blood that appeared around the metal tip revolted him.

"Oh no you don't. I've got the guts, more than you have, 'friend.' I could kill you, but I don't *need* to. You're a part of me, that I admit, one I don't like, but one that I can live with."

Without even knowing that he wanted to, Jared could feel himself reaching out, not to one object, as he had before, but to everything. Instead of fading, the jungle began to glow with a dim phosphorescence that filled the area.

At one moment Jared was one with Larry, the squad members, the Vietnamese hidden in the bushes, the trees, the vines, and the very soil. It was all one, separate and unique but still one, and he was a part of it. He could feel the grass growing under his boots, a monkey poised to leap from branch to branch, the fear that hung heavy on the heart of his blood brother, the men in his squad and even the Vietnamese they faced.

Everything fitted into a proper place here, it all made sense. Everything human, animal, plant, had its place. Had its place to live and to die.

Tears rolled down his face as Jared turned toward the glowing form of his blood brother. This was Larry's place to die. Just as Jared would have his own place someday, when it was time to move on.

The light faded and he looked around. His other self was gone, back into the shadows.

Jared knew the answer, as he looked around. But he had to try anyway, one last time. He owed himself as well as Larry that much.

For more than an hour he examined every angle, played out every possibility, every scenario that he had conceived of over the years. Anything that could have brought the men home. But in the end he knew the answer was the same.

Part of him wanted to pry the weapon out of someone's hand and just start firing. Only that would do no good. Jared knew that as certainly as he knew his own name.

He walked up beside Larry, laying his hand on the shoulder of his oldest friend. "I'll see ya when I see ya, buddy."

As the fog began to swirl around him Will Jared was certain that he could smell the distinctive odor of Jameson's blend tobacco.

*   *   *

Jared ran his finger along the edge of the dish. There was just enough chocolate sauce and melted vanilla ice cream left for one final taste.

"One must have the proper respect and consideration for chocolate," he said grinning.

Jared couldn't remember the last time he had felt so relaxed, so free. He had even locked away the Deutonics; anything he was afraid of now, Jared knew he could handle.

Drawing a deep breath, he reached out with his mind, feeling things around him, the wind, the water, the earth itself, animals moving among the trees and through the water, easily becoming a part of them, letting them become a part of him.

Jared didn't understand everything, even though it all seemed to make a weird sort of sense. He had some vacation time accumulated and with the holidays coming up it might not be a bad idea to visit his family in Tahlequah. He could say it was also a trip to visit the tribal medical facility as well: he still had the cough; it wasn't near as bad now, but it wouldn't hurt to get it looked at.

And as long as he was there a trip to his grandfather's ranch just outside of town, down along the river, and a long talk with the old man would definitely be in order.

For a long time he stood watching the glow on the eastern horizon. The wind had shifted out of the south, bringing with it the heady smell of the lake and something else, the faint sound of a lone musician playing.

Saxophone music?

Logic said that it was more than likely someone's radio.

Jared knew differently.

He smiled and spoke to the wind.

"Thank you, grandfather."

AFTERWORD

And now about Roger.

I first met him when he came to the University of Oklahoma as a guest speaker. After the gig was done I drove him to a con in Wichita Falls, Texas.

During that four-hour drive Roger and I discovered we shared enthusiasms for obscure scientific theories, jazz, and the works of George MacDonald Fraser.

The thing I remember most vividly about that convention is sitting on the floor with Roger, just outside of the room where they were doing a radio play. Someone came up and asked if there was some sort of problem, since we weren't in watching the presentation. Roger explained, very simply, that radio plays such as this were intended to be listened to, not watched.

Over the years we encountered each other a number of times, not to mention trading letters and occasional phone calls.

The last time we had the chance to get together was ironically back at OU. Roger was there as a guest instructor at the Annual Short Course in Professional Writing. My wife and I happened to be in the area to attend a media-con.

It had been four or five years since we had seen each other but Roger made it seem like only a few weeks at the most. The conversation ranged over any number of subjects, jazz, movies, our respective families—and of course we talked shop. (Hey, get two writers in our genre together for more than ten minutes at a time and you know they will be talking shop.)

All too soon we had to leave. Roger still needed to get packed for his flight back to New Mexico that evening. Sue and I needed to get on the road back to Tulsa.

As we drove away she said "That was fun. He's really a nice man."

That he was.

Here's to you Roger. **Salud!**

Wistful and bittersweet, ultimately triumphant, Jennifer Roberson's story takes power, as so many of Roger's did, from allusions to the myths and legends we all share.

■

MAD JACK
Jennifer Roberson

LUSH, UNDULANT COUNTRYSIDE, VERDIGRISED BY SUMMER INTO gilt and gold and green. By train the view was fixed, bound by iron rails; by bus as bound but freer, to curve and sweep and angle, to undulate with the countryside like a serpent's tail, undeterred by such transient barricades as stone, as steel, as water.

He smiled. *Nor am I.*

Else he would not now be here, traveling by bus through the lush, undulant countryside of a land not his own, of a people not his own save they bore perhaps more patience with such as he, who understood the secrets of that land. Their secrets, Scottish secrets, though even they might not know this one.

He smiled again, from inside as well as out, aware of the warm clenching of his belly, of anticipation, of excitement.

Maybe this time. . . . Maybe this time it would be true.

But maybe not. It had not been true in all the other journeys, though the smile had been the same inside and out, the warm clenching of his belly. And the anticipation.

"Hope springs eternal?"

But it was *his* hope, his eternal hope springing from deep inside, always, pushing out the fear, the vicious disbelief of his time, of his people, who refused to see such possibilities. To admit there were things in the world that were not *of* the world.

It was so easy to lose belief, to dismiss trust, to deny such things as he had once believed and now needed—very badly—to believe again. Others cloaked it in runes and rituals designed to destroy fancy and replace it with fact, to label it myth, magic, fantasy: not true, not real, due no place in the world of reality, of responsibility.

He had been real. He had been responsible. The world had closed upon him, and he had welcomed it because it was as they told him it should be. There was no room, no time for fancies, for fantasies; he was a man, an adult; in the parlance of childhood: a *grownup.*

And he had lived among them in the real world, acknowledging and accepting responsibilities of his own making and not; of such small needs as delivering garbage to the curbside, of such larger requisites as delivering a dying child to the hospital.

He had been real, had been responsible, had like a squire embraced the duties of manhood—and yet such dedicated service to that knight had earned him only grief.

—gilt, and gold, and green—

Divorced. An ugly word, a filthy word, a word wrought of the power to alter so many lives, too many. But another word was far worse. And that word was death.

His own he could have dealt with, save for the child he would leave behind. Instead, the child had left him. Had left father, mother, all the detritus of a young life as yet filled with myth, with magic, with fantasy—and now was no more than a statistic. A child, asleep in his bed. A car, driving by. And a shot, a single shot: Was it dare? Was it duty?

A sleeping child dying; dead by the time his father carried him into the hospital, where they said it was too late.

And the woman he once had loved, who once had loved him, was cruelly unkind in the ravages of her grief.

His own was unslaked. But he had learned how to ward it away, how to stave it off. A task. A quest. The ultimate fantasy.

His coworkers expressed understanding; his boss called him mad. His friends said he should go for it; the dead child's mother called him mad.

He supposed he was. But it gave him a task, a quest. It gave him leave to do what he felt he had to do, to justify his survival.

Savings, unsaved. Portfolio plundered. None of it mattered. There was no child who might benefit from his father's fiscal conservatism, who would attend college without the nagging fear there might not be enough money, or that he would, when he graduated, be in debt for a decade as he labored to pay back what was borrowed.

Instead, what was borrowed had been the decade that comprised the child's life, and the debt had been repaid in the guise of a single bullet.

So many places. So many hopes. So much anticipation, and all as yet for naught. His quest was undertaken but the task remained undone.

The bus slowed. He felt his muscles tighten in familiar anticipation; despite all his travels he had never gained the patience of those who knew debarcation at ten *of* the hour—or after—made no difference at all in the ordering of the world.

In his world, it did.

It might.

It *would.*

Please God, it had to.

The bus stopped. He said, "Let it be here."

Each time, the litany. And each time: disappointment.

"This time," he murmured. "*This* time. Yes."

The door folded open. He had little but himself and one small bag. He and the bag got out of the bus and began the ending of his journey. Yet another journey. Another beginning. Ending. In between, he walked.

"Let it be here," he murmured. "This time. Yes."

Lush, undulant countryside, verdigrised by summer into gilt, and gold, and green. He ate of berries on the bushes beside the asphalt roadway, curving and sweeping through the hills like a serpent's tail, undeterred by such transient barricades as stone, as trees, as water. And water there was aplenty.

Jack studied it as he walked. So many legends told of this water, of its secrets, of its truths. And yet to look upon it offered no answers, merely the fact of its being.

"Let it be here," he said.

This time. Yes.

Not so long a walk; he had walked farther. And a castle at the end of it, the ruins of a castle, mortared, mossy stone tumbled in heaps and piles, the remnants of its walls. Grass clothed it now where stone gave way, verdigrised by summer; and beyond it the water; beyond that the sky.

"Here," he said.

They had come as he had come, the others, but not for this reason: these folk laughed in many languages, carried many cameras, called to the water as if it were a dog to come lalloping up to them and collapse upon their feet, panting loyalty.

The water would not come. And what they believed was in it,

what they *wanted* to believe, would not answer to such fools as they, and perhaps not even to him.

Let it be here.

The castle skirted the shoreline, but did not quite encroach. He left them all behind, the laughing strangers camera-weighted, reading aloud of legend, and walked down to the shore. It was a lake fully cognizant of what it was, and what was said of it; he saw it in the cool, quiet confidence, the certitude of its presence and its place in the world.

He set down his bag but did not divest himself of shoes and socks; despite the season, he was born of warmer weather. And it was not in him to pollute the water with his presence.

He waited, and eventually the last bus of the day came and collected the others, and he was left alone. He sat upon a cluster of granite and made himself very still.

"This time," he murmured. As he had murmured every time. And took from his pocket a handful of dross, that was to him gold.

"Here I am," he said. Beyond him stretched the summer: *gilt and gold and green.* "This time," he begged. As he had begged before.

But this time was different. This time he did not think of the dead boy but of the other boy, the only boy, the lonely boy; who was, he supposed, very much like the dead boy, but wasn't.

Although perhaps he *was* dead, if in a different way; the kind of dead that happens when a boy becomes a man, when myth and magic and fantasy are replaced by the swordblade of reality, the knife called responsibility.

That boy too was dead, albeit his heart yet beat. That boy too was dead, in heart, in soul, in mind; but his death needn't be permanent. His day to be buried in the cold, broken ground had not yet come upon him.

"Mad Jack," he murmured; what would they say of him now, to see him like this?

He laughed. But very softly.

And the water laughed back.

At first he could give it no credence. But then he removed himself from reality, despite his physicality, and listened more closely, more deeply, to the voice of the water, the rhythm of its silence.

Wind chafed his scalp, lifting grief-grayed hair. Wind slewed by his ears, seducing like a lover: here, there, another where, then back again to kiss.

And his head was filled with the elusive fragrance of fantasy, the subversive melange of myth.

"It *was* true," he said. "Once. Before I permitted the world to make me blind, to fill my ears with the cacophony of a life I never aspired to."

But no. He had aspired. As all the others aspired, as they had been shaped to aspire, and also to desire.

Bound by shore, by hills, by trees, the water stretched before him: slate and steel and silver. Summer now was banished in the setting of the sun.

"Let it be here," he begged.

And the water acquiesced.

With a hiss of froth on sand, with the tumult of wave on stone, it ran up the shore to his feet. He tensed, but did not move. And when it engulfed his shoes, when it soaked his feet, when it stole away his treasure of strings and sealing wax he did not curse, but rejoiced. Displacement was necessary: water giving up so much required itself to submit, to permit such contained upheaval as the beast, as if it sounded, shouldered through the pale between surface and the air.

It came, did the beast, like a hound to its master's hand, a hand too long denied by far too many years. It came not because he called it as the others had called, but because he had need of it, because his spirit recalled what joys had bound them once, what adventures they had shared, when kings and princes bowed; when pirate ships lowered sails.

Up from the water it came, shaking wing-clad shoulders, snorting through flaring nostrils. The great opaline eye rolled within its socket, beneath the incongruity of delicate, wirelike lashes tempered to gold in the crucible of sunset.

"Oh," Jack breathed, "Oh, but I'd *forgotten*—"

Forgotten everything that now was recalled, and cherished for the memories as much as he grieved for loss.

Fine arched toes broke free of the shoreline froth, and each nail glistened. The scales of the flesh were tightly closed to shed water, sun-heated in the decay of the day like iron within the furnace, an argent heart shining in it ocher and amber and bronze.

The scales of his flesh: *gilt, and gold, and green.*

The glistening verdigrised haunches remained in water; there was no room for more upon the scarpment of shore. And the tail, the serpentlike tail, curved itself across stone, sliced determinedly through sand to touch a shod foot, to drape in blissful familiarity as a dog's paw, wholly undeterred by such transient barricades as a man's shoes, and his tears.

Through them, Mad Jack laughed.

Not Nessie. Never.

"Hello, Puff," he said.

AFTERWORD

I first met Roger in the flesh in 1992, although I'd known him for years via his books, both as a reader and as a bookstore clerk making sure his titles were kept in stock. I was on my way to a small Southern con where Roger and I both were scheduled as a special guests—though the idea of *sharing* billing with Roger Zelazny was inconceivable to me.

And then I met the man, who was sweet and kind and shy and gentle; who went out of his way to put me at ease by simply being himself; who made a point of coming to my reading to encourage and support me. I survived having Roger in the audience, barely; but he said sweet and kind and gentle things when I was done, leaving me to feel worthy after all.

We met a few times after that at various cons, spent some time together, spoke a few times on the phone. I was in awe of the man and the talent, which I think he knew. I *hope* he knew. Because awe carries with it its own homage. And Roger deserves that. From all of us.

In A Night in the Lonesome October, *Roger presented a mixed bag of archetypal figures battling for control of reality. Here Paul Dellinger presents a different cast in a similar battle and reminds us that cinema, too, casts shadows.*

■

MOVERS AND SHAKERS
Paul Dellinger

THE SWORDSMAN REGARDED HIMSELF IN THE FULL-LENGTH MIRROR of the California hacienda, made sure that all his accoutrements were in place from the black mask on his face to the black boots on his feet, turned, and stepped into the shimmering portal in the middle of the opposite wall.

Another Masked Man on a powerful white stallion rode full-tilt across the Texas prairie into an even larger outdoor portal, his ringing signature cry fading even as he disappeared from view. More riders followed—the Duke, the Redhead, the Bullwhip Man, and several others known jointly as the Singers.

From atop one of the tallest trees in a primeval rain forest, the Jungle Man swung from branch to branch to vine and into yet another portal surrounded by steamy vegetation concealing it from anyone it had not called. . . .

The Sleuth penned a message for his biographer to leave in the London apartment they shared, stating that he would be gone for a day or so on one of those journeys about which he could not speak, even afterward. . . .

A shadowy figure whose face was concealed beneath a wide

277

slouch hat disappeared into a portral concealed inside one of the
city subway tunnels, a hollow laugh echoing in the space where
he had stood just before he vanished. . . .

Once more the planets were aligned, the tidal stresses that affected their alternates surfacing, and the latest battle between the
Changers and Maintainers was about to be joined.

It was night on the great plain where the Swordsman emerged.
The stars looked much as he remembered them in the skies of Old
California, but he had no way of knowing on whose world the
morning sun would be rising. The issue would be settled by then,
he knew, at the moment of maximum planetary duress, whenever
it struck. There was never any way of knowing, exactly. In fact,
there had been little time for him to prepare; there had been only
the sudden, instinctive knowing of what was to come, and the
creation of the portal in his own hacienda, and the knowledge that
he would be the leader of those allied to his cause, this time.

What forces, he wondered? He was a leader of men he did not
know, against forces he could not understand, because he was the
prime shade—whatever that meant. He was given to understand
that, in the prime world, he had more incarnations than any of
those summoned to help him, from prose and illustrated literature,
from the flickering shadows that battled across large and small
viewing screens of some kind, and because his own dual identity
had been the basis for so many of the other shades that followed,
the man of action whose real identity was a pretense of timidity
and appeasement. It predated the Man of Steel and his imitators.
Even now, with the enlightenment conferred on him by the calling,
the Swordsman was not sure who the Man of Steel might be but,
from what he gleaned about that man's powers, he wished that
other could have been here instead of himself.

"I can imagine how you feel, sir." A deep and almost rumbling
voice came from behind him.

The Swordsman spun around, surprised that anyone could have
approached so closely without his having heard—but then he realized this man must have just emerged from his own portal. He
found himself facing a large heavily browed man, wearing a suit
of some sort with a loosened cravat knotted around his thick neck
and a look of immense sadness on his face.

"Should I know you?" the Swordsman asked.

"No." The man shook his head, with a cheerless smile. "You
can call me Larry, if you wish. No, I'm on the other side. Or, I
will be, when the moon rises. I won't be able to help myself."

The Swordsman touched the scabbard at his side. "Then why
should I not slay you immediately, señor?"

"Probably you should, if you could. In fact, it would be a relief, to me. Even a man who is pure in heart . . . But never mind that. You haven't the means to kill me, unless that sword of yours is made of purest silver. Only such as that can kill a werewolf."

Werewolf! The word awakened an awareness in the Swordsman's mind, something which had been planted there at his calling but not brought forth until now. This was one of—what were they called?—the Universals. These would be the major antagonists at this alignment.

"Yes, I can see you understand," the tormented man before him said. "I wish I could help you more, while I'm still myself. I can tell you this—the Vlad commands us, by virtue of his many incarnations and powers. His dates go back farther than yours, and are more varied. He has been interpreted by more actors, writers, illustrators, and other creators on the prime world even than you. You will need more than your sword of metal to combat him. You would need, would . . ."

He broke off, as a third figure appeared on the starlit plain. "Enough!" the figure hissed, standing before the man called Larry with his eyes blazing and arms upraised menacingly. "You hatt said enough. You vill obey only me, from this point on."

To the Swordsman, Larry appeared to be the more physically imposing of the two. Yet he cowered back from the smaller, pale man with the dark lips and slicked-back widow's peak. But then the figure changed, growing taller, his eyes becoming redder, his hair thicker and the canine teeth at the corners of his mouth more prominent. "Go your way, werewolf," the man said in a voice that seemed deeper, and with a more English accent than before. "Begone, until I summon you." And then the figure changed again, his legs and body seeming to shrivel up toward his outstretched arms, which became batlike wings on either side of a face which was human no longer . . .

The Swordsman's blade swished out before him, flashing at the batlike thing that dived at him. The point struck true, catching the creature almost directly between its blazing red eyes—but, as he yanked it free, the bloodred hole which it left diminished, growing smaller until it was gone completely, while the creature simply hovered with a gentle flapping of its great bat wings.

"A cross!" Larry called. "Make a cross."

A hissing sound emerged from the creature, seemingly directed at Larry. It rose slightly into the air, then dived again. The Swordsman whipped a long knife from another scabbard on his belt, crossed it over his sword and held them up before him. The bat creature veered away with an awful, moaning sound—and abruptly it was gone. It was nowhere to be seen. And neither was Larry.

Sheathing his weapons, the Swordsman breathed a sigh of relief and readjusted his mask over his eyes. Sometimes it tended to slip at the most inconvenient of times. The instinct implanted in him by the calling through the portal told him to travel east, toward where the sun would rise, signaling the end of the battle. Choosing his direction by the stars, he began to walk.

The plain was by no means empty. Desertlike plants and unnatural-looking rock formations provided plenty of places where Larry could have concealed himself. But the Swordsman had been looking directly at Vlad when he disappeared. Bat creatures . . . werewolves . . . only now was he beginning to realize how far he was out of his depth. It was one thing to match sword skill with a soldier of a corrupt governor, or even a half-dozen such soldiers. But what did he know of supernatural opponents?

On he marched, this time immediately aware of the presence of another, just behind and keeping pace with him. He turned to the newcomer, seeing a tall, ascetic-looking man with a rounded cap upon his head and a coat with a capelike attachment. The Swordsman dropped back to walk beside him. "An unusual uniform for the kind of combat we may expect, señor," he observed.

"Indeed," the man replied. "But more serviceable, perhaps, than a costume which seems more fitting for a mummer's ball. We could reach our destination more quickly had you brought along your horse from the western part of your country instead of a mask."

"How did you know of my horse? Or my country, for that matter?"

"Your boots seem made for riding. And even in this dim light, I can see how the inside of your trousers are slightly frayed in pattern which would match a saddle—an elaborate saddle of the type used in the American West, I believe."

"And your position in this situation?"

"The same as yours, I perceive, although not through any power of reasoning. I seem to have been told in some arcane manner what this battle involves—whether we are to continue to live according to the kinds of scientific laws we can discover and harness, or change to some supernatural sets of laws that change as different elementals assume more or less power over the rest of us. As a sleuth, I am firmly in favor of maintaining discoverable constancy."

"Does your power of reason provide any explanation as to how we have come to be in this situation?"

The Sleuth sighed. "None whatsoever. I have an impression that it involves the positions of the planets, but I know nothing of astronomy. I have always thought the human mind could store only so much data, and I did not wish to clutter my own with extraneous material."

"Perhaps such material was not as extraneous as you had thought."

"I cannot argue the point, given our situation. Can you provide any information about it?"

The Swordsman told him about the encounter with Larry and the creature called Vlad.

"It sounds like a vampire," the Sleuth said. "I once looked into the superstition, when I was asked to investigate the appearance of an incident of vampirism. Its explanation had nothing to do with such creatures, but I do remember what I read of them. In my environs, I would have relegated the idea to the Brothers Grimm. But here . . ." He paused, as though deep in thought. "Tell me," he finally said, "the exact words of this man, Larry, to you."

The Swordsman complied.

By the time he had finished, another man had popped into existence to join them. This one introduced himself as Clayton—first in French, but switching to English as he found that the language his companions had in common—but said he was probably known better as the Jungle Man. Neither name meant anything to the Swordsman, but the man seemed lithe and powerful beneath his clothing, similar to what Larry had worn, and such an ally was not to be dismissed lightly.

His senses also proved sharper. "A band of men await us," he said, "over the next hill. It must be an ambush. They are trying to be very quiet."

"Then how is it you can hear them?" inquired the Sleuth.

Clayton smiled. "I smell them."

As the leader of their growing band, the Swordsman ordered stealth rather than confrontation. He felt their side had not rallied all its supporters yet, and had no idea what the opposition might be like. With the Jungle Man leading—he had stripped off his clothing but for a loincloth, claiming the exposure increased his sensitivity to what lurked around them—they made their way around the hill to avoid those who were expecting them.

The Jungle Man did not have to warn them about their next encounter. The slow, regular pounding of heavy footsteps was audible to them all. In unison, they crouched behind a rock and peeped over its top at what the now-rising moon revealed in the clearing ahead.

The man was gargantuan. Even the fat sergeant on whom the Swordsman occasionally carved an initial would have been dwarfed by him. His arms jutted out in front of him, almost like those of a sleepwalker. His massive, heavy-lidded face had a fixed expression as he passed by their position.

"I don't understand," the Jungle Man whispered. "He has no scent. It's as though he is not a living man."

"Somehow that would not surprise me," the Swordsman replied. "None of those who would change our world, among those I have met so far, are remotely like anyone alive I have ever seen."

"I would suggest that we follow him," the Sleuth said. "At a very safe distance."

That was not difficult. Even if they had not kept him in sight, he generated enough sound as he walked through the bushes and plants rather than around them, with footsteps that sounded like drumbeats. Eventually they saw two others converging on an open area with rock walls on its other three sides, chosen no doubt because it could be well protected. The Swordsman recognized one of them as Vlad, in that first Middle European persona. The other shambled forward with a limp, one arm tucked to his body, and swathed from head to foot in what seemed to be long white wrappings.

"A living mummy," breathed the Sleuth. "What next?"

As though in reply, the Jungle Man pointed to a hirsute manlike figure with the fangs and facial features of a wolf. Larry had not been joking, the Swordsman realized.

"My gypsies still await our enemies," Vlad was proclaiming to them. "Should they elude my human followers, they must still deal with us, the new children of the night," he said, with a dry chuckle. "By sunrise, the prime shade and all its shadows will be our kind. . . ."

"Here!" a new voice called, seemingly right behind the Swordsman. "They are right here, watching you."

"Griffin!" Vlad said. "Where are you?"

The Swordsman was wondering the same thing. He heard the voice right in their midst, but saw no one even in the moonlight.

"When you have eliminated the impossible . . ." murmured the Sleuth. "Jungle Man, can you detect our invisible enemy?"

The reply was a flash of the Jungle Man's clenched fist, which struck something unseen with a meaty thunk and elicited a grunt of pain. An impact like that of a body falling to the ground followed. The Sleuth had produced a pistol with a revolving cylinder from beneath his coat, firing at the approaching wolf, mummy, and automatonlike figures. The Swordsman's surprise at a pistol which fired more than once without reloading was quickly overcome by the realization that those balls were having no effect whatever. "Away from here," he whispered.

"But which way?" said the Sleuth. "They are more masters of the night than we. . . ."

"This way," spoke yet another new voice. The Swordsman could barely see the dim outline of a man with a large hat concealing his face and a great coat hiding the rest of him. He blended in so well with the darkness that he had seemed as invisible as their last antagonist. He lifted an arm and pointed a long gloved finger toward a break in the brush. "I will lead them in another direction," he said, and then began a low, almost-crackling laugh that faded off toward the approaching Universals.

Retreat seemed inglorious to the Swordsman, but it was obvious their weapons would not save them. So he led off the way their new ally had pointed, and his two companions followed. Time seemed to stretch as they pushed their way through bushes, over rocks and, finally, onto a ledge from which it seemed they could see over much of the plain. They saw the fires and wagons of the distant camp of the gypsies mentioned by Vlad. Swords and pistols should be effective against them, all right, but they outnumbered the three—or four—men fighting to maintain their world as it was. And nothing seemed effective against those Universals.

He noticed the bronzed muscles of the Jungle Man tense, then relax. "Our other friend is here," he said.

Only then did the Swordsman see the silhouette of the figure in the wide hat once more. "How do you do that?" he demanded. "Do both of us have invisible warriors on our sides?"

A nasty-sounding laugh answered him. "You might say that," the figure replied. "For the moment, I have them chasing each other. But they will soon be on our trail again, especially that one who is part wolf. He won't have any trouble picking up our track."

"I'm sure," murmured the Jungle Man.

"But he may be the key to our survival," said the half-visible man. "Do any of you know what movies are?"

"I do," the Jungle Man said. "I once tried out for the role of myself in a motion picture. But I didn't get the part."

"I had heard of some experiments in England with projecting moving pictures by Friese-Greene and Paul, and in America by Thomas Edison," the Sleuth said. The Swordsman continued to look blank.

"All right," said the shrouded figure. "Suffice to say movies are one of those art forms from which all of you derive your substance in this shade. That is less true for me—I'm more in the radio and comic books media. Never mind. My point is that movies are the major incarnations or the Universals as well, especially the wolf, mummy and the man of parts, the big man. In fact, the same actor who is famous for the wolf role has also contributed to the others.

Eliminate him, and we may stand a chance of weakening those other two incarnations."

"I don't pretend to understand this," the Jungle Man said, "but I'm willing. How do we do it?"

"That's a good question. In the movies, the best method is a silver bullet."

"Since we are in no position to mine any silver," said the Sleuth, "I would suggest we concentrate on Vlad." He turned to the Swordsman. "From what you told me of Larry's words, I have an idea what he was trying to tell you. The word 'would,' you know, has another spelling and another meaning. If I can borrow the formidable-looking knife of yours, I may be able to fashion an appropriate weapon from some of this tree growth below us."

"Whatever you do, you'd better do it fast," the Jungle Man said. "I smell gypsies approaching again. . . ."

Soft laughter interrupted him. "I'll see if I can't lead them astray, too, while you make your preparations." His voice faded off and, although the Swordsman looked carefully, he did not see his departure.

The Swordsman did not pretend to understand the forces of nature that arrayed these two sides against one another. But it did not seem to fit that one side should have so many more forces to deploy than the other. He was convinced that those who would maintain the world as he knew it had more allies who, he fervently hoped, would show up very soon.

No sooner had the Sleuth returned his knife with another weapon he had made than the sounds of the approaching gypsies could be heard below. The Swordsman stood. "Amigos, I suppose we might as well make our stand here. At least we have the advantage of the high ground. . . ." He noticed the Jungle Man's nose twitching. "Something?"

"Men and animals. Approaching the open area behind us, down below. I have no way of knowing if they are friends or more enemies, but . . ."

"Sí. We know those approaching from this side are enemies. What do we have to lose? Come on."

They scrambled down the back of their ledge, just ahead of Vlad's forces scaling the front—men with heads wrapped in colorful kerchiefs, knives gripped in their hands and teeth, scrambling up toward hem. The stalkers made it to the top, only to find their prey retreating below them on the opposite side. The Swordsman drew his weapons, the Sleuth checked the loads of his pistol, the Jungle Man crouched pantherlike, and the strangely clouded figure in the slouch hat rejoined them as they formed a circle, protecting each other's backs, from those closing in around them.

A ringing cry from the open area behind them was echoed by the sound of hoofbeats and then a volley of gunshots. The Swordsman spun around to see another Masked Man leading the charge of what seemed to be a posse of American cowboys.

And then the gypsies were upon them. The Swordsman's long and short blades flashed in the moonlight, as he slashed with increasing desperation at those who were slashing at him. Someone jumped onto his shoulders, bearing him to the ground. He glimpsed the upraised knife from the corner of his eye, and tried to turn in time to ward off the blow. There was a crack with a different sound than the pistol shots, and he saw the end of a long bullwhip wrapped around the wrist of his attacker. The black-clad man at the other end of the whip gave a pull, and the attacker fell back.

And then it was over. The gypsies were retreating on foot, the horsemen in pursuit. The Swordsman started to breathe a sigh of relief, and found himself staring into the baleful red eyes of Vlad.

"So it comes down to this," he hissed. "The two leaders. There was no way you could have defeated me, Swordsman. The outcome was inevitable this time. Even now, back in the prime world, my incarnations have become more heroic in their depictions. No longer are my kind seen as an evil scourge, but rather as graceful immortals to which the prime humans increasingly aspire. I will treat you as I did the Turkish invaders of my land. One blow . . ."

The Swordsman leaped back, dropping his sword to the ground and reaching for something else stuck in the back of his belt. Before he could draw it, he saw a flash of brownish fur streaking toward him and a flash of yellowish eyes and teeth gleaming with malice. "Larry," he called out. "No!"

A shot rang out. The Swordsman had seen how ineffective previous shots against this creature had been. But this one hurled him back, leaving him growling and pawing at the wound in his upper right shoulder.

The Masked Man on the white horse kept the pistol aimed at the snapping figure, lest it rise and attack again. "I perceive," the Sleuth said to him, "that you carry silver bullets in your weapons?"

Then Vlad was at him again, but the Swordsman had now managed to draw the wooden swordlike weapon which the Sleuth had fashioned for him. With a straight-arm thrust, he plunged it into the heart of the other. It broke in his hand, but most of it remained impaled in the creature, whose shape changed even as he watched. There was a scream, which seemed to hold centuries of evil in its release, and then, on the face, a look of peace. . . .

*   *   *

And then there was nothing but a skeleton beneath the rags of clothing, sprawled on the ground in front of new portal which sprang into being, and drew the Swordsman toward it.

He was lying on a bed in his hacienda, the glow of the portal fading out behind him before he could think to look for it. "A strange dream," he murmured, pulling the mask and wiping perspiration from his face with the back of his hand. "What could have prompted such a nightmare . . . ?"

His voice stopped as he looked down at his other hand, and opened it to drop the broken handle of the wooden sword to the floor.

AFTERWORD

I had listened to Roger Zelazny give a reading once at a convention. It was polished and flawless, and left me with the impression that he was rather stiff, formal and maybe a little shy.

It was not until 1993, when he was guest of honor at a convention in Lynchburg, Virginia, that I got to know him better. I had read his books all the way back to *This Immortal* and *The Dream Master*. In fact, he and I had our first short stories published the same year (1962, by *Amazing/Fantastic* editor Cele Goldsmith). I also had the benefit of having read Jane Lindskold's 1993 book on Zelazny's work by the time I really got to know him.

There was nothing stiff or formal about Roger Zelazny by then. Hopping acrobatically atop tables to give his talks ("Once I attain this measure of heights, my voice appears to project better," he said with a grin. "I just do this for acoustics!"), he regaled us with all kinds of revelations about his career:

How his novel *Damnation Alley* became a movie: A reviewer had described it as featuring bikers, volcanoes and gratuitous violence, he said. Someone in Hollywood saw that, and decided it would make a good picture.

How "For a Breath I Tarry," published in *New Worlds* in 1966, helped classify him as an experimental New Wave writer: "The printer must have been a member of the New Wave also," he said, because the story was garbled, paragraphs transposed and entire sentences left out. Editor Michael Moorcock later apologized, but said he was still getting letters from subscribers about what a wonderful story it was.

A tip for collectors of original manuscripts: Roger had a cat which got into a drawer where he had the manuscript-in-progress for *Deus Irae,* his collaboration with Philip K. Dick, and urinated on it. Roger quickly copied the pages and the stains, fortunately, did not show up. Doubleday was happy with the story but insisted on being sent the original manuscript. So he complied. "I never got a reaction," he said. "I never saw the manuscript again. I don't know what they did with it. It's probably one of those mysteries it's better not to know." But, he advised, if someone at a convention ever offers to sell you that manuscript, there is a way to determine its authenticity.

How the well-received *Creatures of Light and Darkness* had never been meant for publication: "It was only by accident that a publisher found out it existed," Roger said. He wrote it as an experiment, trying out different styles (one entire chapter was in free verse) that he might want to use someday. When he mentioned it to Samuel R. Delany, Delany mentioned it to Lawrence Ashmead at Doubleday, who asked to see it. "You won't like it," Roger insisted. Two weeks later, Ashmead called back: "I like it." It stayed in print for thirty years. "I can only come to the conclusion from this what you never know what will catch on," Roger said.

The success of the Amber series: "I had no idea how many there were going to be, and I was really appalled by how they caught on."

His favorites among his books: *The Immortal*, his first; *Lord of Light*, his most ambitious: *Doorways in the Sand; Eye of Cat;* and his most recent at that time, *A Night in the Lonesome October*, because it was something totally different.

"I wrote *The Lonesome October* in six weeks. It makes me sound like a hack," he said. He found himself skipping meals and losing sleep. "I'm so taken with the story, I can't stop."

When I was offered the opportunity to submit a story for this collection, I wanted to do something like Roger did with Corwin in the first Amber book, where the character had no memory of how he got into his situation and had to rely on his wits to keep others from realizing his handicap. It had a great Raymond Chandleresque mystery tone in its opening chapters. I reread parts of the Lindskold book, hoping to find a way to get a grip on that feel. Instead, her writing about Zelazny's uses of classical and popular mythologies inspired me to try a tribute to *The Lonesome October*.

Roger also helped other writers get published, editing recent anthologies like *Wheel of Fortune* and *The Williamson Effect*. His acceptance note on my story for the latter is the nicest I've ever gotten, from any editor.

And, as you can see by the book you are now holding, he is still helping writers get published.

In a future where virtual reality makes anything possible, a young woman discovers the ultimate thrill.

■

THE HALFWAY HOUSE AT THE HEART OF DARKNESS
William Browning Spencer

KEEL WORE A RAGGED SHIRT WITH THE HOLO *VEED THERE, SIMMED that* shimmering on it. She wore it in and out of the virtual. If she was in an interactive virtual, the other players sometimes complained. Amid the dragons and elves and swords of fire, a bramble-haired girl, obviously spiking her virtual with drugs and refusing to tune her shirt to something suitably medieval, could be distracting.

"Fizz off," Keel would say, in response to all complaints.

Keel was difficult. Rich, self-destructive, beautiful, she was twenty years old and already a case study in virtual psychosis.

She had been rehabbed six times. She could have died that time on Makor when she went blank in the desert. She still bore the teeth marks of the land eels that were gnawing on her shoulder when they found her.

A close one. You can't revive the digested.

No one had to tell Keel that she was in rehab again. She was staring at a green ocean, huge white clouds overhead, white gulls filling the heated air with their cries.

They gave you these serenity mock-ups when they were bringing you around. They were fairly insipid and several shouts behind the

288

technology. This particular V-run was embarrassing. The ocean wasn't continuous, probably a seven-minute repeat, and the sun's heat was patchy on her face.

The beach was empty. She was propped up in a lounge chair— no doubt her position back in the ward. With concentration, focusing on her spine, she could sense the actual contours of the bed, the satiny feel of the sensor pad.

It was work, this focusing, and she let it go. Always better to flow.

Far to her right, she spied a solitary figure. The figure was moving toward her.

It was, she knew, a wilson. She was familiar with the drill. Don't spook the patient. Approach her slowly after she is sedated and in a quiet setting.

The wilson was a fat man in a white suit (*neo-Victorian, dead silly,* Keel thought). He kept his panama hat from taking flight in the wind by clamping it onto his head with his right hand and leaning forward.

Keel recognized him. She even remembered his name, but then it was the kind of name you'd remember: Dr. Max Marx.

He had been her counselor, her wilson, the last time she'd crashed. Which meant she was in Addiction Resources Limited, which was located just outside of New Vegas.

Dr. Marx looked up, waved, and came on again with new purpose.

A pool of sadness welled in her throat. There was nothing like help, and its pale sister hope, to fill Keel's soul with black water.

Fortunately, Dr. Max Marx wasn't one of the hearty ones. The hearty ones were the worst. Marx was, in fact, refreshingly gloomy, his thick black beard and eyebrows creating a doomed stoic's countenance.

"Yes," he said, in response to her criticism of the virtual, "this is a very miserable effect. You should see the sand crabs. They are laughable, like toys." He eased himself down on the sand next to her and took his hat off and fanned it in front of his face. "I apologize. It must be very painful, a connoisseur of the vee like you, to endure this."

Keel remembered that Dr. Marx spoke in a manner subject to interpretation. His words always held a potential for sarcasm.

"We are portable," Dr. Marx said, "we are in a mobile unit, and so, alas, we don't have the powerful stationary AdRes equipment at our command. Even so, we could do better, there are better mockups to be had, but we are not prospering these days. Financially, it has been a year of setbacks, and we have had to settle for some second-rate stuff.''

"I'm not in a hospital?" Keel asked.

Marx shook his head. "No. No hospital."

Keel frowned. Marx, sensing her confusion, put his hat back on his head and studied her through narrowed eyes. "We are on the run, Keel Benning. You have not been following the news, being otherwise occupied, but companies like your beloved Virtvana have won a major legislative battle. They are now empowered to maintain their customer base aggressively. I believe the wording is 'protecting customer assets against invasive alienation by third-party services.' Virtvana can come and get you."

Keel blinked at Dr. Marx's dark countenance. "You can't seriously think someone would . . . what? . . . kidnap me?"

Dr. Marx shrugged. "Virtvana might. For the precedent. You're a good customer."

"Vee moguls are going to sweat the loss of one spike? That's crazy."

Dr. Marx sighed, stood up, whacked sand from his trousers with his hands. "You noticed then? That's good. Being able to recognize crazy, that is a good sign. It means there is hope for your own sanity."

Her days were spent at the edge of the second-rate ocean. She longed for something that would silence the Need. She would have settled for a primitive bird-in-flight simulation. Anything. Some corny sex-with-dolphins loop—or something abstract, the color red leaking into blue, enhanced with aural-D.

She would have given ten years of her life for a game of Apes and Angels, Virtvana's most popular package. Apes and Angels wasn't just another smooth metaphysical mix—it was the true religion to its fans. A gamer started out down in the muck on Libido Island, where the senses were indulged with perfect, shimmerless sims. Not bad, Libido Island, and some gamers stayed there a long, long time. But what put Apes and Angels above the best pleasure pops was this: A player could *evolve spiritually*. If you followed the Path, if you were steadfast, you became more compassionate, more aware, at one with the universe . . . all of which was accompanied by feelings of euphoria.

Keel would have settled for a legal rig. Apes and Angels was a chemically enhanced virtual, and the gear that true believers wore was stripped of most safeguards, tuned to a higher reality.

It was one of these hot pads that had landed Keel in Addiction Resources again.

"It's the street stuff that gets you in trouble," Keel said. "I've just got to stay clear of that."

"You said that last time," the wilson said. "You almost died, you know."

Keel felt suddenly hollowed, beaten. "Maybe I want to die," she said.

Dr. Marx shrugged. Several translucent seagulls appeared, hovered over him, and then winked out. "Bah," he muttered. "Bad therapy-v, bad, death-wishing clients, bad career choice. Who doesn't want to die? And who doesn't get that wish, sooner or later?"

One day, Dr. Marx said, "You are ready for swimming."

It was morning, full of a phony, golden light. The nights were black and dreamless, nothing, and the days that grew out of them were pale and untaxing. It was an intentionally bland virtual, its sameness designed for healing.

Keel was wearing a one-piece, white bathing suit. Her counselor wore bathing trunks, baggy with thick black vertical stripes; he looked particularly solemn, in an effort, no doubt, to counteract the farcical elements of rotund belly and sticklike legs.

Keel sighed. She knew better than to protest. This was necessary. She took her wilson's proffered hand, and they walked down to the water's edge. The sand changed from white to gray where the water rolled over it, and they stepped forward into the salt-smelling foam.

Her legs felt cold when the water enclosed them. The wetness was now more than virtual. As she leaned forward and kicked, her muscles, taut and frayed, howled.

She knew the machines were exercising her now. Somewhere her real body, emaciated from long neglect, was swimming in a six-foot aquarium whose heavy seas circulated to create a kind of liquid treadmill. Her lungs ached; her shoulders twisted into monstrous knots of pain.

In the evening, they would talk, sitting in their chairs and watching the ocean swallow the sun, the clouds turning orange, the sky occasionally spotting badly, some sort of pixel fatigue.

"If human beings are the universe's way of looking at itself," Dr. Marx said, "then virtual reality is the universe's way of *pretending* to look at itself."

"You wilsons are all so down on virtual reality," Keel said. "But maybe it is the natural evolution of perception. I mean, everything we see is a product of the equipment we see it with. Biological, mechanical, whatever."

Dr. Marx snorted. "Bah. The old 'everything-is-virtual' argument. I am ashamed of you, Keel Benning. Something more original, please. We wilsons are down on virtual addiction because everywhere we look we see dead philosophers. We see them and they don't look so good. We smell them, and they stink. That is our perception, our primitive reality."

The healing was slow, and the sameness, the boredom, was a hole to be filled with words. Keel talked, again, about the death of her parents and her brother. They had been over this ground the last time she'd been in treatment, but she was here again, and so it was said again.

"I'm rich because they are dead," she said.

It was true, of course, and Dr. Marx merely nodded, staring in front of him. Her father had been a wealthy man, and he and his young wife and Keel's brother, Calder, had died in a freak airdocking accident while vacationing at Keypond Terraforms. A "sole survivor" clause in her father's life insurance policy had left Keel a vast sum.

She had been eleven at the time—and would have died with her family had she not been sulking that day, refusing to leave the hotel suite.

She knew she was not responsible, of course. But it was not an event you wished to dwell on. You looked, naturally, for powerful distractions.

"It is a good excuse for your addiction," Dr. Marx said. "If you die, maybe God will say, 'I don't blame you.' Or maybe God will say, 'Get real. Life's hard.' I don't know. Addiction is in the present, not the past. It's the addiction itself that leads to more addictive behavior."

Keel had heard all this before. She barely heard it this time. The weariness of the evening was real, brought on by the day's physical exertions. She spoke in a kind of woozy, presleep fog, finding no power in her words, no emotional release.

Of more interest were her counselor's words. He spoke with rare candor, the result, perhaps, of their fugitive status, their isolation.

It was after a long silence that he said, "To tell you the truth, I'm thinking of getting out of the addiction treatment business. I'm sick of being on the losing side."

Keel felt a coldness in her then, which, later, she identified as fear.

He continued: "They are winning. Virtvana, MindSlide, Right to Flight. They've got the sex, the style, the flash. All we wilsons have is a sense of mission, this knowledge that people are dying, and the ones that don't die are being lost to lives of purpose.

"Maybe we're right—sure, we're right—but we can't sell it. In two, three days we'll come to our destination and you'll have to come into Big R and meet your fellow addicts. You won't be impressed. It's a henry-hovel in the Slash. It's not a terrific advertisement for Big R."

Keel felt strange, comforting her wilson. Nonetheless, she reached forward and touched his bare shoulder. "You want to help people. That is a good and noble impulse."

He looked up at her, a curious nakedness in his eyes. "Maybe that is hubris."

"Hubris?"

"Are you not familiar with the word? It means to try to steal the work of the gods."

Keel thought about that in the brief moment between the dimming of the seascape and the nothingness of night. She thought it would be a fine thing to do, to steal the work of the gods.

Dr. Marx checked the perimeter, the security net. All seemed to be in order. The air was heavy with moisture and the cloying odor of mint. This mint scent was the olfactory love song of an insectlike creature that flourished in the tropical belt. The creature looked like an unpleasant mix of spider and wasp. Knowing that the sweet scent came from it, Dr. Marx breathed shallowly and had to fight against an inclination to gag. Interesting, the way knowledge affected one. An odor, pleasant in itself, could induce nausea when its source was identified.

He was too weary to pursue the thought. He returned to the mobile unit, climbed in and locked the door behind him. He walked down the corridor, paused to peer into the room where Keel rested, sedated electrically.

He should not have spoken his doubts. He was weary, depressed, and it was true that he might very well abandon this crumbling profession. But he had no right to be so self-revealing to a client. As long as he was employed, it behooved him to conduct himself in a professional manner.

Keel's head rested quietly on the pillow. Behind her, on the green panels, her heart and lungs created cool, luminous graphics. Physically, she was restored. Emotionally, mentally, spiritually, she might be damaged beyond repair.

He turned away from the window and walked on down the corridor. He walked past his sleeping quarters to the control room. He undressed and lay down on the utilitarian flat and let the neuronet embrace him. He was aware, as always, of guilt and a hangdog sense of betrayal.

The virtual had come on the Highway two weeks ago. He'd

already left Addiction Resources with Keel, traveling west into the wilderness of Pit Finitum, away from the treatment center and New Vegas.

Know the enemy. He'd sampled all the vees, played at lowest res with all the safeguards maxed, so that he could talk knowledgeably with his clients. But he'd never heard of this virtual—and it had a special fascination for him. It was called *Halfway House.*

A training vee, not a recreational one, it consisted of a series of step-motivated, instructional virtuals designed to teach the apprentice addictions counselor his trade.

So why this guilt attached to methodically running the course?
What guilt?
That guilt.
Okay. Well . . .

The answer was simple enough: Here all interventions came to a good end, all problems were resolved, all clients were healed.

So far he had intervened on a fourteen-year-old boy addicted to Clawhammer Comix, masterfully diagnosed a woman suffering from Leary's syndrome, and led an entire Group of mix-feeders through a nasty withdrawal episode.

He could tell himself he was learning valuable healing techniques.

Or he could tell himself that he was succumbing to the world that killed his clients, the hurt-free world where everything worked out for the best, good triumphed, bad withered and died, rewards came effortlessly—and if that was not enough, the volume could always be turned up.

He had reservations. Adjusting the neuronet, he thought, "I will be careful." It was what his clients always said.

Keel watched the insipid ocean, waited. Generally, Dr. Marx arrived soon after the darkness of sleep had fled.

He did not come at all. When the sun was high in the sky, she began to shout for him. That was useless, of course.

She ran into the ocean, but it was a low res ghost and only filled her with vee-panic. She stumbled back to the beach chair, tried to calm herself with a rational voice: *Someone will come.*

But would they? She was, according to her wilson, in the wilds of Pit Finitum, hundreds of miles to the west of New Vegas, traveling toward a halfway house hidden in some dirty corner of the mining warren known as the Slash.

Darkness came, and the programmed current took her into unconsciousness.

The second day was the same, although she sensed a physical

weakness that emanated from Big R. Probably nutrients in one of the IV pockets had been depleted. *I'll die,* she thought. Night snuffed the thought.

A new dawn arrived without Dr. Marx. Was he dead? And if so, was he dead by accident or design? And if by design, whose? Perhaps he had killed himself; perhaps this whole business of Virtvana's persecution was a delusion.

Keel remembered the wilson's despair, felt a sudden conviction that Dr. Marx had fled Addiction Resources without that center's knowledge, a victim of the evangelism/paranoia psychosis that sometimes accompanied counselor burnout.

Keel had survived much in her twenty years. She had donned some deadly v-gear and made it back to Big R intact. True, she had been saved a couple of times, and she probably wasn't what anyone would call psychologically sound, but . . . it would be an ugly irony if it was an addictions rehab, an unhinged wilson, that finally killed her.

Keel hated irony, and it was this disgust that pressed her into action.

She went looking for the plug. She began by focusing on her spine, the patches, the slightly off-body temp of the sensor pad. Had her v-universe been more engrossing, this would have been harder to do, but the ocean was deteriorating daily, the seagulls now no more than scissoring disruptions in the mottled sky.

On the third afternoon of her imposed solitude, she was able to sit upright in Big R. It required all her strength, the double-think of real Big-R motion while in the virtual. The affect in vee was to momentarily tilt the ocean and cause the sky to leak blue pixels into the sand.

Had her arms been locked, had her body been glove-secured, it would have been wasted effort, of course, but Keel's willing participation in her treatment, her daily exercise regimen, had allowed relaxed physical inhibitors. There had been no reason for Dr. Marx to anticipate Keel's attempting a Big-R disruption.

She certainly didn't want to.

The nausea and terror induced by contrary motion in Big R while simulating a virtual was considerable.

Keel relied on gravity, shifting, leaning to the right. The bed shifted to regain balance.

She screamed, twisted, hurled herself sideways into Big R.

And her world exploded. The ocean raced up the beach, a black tidal wave that screeched and rattled as though some monstrous mechanical beast were being demolished by giant pistons.

Black water engulfed her. She coughed and it filled her lungs.

She flayed; her right fist slammed painfully against the side of the container, making it hum.

She clambered out of the exercise vat, placed conveniently next to the bed, stumbled, and sprawled on the floor in naked triumph.

"Hello Big R," she said, tasting blood on her lips.

Dr. Marx had let the system ease him back into Big R. The sessions room dimmed to glittering black, then the light returned. He was back in the bright control room. He removed the neuronet, swung his legs to the side of the flatbed, stretched. It had been a good session. He had learned something about distinguishing (behaviorially) the transitory feedback psychosis called frets from the organic v-disease, Viller's Pathway.

This Halfway House was proving to be a remarkable instructional tool. In retrospect, his fear of its virtual form had been pure superstition. He smiled at his own irrationality.

He would have slept that night in ignorance, but he decided to give the perimeter of his makeshift compound a last security check before retiring.

To that effect, he dressed and went outside.

In the flare of the compound lights, the jungle's purple vegetation looked particularly unpleasant, like the swollen limbs of long-drowned corpses. The usual skittering things made a racket. There was nothing in the area inclined to attack a man, but the planet's evolution hadn't stinted on biting and stinging vermin, and . . .

And one of the vermin was missing.

He had, as always, been frugal in his breathing, gathering into his lungs as little of the noxious atmosphere as possible. The cloying mint scent never failed to sicken him.

But the odor was gone.

It had been there earlier in the evening, and now it was gone. He stood in jungle night, in the glare of the compound lights, waiting for his brain to process this piece of information, but his brain told him only that the odor had been there and now it was gone.

Still, some knowledge of what this meant was leaking through, creating a roiling fear.

If you knew what to look for, you could find it. No vee was as detailed as nature.

You only had to find one seam, one faint oscillation in a rock, one incongruent shadow.

It was a first-rate sim, and it would have fooled him. But they had had to work fast, fabricating and downloading it, and no one had noted that a nasty alien-bug filled the Big-R air with its mating fragrance.

Dr. Marx knew he was still in the vee. That meant, of course, that he had not walked outside at all. He was still lying on the flat. And, thanks to his blessed paranoia, there was a button at the base of the flat, two inches from where his left hand naturally lay. Pushing it would disrupt all current and activate a hypodermic containing twenty cc's of hapotile-4. Hapotile-4 could get the attention of the deepest v-diver. The aftereffects were not pleasant, but, for many v-devotees, there wouldn't have been an "after" without hapotile.

Dr. Marx didn't hesitate. He strained for the Big R, traced the line of his arm, moved. It was there; he found it. Pressed.

Nothing.

Then, out of the jungle, a figure came.

Eight feet tall, carved from black steel, the vee soldier bowed at the waist. Then, standing erect, it spoke: "We deactivated your failsafe before you embarked, Doctor."

"Who are you?" He was not intimidated by this military mockup, the boom of its metal voice, the faint whine of its servos. It was a virtual puppet, of course. Its masters were the thing to fear.

"We are concerned citizens," the soldier said. "We have reason to believe that you are preventing a client of ours, a client-in-good-credit, from satisfying her constitutionally sanctioned appetites."

"Keel Benning came to us of her own free will. Ask her and she will tell you as much."

"We will ask her. And that is not what she will say. She will say, for all the world to hear, that her freedom was compromised by so-called caregivers."

"Leave her alone."

The soldier came closer. It looked up at the dark blanket of the sky. "Too late to leave anyone alone, Doctor. Everyone is in the path of progress. One day we will all live in the vee. It is the natural home of gods."

The sky began to glow as the black giant raised its gleaming arms.

"You act largely out of ignorance," the soldier said. "The god-seekers come, and you treat them like aberrations, like madmen burning with sickness. This is because you do not know the virtual yourself. Fearing it, you have confined and studied it. You have refused to taste it, to savor it."

The sky was glowing gold, and figures seemed to move in it, beautiful, winged humanforms.

Virtvana, Marx thought. *Apes and Angels.*

It was his last coherent thought before enlightenment.

"I give you a feast," the soldier roared. And all the denizens of heaven swarmed down, surrounding Dr. Marx with love and compassion and that absolute, impossible distillation of a hundred thousand insights that formed a single, tear-shaped truth: Euphoria.

Keel found she could stand. A couple of days of inaction hadn't entirely destroyed the work of all that exercise. Shakily, she navigated the small room. The room had the sanitized, hospital look she'd grown to know and loathe. If this room followed the general scheme, the shelves over the bed should contain . . . They did, and Keel donned one of the gray, disposable client suits.

She found Dr. Marx by the noise he was making, a kind of *huh, huh, huh* delivered in a monotonous chant and punctuated by an occasional *Ah!* The sounds, and the writhing, near-naked body that lay on the table emitting these sounds, suggested to Keel that her doctor, naughty man, might be auditing something sexual on the virtual.

But a closer look showed signs of v-overload epilepsy. Keel had seen it before and knew that one's first inclination, to shut down every incoming signal, was not the way to go. First you shut down any chemical enhancers—and, if you happened to have a hospital handy (as she did), you slowed the system more with something like clemadine or hetlin—then, if you were truly fortunate and your spike was epping in a high-tech detox (again, she was so fortunate), you plugged in a regulator, spliced it and started running the signals through that, toning them down.

Keel got to it. As she moved, quickly, confidently, she had time to think that this was something she knew about (a consumer's knowledge, not a tech's, but still, her knowledge was extensive).

Dr. Marx had been freed from the virtual for approximately ten minutes (but was obviously not about to break the surface of Big R), when Keel heard the whine of the security alarm. The front door of the unit was being breached with an L-saw.

Keel scrambled to the corridor where she'd seen the habitat sweep. She swung the ungainly tool around, falling to one knee as she struggled to unbolt the barrel lock. *Fizzing pocky low-tech grubber.*

The barrel-locking casing clattered to the floor just as the door collapsed.

The man in the doorway held a weapon, which, in retrospect, made Keel feel a little better. Had he been weaponless, she would still have done what she did.

She swept him out the door. The sonic blast scattered him across the cleared area, a tumbling, bloody mass of rags and unraveling flesh, a thigh bone tumbling into smaller bits as it rolled under frayed vegetation.

She was standing in the doorway when an explosion rocked the unit and sent her crashing backward. She crawled down the corridor, still lugging the habitat gun, and fell into the doorway of a cluttered storage room. An alarm continued to shriek somewhere.

The mobile now lay on its side. She fired in front of her. The roof rippled and roared, looked like it might hold, and then flapped away like an unholy, howling v-demon, a vast silver blade that smoothly severed the leafy tops of the jungle's tallest sentinels. Keel plunged into the night, ran to the edge of the unit and peered out into the glare of the compound lights.

The man was crossing the clearing.

She crouched, and he turned, sensing motion. He was trained to fire reflexively but he was too late. The rolling sonic blast from Keel's habitat gun swept man and weapon and weapon's discharge into rolling motes that mixed with rock and sand and vegetation, a stew of organic and inorganic matter for the wind to stir.

Keel waited for others to come but none did.

Finally, she reentered the mobile to retrieve her wilson, dragging him (unconscious) into the scuffed arena of the compound.

Later that night, exhausted, she discovered the aircraft that had brought the two men. She hesitated, then decided to destroy it. It would do her no good; it was not a vehicle she could operate, and its continued existence might bring others.

The next morning, Keel's mood improved when she found a pair of boots that almost fit. They were a little tight but, she reasoned, that was probably better than a little loose. They had, according to Dr. Marx, a four-day trek ahead of them.

Dr. Marx was now conscious but fairly insufferable. He could talk about nothing but angels and the Light. A long, hard dose of Apes and Angels had filled him with fuzzy love and an uncomplicated metaphysics in which smiling angels fixed bad stuff and protected all good people (and, it went without saying, all people were good).

Keel had managed to dress Dr. Marx in a suit again, and this restored a professional appearance to the wilson. But, to Keel's dismay, Dr. Marx in virtual-withdrawal was a shameless whiner.

"Please," he would implore. "Please, I am in terrible terrible Neeeeeeed."

He complained that the therapy-v was too weak, that he was

sinking into a catatonic state. Later, he would stop entirely, *of course,* but now, please, something stronger . . .

No.

He told her she was heartless, cruel, sadistic, vengeful. She was taking revenge for her own treatment program, although, if she would just recall, he had been the soul of gentleness and solicitude.

"You can't be in virtual and make the journey," Keel said. "I need you to navigate. We will take breaks, but I'm afraid they will be brief. Say goodbye to your mobile."

She destroyed it with the habitat sweep, and they were on their way. It was a limping, difficult progress, for they took much with them: food, emergency camping and sleeping gear, a portable, two-feed v-rig, the virtual black box, and the security image grabs. And Dr. Marx was not a good traveler.

It took six days to get to the Slash, and then Dr. Marx said he wasn't sure just where the halfway house was.

"What?"

"I don't know. I'm disoriented."

"You'll never be a good v-addict," Keel said. "You can't lie."

"I'm not lying!" Dr. Marx snapped, goggle-eyed with feigned innocence.

Keel knew what was going on, of course. He wanted to give her the slip and find a v-hovel where he could swap good feelings with his old angel buddies. Keel knew.

"I'm not letting you out of my sight," she said.

The Slash was a squalid mining town with every vice a disenfranchised population could buy. It had meaner toys than New Vegas, and no semblance of law.

Keel couldn't just ask around for a treatment house. You could get hurt that way.

But luck was with her. She spied the symbol of a triangle inside a circle on the side of what looked like an abandoned office. She watched a man descend a flight of stairs directly beneath the painted triangle. She followed him.

"Where are we going?" Dr. Marx said. He was still a bundle of tics from angel-deprivation.

Keel didn't answer, just dragged him along. Inside, she saw the "Easy Does It" sign and knew everything was going to be okay.

An old man saw her and waved. Incredibly, he knew her, even knew her name. "Keel," he shouted. "I'm delighted to see you."

"It's a small world, Solly."

"It's that. But you get around some too. You cover some ground, you know. I figured ground might be covering you by now."

Keel laughed. "Yeah." She reached out and touched the old man's arm. "I'm looking for a house," she said.

In Group they couldn't get over it. Dr. Max Marx was a fizzing *client*. This amazed everyone, but two identical twins, Sere and Shona, were so dazed by this event that they insisted on dogging the wilson's every move. They'd flank him, peering up into his eyes, trying to fathom this mystery by an act of unrelenting scrutiny.

Brake Madders thought it was a narc thing and wanted to hurt Marx.

"No, he's one of us," Keel said.

And so, Keel thought, *am I.*

When Dr. Max Marx was an old man, one of his favorite occupations was to reminisce. One of his favorite topics was Keel Benning. He gave her credit for saving his life, not only in the jungles of Pit Finitum but during the rocky days that followed when he wanted to flee the halfway house and find, again, virtual nirvana.

She had recognized every denial system and thwarted it with logic. When logic was not enough, she had simply shared his sadness and pain and doubt.

"I've been there," she had said.

The young wilsons and addiction activists knew Keel Benning only as the woman who had fought Virtvana and MindSlip and the vast lobby of Right to Flight, the woman who had secured a resounding victory for addicts' rights and challenged the spurious thinking that suggested a drowning person was drowning by choice. She was a hero, but, like many heroes, she was not, to a newer generation, entirely real.

"I was preoccupied at the time," Dr. Marx would tell young listeners. "I kept making plans to slip out and find some Apes and Angels. You weren't hard pressed then—and you aren't now—to find some mind-flaming vee in the Slack. My thoughts would go that way a lot.

"So I didn't stop and think, 'Here's a woman who's been rehabbed six times; it's not likely she'll stop on the seventh. She's just endured some genuine nasty events, and she's probably feeling the need for some quality downtime.'

"What I saw was a woman who spent every waking moment working on her recovery. And when she wasn't doing mental, spiritual, or physical push-ups she was helping those around her, all us shaking, vision-hungry, fizz-headed needers.

"I didn't think, 'What the hell is this?' back then. But I thought it later. I thought it when I saw her graduate from medical school.

"When she went back and got a law degree, so she could fight the bastards who wouldn't let her practice addiction medicine properly, I thought it again. That time, I asked her. I asked her what had wrought the change."

Dr. Marx would wait as long as it took for someone to ask, "What did she say?"

"It unsettled me some," he would say, then wait again to be prompted.

They'd prompt.

" 'Helping people,' she'd said. She'd found it was a thing she could do, she had a gift for it. All those no-counts and dead-enders in a halfway house in the Slack. She found she could help them all."

Dr. Marx saw it then, and saw it every time after that, every time he'd seen her speaking on some monolith grid at some rally, some hearing, some whatever. Once he'd seen it, he saw it every time: that glint in her eye, the incorrigible, unsinkable addict.

"People," she had said. "What a rush."

AFTERWORD

If you go to science fiction/fantasy conventions, you've heard us on panels talking about our books. Perhaps you have been on such a panel, talking about your books. It generally goes something like this: "While my Elves of the Azure Vortex cycle contains many of the trappings of traditional fantasy, it owes more to Dostoyevsky and Tolstoy than to Tolkien. I've tried to create a resonating thematic structure that forces the reader to assume an existential stance in relation to the work." There's a chance we'll throw in some reference to Melville.

We are not bad people, we panel pontificaters. We are, as are all artists, fighting the dread of anonymity. We have discovered that this convention we have attended contains hundreds of professional writers, many of whom have written fifty or more books, many of them with avid followings, some with followings that have fashioned whole cultures around the author's work. These fans sing the author's folksongs, laugh heartily at jokes in the ersatz language of the Azure Vortex, and wear T-shirts that are incomprehensible to the uninitiated.

We do not recognize any of these authors' names.

This is appalling. The writing of novels is, after all, a way we have discovered to talk at great length without being interrupted. And now here, surrounding us, are all these people who have written all these blathering books.

Place us on a panel, give us a book of our own to hold, and we are apt—helpless perhaps—to begin speaking of that book in exalted terms. We are not the hoi polloi; we are not slapping out some forgettable product for indiscriminate hordes. We are creating something a little more distinctive.

The inclination to wax pompous is irresistible.

When a reviewer writing in *The New York Times Book Review* referred to my novel, *Zod Wallop* a "clunkily wonderful entertainment," I objected to the use of clunkily. Wonderful, certainly, but *clunky?* I thought *Zod Wallop* was artful, streamlined. Hadn't *Kirkus,* in a review of that very same novel, called me "a brilliant writer of fantasy who's also a very considerable serious novelist"? Note that "very considerable serious."

On reflection, *clunky* is just fine.

It is always easier to write about the small things. Young writers sense this, and since they are often afraid of looking foolish, many of them stick to the smooth well-traveled highways, the quiet coming-of-age story, the unhappy marriage unraveling in the suburbs, the keenly observed slice of life.

Roger Zelazny always went after big themes, slapped together in fantasy/sf worlds that, he told me, made some of his critics uncomfortable. Is this science fiction or fantasy? Clunky stuff, maybe. A nod to science here, a ghost there that looked more like a supernatural element than a hologram.

He wrote beautifully; powerfully because his words were always fueled by passion, brilliantly because he had a fearless imagination and trusted his audience to follow him.

Roger fashioned wonderful entertainment out of big ideas, and when I was asked to write a story that would somehow fit into an anthology that was an homage to his talent, I thought I would write—here comes the pontificating—something driven by a big theme that had, at its heart, an individual's struggle for salvation.

Roger's done it better than I, and, fortunately, his novels and stories are there to read and reread. His innovation, his influence, was immense—on the field and on my personal journey as a writer. One of the great moments of my life was discovering that he admired my work. It's a privilege to be in this collection, in the company of his friends and admirers.

A weary werewolf once again joins in the eternal battle to prevent the freeing of dark forces that was first revealed in A Night in the Lonesome October—*but this time, none of the other good guys shows up.*

■

ONLY THE END OF THE WORLD AGAIN
Neil Gaiman

IT WAS A BAD DAY: I WOKE UP NAKED IN THE BED, WITH A CRAMP in my stomach, feeling more or less like hell. Something about the quality of the light, stretched and metallic, like the color of a migraine, told me it was afternoon.

The room was freezing—literally: there was a thin crust of ice on the inside of the windows. The sheets on the bed around me were ripped and clawed, and there was animal hair in the bed. It itched.

I was thinking about staying in bed for the next week—I'm always tired after a change—but a wave of nausea forced me to disentangle myself from the bedding, and to stumble, hurriedly, into the apartment's tiny bathroom.

The cramps hit me again as I got to the bathroom door. I held on to the door-frame and I started to sweat. Maybe it was a fever; I hoped I wasn't coming down with something.

The cramping was sharp in my guts. My head felt swimmy. I crumpled to the floor, and, before I could manage to raise my head enough to find the toilet bowl, I began to spew.

304

I vomited a foul-smelling thin yellow liquid; in it was a dog's paw—my guess was a Doberman's, but I'm not really a dog person; a tomato peel; some diced carrots and sweet corn; some lump of half-chewed meat, raw; and some fingers. They were fairly small, pale fingers, obviously a child's.

"Shit."

The cramps eased up, and the nausea subsided. I lay on the floor, with stinking drool coming out of my mouth and nose, with the tears you cry when you're being sick drying on my cheeks.

When I felt a little better I picked up the paw and the fingers from the pool of spew and threw them into the toilet bowl, flushed them away.

I turned on the tap, rinsed out my mouth with the briny Innsmouth water, and spat it into the sink. I mopped up the rest of the sick as best I could with washcloth and toilet paper. Then I turned on the shower, and stood in the bathtub like a zombie as the hot water sluiced over me.

I soaped myself down, body and hair. The meager lather turned gray; I must have been filthy. My hair was matted with something that felt like dried blood, and I worked at it with the bar of soap until it was gone. Then I stood under the shower until the water turned icy.

There was a note under the door from my landlady. It said that I owed her for two weeks' rent. It said that all the answers were in the Book of Revelations. It said that I made a lot of noise coming home in the early hours of this morning, and she'd thank me to be quieter in the future. It said that when the Elder Gods rose up from the ocean, all the scum of the Earth, all the nonbelievers, all the human garbage and the wastrels and deadbeats would be swept away, and the world would be cleansed by ice and deep water. It said that she felt she ought to remind me that she had assigned me a shelf in the refrigerator when I arrived and she'd thank me if in the future I'd keep to it.

I crumpled the note, dropped it on the floor, where it lay alongside the Big Mac cartons and the empty pizza cartons, and the long-dead dried slices of pizza.

It was time to go to work.

I'd been in Innsmouth for two weeks, and I disliked it. It smelled fishy. It was a claustrophobic little town: marshland to the east, cliffs to the west, and, in the center, a harbor that held a few rotting fishing boats, and was not even scenic at sunset. The yuppies had come to Innsmouth in the Eighties anyway, bought their picturesque fishermen's cottages overlooking the harbor. The yuppies had been gone for some years, now, and the cottages by the bay were crumbling, abandoned.

The inhabitants of Innsmouth lived here and there in and around the town, and in the trailer parks that ringed it, filled with dank mobile homes that were never going anywhere.

I got dressed, pulled on my boots and put on my coat and left my room. My landlady was nowhere to be seen. She was a short, pop-eyed woman, who spoke little, although she left extensive notes for me pinned to doors and placed where I might see them; she kept the house filled with the smell of boiling seafood: huge pots were always simmering on the kitchen stove, filled with things with too many legs and other things with no legs at all.

There were other rooms in the house, but no one else rented them. No one in their right mind would come to Innsmouth in winter.

Outside the house it didn't smell much better. It was colder, though, and my breath steamed in the sea air. The snow on the streets was crusty and filthy; the clouds promised more snow.

A cold, salty wind came up off the bay. The gulls were screaming miserably. I felt shitty. My office would be freezing, too. On the corner of Marsh Street and Leng Avenue was a bar, The Opener, a squat building with small, dark windows that I'd passed two dozen times in the last couple of weeks. I hadn't been in before, but I really needed a drink, and besides, it might be warmer in there. I pushed open the door.

The bar was indeed warm. I stamped the snow off my boots and went inside. It was almost empty and smelled of old ashtrays and stale beer. A couple of elderly men were playing chess by the bar. The barman was reading a battered old gilt-and-green-leather edition of the poetical works of Alfred, Lord Tennyson.

"Hey. How about a Jack Daniel's straight up?"

"Sure thing. You're new in town," he told me, putting his book face down on the bar, pouring the drink into a glass.

"Does it show?"

He smiled, passed me the Jack Daniel's. The glass was filthy, with a greasy thumb-print on the side, and I shrugged and knocked back the drink anyway. I could barely taste it.

"Hair of the dog?" he said.

"In a manner of speaking."

"There is a belief," said the barman, whose fox-red hair was tightly greased back, "that the *lykanthropoi* can be returned to their natural forms by thanking them, while they're in wolf form, or by calling them by their given names."

"Yeah? Well, thanks."

He poured another shot for me, unasked. He looked a little like Peter Lorre, but then, most of the folk in Innsmouth look a little like Peter Lorre, including my landlady.

I sank the Jack Daniel's, this time felt it burning down into my stomach, the way it should.

"It's what they say. I never said I believed it."

"What *do* you believe?"

"Burn the girdle."

"Pardon?"

"The *lykanthropoi* have girdles of human skin, given to them at their first transformation, by their masters in hell. Burn the girdle."

One of the old chess-players turned to me then, his eyes huge and blind and protruding. "If you drink rainwater out of warg-wolf's paw-print, that'll make a wolf of you, when the moon is full," he said. "The only cure is to hunt down the wolf that made the print in the first place and cut off its head with a knife forged of virgin silver."

"Virgin, huh?" I smiled.

His chess partner, bald and wrinkled, shook his head and croaked a single sad sound. Then he moved his queen, and croaked again.

There are people like him all over Innsmouth.

I paid for the drinks, and left a dollar tip on the bar. The barman was reading his book once more, and ignored it.

Outside the bar big wet kissy flakes of snow had begun to fall, settling in my hair and eyelashes. I hate snow. I hate New England. I hate Innsmouth: it's no place to be alone, but if there's a good place to be alone I've not found it yet. Still, business has kept me on the move for more moons than I like to think about. Business, and other things.

I walked a couple of blocks down Marsh Street—like most of Innsmouth, an unattractive mixture of eighteenth-century American Gothic houses, late-nineteenth-century stunted brownstones, and late-twentieth prefab gray-brick boxes—until I got to a boarded-up fried chicken joint, and I went up the stone steps next to the store and unlocked the rusting metal security door.

There was a liquor store across the street; a palmist was operating on the second floor.

Someone had scrawled graffiti in black marker on the metal: JUST DIE, it said. Like it was easy.

The stairs were bare wood; the plaster was stained and peeling. My one-room office was at the top of the stairs.

I don't stay anywhere long enough to bother with my name in gilt on glass. It was handwritten in block letters on a piece of ripped cardboard that I'd thumbtacked to the door.

LAWRENCE TALBOT.

ADJUSTOR.

I unlocked the door to my office and went in.

I inspected my office, while adjectives like *seedy* and *rancid* and *squalid* wandered through my head, then gave up, outclassed. It was fairly unpreposessing—a desk, an office chair, an empty filing cabinet: a window, which gave you a terrific view of the liquor store and the empty palmist's. The smell of old cooking grease permeated from the store below. I wondered how long the fried chicken joint had been boarded up; I imagined a multitude of black cockroaches swarming over every surface in the darkness beneath me.

"That's the shape of the world that you're thinking of there," said a deep, dark voice, deep enough that I felt it in the pit of my stomach.

There was an old armchair in one corner of the office. The remains of a pattern showed through the patina of age and grease the years had given it. It was the color of dust.

The fat man sitting in the armchair, his eyes still tightly closed, continued, "We look about in puzzlement at our world, with a sense of unease and disquiet. We think of ourselves as scholars in arcane liturgies, single men trapped in worlds beyond our devising. The truth is far simpler: there are things in the darkness beneath us that wish us harm."

His head was lolled back on the armchair, and the tip of his tongue poked out of the corner of his mouth.

"You read my mind?"

The man in the armchair took a slow deep breath that rattled in the back of his throat. He really was immensely fat, with stubby fingers like discolored sausages. He wore a thick old coat, once black, now an indeterminate gray. The snow on his boots had not entirely melted.

"Perhaps. The end of the world is a strange concept. The world is always ending, and the end is always being averted, by love or foolishness or just plain old dumb luck.

"Ah well. It's too late now: the Elder Gods have chosen their vessels. When the moon rises . . ."

A thin trickle of drool came from one corner of his mouth, trickled down in a thread of silver to his collar. Something scuttled down into the shadows of his coat.

"Yeah? What happens when the moon rises?"

The man in the armchair stirred, opened two little eyes, red and swollen, and blinked them in waking.

"I dreamed I had many mouths," he said, his new voice oddly small and breathy for such a huge man. "I dreamed every mouth was opening and closing independently. Some mouths were talking, some whispering, some eating, some waiting in silence."

He looked around, wiped the spittle from the corner of his mouth, sat back in the chair, blinking puzzledly. "Who are you?"

"I'm the guy that rents this office," I told him.

He belched suddenly, loudly. "I'm sorry," he said, in his breathy voice, and lifted himself heavily from the armchair. He was shorter than I was, when he was standing. He looked me up and down blearily. "Silver bullets," he pronounced, after a short pause. "Old-fashioned remedy."

"Yeah," I told him. "That's so obvious—must be why I didn't think of it. Gee. I could just kick myself. I really could."

"You're making fun of an old man," he told me.

"Not really. I'm sorry. Now, out of here. Some of us have work to do."

He shambled out. I sat down in the swivel chair at the desk by the window, and discovered after some minutes, through trial and error, that if I swiveled to the chair to the left it fell off its base.

So I sat still and waited for the dusty black telephone on my desk to ring, while the light slowly leaked away from the winter sky.

Ring.

A man's voice: *Had I thought about aluminum siding?* I put down the phone.

There was no heating in the office. I wondered how long the fat man had been asleep in the armchair.

Twenty minutes later the phone rang again. A crying woman implored me to help her find her five-year-old daughter, missing since last night, stolen from her bed. The family dog had vanished too.

I don't do missing children, I told her. *I'm sorry: too many bad memories.* I put down the telephone, feeling sick again.

It was getting dark now, and, for the first time since I had been in Innsmouth, the neon sign across the street flicked on. It told me that Madame Ezekiel performed Tarot Readings and Palmistry. Red neon stained the falling snow the color of new blood.

Armageddon is averted by small actions. That's the way it was. That's the way it always has to be.

The phone rang a third time. I recognized the voice; it was the aluminum-siding man again. "You know," he said, chattily, "transformation from man to animal and back being, by definition, impossible, we need to look for other solutions. Depersonalization, obviously, and likewise some form of projection. Brain damage? Perhaps. Pseudoneurotic schizophrenia? Laughably so. Some cases have been treated with intravenous thioridazine hydrochloride."

"Successfully?"

He chuckled. "That's what I like. A man with a sense of humor. I'm sure we can do business."

"I told you already. I don't need aluminum siding."

"Our business is more remarkable than that, and of far greater importance. You're new in town, Mr. Talbot. It would be a pity if we found ourselves at, shall we say, loggerheads?"

"You can say whatever you like, pal. In my book you're just another adjustment, waiting to be made."

"We're ending the world, Mr. Talbot. The Deep Ones will rise out of their ocean graves and eat the moon like a ripe plum."

"Then I won't ever have to worry about full moons anymore, will I?"

"Don't try and cross us," he began, but I growled at him, and he fell silent.

Outside my window the snow was still falling.

Across Marsh Street, in the window directly opposite mine, the most beautiful woman I had ever seen stood in the ruby glare of her neon sign, and she stared at me.

She beckoned, with one finger.

I put down the phone on the aluminum-siding man for the second time that afternoon, and went downstairs, and crossed the street at something close to a run; but I looked both ways before I crossed.

She was dressed in silks. The room was lit only by candles, and stank of incense and patchouli oil.

She smiled at me as I walked in, beckoned me over to her seat by the window. She was playing a card game with a tarot deck, some version of solitaire. As I reached her, one hand swept up the cards, wrapped them in a silk scarf, placed them gently in a wooden box.

The scents of the room made my head pound. I hadn't eaten anything today, I realized; perhaps that was what was making me light-headed. I sat down, across the table from her, in the candlelight.

She extended her hand, and took my hand in hers.

She stared at my palm, touched it, softly, with her forefinger.

"Hair?" She was puzzled.

"Yeah, well, I'm on my own a lot." I grinned. I had hoped it was a friendly grin, but she raised an eyebrow at me anyway.

"When I look at you," said Madame Ezekiel, "this is what I see. I see the eye of a man. Also I see the eye of a wolf. In the eye of a man I see honesty, decency, innocence. I see an upright man who walks on the square. And in the eye of wolf I see a groaning and a growling, night howls and cries, I see a monster running with blood-flecked spittle in the darkness of the borders of the town."

"How can you see a growl or a cry?"

She smiled. "It is not hard," she said. Her accent was not American. It was Russian, or Maltese, or Egyptian perhaps. "In the eye of the mind we see many things."

Madame Ezekiel closed her green eyes. She had remarkably long eyelashes; her skin was pale, and her black hair was never still—it drifted gently around her head, in the silks, as if it were floating on distant tides.

"There is a traditional way," she told me. "A way to wash off a bad shape. You stand in running water, in clear spring water, while eating white rose petals."

"And then?"

"The shape of darkness will be washed from you."

"It will return," I told her, "with the next full of the moon."

"So," said Madame Ezekiel, "once the shape is washed from you, you open your veins in the running water. It will sting mightily, of course. But the river will carry the blood away."

She was dressed in silks, in scarves and cloths of a hundred different colors, each bright and vivid, even in the muted light of the candles.

Her eyes opened.

"Now," she said. "The Tarot." She unwrapped her deck from the black silk scarf that held it, passed me the cards to shuffle. I fanned them, riffed and bridged them.

"Slower, slower," she said. "Let them get to know you. Let them love you, like . . . like a woman would love you."

I held them tightly, then passed them back to her.

She turned over the first card. It was called *The Warwolf.* It showed darkness and amber eyes, a smile in white and red.

Her green eyes showed confusion. They were the green of emeralds. "This is not a card from my deck," she said, and turned over the next card. "What did you do to my cards?"

"Nothing, ma'am. I just held them. That's all."

The card she had turned over was *The Deep One.* It showed something green and faintly octopoid. The thing's mouths—if they were indeed mouths and not tentacles—began to writhe on the card as I watched.

She covered it with another card, and then another, and another. The rest of the cards were blank pasteboard.

"Did you do that?" She sounded on the verge of tears.

"No."

"Go now," she said.

"But—"

"Go." She looked down, as if trying to convince herself I no longer existed.

I stood up, in the room that smelled of incense and candlewax, and looked out of her window, across the street. A light flashed, briefly, in my office window. Two men, with flashlights, were walking around. They opened the empty filing cabinet, peered around, then took up their positions, one in the armchair, the other behind the door, waiting for me to return. I smiled to myself. It was cold and inhospitable in my office, and with any luck they would wait there for hours until they finally decided I wasn't coming back.

So I left Madame Ezekiel turning over her cards, one by one, staring at them as if that would make the pictures return; and I went downstairs, and walked back down Marsh Street until I reached the bar.

The place was empty, now; the barman was smoking a cigarette, which he stubbed out as I came in.

"Where are the chess fiends?"

"It's a big night for them tonight. They'll be down at the bay. Lets see: you're a Jack Daniel's? Right?"

"Sounds good."

He poured it for me. I recognized the thumbprint from the last time I had the glass. I picked up the volume of Tennyson poems from the bartop.

"Good book?"

The fox-haired barman took his book from me, opened it and read:

> *"Below the thunders of the upper deep;*
> *Far, far beneath in the abysmal sea,*
> *His ancient dreamless, uninvaded sleep*
> *The Kraken sleepeth . . ."*

I'd finished my drink. "So? What's your point?"

He walked around the bar, took me over to the window. "See? Out there?"

He pointed toward the west of the town, toward the cliffs. As I stared a bonfire was kindled on the cliff-tops; it flared and began to burn with a copper-green flame.

"They're going to wake the Deep Ones," said the barman. "The stars and the planets and the moon are all in the right places. It's time. The dry lands will sink, and the seas shall rise . . ."

"For the world shall be cleansed with ice and floods and I'll thank you to keep to your own shelf in the refrigerator," I said.

"Sorry?"

"Nothing. What's the quickest way to get up to those cliffs?"

"Back up Marsh Street. Hang a left at the Church of Dagon, till you reach Manuxet Way and then just keep on going." He pulled a coat off the back of the door, and put it on. "C'mon. I'll walk up there. I'd hate to miss any of the fun."

"You sure?"

"No one in town's going to be drinking tonight." We stepped out, and he locked the door to the bar behind us.

It was chilly in the street, and fallen snow blew about the ground, like white mists. From street level I could no longer tell if Madame Ezekiel was in her den above her neon sign, or if my guests were still waiting for me in my office.

We put our heads down against the wind, and we walked.

Over the noise of the wind I heard the barman talking to himself: *"Winnow with giant arms the slumbering green,"* he was saying.

> *"There hath he lain for ages and will lie*
> *Battening upon huge seaworms in his sleep,*
> *Until the latter fire shall heat the deep;*
> *Then once by men and angels to be seen,*
> *In roaring he shall rise . . ."*

He stopped there, and we walked on together in silence, with blown snow stinging our faces.

And on the surface die, I thought, but said nothing out loud.

Twenty minutes' walking and we were out of Innsmouth. The Manuxet Way stopped when we left the town, and it became a narrow dirt path, partly covered with snow and ice, and we slipped and slid our way up it in the darkness.

The moon was not yet up, but the stars had already begun to come out. There were so many of them. They were sprinkled like diamond dust and crushed sapphires across the night sky. You can see so many stars from the seashore, more than you could ever see back in the city.

At the top of the cliff, behind the bonfire, two people were waiting—one huge and fat, one much smaller. The barman left my side and walked over to stand beside them, facing me.

"Behold," he said, "the sacrificial wolf." There was now an oddly familiar quality to his voice.

I didn't say anything. The fire was burning with green flames, and it lit the three of them from below: classic spook lighting.

"Do you know why I brought you up here?" asked the barman, and I knew then why his voice was familiar: it was the voice of the man who had attempted to sell me aluminum siding.

"To stop the world ending?"

He laughed at me, then.

The second figure was the fat man I had found asleep in my office chair. "Well, if you're going to get eschatalogical about it . . ." he murmured, in a voice deep enough to rattle walls. His eyes were closed. He was fast asleep.

The third figure was shrouded in dark silks and smelled of patchouli oil. It held a knife. It said nothing.

"This night," said the barman, "the moon is the moon of the deep ones. This night are the stars configured in the shapes and patterns of the dark, old times. This night, if we call them, they will come. If our sacrifice is worthy. If our cries are heard."

The moon rose, huge and amber and heavy, on the other side of the bay, and a chorus of low croaking rose with it from the ocean far beneath us.

Moonlight on snow and ice is not daylight, but it will do. And my eyes were getting sharper with the moon: in the cold waters men like frogs were surfacing and submerging in a slow water-dance. Men like frogs, and women, too: it seemed to me that I could see my landlady down there, writhing and croaking in the bay with the rest of them.

It was too soon for another change; I was still exhausted from the night before; but I felt strange under that amber moon.

"Poor wolf-man," came a whisper from the silks. "All his dreams have come to this; a lonely death upon a distant cliff."

I will dream if I want to, I said, *and my death is my own affair.* But I was unsure if I had said it out loud.

Senses heighten in the moon's light; I heard the roar of the ocean still, but now, overlaid on top of it, I could hear each wave rise and crash; I heard the splash of the frog people; I heard the drowned whispers of the dead in the bay; I heard the creak of green wrecks far beneath the ocean.

Smell improves, too. The aluminum-siding man was human, while the fat man had other blood in him.

And the figure in the silks . . .

I had smelled her perfume when I wore man-shape. Now I could smell something else, less heady, beneath it. A smell of decay, of putrefying meat, and rotten flesh.

The silks fluttered. She was moving toward me. She held the knife.

"Madame Ezekiel?" My voice was roughening and coarsening. Soon I would lose it all. I didn't understand what was happening, but the moon was rising higher and higher, losing its amber color, and filling my mind with its pale light.

"Madame Ezekiel?"

"You deserve to die," she said, her voice cold and low. "If only for what you did to my cards. They were old."

"I don't die," I told her. *"Even a man who is pure in heart, and says his prayers by night.* Remember?"

"It's bullshit," she said. "You know what the oldest way to end the curse of the werewolf is?"

"No."

The bonfire burned brighter now, burned with the green of the world beneath the sea, the green of algae, and of slowly drifting weed; burned with the color of emeralds.

"You simply wait till they're in human shape, a whole month away from another change; then you take the sacrificial knife, and you kill them. That's all."

I turned to run, but the barman was behind me, pulling my arms, twisting my wrists up into the small of my back. The knife glinted pale silver in the moonlight. Madame Ezekiel smiled.

She sliced across my throat.

Blood began to gush, and then to flow. And then it slowed, and stopped . . .

—The pounding in the front of my head, the pressure in the back. All a roiling change a how-wow-row-now change a red wall coming towards me from the night
—I tasted stars dissolved in brine, fizzy and distant and salt
—my fingers prickled with pins and my skin was lashed with tongues of flame my eyes were topaz I could taste the night

My breath steamed and billowed in the icy air.

I growled involuntarily, low in my throat. My forepaws were touching the snow.

I pulled back, tensed, and sprang at her.

There was a sense of corruption that hung in the air, like a mist, surrounding me. High in my leap I seemed to pause, and something burst like a soap bubble. . . .

I was deep, deep in the darkness under the sea, standing on all fours on a slimy rock floor, at the entrance of some kind of citadel, built of enormous, rough-hewn stones. The stones gave off a pale glow-in-the-dark light; a ghostly luminescence, like the hands of a watch.

A cloud of black blood trickled from my neck.

She was standing in the doorway, in front of me. She was now six, maybe seven feet high. There was flesh on her skeletal bones, pitted and gnawed, but the silks were weeds, drifting in the cold water, down there in the dreamless deeps. They hid her face like a slow green veil.

There were limpets growing on the upper surfaces of her arms, and on the flesh that hung from her rib cage.

I felt like I was being crushed. I couldn't think anymore.

She moved toward me. The weed that surrounded her head shifted. She had a face like the stuff you don't want to eat in a sushi counter, all suckers and spines and drifting anemone fronds; and somewhere in all that I knew she was smiling.

I pushed with my hind legs. We met there, in the deep, and we struggled. It was so cold, so dark. I closed my jaws on her face, and felt something rend and tear.

It was almost a kiss, down there in the abysmal deep. . . .

I landed softly on the snow, a silk scarf locked between my jaws.

The other scarves were fluttering to the ground. Madame Ezekiel was nowhere to be seen.

The silver knife lay on the ground, in the snow. I waited on all fours, in the moonlight, soaking wet. I shook myself, spraying the brine about. I heard it hiss and spit when it hit the fire.

I was dizzy, and weak. I pulled the air deep into my lungs.

Down, far below, in the bay, I could see the frog people hanging on the surface of the sea like dead things; for a handful of seconds they drifted back and forth on the tide, then they twisted and leapt, and each by each they *plop-plopped* down into the bay and vanished beneath the sea.

There was a scream. It was the fox-haired bartender, the pop-eyed aluminum-siding salesman, and he was staring at the night sky, at the clouds that were drifting in, covering the stars, and he was screaming. There was rage and there was frustration in that cry, and it scared me.

He picked up the knife from the ground, wiped the snow from the handle with his fingers, wiped the blood from the blade with his coat. Then he looked across at me. He was crying. "You bastard," he said. "What did you do to her?"

I would have told him I didn't do anything to her, that she was still on guard far beneath the ocean, but I couldn't talk anymore, only growl and whine and howl.

He was crying. He stank of insanity, and of disappointment. He raised the knife and ran at me, and I moved to one side.

Some people just can't adjust even to tiny changes. The barman stumbled past me, off the cliff, into nothing.

In the moonlight blood is black, not red, and the marks he left on the cliff-side as he fell and bounced and fell were smudges of black and dark gray. Then, finally, he lay still on the icy rocks at the base of the cliff, until an arm reached out from the sea and dragged him, with a slowness that was almost painful to watch, under the dark water.

A hand scratched the back of my head. It felt good.

"What was she? Just an avatar of the Deep Ones, sir. An eidolon, a manifestation, if you will, sent up to us from the uttermost deeps to bring about the end of the world."

I bristled.

"No, it's over, for now. You disrupted her, sir. And the ritual is most specific. Three of us must stand together and call the sacred names, while innocent blood pools and pulses at our feet."

I looked up at the fat man, and whined a query. He patted me on the back of the neck, sleepily.

"Of course she doesn't love you, boy. She hardly even exists on this plane, in any material sense."

The snow began to fall once more. The bonfire was going out.

"Your change tonight, incidentally, I would opine, is a direct result of the self-same celestial configurations and lunar forces that made tonight such a perfect night to bring back my old friends from Underneath. . . ."

He continued talking, in his deep voice, and perhaps he was telling me important things. I'll never know, for the appetite was growing inside me, and his words had lost all but the shadow of any meaning; I had no further interest in the sea or the clifftop or the fat man.

There were deer running in the woods beyond the meadow: I could smell them on the winter's night air.

And I was, above all things, hungry.

I was naked when I came to myself again, early the next morning, a half-eaten deer next to me in the snow. A fly crawled across its eye, and its tongue lolled out of its dead mouth, making it look comical and pathetic, like an animal in a newspaper cartoon.

The snow was stained a fluorescent crimson where the deer's belly had been torn out.

My face and chest were sticky and red with the stuff. My throat was scabbed and scarred. And it stung; by the next full moon it would be whole once more.

The sun was a long way away, small and yellow, but the sky was blue and cloudless, and there was no breeze. I could hear the roar of the sea some distance away.

I was cold and naked and bloody and alone; ah well, I thought: it happens to all of us, in the beginning. I just get it once a month.

I was painfully exhausted, but I would hold out until I found a deserted barn, or a cave; and then I was going to sleep for a couple of weeks.

A hawk flew low over the snow toward me, with something dangling from its talons. It hovered above me for a heartbeat, then dropped a small gray squid in the snow at my feet, and flew upward. The flaccid thing lay there, still and silent and tentacled in the bloody snow.

I took it as an omen, but whether good or bad I couldn't say and I didn't really care anymore; I turned my back to the sea, and on the shadowy town of Innsmouth, and began to make my way toward the city.

AFTERWORD

I first met Roger Zelazny in 1990, at a convention in Dallas, Texas. We were signing books at the same time, at the same table. This had excited me when I had heard about it: I imagined that I would get to talk to him, and Roger had been a hero of mine since, at the age of eleven, I had read *Lord of Light.* Actually, we both sat and signed books for a line of people, and all I managed to do was mumble something about being an enormous fan of his, and I thrust a copy of the Sandman collection *The Doll's House* at him, saying something about the Sandman being one of Roger's illegitimate godchildren.

We did not talk for another year, and then, in 1991, at a World Fantasy Convention in Tucson, Arizona, my friend Steve Brust sat me down in the bar with Roger, and the three of us spoke about short story structure for most of the evening. When Roger spoke Steve and I listened.

"Many of my better short stories," said Roger, pulling on his pipe, explaining how to write short stories, "are just the last chapters of novels I did not write."

The next time I saw Roger he was a guest of honor at the 1993 World Fantasy Convention, in Minneapolis. I was toastmaster, and we were both working hard, doing panels and readings and whatever else one does at conventions. We bumped into each other in the book dealers' room, and exchanged books: I gave him a copy of *Angels and Visitations,* the miscellany of my work that had just been published, and he gave me a copy of his novel, *A Night in the Lonesome October.*

I got the impression that it was the first novel he had written in some time that he felt had worked as he had wanted it to. Or at least, that it had been as much of a surprise to him as to his readers.

I remember how tired I was that night, and I remember planning only to read the first few pages of *A Night in the Lonesome October.* I read them and I was hooked, unable to stop reading, and I read until I fell asleep.

I loved a number of things about the book—the delight in a story told from the wrong point of view (Jack the Ripper's dog), the fun in assembling a cast out of stock characters (including Sherlock Holmes and Larry Talbot), and the sense of Lovecraftian nastiness as a sort of a dance, in which everyone knows the moves they should make and in which the door to permit the Great Old Ones in to eat the world is, always, ultimately, opened a crack, but never all the way.

I wrote this story in February 1994, and sent it to Roger to read. It was directly inspired by what he had done in *A Night in the Lonesome October,* although my Larry Talbot was no more Roger's than he was the original Wolfman of the movies, or Harlan Ellison's marvelous Talbot in "Adrift Just off the Islets of Langerhans, Latitude 38° 54' N, Longitude 77° 00' 13" W." I was inspired in the way Roger inspired you: he made it look like so much fun, you wanted to do it too, and do it your own way, not his.

It's the last chapter of a novel I did not write.

This was the only time I had ever sent Roger a story (he was, after all, a man who had written five or six of my favorite short stories in all the world). And he liked it, which is why, when I was asked for a story for this book, this was the only one it could have been.

We saw each other—were on a panel together, and spent part of an evening on a roof beside a swimming pool, talking to Mike Moorcock—in New Orleans at World Fantasy in 1994. We spoke again, on the phone, early in the New Year, following the birth of my daughter, Maddy. Roger had sent her a dreamcatcher, from New Mexico, a web of cord and feathers and beads, to hang over her bed, and catch any bad dreams, letting only the good dreams through, and I phoned him to say thank you. We spoke for an hour, about fiction, and stories, and promised each other that sooner or later we would make the time to see each other properly, for a visit. There was, after all, plenty of time.

We did not speak again.

The dreamcatcher hangs there still, above my daughter's bed.

At Roger's memorial in Santa Fe, shortly after his death, we sat on the floor, and on the chairs, and we stood, crowded together in the Saberhagens' front room, remembering Roger. I forget much of what I said, but one thing I do recall is pointing out that Roger Zelazny was the kind of writer who made you want to write too. He made it look so damned fun, and so damned cool. There are many of us who would not have begun to write, if we had not read Roger's stories: the bastard writer-children of Roger Zelazny are a huge and motley group, with little else in common.

I'm proud to be one of them.

Shades of Roger's "The Graveyard Heart" and Isle of the
Dead *combine with Greg Benford's singular talent of scientific
extrapolation to create a fevered chase through mass and time
that is anything but "slow."*

■

SLOW SYMPHONIES OF MASS AND TIME
Gregory Benford

THE CHASE ACROSS AN ENTIRE GALAXY STARTED AT A SWANKY PRI-
vate party.

Think of the galaxy as a swarm of gaudy bees, bright colors
hovering in a ball. Then stomp them somehow in midair, so they
bank and turn in a compressed disk. Dark bees fly with them too,
so that somber lanes churn in the swiftly rotating cloud.

Angry bees, buzzing, stingers out. Churning endlessly in their
search.

That is the galaxy, seen whole and quick. Stars have no will,
but their courses and destinies were now guided by small entities
of great pretension: humans, now lording it over the All.

Or such is the viewpoint of the lords and ladies of a galactic
empire that stretches across that bee swarm disk: they loom above
it all, oblivious. Stars do their bidding. The bees swarm at the lift
of an Imperial eyebrow.

Until one lord turns upon another. Then they are as their origins
made them: savvy omnivores, primates reared up and grimacing,

teeth bared at each other. Across the span of a hundred billion worlds, ancient blood sings in pounding vessels.

Despite appearances, some of these primordial creatures were present at the party, yet seeming mild and splendid in their finery.

Of course, it all began innocently enough.

An ample, powerful woman named Vissian grasped his sleeve and tugged him back to the ornate reception. "Sir Zeb, you are the *point* of this affair! Sir Zeb, my guests have so much to *tell* you."

And to think that he had *wanted* to come here! To get the scent of change. But already he was tiring of this world, Syrna. Sir Zeb, indeed. He truly did not enjoy travel all that much, a fact he often forgot.

Even here, in a distant Sector, the heavy hand of the Imperium lay upon style and art. The Imperium's essence lay in its solidity; its taste ran to the monumental. Rigorous straight lines in ascending slabs, the exact parabolas of arching purple water fountains, heavy masonry—all entirely proper and devoid of embarrassing challenge. He sniffed at the hyperbolic draperies and moved toward the crowd, their faces terminally bland.

Vissian nattered on. "—and our most brilliant minds are waiting to meet you! Do come!"

He suppressed a groan and looked beseechingly at Fyrna, his consort now of a full decade; something of a record in Imperial circles. She smiled and shook her head. From this hazard she could not save him.

"Sir Zeb, what of the mysteries at galactic center?"

"I savor them."

"But are those magnetic entities a threat? They are huge!"

"And wise. Think of them as great slumbering libraries."

"But they command such energies!"

"Then think of them as natural wonders, like waterfalls."

This provoked a chorus of laughter in the polite half-moon crowd around him. "Some on the Council believe we should take action against them!" a narrow woman in flocked velvet called from the crowd's edge.

"I would sooner joust with the wind," Zeb said, taking a stim from a passing dwarf servant.

"Sir Zeb, surely you cannot take lightly—"

"I am on holiday, sir, and can take things as they are."

"But you, Sir Zeb, have seen these magnetic structures?"

"Filaments, hundreds of light-years long—yes. Lovely, they are."

Wide-eyed: "Was it dangerous?"

"Of course. Nobody goes to the galactic center. Hard protons sleet through it, virulent X rays light its pathways."

"Why did you risk it?"

"I am a fool, madam, who works for you, the people."

And so on.

If Vissian had begun as a grain of sand in his shoe, she became a boulder. An hour later, Fyrna whisked him into an alcove and said curtly, "I am concerned about someone tracking us here. We're just one worm-jump away from fleet's quadrant assembly point."

Zeb had allowed himself to forget about politics: the only vacation a statesman had. "My protection should be good here. I can get a quick message out, using a wormlink to—"

"No, you can't work using a link. The Speculists could trace that easily."

Factions, factions. The situation had shifted while he was idling away here. As Governor of another Sector, he was a guest here, given nominal protection. He had his own bodyguards, too, salted among the crowd here. But the Speculists had strong support in this region of the galaxy and were quite blithely ruthless. Zeb stared out at the view, which he had to admit was spectacular. Great, stretching vistas. Riotous growth.

But more fires boiled up on the horizon. There was gaiety in the streets here—and angst. Their laboratories seethed with fresh energies, innovation bristled everywhere, the air seemed to sing with change and chaos.

The extremes of wealth and destitution were appalling. Change brought that, he knew.

As a boy he had seen poverty—and lived it, too. His grandmother had insisted on buying him a raincoat several sizes too large, "to get more use out of it." His mother didn't like him playing kickball because he wore out his shoes too quickly.

Here, too, the truly poor were off in the hinterlands. Sometimes they couldn't even afford fossil fuels. Men and women peered over a mule's ass all day as it plodded down a furrow, while overhead starships screamed through velvet skies.

And here . . . Among these fast-track circles, body language was taught. There were carefully designed poses for Confidence, Impatience, Submission (four shadings), Threat, Esteem, Coyness, and dozens more. Codified and understood unconsciously, each induced a specific desired neurological state in both self and others. The rudiments lay in dance, politics, and the martial arts, but by being systematic, much more could be conveyed. As with language, a dictionary helped.

Zeb felt an unease in the reception party. Reading some veiled threat-postures? Or was he projecting?

Quickly he adjusted his own stance—radiating confidence, he

hoped. But still, he had picked up a subconscious alarm. And he knew enough from decades of politics to trust his instincts.

"Governor!" Vissian's penetrating voice snatched away his thoughts.

"Uh, that tour of the precincts. I, I really don't feel—"

"Oh, that is not possible, I fear. A domestic disturbance, most unfortunate."

Zeb felt relief but Vissian went right on, bubbling over new ventures, balls, and tours to come tomorrow. Then her eyebrows lifted and she said brightly, "Oh yes—I do have even more welcome news. An Imperial squadron has just come to call."

"Oh?" Fyrna shot back. "Under whose command?"

"An Admiral Kafalan. I just spoke to him—"

"Damn!" Fyrna said. "He's a Speculist henchman."

"You're sure?" Zeb asked. He knew her slight pause had been to consult her internal files.

Fyrna nodded. Vissian said gaily, "Well, I am sure he will be honored to return you to your sector when you are finished with your visit here. Which we hope will not be soon, of—"

"He mentioned us?" Fyrna asked.

"He asked if you were enjoying—"

"Damn!" Zeb said.

"An Admiral commands all the worm links, if he wishes—yes?" Fyrna asked.

"Well, I suppose so." Vissian looked puzzled.

"We're trapped," Zeb said.

Vissian's eyes widened in shock. "But surely you, Governor, need fear no—"

"Quiet." Fyrna silenced the woman with a stern glance. "At best this Kafalan will bottle us up here."

Fyrna pushed them both into a side gallery. Vissian seemed startled by this, though Fyrna was both consort and bodyguard. Indeed, she and Zeb might as well have been married, but for the social impossibilities.

This side gallery featured storm-tossed jungles of an unnamed world lashed by sleeting rain, lit by jagged purple lightning. Strange howls called through the lashing winds.

"Note that if Imperial artists do show you an exterior, it is alarming," Fyrna said clinically as she checked her detectors, set into her spine and arms.

"They're still nearby?" Zeb asked, shushing Vissian.

"Yes, but of course they are beards."

To his puzzled look she said, "Meaning, the disguise we are meant to see."

"Ah." They strolled into the next gallery, trying to look casual.

This sensor was milder, a grandiose streetscape and hanging gardens. "Ummm, still poorly attended. And the real shadows?"

"I have spotted one. There must be more."

Vissian said, "But surely no one would dare kidnap you from my reception—"

"No, probably there will be an 'accident,' " Zeb said.

"Why has this Admiral moved to block you just now?"

"Nova triggers," Zeb said.

Once invented, triggers had made war far more dangerous. A solar system could be "cleansed"—a horrifyingly bland term used by aggressors of the time—by inducing a mild nova burst in a balmy sun. This roasted worlds just enough to kill all but those who could swiftly find caverns and store food for the few years of the nova stage. Fleet wanted a supply of them, and Zeb led opposition to the weapon.

"Admirals love their toys," he said sourly, fingering a stim but not inhaling it. They returned to the main party, not wanting to seem perturbed by the news.

"Is there no other way to get off Syrna?" Fyrna demanded of Vissian.

"No, I can't recall—"

"Think!"

Startled, Vissian said, "Well, of course, we do have privateers who at times use the wild worms, an activity that is at best quasi-legal, but—"

In Zeb's career he had discovered a curious little law. Now he turned it in his favor.

Bureaucracy increases as a doubling function in time, given resources. At the personal level, the cause is the persistent desire of every manager to hire at least one assistant. This provides the time constant for growth.

Eventually this collides with the carrying capacity of society. Given the time constant and the capacity, one could predict a plateau level of bureaucratic overhead—or else, if growth persists, the date of collapse. Predictions of the longevity of bureaucracy-driven societies fit a precise curve. Surprisingly, the same scaling laws worked for micro-societies such as large agencies.

The corpulent Imperial bureaus on Syrna could not move swiftly. Admiral Kafalan's squadron had to stay in planetary space, since it was paying a purely formal visit. Niceties were still observed. Kafalan did not want to use brute force when a waiting game would work.

"I see. That gives us a few days," Fyrna concluded.

Zeb nodded. He had done the required speaking, negotiating,

dealing, promising favors—all activities he disliked intensely. Fyrna had done the background digging. "To . . . ?"

"Train."

The wormhole web had built the galactic empire. Made in the first blaring instant of the Great Emergence, found (rarely) floating between stars, they now were the most precious resources of all.

Of course, worms ended and began as they liked. A worm jump could bring you to a black vacuum still many years from a far-flung world. Hyperships flitted through wormholes in mere seconds, then exhausted themselves hauling their cargoes across empty voids, years and decades in the labor.

Wormholes were labyrinths, not mere tunnels with two ends. The large ones held firm for perhaps billions of years—none larger than a hundred meters across had yet collapsed. The smallest could sometimes last only hours, at best a year. In the thinner worms, flexes in the wormwalls *during* passage could alter the end point of a traveler's trajectory.

Worse, worms in their last stages spawned transient, doomed young—the wild worms. As deformations in space-time, supported by negative energy-density "struts," all wormholes were inherently rickety. As they failed, smaller deformations twisted away.

Syrna had seven wormholes. One was dying in gorgeous agonies.

It hung a light-hour away, spitting out wild worms that ranged from a hand's-width size up to several meters. In the spongy space-time of the negative-energy-density struts, time could crawl or zip, quite unpredictably. This worm was departing our universe in molasses-slow torment.

A fairly sizable wild worm had sprouted out of the side of the dying worm several months before. The Imperial squadron did not know of this, of course. All worms were taxed, so a fresh, free wormhole was a bonanza. Reporting their existence, well . . . often a planet simply didn't get around to that until the wild worm had fizzled away in a spray of subatomic surf.

Until then, pilots carried cargo through them. That wild worms could evaporate with only seconds' warning made their trade dangerous, highly paid, and legendary.

Wormriders were the sort of people who as children liked to ride their bicycles no-handed, but with a difference—they rode off rooftops.

By an odd logic, that kind of child grew up and got trained and even paid taxes—but inside, they stayed the same.

Only risk takers could power through the chaotic flux of a transient worm and take the risks that worked, *not* take those that didn't, and live. They had elevated bravado to its finer points.

"This wild worm, it's tricky," a grizzled woman told Zeb and Fyrna. "No room for a pilot if you both go."

"We must stay together,'" Fyrna said with finality.

"Then you'll have to pilot."

"We don't know how," Zeb said.

"You're in luck." The lined woman grinned without humor. "This wildy's short, easy."

"What are the risks?" Fyrna demanded stiffly.

"I'm not an insurance agent, lady."

"I insist that we know—"

"Look, lady, we'll teach you. That's the deal."

"I had hoped for a more—"

"Give it a rest or it's no deal at all."

In the men's room, above the urinal he used, Zeb saw a small gold plaque: *Senior Pilot Joquan Beunn relieved himself here Octdent 4, 13,435.*

Every urinal had a similar plaque. There was a washing machine in the locker room with a large plaque over it, reading *The Entire 43d Pilot Corps relieved themselves here Marlass 18, 13,675.*

Pilot humor. It turned out to be absolutely predictive. He messed himself on his first training run.

As if to make the absolutely fatal length of a closing wormhole less daunting, the worm flyers had escape plans. These could only work in the fringing fields of the worm, where gravity was beginning to wrap, and space-time was only mildly curved. Under the seat was a small, powerful rocket that propelled the entire cockpit out, automatically heading away from the worm.

There is a limit to how much self-actuated tech one can pack into a small cockpit, though. Worse, worm mouths were alive with electrodynamic "weather"—writhing forks of lightning, blue discharges, red magnetic whorls like tornadoes. Electrical gear didn't work well if a bad storm was brewing at the mouth. So most of the emergency controls were manual. Hopelessly archaic, but unavoidable.

He and Fyrna went through a bail-out training program. Quite soon it was clear that if he used the EJECT command he had better be sure that he had his head tilted back. That is, unless he wanted his kneecaps to slam up into his chin, which would be unfortunate, because he would be trying to check if his canopy had gone into a spin. This would be bad news, because his trajectory might get warped back into the worm. To correct any spin he had to yank on a red lever, and if that failed he had to then very quickly—in pilot's terms, this meant about half a second—punch two blue knobs. When the spindown came, he then had to be sure to release the automatic actuator by pulling down on two yellow tabs, being certain that he was sitting up straight with his hands between knees to avoid . . .

. . . and so on for three hours. Everyone seemed to assume that since he was this famous politician trained in intricate galactic protocols he could of course keep an entire menu of instructions straight, timed down to fractions of seconds.

After the first ten minutes he saw no point in destroying their illusions, and simply nodded and squinted to show that he was carefully keeping track and absolutely enthralled. Meanwhile he solved chess puzzles in his head for practice.

He was taking a stroll with his bodyguards when the Admiral sent a greeting card.

The guard nearest him, one Ladoro, was saying something into his wrist comm as they ambled through a park. It was an Imperial distraction, with babbling brooks that ran uphill, this artful effect arising from intricately charged electrodynamic streams that countered gravity. His guards liked the effect; Zeb found it rather obvious.

He chanced to be looking toward Ladoro, his oldest guard, a stout fellow whose personal service went back a full century. Later Zeb reflected that the Admiral probably knew that. It made what happened more pointed.

Ladoro went down with his head jerked back, as if he were looking up at the sky, a quizzical expression flickering. Over backwards, twisting, then down hard. He hit face first on the carpet-moss. Ladoro had not lifted his hands to break the fall.

Two other guards had Zeb behind a wall within two seconds. There was too much open space and too little shelter to try a move. He squatted and fumed and could not see what had fired the shot. Zeb risked a quick look over the wall's low edge and saw Ladoro sprawled flat without a twitch.

Then a lot of nothing happened. No following pulses.

Zeb replayed the image. From Ladoro had spouted rosy blood from a punch high in the spine. Absolutely dead center, four centimeters below the neck. Kilojoules of energy focused to a spot the size of a fingernail.

That much energy delivered so precisely would have done the job even if it hit the hip or gut. Delivered so exactly, it burst the big bony axis of the man, massive pressures in the spinal fluid, a sudden breeze blowing out a candle, the brain going black in a millisecond.

Ladoro had gone down boneless, erased. A soft, liquid thump, then eternal silence.

Zeb held up his hand and watched it tremble for a while. Enough waiting. "Let's go. They can lob anything they want here."

A guard said, "Sir Zeb, I don't advise—"

"I've been shot at before, kid."

"Well, I suppose we could fire as we move—"

"You do that. Go."

They worked their way along a creek frothing uphill. More guards arrived and spilled out across the park. The pulse had come from behind Ladoro. Zeb kept plenty of rock between him and that direction. He got to Ladoro and studied the face from behind a boulder nearby. The head was cocked to one side, eyes still open, mouth seeping moisture into the dry dirt. The eyes were the worst, staring into an infinity nobody glimpses more than once.

Goodbye, friend. We had our time, some laughs and light-years. You saved my ass more than once. And now I can't do a damn thing for you.

Something moved to his right, a gossamer ball of motes. Cops, or rather, a local manifestation of them.

It flickered, spun, and said in a low, bass voice, "We regret."

"Who did this?"

"We suspect an Imperial source. Our defenses were compromised in a characteristic way. Sir."

"And what can you do?"

"I will protect you."

"You didn't do a great job for Ladoro."

"I arrived here slightly late."

"Slightly?"

"You must forgive errors. We are finite, all."

"Damn finite."

"No place is safe. This is safer, however. I extend the apologies of Madame Vissian—"

"Tell the Admiral I got his calling card."

"Sir?"

"I'm sure you will be all right," Vissian said fulsomely to them in the departure lounge.

Zeb had to admit this woman had proven better than he had hoped. She had cleared the way, stalled the Imperial officers. Probably she shrewdly expected a payoff from him, and she had every right to do so.

"I hope I can handle a wormship," Zeb said.

"And I," Fyrna added.

"Our training is the very best," Vissian said, brow furrowing. "I do hope you're not worried about the wild worm, Governor?"

"It's a tight fit," he said.

They had to fly in a slender cylinder, Fyrna co-piloting. Splitting the job had proved the only way to get them up to a barely competent level.

"I think it's *marvelous,* how courageous you two are."

"We have little choice," Fyrna said. This was artful understatement. Another day and the Admiral's officers would have Zeb and Fyrna under arrest, then dead.

"Riding in a little pencil ship. *Such* primitive means!"

"Uh, time to go," Zeb said behind a fixed smile. She was wearing thin again.

"*I* agree with the Emperor. Any technology distinguishable from magic is insufficiently advanced."

Zeb felt his stomach flutter with dread. "You've got a point."

He had brushed off the remark.

Four hours later, closing at high velocity with the big wormhole complex, he saw her side of it.

He spoke on suitcomm to Fyrna. "In one of my classes—Nonlinear Philosophy, I believe—the professor said something I'll never forget. 'Ideas about existence pale, beside the fact of existence.' Quite true."

"Bearing oh six nine five," she said rigorously. "No small talk."

"Nothing's small out here—except that wild worm mouth."

The wild worm was a fizzing point of vibrant agitation. It orbited the main worm mouth, a distant bright speck.

Imperial ships patrolled the main mouth, ignoring this wild worm. They had been paid off long ago, and expected a steady train of slimships to slip through the Imperial guard.

The galaxy was, after all, a collection of debris, swirling at the bottom of a gravitational pothole in the cosmos. The worms made it traversable.

Below, the planet beckoned with its lush beauties.

At the terminator, valleys sank into darkness while a chain of snowy mountains gleamed beyond. Late in the evening, just beyond the terminator, the fresh, peaked mountains glowed red-orange, like live coals. Mountaintops cleaved the sheets of clouds, leaving a wake like that of a ship. Tropical thunderheads, lit by lightning flashes at night, recalled the blooming buds of white roses.

The glories of humanity were just as striking. The shining constellations of cities at night, enmeshed by a glittering web of highways. His heart filled with pride at human accomplishments. Here the hand of his fellow Empire citizens was still casting spacious designs upon the planet's crust. They had shaped artificial seas and elliptical water basins, great squared plains of cultivated fields, immaculate order arising from once-virgin lands.

"So beautiful," he mused. "And we are fleeing for our lives from it."

Fyrna sniffed. "You are losing your taste for politics."

"You have no poetry left in your soul?"

"Only when I'm not working."

He saw distant ships begin to accelerate, their yellow exhausts flaring. "Many believe that the early Empire was a far better affair, serene and lovely, with a few conflicts and certainly fewer people."

"Fine feelings and bad history," Fyrna said, dismissing all such talk.

"No doubt you are correct. Note the Admiral's approach."

Fyrna saw them now. "Damn! They've spotted us already."

"We'll have one chance to make the worm run."

"But they know—and they'll follow."

Zeb had passed through worm gates before, but always in big cruisers plying routes through wormholes tens of meters across. Every hole of that size was the hub of a complex which buzzed with carefully orchestrated traffic. He could see the staging yards and injection corridors of the main route gleaming far away.

Their wild worm, a renegade spinoff, could vanish at any moment. Its quantum froth advertised its mortality. *And maybe ours . . .* Zeb thought.

"Vector null sum coming up," he called.

"Convergent asymptotes, check," Fyrna answered.

Just like the drills they had gone through.

But coming at them was a sphere fizzing orange and purple at its rim. A neon-lit mouth. Tight, dark at the very center—

Zeb felt a sudden desire to swerve, not dive into that impossibly narrow gullet.

Fyrna called numbers. Computers angled them in. He adjusted with a nudge here and a twist there.

It did not help that he knew some of the underlying physics. Wormholes were held open with onion-skin layers of negative energy, sheets of anti-pressure made in the first convulsion of the universe. The negative energy in the "struts" was equivalent to the mass needed to make a black hole of the same radius.

So they were plunging toward a region of space of unimaginable density. But the danger lurked only at the rim, where stresses could tear them into atoms.

A bull's-eye hit was perfectly safe. But an error—

Don't hit the walls . . .

Thrusters pulsed. The wild worm was now a black sphere rimmed in quantum fire.

Growing.

Zeb felt suddenly the helpless constriction of the pencil ship.

Barely two meters across, its insulation was thin, safety buffers minimal. Behind him, Fyrna kept murmuring data and he checked . . . but part of him was screaming at the crushing sense of confinement, of helplessness.

He had never really liked travel all that much. . . . A sudden swampy fear squeezed his throat.

"Vectors summing to within zero seven three," Fyrna called.

Her voice was calm, steady, a marvelous balm. He clung to its serene certainties and fought down his own panic.

"Let's have your calculation," she called.

He was behind! Musing, he had lost track.

With a moment's hard thought he could make his mind bicameral. The two liberated subselves did their tasks, speaking back and forth only if they wished. The results merged when each was done.

"There." He squirted her the answers, last-moment computations of the changing tidal stresses into which they now plunged.

Squeals of last-second correction echoed in his cramped chamber. A quick kick in the pants—

Lightning curling snakelike blue and gold at them—

—Tumbling. Out the other end, in a worm complex fifteen thousand light-years away.

"That old professor . . . damn right, he was," he said.

Fyrna sighed, her only sign of stress. "Ideas about existence pale . . . beside the fact of existence. Yes, my love. Living is bigger than any talk about it."

A yellow-green sun greeted them. And soon enough, an Imperial picket craft. The Admiral had been right behind them and he had called ahead somehow.

So they ducked and ran. A quick serve, and they angled into the traffic-train headed for a large wormhole mouth. The commercial charge-computers accepted his Imperial override without a murmur. Zeb had learned well. Fyrna corrected him if he got mixed up.

Their second hyperspace jump took a mere three minutes. They popped out far from a dim red dwarf.

By the fourth jump they knew the drill. Having the code-status of the Imperial court banished objections.

But being on the run meant that they had to take whatever wormhole mouths they could get. Kafalan's people could not be too far behind.

A wormhole could take traffic only one way at a time. High-velocity ships plowed down the wormhole throats, which could vary from a finger's length to a star's diameter.

Zeb had known the numbers, of course. There were a few billion wormholes in the galactic disk, spread among several hundred billion stars. The average Imperial Sector was about fifty light years in radius. A jump could bring you out still many years from a far-flung world.

This influenced planetary development. Some verdant planets were green fortresses against an isolation quite profound. For them the Empire was a remote dream, the source of exotic products and odd ideas.

The worm web had many openings near inhabitable worlds, but also many near mysteriously useless solar systems. By brute force interstellar hauling the Empire had positioned the smaller worm mouths—those massing perhaps as much as a mountain range—near rich planets. But some worm mouths of gargantuan mass orbited near solar systems as barren and pointless as any surveyed.

Was this random, or a network left by some earlier civilization? Archaeologists thought so. Certainly the wormholes themselves were leftovers from the Great Emergence, when space and time alike began. They linked distant realms which had once been nearby, when the galaxy was young and smaller. The differential churn of the disk had redistributed the wormholes. But someone— or rather, something—had made sure they at least orbited reasonably near a star.

They developed a rhythm. Pop through a worm mouth, make comm contact, get in line for the next departure. Imperial watchdogs would not pull anyone of high class from a queue. So their most dangerous moments came as they negotiated clearance.

At this Fyrna became adept. She sent the WormMaster computers blurts of data and—*whisk*—they were edging into orbital vectors, bound for their next jump.

They caught a glimpse of Admiral Kafalan's baroque ship winking forth from a wormhole mouth they had left only minutes before. In the scurry-scurry of commerce they lost themselves, while they waited their turn. Then they ducked through their next hole, a minor mouth, hoping Kafalan had not noticed.

For once, the snaky, shiny innards of the worm were almost relaxing to Zeb. This one was small of mouth but long of throat; their journey took dragging, heart-thumping moments.

Matter could flow only one way at a time in a wormhole. The few experiments with simultaneous two-day transport ended in disaster. No matter how ingenious engineers tried to steer ships around each other, the sheer flexibility of worm-tunnels spelled doom. Each worm mouth kept the other "informed" of what it had just eaten. This information flowed as a wave, not in physical matter, but in the tension of the wormhole itself—a ripple in the "stress tensor," as physicists termed it.

Flying ships through both mouths sent stress waves propagating toward each other, at speeds which depended on the location and velocity of the ships. The stress constricted the throat, so that when the waves met, a clenching squeezed down the walls.

The essential point was that the two waves moved differently after they met. They interacted, one slowing and the other speeding up, in highly nonlinear fashion.

One wave could grow, the other shrink. The big one made the throat clench down into sausages. When a sausage neck met a ship, the craft *might* slip through—but calculating that was a prodigious job. If the sausage neck happened to meet the two ships when they passed—*crunch.*

This was no mere technical problem. It was a real limitation, imposed by the laws of quantum gravity. From that firm fact arose an elaborate system of safeguards, taxes, regulators, and hangers-on—all the apparatus of a bureaucracy which does indeed have a purpose, and makes the most of it.

Zeb learned to dispel his apprehension by watching the views. Suns and planets of great, luminous beauty floated in the blackness.

Behind the resplendence, he knew, lurked necessity.

From the wormhole calculus arose blunt economic facts. Between worlds A and B there might be half a dozen wormhole jumps—the Nest was not simply connected, a mere astrophysical subway system. Each worm mouth imposed added fees and charges on each shipment.

Control of an entire trade route yielded the maximum profit. The struggle for control was unending, often violent. From the viewpoint of economics, politics, and "historical momentum"—which meant a sort of imposed inertia on events—a local empire which controlled a whole constellation of nodes should be solid, enduring.

Not so. Time and again, regional satrapies went toes-up. As Governor, he had been forced to bail some of them out. That amounted to local politics, where he had proved reasonably adept. Alas, Kafalan pursued them for global, galactic reasons.

Many worlds that feasted on the largesse of a wormhole mouth perished, or at least suffered repeated boom-and-bust cycles, because they were elaborately controlled. It seemed natural to squeeze every worm passage for the maximum fee, by coordinating every worm to optimize traffic. But that degree of control made people restive.

The system could not deliver the best benefits. Over-control failed.

On their seventeenth jump, they met a case in point.

*   *   *

"Vector aside for search," came an automatic command from an Imperial vessel.

They had no choice. The big-bellied Imperial sentry craft scooped them up within seconds after their emergence from a medium-sized wormhole mouth.

"Transgression tax," a computerized system announced. "Planet Alacaran demands that special carriers pay—" A blur of computer language.

"Let's pay it," Zeb said.

"I wonder if it will provide a tracer for Kafalan's use," Fyrna said over comm.

"What is our option?"

"I shall use my own personal indices."

"For a wormhole transit? That will bankrupt you!"

"It is safer."

Zeb fumed while they floated in magnetic grapplers beneath the Imperial picket ship. The wormhole orbited a heavily industrialized world. Gray cities sprawled over the continents and webbed across the seas in huge hexagonals.

The Empire had two planetary modes: rural and urban. Farm worlds were socially stable because of its time-honored lineages and stable economic modes. They, and the similar Femo-rustics, lasted.

This planet Alacaran, on the other hand, seemed to cater to the other basic human impulse: clumping, seeking the rub of one's fellows, a pinnacle of city-clustering.

Zeb had always thought it odd that humanity broke so easily into two modes. Now, though, his political experience clarified these proclivities. Most people were truly primates, seeking a leader. Countless planets congealed into the same basic Feudalist attractor groups—Macho, Socialist, Paternal. Even the odd Thanatocracies fit the pattern. They had Pharaoh-figures promising admission to an afterlife, and detailed rankings descending from his exalted peak in the rigid social pyramid.

"They're paid off," Fyrna sent over comm. "Such corruption!"

"Ummm, yes, shocking." Was he getting cynical? He wanted to turn and speak with her, but their pencil ship allowed scant socializing.

"Let's go."

"Where to?"

"To . . ." He realized that he had no idea.

"We have probably eluded pursuit." Fyrna's voice came through stiff and tight. He had learned to recognize these signs of her own tension.

"We could work a route back to our Sector."

"They would expect that and block it."

He felt a stab of disappointment. But she was the professional bodyguard and she was undoubtedly right. "Where, then?"

"I took advantage of this pause to alert a friend, by wormlink," she said. "We may be able to return, though through a devious route."

"The Speculists—"

"May not expect such audacity."

"Which recommends the idea."

Dizzying indeed—leaping about the entire galaxy, trapped in a casket-sized container.

They jumped and dodged and jumped again. At several more wormhole yards Fyrna made "deals." Payoffs, actually. She deftly dealt combinations of his cygnets, the Imperial passage indices, and her private numbers.

"Costly," Zeb fretted. "How will I ever pay—"

"The dead do not worry about debts," she said.

"You have such an engaging way of putting matters."

"Subtlety is wasted here."

They emerged from one jump in close orbit about a sublimely tortured star. Streamers lush with light raced by them.

"How long can this worm last here?" he wondered.

"It will be rescued, I'm sure. Imagine the chaos in the system if a worm mouth begins to gush hot plasma."

Zeb knew the wormhole system, though discovered in pre-Empire ages, had not always been used. After the underlying physics of the wormhole calculus came to be known, ships could ply the galaxy by invoking wormhole states around themselves. This afforded exploration of reaches devoid of wormholes, but at high energy costs and some danger. Further, such ship-local hyperdrives were far slower than simply slipping through a worm.

And if the Empire eroded? Lost the worm network? Would the slim attack fighters and snakelike weapons fleets give way to lumbering hypership dreadnoughts?

The next destination swam amid an eerie black void, far out in the halo of red dwarfs above the galactic plane. The disk stretched in luminous splendor. Zeb remembered holding a coin and thinking of how a mere speck on it stood for a vast volume, like a large Zone. Here such human terms seemed pointless. The galaxy was one serene entity, grander than any human perspective.

"Ravishing," Fyrna said.

"See Andromeda? It looks nearly as close."

The spiral, twin to their own galaxy, hung above them. Its lanes of clotted dust framed stars azure and crimson and emerald. A slow symphony of mass and time.

"Here comes our connection," Zeb warned.

This wormhole intersection afforded five branches. Three black spheres orbited closely together like circling leopards, blaring bright by their quantum rim radiation. Two cubic wormholes circled further out. Zeb knew that one of the rare variant forms was cubical, but he had never seen any. Two together suggested that they were born at the edge of galaxies, but such matters were beyond his shaky understanding.

"We go—there," Fyrna pointed a laser beam at one of the cubes, guiding the pencil ship.

They thrust toward the smaller cube, gingerly inching up. The wormyard here was automatic and no one hailed them.

"Tight fit," Zeb said nervously.

"Five fingers to spare."

He thought she was joking, then realized that if anything, she was underestimating the fit. At this less-used wormhole intersection slow speeds were essential. Good physics, unfortunate economics. The slowdown cut the net flux of mass, making them backwater intersections.

He gazed at Andromeda to take his mind off the piloting. No wormholes emerged in other galaxies, for arcane reasons of quantum gravity. Or perhaps by some ancient alien design?

They flew directly into a flat face of a cubic worm. The negative-energy-density struts which held the wormhole open were in the edges, so the faces were free of tidal forces.

A smooth ride took them quickly to several wormyards in close orbit about planets. One Zeb recognized as a rare type with an old but ruined biosphere. There are plenty of ways to kill a world. Or a man, he reflected.

Another jump—into the working zone of a true, natural black hole. He watched the enormous energy-harvesting disks glow with fermenting scarlets and virulent purples. The Empire had stationed great conduits of magnetic field around the hole. These sucked and drew interstellar dust clouds. The dark cyclones narrowed toward the brilliant accretion disk around the hole. Radiation from the friction and infalling of that great disk was in turn captured by vast grids and reflectors.

The crop of raw photon energy itself became trapped and flushed into the waiting maws of wormholes. These carried the flux to distant worlds in need of cutting lances of light, for the business of planet-shaping, world-raking, moon-carving.

"Time to run," she said.

"We can't get back to our home Sector?"

"I have eavesdropped on the signals sent between worm sites. We are wanted at all domains adjacent to our Sector."

"Damn!"

"I suspect they have many allies."

"They must, to get this quick cooperation. They've staged a fine little manhunt."

"Perhaps the nova trigger issue is but a pretext?"

"How so?"

"Many like the present system of wormhole use," she said delicately. She never let her own views of politics seep into their relationship. Even this oblique reference plainly made her uncomfortable. Her concern was him as a breathing man, not as a bundle of political abstractions.

She had a point, too. Zeb wanted free wormholes, governed only by market forces. The Speculists wanted tariffs and favors, preferences and paybacks. And guess who would control all that bureaucracy?

He floated and thought. She wanted for the decision.

"Precious little running room left."

"I do not urge compromise. I merely advise."

"Ladoro . . ."

"They would not have bothered to kill him unless they wanted to deal."

"I don't like dealing with a knife at my throat."

"We need to decide," she said edgily.

Time ran against them. He bit his lip. Give up? He couldn't, even if it seemed smart. "Our Sector is pretty far out. What if we run inward?"

"To what end?"

"I'll be working on that. Let's go."

Pellucid, a mere dozen light-years from Galactic Center, had seventeen wormhole mouths orbiting within its solar system—the highest hole density in the galaxy. The system had originally held only two, but a gargantuan technology of brute interstellar flight had tugged the rest there, to make the nexus.

Each of the seventeen spawned occasional wild worms. One of these was Fyrna's target.

But to reach it, they had to venture where few did.

"The galactic center is dangerous," Fyrna said as they coasted toward the decisive wormhole mouth. They curved above a barren mining planet. "But necessary."

"The Admiral pursuing us worries me more—" Their jump cut him off.

—and the spectacle silenced him.

The filaments were so large the eye could not take them in. They stretched fore and aft, shot through with immense luminous corridors and dusky lanes. These arches yawned over tens of light-years. Immense curves descended toward the white-hot True Center. There matter frothed and fumed and burst into dazzling fountains.

"The black hole," he said simply.

The small black hole they had seen only an hour before had trapped a few stellar masses. At True Center, three million suns had died to feed gravity's gullet.

The orderly arrays of radiance were thin, only a light-year across. Yet they sustained themselves along hundreds of light-years as they churned with change. Zeb switched the polarized walls to see in different frequency ranges. Though the curves were hot and roiling in the visible, human spectrum, the radio revealed hidden intricacy. Threads laced among convoluted spindles. He had a powerful impression of layers, of labyrinthine order ascending beyond his view, beyond simple understanding.

"Particle flux is high," Fyrna said tensely. "And rising."

"Where's our junction?"

"I'm having trouble vector-fixing—ah! There."

Hard acceleration rammed him back into his flow-couch. Fyrna took them diving down into a mottled pyramid-shaped wormhole.

This was an even rarer geometry. Zeb had time to marvel at how accidents of the universal birth-pang had shaped these serene geometries, like exhibits in some god's Euclidean museum of the mind.

The wild worm they had used fizzled and glowed behind them. Something emerged on their tall.

Fyrna sped them toward a ramshackle, temporary wormyard. He said nothing, but felt her tense calculations.

The sky filled with light.

"They have detonated the worm!" Fyrna cried.

Breaking hard, veering left—

—into a debris cloud. Thumps, crashes.

Zeb said, "How could the Admiral blow a *worm*?"

"He carries considerable weaponry. Evidently the Empire knows how to trigger the negative-energy-density struts inside a worm mouth."

"Can they see us?"

"Not inside this cloud—I hope."

"Head for that bigger cloud—there."

A huge blot beckoned, coal-sack sullen. They were close in here, near the hole's accretion disk. Around them churned the deaths of stars, all orchestrated by the magnetic filaments.

Here stars were ripped open, spilled, smelted down into fusing globs. They lit up the dark, orbiting masses of debris like tiny crimson match heads flaring in a filthy coal sack.

Amid all that moved the strangest stars of all. Each was half-covered by a hanging hemispherical mask. The mask gave off infra-red from this strange screen, which hung at a fixed distance from the star. It hovered on light, gravity just balancing the outward light pressure. The mask reflected half the star's flux back on it, turning up the heat on the cooker, sending virulent arcs jetting from the corona.

Light escaped freely on one side while the mask bottled it up on the other. This pushed the star toward the mask, but the mask was bound to the star by gravitation. It adjusted and kept the right distance. The forlorn star was able to eject light in only one direction, so it recoiled oppositely.

The filaments were herding these stars: sluggish, but effective. Herded toward the accretion disk, stoking the black hole's appetite.

"The Admiral is after us."

Zeb could see nothing, but she had the instruments to peer through the dust cloaking them. "Can he shoot?"

"Not if we damp engines."

"Do it."

Drifting . . . into a narrow gulf, overlooking the splendor below.

Blackness dwelled at the core, but friction heated the infalling gas and dust. These brimmed with forced radiation. Storms worried the great banks; white-hot tornadoes whirled. A virulent glow hammered outward, shoving incessantly at the crowded masses jostling in their doomed orbits. Gravity's gullet forced the streams into a disk, churning ever inward.

Amid this deadly torrent, life persisted. Of a sort.

Zeb peered through the gaudy view, seeking the machine-beasts who ate and dwelled and died here.

Suffering the press of hot photons, the grazer waited. To these photovores, the great grinding disk was a source of food. Above the searing accretion disk, in hovering clouds, gossamer herds fed.

"Vector that way," Zeb said. "I remember seeing these on my visit. . . ."

"We run a risk, using our drive."

"So be it."

Sheets of the photovores billowed in the electromagnetic winds, basking in the sting. Some were tuned to soak up particular slices of the electromagnetic spectrum, each species with a characteristic polish and shape, deploying great flat receptor planes to maintain orbit and angle in the eternal brimming day.

Their ship slipped among great wings of high-gloss moly-sheet spread. The photovore herds skated on winds and magnetic torques in a complex dynamical sum. They were machines, of course, descended from robot craft which had explored this center billions of years before. More complex machines, evolved in this richness, prowled the darker lanes further out.

"Let's hide here."

"We're over-heating already," she said.

"Duck into the shade of that big-winged one."

She called, "Our own ship magnetic fields are barely able to hold back the proton hail."

"Where's the nearest worm?"

"Not far, but—"

"The Admiral will be covering it."

"Of course." A chess game with obvious moves.

A bolt seared across the dust ball behind them and struck some photovores. They burst open and flared with fatal energies.

"He's shooting on spec," Zeb said.

"Perhaps as he does not like the weather here."

They hugged the shadow and waited. Moments tiptoed by.

The Admiral's ship emerged from a dust bank, baroquely elegant and foppishly ornate, glowing with purpose, spiraling lazily down.

Zeb saw a spindly radiance below the photovore sheets. "A magnetic filament."

"Looks dangerous," she said.

"Let's head for it."

"What?"

"We're doomed if we stay here. If you're losing at a game, change the game."

They slipped below vast sheets of photovores with outstretched wings, banking gracefully on the photon breeze. Lenses swiveled to follow the human ship: prey? Here a pack of photovores had clumped, caught in a magnetic flux tube that eased down along the axis of the galaxy itself.

Among them glided steel-blue gamma-vores, feeders on the harder gamma-ray emission from the accretion disk. They sometimes came this far up, he knew, perhaps to hunt the silicate-creatures who dwelled in the darker dust clouds. Much of the ecology here was still unknown.

He stopped musing. Nature red in tooth and claw, after all. Time to move. Where?

"Slip into the magnetic tube."

She said sharply, "But the electrodynamic potentials there—"

"Let's draw a little cover."

She swooped them forward toward the filament. This also took them angling toward a huge sailcraft photovore. It sighted them, pursued.

Here navigation was simple. Far below them, the rotational pole of the Eater of All Things, the black hole of three million stellar masses, was a pinprick of absolute black at the center of a slowly revolving incandescent disk.

The photovore descended after them, through thin planes of burnt-gold light seekers. They all lived to ingest light and excrete microwave beams, placid conduits, but some—like the one gliding after the tiny human ship—had developed a taste for metals: a metallovre. It folded its mirror wings, now angular and swift, accelerating.

"The Admiral has noticed us," she announced in flat tones.

"Good. Into the flux tube. Quick!"

"That big alien machine is going to reach us first."

"Even better."

He had heard the lecture, while on his "tour" here. Fusion fires inside the photovores could digest the ruined carcasses of other machines. Exquisitely tuned, their innards yielded pure ingots of any alloy desired.

The ultimate resources here were mass and light. The photovores lived for light, and the sleek metallovore lived to eat them, or even better, the human ship, an exotic variant. It now gave gigahertz cries of joy as it followed them into the magnetic fields of the filament.

"These magnetic entities are intelligent?" she asked.

"Yes, though not in the sense we short-term thinkers recognize. They are more like fitfully sleeping libraries." A glimmer of an idea. "But it's their thinking processes that might save us."

"How?"

"They trigger their thinking with electrodynamic potentials. We're irritating them, I'm sure, by flying in hell-bent like this."

"How wonderful."

"Watch that metallovore. Let it get close, then evade it."

Banks, swoops, all amid radiance. Magnetic strands glowed like ivory.

It would ingest them with relish, but the metal-seeker could not maneuver as swiftly as their sleek ship. Deftly they zoomed through magnetic entrails—and the Admiral followed.

"How soon will these magnetic beings react?"

Zeb shrugged. "Soon, if experience is a guide."

"And we—"

"Hug the metallovore now. Quick!"

"But don't let him grab us?"

"That's the idea."

The metallovore, too, was part of an intricate balance. Without it, the ancient community orbiting the Eater would decay to a less diverse state, one of monotonous simplicity, unable to adjust to the Eater's vagaries. Less energy would be harnessed, less mass recovered.

The metallovore skirted over them. Zeb gazed out at it. Predators always had parasites, scavengers. Here and there on the metallovore's polished skin were limpets and barnacles, lumps of orange-brown and soiled yellow that fed on chance debris, purging the metallovore of unwanted elements—wreckage and dust which can jam even the most robust mechanisms, given time.

It banked, trying to reach them. The Admiral's glossy ship came angling in, too, along the magnetic strands.

"Let it get closer," Zeb ordered.

"It'll grab us!"

"True, unless the Admiral kills it first."

"Some choice," she said sardonically.

A dance to the pressure of photons. Light was the fluid here, spilling up from the blistering storms far below in the great grinding disk. This rich harvest supported the great sphere which stretched for hundreds of cubic light-years, its sectors and spans like armatures of an unimaginable city. Why had he gone into politics, Zeb asked himself—he was always rather abstract when in a crisis—when all *this* beckoned?

All this, centered on a core of black oblivion, the dark font of vast wealth.

"I'm getting a lot of electrodynamic static," she called.

"Ah, good."

"Good? My instruments are sluggish—"

The metallovore loomed. Pincers flexed forth from it.

The jolt came first as a small refraction in the howling virulence. Slow tightening arced along the magnetic filament, annihilating riding down.

"It'll fry us!"

"Not us," he said. "We're a minor mote here. Much bigger conductors will draw this fire."

Another jarring jolt. The metallovore arced and writhed and died in a dancing fire.

No differently could the laws of electrodynamics treat an ever bigger conductor, closing in. The Admiral's fine glowing ship drew flashes of discharge, dancing ruby-red and bile-green.

It coasted, dead. The larger surface areas of both metallovore and starship had intercepted the electrical circuitry of the filaments.

"I . . . You really did know what you were doing," she said weakly.

"Not actually. I was just following my intuition."

"The one that got you the Governorship?"

"No, something more primitive."

Coasting now, out of the gossamer filaments. There might be more bolts of high voltage.

"Is everyone on that ship dead?" she asked.

"Oh no. You have forgotten your elementary physics. A charge deposits only on the outside of a conductor. Electrons will not enter it."

"But why are they drifting then?"

"Any antenna will draw the charge in, if the line is active; that's its job. Like having your hand on the knob of a radio in a lightning storm, a chancy act."

"So they're inert?"

"A few may have been standing too close to the instruments."

"They would be . . . ?"

He shrugged. "Fried. Luck of the game."

"The Admiral—"

"Let us hope he was unlucky. Even if not, I suspect the Speculists will not look kindly upon one who has raised such a rowdy chase and then caught nothing."

She laughed. They coasted in the gorgeous splendor.

Then he yawned, stretched, and said, "Getting cramped in here. Shall we find that wormhole you mentioned?"

He really didn't like travel all that much, indeed.

Think of the galaxy as a swarm of gaudy bees, bright colors hovering in a ball. Stomp them somehow in midair, so they bank and turn in a furious, compressed disk. Yet their courses and destinies are now guided by small entities of great pretension: humans, at times no better than bees. Across the span of a hundred billion worlds, rich and ancient blood sings in pounding vessels. Even on so great a scale, the hunt is always on.

AFTERWORD

I so loved Roger Zelazny's liquid grace, his fervent sense of narrative momentum, that I have tried in this piece to emulate some of his moments and moves.

Like many, my first Zelazny story was "A Rose for Ecclesiastes." Who can forget reading that opening voice? It evoked a romantic, daring world seen through a poet's eyes. I followed his career eagerly, through novels and novellas of great power. He was the brightest light in a burning decade, the sixties.

When I met Roger in the 1970s he proved to be an affable, witty, wiry man. We became friends and I visited him and family, often having dinner in Santa Fe when I was consulting at Los Alamos. Restless of mind, he always probed for the latest from the grand canvas of science.

I saw him twice in the last year and a half of his life, when we were both guests of honor at two cons. The last time, in Idaho, I found him as quick and funny, eyes glittery, as ever, though gaunt and at times sobered. His spirit was so firm I did not seriously suppose that he would falter and vanish from us so quickly.

Deaths diminish us all. Among the science fiction community, I missed terribly Robert Heinlein and Terry Carr and had persistent dreams about them for over a year after they departed. For Roger it was the same: dreams of flying somewhere with him, always in air sunny and resplendent with long, high perspectives.

So when asked to write a story in tribute to him, I took from my stock of ideas at hand, using pieces of ideas I was working on, and tried to see what Roger would like to fashion from them. He loved the bare and the swanky alike, so I thought of a rather Roger-like character, comfortable in his opulent world, who gets to flee and fight across the sort of wondrous galaxy Roger would have enjoyed. It's been fun to go along with him this one last time.

In Lord of Light *fabulous technology makes gods of mortal men. In Michael Stackpole's ironic tale, forgotten gods employ modern media for their own ends.*

■

ASGARD UNLIMITED
Michael A. Stackpole

ASIDE FROM THE RAVEN-SHIT ON HIS SHOULDERS, ODIN LOOKED pretty good in the Armani suit. The matching blue pin-striping on the eyepatch was a nice touch. Odin had never been a slouch, but even I was impressed at how quickly he was picking up on the ways of this new age.

He looked down on me from a composite video screen taller than he had ever been in life. He wore a smile that I knew was for the benefit of his audience, but the spectators in Valhalla assumed the smile was for them. If it pleased them to think so, I saw no reason to disabuse them of this notion. I was feeling too good to indulge myself.

I stood in the Grand Foyer of Valhalla and smiled at what I had wrought. Massive steel spears were bound together to form pillars and rafters, giving the grand hall the retro-martial look all the architectural journals had raved about. In the old Valhalla the roof had been made of shields, but I had them cast in lexan so they let light in during the day and allowed people permitted into the upper reaches to see the stars at night. Carefully crafted sword-shaped sconces hid halogen lights that provided the lower levels with a constant, timeless glow.

The old, tired wooden benches, moth-eaten tapestries and well-worn animal skins had been replaced with more modern Scandinavian furnishings. Shields, swords, spears, and armor all still figured into the motifs, but that's because they were familiar to people. One of the special aspects of the new Valhalla allowed everyone to see some decorations as those things with which they were most familiar—the Christers spoke in tongues, we provided Icons-for-all.

Valhalla was a beautiful place no one would mind dwelling in for eternity. The Valkyries were certainly striking and one of our better attractions. It took me a while to convince Odin that bringing in men to wear similarly brief outfits would be a good way to offer something to the female market. He finally succumbed after I convinced him that he thought up the name by which the beef-cake would be known. "Valiants" were now one of our more popular features.

Then again, Odin had not been the reactionary element among the Aesir. At the very first briefing I gave the others just over a year ago, Odin had already begun to adapt to the changed circumstances. The Perry Ellis ensemble he wore had been a season out of date, but of a conservative enough cut to enhance the patriarchal nobility that had long been his trademark.

The others were a bit slower to adjust, but that was how it always had been. Thor, wearing some urban commando fatigues, began to do a wonderful imitation of a beached fish gasping for oxygen the moment I walked into the room. Tyr noticed my entrance, but returned to studying the biomechanical prosthesis replacing his right hand. He opened and closed the fist in rough time with the opening and closing of Thor's mouth.

And Heimdall, well, that venomous glare took me back centuries.

Thor slammed a fist onto the conference room table, pulverizing formica and particle board. "What is *he* doing here?" Wood dust rose up in a great cloud and lodged firmly in Thor's red beard. "It's his trickery that has woven these illusions that mask Asgard's true nature."

Odin slowly shook his snow-maned head. "No, Loki is the reason we are all here, hence his place with us."

Little lightning-bolts trickled from Thor's eyes as he glanced at me. "It is a trick, Odin Val-father. This is the one who had Baldur slain. It was he who caused the Ragnarok, in which we were slain. . . ."

"Is that so, Thunderer?" I smiled and seated myself in the chair at the opposite end of the lozenge table from Odin. "I triggered Ragnarok?"

"Don't seek to deny it." Thor folded his arms over his chest, his bulging muscles sorely testing the resiliency of his jacket's synthetic fibers. "We know this is true. The serpent and I slew each other. Odin died in Fenris's maw and Tyr slew the hell-hound Garm, but was slain by him. Heimdall killed you and you him. This we know."

I allowed myself a little laugh and had Odin not smiled and nodded in my direction, any of my brethren would have gladly torn me apart. "How do you know this, Thor? Do you recall smiting the serpent with Mjolnir? And you, Tyr, do you recall Garm's bite?" My smile died a bit as I regarded Heimdall. "And you, do you recall the twisting agony of my sword in your guts?"

Heimdall's smile revealed a glittering mouthful of golden teeth. "No more than my hands remember twisting your head off."

I shot the cuffs of my shirt to cover the momentary difficulty I had swallowing. "None of us have memories of the events of Ragnarok actually happening. We knew what *would* happen, how the world would end, because of Odin's wisdom and the various oracles that predicted the twilight of the gods, but we did not live through that predicted end."

Tyr's hand snapped shut. "Do not try to tell me Baldur did not die. I feel the pain of his loss still in my heart."

"You are absolutely right, Tyr, he did die, but the events his death presaged did not come to pass. There was no Ragnarok."

"Impossible!" Thor started to pound the table again, but a rare bit of restraint left his fist poised to strike. "Ragnarok must have happened. There has been so much nothing—I must have been dead. I will not believe there was no twilight of the gods."

I gave him my most disarming smile and his fist began to slowly drift down. "There was a twilight, but not the one we expected."

Thor's red eyebrows collided with confusion. "Was there or was there not a Ragnarok?"

"*Our* Ragnarok, no." Odin laid his left hand on Thor's arm. "Allow Loki to explain."

Thor grumbled and glowered at me. "Speak on, Deceiver."

"For forever and a day we have known of other gods and their realms. We have also known that we draw life from the belief of our worshipers in us. Their prayers and invocations, sacrifices and vows sustain us." I opened my hands. "We use the power they give us to grant boons to our favorites, inspiring others to greater belief and sacrifice in the hopes we will favor them, too."

My fellow gods squirmed a bit in their chairs. Though they knew nothing of B. F. Skinner, they had intuitively grasped the fact that random interval reinforcement was truly the most powerful inducement to create and maintain a behavior pattern. Often, in fact, we received credit for things we did not do. If a tree fell on a longhouse during a storm, the enemies of the person so afflicted would offer thanks to me or another god for our smiting of their enemy.

There may be no such thing as a free lunch, but people are much more protective about their food than they are their devotion.

"Well to the south of our Midgard holdings, in the desert crossroads, Jehovah decided to retire."

Heimdall's treasure-trove smile broadened. "Had I created the world in six days, I would have chosen more than one day's rest, too."

We all laughed. While it was true most of us could not remember where we had come from, and therefore made up rather elaborate stories about our antecedents, only Jehovah had come up with the tale of his being the end-all and be-all of existence. While claiming to have killed your own parents wasn't necessarily the most attractive story we could have come up with, it was easier for humans to relate to than a tale of willing oneself into full-blown, egotistical existence.

"I'm certain that had something to do with it, Heimdall. In any event, to facilitate his retirement, he had a fling with a human and she gave birth to a son, Joshua—though he is now more commonly known as Jesus and the Christ. He performed some miracles, gave his people the benefit of his wisdom, then hung from a tree until dead."

Thor frowned. "How long was he on the tree?"

"An afternoon."

The god of thunder snickered. "An afternoon? That's nothing compared to Odin's nine days, and he was stuck on his own spear at the time."

"Josh may well have heard of the tale, or his followers did, because there was a spear-sticking involved in the whole incident, too. His disciples bundled him off to a tomb, and after a day and a half, Josh came back to life." I shrugged my shoulders. "Again, a substandard performance, but one that was convincing for his people."

Tyr swept golden locks away from his blue eyes. "I recall hearing of the Christ when some of his followers were slain for spreading his story among my people."

My eyes narrowed. "Would that we had realized the danger of his cult. The Christ demanded two things of his followers. The first he borrowed from his father: they were to have no gods but him before them. This demand of exclusivity is fine when you are a lonely godling ruling over nomads in featureless wastes—there were no other gods who wanted those people."

Odin frowned. "When Jehovah's people were captive in Thothheim and Baalheim, they were no threat to the indigenous gods."

"No, but the Christ's second demand of his believers is what made them malignant." I put an edge into my voice so even Thor could understand what I was saying was important. "The Christ demanded they share their religion with others, who would then become exclusively his and spread the faith further."

Thor shook his head. "I don't believe you. I would remember such a thing."

"You don't remember because the Christ movement took hold in our realm almost overnight. As we concerned ourselves with the coming of Ragnarok, the Christers stole into our lands. Our believers dwindled, then abandoned us. We fell into the sleep of the forgotten."

Heimdall cocked an eyebrow at me. "If this is true, if we all became forgotten, how is it you know this story?"

I pressed my hands together, fingertip to fingertip. "In their zeal to spread Christism, they linked me with Lucifer, the ancient enemy Jehovah spawned and who tormented Joshua. There are those humans who always go against the prevailing sentiment of society, and worshiping me became a viable alternative for them."

Tyr reached up with his mechanical hand and tried to pluck a fly out of the air. "If these Christers hold sway, how are we here, now?"

My smile broadened. "Christism did become quite widespread and certainly become the dominant religion in the world, but it is based on tolerance and pacifism. As a result, some evils in the world go unchecked. I believe it was the slaughter of Jehovah's core constituency in central Europe that first alarmed Jehovah. He took a look at what the Christ had done with the family firm and initiated a hostile takeover of the enterprise. He forced Joshua out and returned things to the way they had been. Joshua immediately struck out on his own, but his people had become fragmented and his doctrine muddled. At the same time Christism became seen by any number of people as theological imperialism, so they rejected it and returned to the old ways.

"Our ways."

"I cannot believe it." Thor frowned mightily. "You say this Christ was a pacifist who preached tolerance."

"Exactly."

"No fighting? No warrior tradition?"

"No, he was a pacifist. He completely eschewed violence."

Thor's lower lip quivered for a moment. "If he was a pacifist, how were we defeated?"

I smiled. "He offered people something they wanted. He promised them life after death."

"So did we."

Odin pressed his hands to the tabletop. "This brings us to the point of this meeting. The return of people to the old faiths has given us another chance at life, but these people are not the people we knew of old. Things are different, now, and we must avail ourselves of the means we have today to guarantee we do not go away again."

Thor shook his head. "I don't understand. We are the gods. We do not change. People worship us for what we are, what we offer them."

"And there is the problem." I frowned. "Quite frankly, the Aesir are a public relations nightmare. All of us here have our warrior aspects, but war just isn't in vogue any more."

Thor's eyes blazed. "War is the most noble and lofty pursuit to which a man can aspire. This is why the boldest and most brave warriors are plucked by the Valkyries from the fields of the dead and brought to Valhalla. Odin himself ordered warriors to be buried with their arms and armor so they would be prepared to join us in the last days, fighting against our foes at Ragnarok!"

I sighed. "Look, we really need to rethink this Ragnarok thing. The Christers pretty much own the idea of a grand battle to usher in the end of the world, so our Ragnarok just comes across as a pale imitation of their Armageddon. And this warriors-only thing, that's got to go, too."

The god of thunder's voice boomed. "What? You want to admit other than warriors to Valhalla?"

"Thor, what you would recognize as warriors in this era carry weapons that can kill a man at over a mile. Most of the wars now are called police actions, which means people far away use weapons that hit with the force of Mjolnir to shatter their enemy's cities. The heroic nature of combat you recall so fondly is no more."

Thor's florid face drained of color. "There are no more humans who bravely venture out, risking life and limb, to defeat their enemies and reap riches for themselves?"

"There are, but they battle away in commercial wars."

"Merchants?"

"Think of them as captains of industry."

"You want to admit *merchants* to Valhalla?" Thor shook his head. "Next you will want to allow women into that hallowed hall."

I winced. "Actually, I *did* want to bring women in, but several of the mother-goddess cults have combined with feminism to really block our inroads there. Face it, while all of your wives were wonderful, they're not as inspiring as the Mediterranean goddesses. Still, focusing on men gives us a potential market of roughly half the world's population, and that half controls the majority of the wealth in the world."

"Wealth?" Tyr frowned. "I agree with Thor. We want nobility and courage."

"No, we want *believers.* To attract them, we have to give them something the Christers won't." I smiled. "One of the Christ's pronouncements is that it will be easier for a camel to pass through the eye of a needle than it will for a rich man to enter Paradise. We've got a long-standing tradition of having a person buried with his material possessions so he can have them in the afterlife. We'll build on that tradition and have people flocking in."

I leaned forward. "Welcome to Asgard Unlimited. We're in the religion business. Our slogan is this: Asgard Unlimited—you *can* take it with you."

Heimdall's visage darkened. "The people you speak of attracting sound less like worshipers than pillagers and scavengers, coming to us to see what we can give them."

"You have to understand, all of you, that the human of today is less a worshiper than a fan. They don't so much believe in anyone or thing as much as they believe in and worship the myth surrounding a phenomenon. Being gods is certainly impressive, but we need to become more, something that allows everyone to participate in our mystique."

I nodded toward the head of the table. "The three of you will form a trinity—the Christers made that popular and we can use the pattern. Odin will be the head of things and preside over Valhalla. His job will be to dispense wisdom and help our people prosper in their endeavors.

"We'll remake Valhalla into something new and sophisticated. As we have in the past, we'll thin the line between the living and the dead, bringing in dead celebrities to meet and greet folks. This will provide our claims of the afterlife—something the Christers never do. We also want Valhalla to be a fun place—with family entertainment as well as more adult pursuits."

"Adult pursuits?"

I looked at Tyr. "You've not forgotten Odin's taste for hot and cold running Valkyries, have you? One part of Valhalla will be Hooters of the Gods. Another section will be devoted to weekend warriors—people who always wanted to fight but never had the chance. Add in a casino, an amusement park, a 'Warfare of the Ages' exhibit area and we have pretty much everything covered. Since Valhalla has five hundred and forty doors, we'll franchise them out to the major population centers of the world, meaning the site stays centralized, but people can get together instantly. That will greatly boost our commercial bookings—conventions every-where will be coming to us."

I pointed at Tyr. "Your role is going to be that of the divine Princeling. Royalty has gotten a bad name of late, but Tyr, you're the one who can bring nobility back to it. Tragically wounded while saving the rest of the gods, you're already a heroic figure. You're also favored by sportsmen, and sports is big business. You're a natural for skiing and other winter sports at the more exclusive hideways in the world. If you can pick up golf, cricket, and yachting, you'll be pitching straight to our core market."

Tyr slowly smiled. "All I have to do is spend my time involved in sport, associating with the rich and beautiful?"

"That's it."

"I'm willing to listen—more."

I turned to Heimdall. "Though I ridiculed you in the past for the job of being the Aesir's watchman, now is a time we need your keen eyes and ears to safeguard our enterprise. Before you listened for enemies approaching Bifrost on their way to Asgard. Now we will have many more bridges, and each of them will bear watching."

The smile that had begun to blossom on Heimdall's face with my initial remarks froze. "I may be a god, but I cannot monitor the whole world without help."

"And help you shall have." From my pocket I fished a remote control and pointed it at the wall to my right. Hitting a button I brought a dancing picture to life. "This is television. In our Valhalla you will be able to watch hundreds of such monitors, seeing what they see, hearing the sounds they hear. There is no corner of Mid-gard that you will not be able to see immediately. When you see danger, you get on the horn—ah, the telephone, not Gjallarhorn—and warn us what is going on.

"It is a grave responsibility," I said, handing him the remote, "but no one else can handle it."

Heimdall brandished the plastic box as if it were Hofud, his sword. "I shall be ever vigilant."

Thor thrust his lower lip out in a pout. "You say war is revered no more. There is nothing for me in your Asgard Unlimited."

"Ah, but there is—a very special role indeed." I gave him a genuine smile. "Among humans there is a need for idols. Many of them come out of sports, and Tyr will cover them, but others come from the entertainment industry. James Dean, Marilyn Mon-roe, Bruce Lee, Elvis—each of them has attained a near divinity because of how they entertained people."

"But I am a warrior! There is no entertainment for which I am suited."

"You're so wrong, my friend. There is a form of entertainment here that was made for you." I rubbed my hands together. "It's called professional wrestling."

Gunnar, my aide, cleared his throat and brought me back to the present. "If you have a moment, Divinity."

"Always." I reached back and rubbed at the sore spot on my spine. "What do you have?"

"We got our shipment of the new summer-color eyepatches in and they're set to go on sale in our boutiques this afternoon. This includes the ones that allow you to tan beneath them."

"Good. What about the Odin jackets?"

Gunnar frowned. "The supplier says the subcontractor they've got making the ravens has really done a poor job. They're able to join the ravens to the jacket's shoulders and they stand up, but they lose feathers and the eyes fall out."

"You tell them more than their eyes will fall out if they don't fix the problem." I glanced at the video screen behind me and then at my watch. "When is Odin due back?"

"Not for a couple of hours. He's just begun speaking in Tokyo and won't come through from our doorway there for at least another three hours." Gunnar smiled. "By the way, we got the fax this morning: *The One-eyed God's Business Wisdom* is going to start at number one on the Times list. It's bumping Jesus' *Business Beatitudes: Charity Before Profit* from the top spot. Herakles' *Twelve Labors' Lessons* will be out in two weeks, but pre-orders are soft, so we'll remain at number one for a while. We'll be selling a lot of books. And Letterman wants Odin in to help host a segment of 'stupid demigod tricks.' "

"Tell Letterman's people it's a deal, but questions about CBS are off-limits." Struck by the symbology of the network's logo, Odin bought it and didn't take well to criticism from his employees. I sighed, anticipating another long lecture from the Val-father about my making bookings for him. In the end I knew he'd see reason, but enduring the discussion would be torture.

Still, it was all in service to a worthy cause.

"Anything else?"

"Yes, Divinity." He looked down at the personal digital assistant he carried, then grinned. "Ticket sales are way up for the Great Battles of History Symposium series. The Rommel/Patton debate really got people juiced to hear more."

"Who is up next?"

"Hannibal and the two Scipios, Elder and Younger. Nike is going to underwrite part of the cost."

"Right, they have those Air Hannibal hiking boots." I nodded.

"Very good. Make sure we have plenty of them stocked in our gift shops before and after that debate. I take it Tyr's still in court?"

Gunnar nodded. "Case should go to the jury in two weeks. We anticipate a victory. The other side has good lawyers, but ours are devilishly clever and even the most stone-hearted troll would side with Tyr against a tabloid."

"Good. Keep on top of these things and keep me informed." I gave Gunnar a pat on the shoulder. "I'm going to see my daughter, but I should be back in an hour or so."

I felt the shudder run through him, but I ignored it and wended my way through the crowd waiting in line to get into the Thor memorial. I was tempted to shift my shape into that of my lost comrade, just to give them a thrill, but the chances of starting a riot weren't worth it. I passed through them unnoticed, smiling as every third or fourth person remarked on what a pity his death had been.

I thought it was more tragic—grandly tragic at that. Thor had taken to professional wrestling like a fly to carrion. He knew there was no one who could best him in a fight, and the audience knew that as well. Every night, every bout, was a morality play. It was a reenactment of the classic solar hero struggle to overcome the forces of evil and return to a new day and dawn. The bouts would start even, then Thor's foe would use some underhanded trick to gain a temporary advantage. Thor would take a beating and while his foe danced around the arena, exultant and triumphant, Thor would crawl to his corner and pull on his belt of might and gloves of iron.

I used to thrill to it. His enemy—some steroided mutant man or odd demigod from pantheons best left to their obscurity—would remain innocently unaware of his danger. The crowd would begin to pound their feet in a thunderous cadence and Thor would draw power from it. Their desire to see him win, their belief in his invincibility fueled him. He would slam his gloves together, letting their peal spread through the crowd, then he would turn and vanquish his foe.

The end came when he fought Louis the Serpent. Louis was yet another in a line of forgettable foes to face Thor, but we'd arranged for a worldwide satellite hook-up. Thor's fame and popularity was peaking—ninety-five percent of the people on the planet could identify him. This bout would solidify his place in the minds of all humanity. Thor had known from the first moment of sentience that he was meant to fight a great serpent, and Louis became it.

And Louis killed him.

After three rounds of battering each other silly, Louis picked him up in big bear hug and snapped his spine. He cast Thor aside and laughed at his fallen foe. Then he laughed at Thor's fans, called them weak and stupid. He said they were pathetic for having believed in him and that they were losers because their god was dead.

Thor's death was a crushing blow for us, but not for long. Little by little stories began to filter in about Thor having been seen here and there. There was no mistaking him, of course. He helped people out of difficult situations, averted disasters, and made the impossible happen for them. To each and every one of his worshipers these stories were proof that he lived and that their faith was anything but false.

In death Thor became bigger than he ever was in life. Caps, shirts, the Craftsman line of Mjolnir tools, the comics, videos, and action figures all went through the roof in sales. While Odin was doing very well with his books and motivational speaking engagements, and Tyr added a layer of respectability to Asgard Unlimited, Thor was the backbone of its popularity.

Past the memorial I stepped up to a door few could see and fewer could open. I could and did, passing through and petting Garm as I did so. The hell-hound would have gladly taken my hand off at the shoulder, but he feared my son Fenris, so I was safe. Past him I headed down the spiral stairs that took me to Niflhel, my daughter Hel's domain. I tossed a quick salute to Baldur—making as if I was going to flick my mistletoe boutonniere at him. He flinched and I laughed.

Compared to Valhalla, the mist-shrouded depths of Niflhel were cold and claustrophobic, but I found it bracing and cozy at the same time. The vaporous veils softened the light and dulled sound, though I was certain my laughter had penetrated into the depths.

Confirmation of that fact came from the rising and incoherent growl on my left. Through the mists a huge shadowed form lunged at me. Its eyes blazed and its teeth flashed, then the length of chain binding it to the heart of the underworld ran out of slack. It tightened, jerking the collar and creature back. It landed with a heavy thud, shaking the ground, then lay there with sobs wracking its chest.

I squatted down at the very edge of its range. "Will you never learn, Thor?"

"This chain *will* break."

I shook my head. "I think not. If you will recall, the chain forged to restrain Fenris resisted the efforts of any of the gods to break it, yourself included. That chain was made from the meow of a cat, the beard of a woman, the roots of a mountain, the tendons of a bear, the breath of a fish, and the spittle of a bird. For you I alloyed in yet other things, both tangible and intangible. There's Nixon's belief in his own innocence, the true identity of the man on the grassy knoll, and not a little bit of kevlar. The same goes for the collar. You are here until I decide you are to be released."

Thor pulled himself up into a sitting position. "I know how you did it. You invited me in for a celebratory drink before my match and drugged me, then took my shape and were killed by the serpent."

"Very good—you've been using your head for something more than a helm-filler."

"You won't get away with it. Heimdall has to have seen what you did, and what you have been doing. He knows you have been masquerading as me. He will expose you."

"Ha!" I stood and looked down upon him. "Heimdall spends every hour of every day watching the programming on over five hundred television stations. Even a god cannot escape transformation into a drooling idiot when subjected to that much television. He's so mesmerized he couldn't blow his nose, much less blow his horn."

"Why?"

"Why what? Why fake your death?" I shook my head. "How often do I have to go over this with you? Every human idol must pass through the mystery of death. Death absolves you of guilt and hides your blemishes. You're more perfect in death than you ever were in life, just like Elvis and Marilyn, Bruce Lee and Kurt Cobain. From the start I knew I needed someone to die, and you were it. Odin had already done it and hadn't had very good results, and death is just too inelegant for Tyr. That left you—Mr. Big, Dumb, and Vulnerable."

"*That* I understand." Electricity sparked in Thor's eyes. "I want to know why the deceptions? Why do I appear everywhere? Why build up my army of believers?"

"Because they aren't *your* believers." I snorted derisively at him. "If all those people who worship Thor were worshiping you, this chain would be like a spiderweb to you. You could tear it and me apart. You can't because they don't worship you. They worship the *image* of you—the romanticized image of you that *I* project."

I smiled. "My friend Louis and I, after having been so long linked and vilified by the Christers, realized we could never be transformed into the noble and hunky sort of god that people would accept. Lucifer had a constituency—hedonists, anarchists, selfish, venal people, and impotent people who wanted a shortcut to power. As Louis the Serpent he fed all those 'get it now and easy' fantasies. In showing contempt for your believers, he earned the respect of those who hated your image, and he earned quite a bit of hatred from your people. That was his payoff."

I pressed my hands to my chest. "And I became the Thor I helped create through the media. What you sowed, I reap."

Thor hung his head. "When you said we needed to rethink Ragnarok . . ."

"I wanted it rethought because the way it was scripted before, I *lost*. No more. Odin is distracted by his writing and speaking and running his network. Tyr has his diversions—and I do like that Diana; she looks very good on the arm of a god. He spends most of his time suing tabloids for stories they print about him, attending parties, and running that football team he bought. Neither of them is a threat to me. Odin's star will fade soon enough—seldom does a business guru survive more than a dozen years before being completely eclipsed, and there's nothing more boring than yesterday's financial genius. As for Tyr, a sportsman gigolo who bumps indolently from one resort to another becomes pitiful rather quickly. He'll get a talk show, it will be canceled, then he can join George Hamilton on the beach."

"And you win."

"At least the preliminary round."

Thor raised his head. "Why keep me around? Is it pity or contempt you have for me?"

"Neither, my friend." I squatted again and tugged at the fringe of his beard. "I only have the utmost of respect for you. You, I need."

"What?"

"As I said, I win the preliminary round, which means I'm going up against other gods. The Meso-Americans appear to be consolidating their pantheons. I expect the war between the Buddhists and Maoists in China will soon be resolved. Jehovah is holding his own and appears to be usurping Allah's position. The Christ is still strong. And then there's the serpent of Eden."

I saw the lightning again spark in Thor's eyes. "Yes, Thor, war might not be in vogue in this world right now, but I think the gods will change that. There's going to be a new Ragnarok, a bigger, nastier one, and in it, my friend, you will get your crack at a serpent."

His hunger was such that I could taste its bitterness. "Promise?"

"You have my solemn oath on it." I smiled, then stood and let the mist hide him from me. "The *true* Twilight of the gods fast approaches and this time, I mean to survive to the dawn."

AFTERWORD

There is something Messianic about Roger Zelazny—and part of it is the fact that he'd reject that idea out of hand, while still being entertained by it. I feel that incipient Zelazny cultus whenever those who knew Roger get together and talk about him, or tell others about him. The man's impact on us was such that it must be shared.

I met Roger only three years before his death, but I get the impression that knowing him for an hour was knowing him for a lifetime—at least as much as any of us could know him. His genius was palpable, likewise his keen interest in anything and everything. And that included us. I can't recall a phone conversation with him, no matter how brief, that didn't include him asking me what I was working on and how it was going. He seemed less interested in the nature of the work than he was in how I felt about it as a writer.

This sense of the Messianic is not the reason I wrote this particular story, however. I have no doubt that in the world of Asgard Unlimited there is a Church of Roger duking it out with the First Assembly of Elvis or showing the Church of Scientology what kind of religion you can get out of a *real* writer. I wrote this story because I felt it was the kind of story Roger *could have* written— and I would have loved to see what he would have done with the concept.

The other reason I wrote it was because I think it was the kind of story Roger would have enjoyed reading. Trying to produce a story that lives up to that kind of billing is very tough. I remember fighting that battle when I wrote my portion of *Forever After,* pushing myself to come up with something that would do justice to the assignment Roger had given me. As difficult a task as that was, it's one that really pushed me as a writer, and *that* is something I know would have made Roger very pleased.

Barring the establishment of a Church of Roger (I keep seeing Robert Schuler's Crystal Cathedral and wondering what it would look like in amber), I guess writing stories that would have entertained the man is the only way to pay homage to him. Too little, perhaps, and way too late, but it works, and for now that will have to be enough.

WHEREFORE THE REST IS SILENCE
by Gerald Hausman

In Ketchum, Idaho, the little town where Ernest Hemingway had taken his life, I lay stretched out in the sun, enjoying the clear cold mountain air, and the only thing moving around in the desolated cottonwood trees was the eye of a magpie. I was thinking, however, not about Hemingway but of my friend, Roger Zelazny, and how he had urged me to take this trip.

We were talking about daemons one day, and he said in that cellar-deep voice of his, "Yes, I've seen a few."

I asked him if he had ever done battle with a daemon, a real one.

"As a matter of fact, I have," he said. And said no more.

So I explained that one of my personal daemons was Ernest Hemingway.

"Why Hemingway?" Roger asked.

So I told him that my father had physically resembled Hemingway, and that, from the earliest time that I could remember, I always identified with Hemingway as a father figure.

"In the literary sense?" Roger queried.

"I'm afraid not," I said. "You see, he looked so much like my dad that I sometimes thought they were the same man. An overactive imagination will do that for you when you are a kid."

"So Hemingway," he mused, "is someone you must meet, if

not in the flesh, then in the spirit. And if only to find out that you are wrong—that he is nothing like your own father.''

I nodded. Then, "Do you believe that the spirit lives on after death?''

He chuckled. "The spirit lives before, during, and after death, and it is no more confined to our definitions of existence than we are bound by our limitations in not being able to see it with our eyes. For some people, there is only spirit; for others there is only flesh. Your man Hemingway had a great deal of spirit, of life-force, we might say, and something of that must live on in that place that he loved up there in Idaho.''

"It was the wrong place," I suggested. "Ray Bradbury said as much in a short story that he wrote, 'The Kilimanjaro Machine.' In the story, Hemingway is returned to Africa, to the place where he almost died in one of several airplane crashes.''

Roger smiled. "You certainly know a lot about the great white hunter, don't you? I have to confess, I have hardly looked at any of his books. Maybe because his persona got too much in the way of his well-chosen words.''

"Have you ever read *Islands in the Stream*?''

"No. Is it good?''

"I think it's his greatest book. But then I am a bit hung up on blue water and white sand.''

"Do you have a copy I could read?''

"Yes.''

So, here it was a few months later, and I was up in Idaho, in Ketchum where there was no blue water or white sand. There was, however, white snow and blue sky. It seemed odd now that I had asked Roger for permission, as it were, to visit the Hemingway house, to meet an old daemon, to kill off perhaps, once and for all, a false father-figure, a writer whose ghost had loomed large in my adolescence, and had haunted me even now. But Roger had urged me to meet the ghost. And then I had asked him, point blank, how much of Amber Castle was real, and how much of it was ghostly vision. He took a long time to answer that one, but he finally said this: "I have been in Amber Castle, I have set foot in it.''

I pushed it a bit further. "Have you ever laid hands on any of the daemons that you've written about. I mean, actually put your hands upon them?''

His face furrowed. "Yes," he said. "I have done violence with a few of them.''

I wondered about this; wondered if he were kidding me. A couple days later, however, I was talking with Roger's son, Trent, who had asked me what my favorite movie was, and I had told him, without hesitation, *Black Orpheus.* No sooner had I said this than I looked up, and, about one hundred yards away, we both saw Roger's van pull into the parking lot. He got out and stood for a moment in the bright sun, leaning against the van.

I said to Trent, "One would almost think, even at this distance, that Roger could hear us talking."

Trent laughed, "He probably can."

We walked to where Roger was, and he greeted us warmly. Then he whispered two words in my ear. *"Black Orpheus,"* he said, his face lit with a grin that quickly faded as he got into the van. I think that was the precise moment when I knew that I was going to visit the Hemingway house in Ketchum and see what was there. And now, as fate, or will, or writer's madness, would have it, I was there, or at least I was on my way. Actually, I was sitting in front of a vast woodpile in the Sun Valley sun, watching the darting eyes of a magpie, feeling quite foolish. Here I was a thousand miles from home on a crazy quest—to see if a writer whose face resembled my father's had left any part of his spirit behind when thirty years ago he had taken his life. I wanted, perhaps, to see if that shotgun blast was trapped in the walls of the house; I wanted to touch Amber Castle, too, but the Hemingway house was a tangible place, and if a spirit resided within it, I felt that somehow I would know it.

Later that afternoon I drove over to the big house on the Big Wood River, and saw it for the first time, sitting like a grayish bunker against the snow. A two-story cinderblock structure built above the river about a mile north of Ketchum. Aspen, cottonwood, and spruce hemmed the house, sheltered it, and the river ran below. All round the house were great white breadloaf hills. As I looked upon it, I realized this house was as far as one might get from the Cuban farm called Finca Vigia where Hemingway had spent the latter part of his life. And yet there was something fitting in the gray building's shape, so square and blocky, against the northern sky of Idaho. Its lonely massivity against the steely winter landscape was like the old man himself. I drew an odd sigh of relief when I first beheld the sight, for it was, somehow, just what I expected.

Inside, it was a hunter's house. It had all the requisite hides and heads and trophy items from Hemingway's life with his gun. However, there were also paintings from the Paris days, bookshelves laden with faded hardcovers, a writing desk with green-globed desk lamp on top of which hung a slightly soiled duckbill hunting cap. I was drawn, of course, to the bookshelves. Touching them with my fingers, I heard my host, who was the caretaker of the estate, remark, "I'm sorry but you won't find anything of literary value here. All of the limited editions of the Hemingway house-hold have been sold off or donated to the Kennedy Library.''

"Is that so?" I said. And I remembered that Roger told me that when he entered Amber Castle, he had placed his hand upon a tapestry and felt of the cloth with his fingers to be assured that he was really there. I reached for a book, any book, and withdrew it from the shelf. The cover was black cloth, the book was small and quite old. I opened it to the flyleaf, discovering that this was a collection of poems by Archibald MacLeish. There was a poem written in MacLeish's hand and dedicated to Hemingway and it was dated 1926. The poem went thus:

At the very bottom of the yellowed page, MacLeish had penned a personal message: "Dear Ernest, I don't want to make it awk-ward: and anything else would be inadequate—wherefore the rest is silence.''

My host came over to where I was standing and peeked over my shoulder. "Here's one the literary vultures seem to have over-looked,'' I said, chuckling.

"Good grief,'' the man said. "You've really found something there, haven't you?"

A message, I thought, from that good undiscovered country that Hemingway always wrote about, the land beyond the islands, be-yond Bimini blue, beyond the Caribbean archipelago, beyond books, beyond time, beyond Bradbury's Kilimanjaro Machine, be-yond the resemblance of the great author to an incidental father whom he had never met. Beyond all coincidences and fateful cir-cumstances, the message traveled straight to the heart. I had really found something, I imagined, and my host, astonished and pleased, announced that my find was going to create a few ripples at the Kennedy Library. "There are scholars who will be all over this,'' he said, holding the book reverently.

Back home in Santa Fe, I told Roger what had happened, and he listened eagerly, becoming very interested in the poem. He asked that I write it down for him, and, when a copy turned up in the mail from the caretaker of the Hemingway estate, I took it over to Roger and gave it to him. He read it over and over, and then smiled. "There's a key in this,'' he said approvingly.

"A key?"

"Yes. The key to Hemingway's passing is in this poem.''

I felt so myself, but I said nothing, waiting for him to go on. But he said no more about it, content that he had recognized the key. "Now you can go on,'' Roger said, "with whatever it is you are going to write, for the daemon is gone, burned away by that poem.''

"Do you think Hemingway's ghost gave me that book?" I asked.

Roger laughed. "Nothing so one-dimensional as that, I wouldn't think. However, I'd say his spirit is still moving through the work that he did in this life. Still moving, still very much alive."

"Why do you think no one else ever saw it before? I mean, from what I was told, they'd picked the place clean."

Roger pondered for a moment, looking down at the floor. "Hmm. That's a question for you to answer and I suppose you already know the answer. After all, you went up there looking for something, didn't you?" Then, he asked, "So what is it that you are going to write yourself?"

"To tell you the truth, I don't know. But I am going to write something."

"And did anything else happen up there in Ketchum?" he wanted to know. "Anything you haven't told me?"

I thought about this for a while. We were sipping strong black coffee from the Blue Mountains of Jamaica and nibbling on Scottish scones that Roger had bought that morning at the bakery, and I watched the steam rise off his cup. His eyes were agleam, and I remembered that he had once told me the derivation of his name: it came from Poland, as did his family. Sparks thrown off by the hot iron of the blacksmith's hammer. Roger's eyes, sparkling with blue fire, reminded me that he himself was forged within the power of his birth name: Zelazny. Spark-maker, smithy of words.

"There is something I haven't told you," I recalled. "Something that someone said to me just before I left Idaho. It was weird, too. There was this old man at the airport, who came up to me and asked what I did for a living, and I mumbled, half-heartedly, that I was a teacher. And do you know what he said, that old man? He asked if I were a storyteller. And I told him that, being a teacher, I had to be. Then, while we waited for the plane, he told me a story. It was about a mountain man named John Colter, who ran half-naked across three hundred miles of wilderness while being pursued by half the Blackfeet nation."

Roger said, "That's worth more than the MacLeish poem, I'd wager."

He said nothing more about this, and I did not mention it myself for at least a year. Then, one night, while we were having dinner together, I showed him the first chapter of John Colter's race for life. Once again, we were sipping coffee. He smiled and put down his mug.

"That's good writing," he said.

"I wanted you to see it for a special reason," I told him.

"Oh?" He took another sip of coffee, set the mug down again.

"I would like to know if you would write this tale with me, if we could possibly write it together?"

"What's the main thread?" he asked curiously.

"Two men," I said, "two mountain men, John Colter and Hugh Glass. Colter, pursued by Indians, runs a hundred fifty miles to safety; Glass is mauled by a grizzly bear, and crawls an equal distance. That is about all I know at the moment. But I know that I want to write it with you."

Roger's interest seemed to cool before my eyes. He told me that he had so much to do, contracts to fulfill for books as yet unwritten, and there was just no time for this one. "Maybe in a few years," he said. Then he changed the subject to what a good book *Islands in the Stream* had turned out to be, and how much he liked the poem by MacLeish. And that was all he said about Colter/Glass for quite some time.

Then, one day, two years later, while we were discussing an audio project of his which I was busy putting together, he showed me something that he was working on. At the top of the page was the word "Glass." Amazed, I read on, discovering that this was chapter two of the novel I had proposed that we would write together, a book about two men fighting their own personal daemons in the American West; one turning hawk, the other turning bear, both switching identities somewhere near the end of their travail, so that Colter crawled upon his belly and Glass danced across the snow.

I remember well the day we finished the book. Well, it wasn't "we," it was "he." For when I received the last sheet of typing paper from him, he had written something at the bottom of the page. It was there in his neat and tidy, scrunched-down script: "Wherefore the rest is silence."

ABOUT THE AUTHORS

Fred Saberhagen is the author of several popular science fiction and fantasy series, including the *Berserker* series and the *Swords* and *Lost Swords* series. He coauthored the novels *Coils* and *The Black Throne* with Roger Zelazny. He lives in Albuquerque, New Mexico.

Walter Jon Williams is adept at writing hard science fiction, allegorical fantasy, or just about anything in between. He has published more than a dozen novels, among them *City on Fire, Angel Station, Metropolitan,* and *Rock of Ages.* His novella "Elegy for Angels and Dogs" is a sequel to Roger Zelazny's "The Graveyard Heart," and the two stories were packaged together in 1990.

Jack Williamson was born in 1908 and has been writing science fiction for the past half-century, with the novels *Darker Than You Think, The Humanoids, Star Bridge,* and *Lifeburst,* as well as many others, as a result. He has also written nonfiction on such topics as the teaching of science fiction, and a study of H. G. Wells. A winner of the Nebula Grandmaster award and the Hugo award, he lives in New Mexico.

Nina Kiriki Hoffman has been nominated for several awards for her fiction, the most recent being for the World Fantasy award for her novel *The Silent Strength of Stones* and her novelette "Home for Christmas." She also has stories in *Tarot Fantastic, Enchanted Forests,* and *Wizard Fantastic.*

Steven Brust was born in November 1955, and currently lives in Minneapolis, Minnesota. His latest novel is *Freedom and Necessity,* a collaboration with Emma Bull.

Katharine Eliska Kimbriel's credits include stories in the anthologies *Against the Wind, Arabesques 2,* and *Werewolves.* She is also the author of five novels, the most recent titled *Night Calls* and *Kindred Rites.* She lives in Austin, Texas.

Jane M. Lindskold resides in Albuquerque, New Mexico. Her published works include the novels *Brother to Dragons, Companion to Owls; Marks of Our Brothers; The Pipes of Orpheus; Smoke and Mirrors;* and *When the Gods Are Silent. Donnerjack,* the first of two novels left unfinished by Roger Zelazny and completed by Lindskold, was published in 1997. Her latest solo work, *Changer,* will be published in the fall of 1998.

Robert Sheckley was born in New York and raised in New Jersey. Several of his stories have been made into movies. *The Tenth Victim,* based on his short story "The Seventh Victim," has become a cult film. The author of many books of science fiction and fantasy, including three collaborations with Roger himself, he lives in Portland, Oregon, with his wife, journalist Gail Dana.

Jack C. Haldeman II began his writing career combining science fiction and sports, and soon progressed into writing novels such as *High Steel,* coauthored with Jack Dann, which examines the construction of a space station from the view of one of the men who build it. His short fiction appears in *By Any Other Flame, Warriors of Blood and Dream,* and *Alternate Tyrants.* He lives in Gainesville, Florida, with his wife, author Barbara Delaplace.

John J. Miller has had a number of stories published in George R. R. Martin's *Wild Cards* anthology series. He has also had five science fiction novels published, including two *Ray Bradbury's Dinosaur World* novels, and has written a number of nonfiction articles about the history of baseball. He lives in Albuquerque, New Mexico.

Robert Wayne McCoy's work has received an honorable mention in *The Year's Best Fantasy and Horror 1995* for his collaboration with Thomas Monteleone. His work also appears in *Borderlands 5*. He lives in Owings Mills, Maryland.

Thomas F. Monteleone is the co-editor of the critically acclaimed *Borderlands* anthology series, collections of dark fantasy and horror that push the traditional boundaries of the genres. He is also an accomplished author, having published over a dozen books, as well as a short story collection, plays, and screenplays. He and his wife Elizabeth own and operate Borderlands Press.

John Varley's small body of work nevertheless marks him as an inventive science fiction author. He has won the Locus award six times, as well as the Jupiter, Nebula, and Hugo awards. His best known work is the Gaea trilogy, consisting of *Titan, Wizard,* and *Demon*. His 1985 novel *Millennium* was made into a movie of the same name. He lives in Portland, Oregon.

William Sanders writes offbeat fiction, notably the novels *Journey to Fusang* and *The Wild Blue and the Gray*. His short work appears in numerous magazines and anthologies. He currently lives in Tahlequah, Oklahoma.

Robert Silverberg is a science fiction writer and editor with few peers. His dozens of novels have addressed such social issues as overpopulation, war, drug abuse, man's use of technology, and other themes. He has also created many worlds of wonder with fantastic, detailed alien races and societies, garnering him four Hugo awards and five Nebula awards. His most recent creation is the planet of Majipoor, a world with over twenty million human and alien beings. His latest novel, *Sorcerers of Majipoor,* was released in 1997.

Andre Norton has written and collaborated on over 100 novels in her sixty years as a writer, working with such authors as Robert Bloch, Marion Zimmer Bradley, Mercedes Lackey, and Julian May. Her best-known creation is the Witch World, which has been the subject of several novels and anthologies. She has received the Nebula Grandmaster award, the Fritz Leiber award, and the Daedalus award, and lives in Monterey, Tennessee, where she oversees a genre writers' research library, High Hallack.

Pati Nagle has been published in *The Magazine of Fantasy & Science Fiction, The Williamson Effect, An Armory of Swords* and *Elf Magic*. Her first novel, *Glorieta,* will be released in October 1998. She lives in Albuquerque, New Mexico.

Bradley H. Sinor has seen his work appear in the *Merovigan Nights* anthologies, *Time of the Vampires,* and other places. He lives in Oklahoma with his wife Sue and three strange cats.

Jennifer Roberson is an accomplished storyteller with numerous novels and stories to her credit. To date she has written two series, *The Chronicles of the Cheysuli* and the *Sword—Dancer* novels. Recently she collaborated with Melanie Rawn and Kate Elliott on *The Golden Key.* She also edited the anthology *Return to Avalon,* a tribute book to Marion Zimmer Bradley.

Paul Dellinger is the author of a number of short stories, including science fiction, fantasy, and mysteries, along with two plays and a comedy-adventure radio series. Recent fiction appears in *The Williamson Effect* and *Future Net.* He lives in Virginia.

William Browning Spencer's works include *Maybe I'll Call Anna, Zod Wallop, Irrational Fears,* and a collection of short fiction, *The Return of Count Electric and Other Stories.* He lives in Austin, Texas.

Neil Gaiman's comic book series *Sandman* gained worldwide acclaim during its run from 1988–96. He combined mythic figures with lyrical imagery and brooding, dark artwork to create a visual experience unlike anything else. But amazing comic books aren't all the British author is known for. He is the author of the novel *Neverwhere* and the short story collection *Angels and Reflections,* and collaborated on the novel *Good Omens* with Terry Pratchett. *Neverwhere* was broadcast as a BBC miniseries in 1996, and a motion picture of the novel is also planned. In addition, Neil Gaiman has edited anthologies with Kim Newman and Stephen Jones. Gaiman's newest short story collection is due out in late 1998.

Gregory Benford is a professor of physics at the University of California, Irvine, where he conducts research in plasma turbulence theory and astrophysics. He has served as an advisor to the Department of Energy, NASA, and the White House Council on Space Policy. Benford is also the author of more than a dozen novels, including *Cosm, Jupiter Project, Against Infinity, Great Sky River,* and *Timescape.* A two-time winner of the Nebula award, Benford has also won the John W. Campbell award, the Australian Ditmar award, and the United Nations Medal in Literature.

Michael A. Stackpole is an award-winning game and computer game designer who has worked with such companies as TSR, Inc.,

FASA, Corp., West End Games, and Wizards of the Coast. He was inducted into the Academy of Gaming Arts and Design's Hall of Fame in 1994. He has published twenty-five novels to date, the most recent fantasy titled *Talion: Revenant*. He lives in Arizona.

Gerald Hausman, is an award-winning writer of children's and adult books. With Roger Zelazny, he wrote *Wilderness,* the tale of Colter/Glass, which was was honored as a New York Public Library Best Adventure Book for the Teenage in 1995. Mr. Hausman lives in Bokeelia, Florida, where he writes animal books with his wife, Loretta.

Permissions

"Introduction" by Fred Saberhagen. Copyright © 1998 by Fred Saberhagen.

"Lethe" by Walter Jon Williams. Copyright © 1997 by Walter Jon Williams. First published in *Isaac Asimov's Science Fiction Magazine*. Reprinted by permission of the author.

"The Story Roger Never Told" by Jack Williamson. Copyright © 1998 by Jack Williamson.

"The Somehow Not Yet Dead" by Nina Kiriki Hoffman. Copyright © 1998 by Nina Kiriki Hoffman.

"Calling Pittsburgh" by Steven Brust. Copyright © 1998 by Steven Brust.

"If I Take the Wings of Morning" by Katharine Eliska Kimbriel. Copyright © 1998 by Katharine Eliska Kimbriel.

"Ki'rin and the Blue and White Tiger" by Jane M. Lindskold. Copyright © 1998 by Jane Lindskold.

"The Eryx" by Robert Sheckley. Copyright © 1998 by Robert Sheckley.